DEVILLE'S CONTRACT

Scott Zarcinas

Other Titles by
Scott Zarcinas

The Pilgrim Chronicles:
Samantha Honeycomb
The Golden Chalice

Fiction:
*Ananda (*Thanksgiving Day)*
Roadman

Non-Fiction:
Your Natural State of Being

DEVILLE'S CONTRACT

Scott Zarcinas

DoctorZed
Publishing
www.doctorzed.com

First published 2015 by DoctorZed Publishing.

DoctorZed Publishing books may be ordered through booksellers or by contacting:

DoctorZed Publishing
IDAHO
10 Vista Ave
Skye, South Australia 5072
www.doctorzed.com
61-(0)8 8431-4965

ISBN: 978-0-9924473-5-9 (sc)
ISBN: 978-0-9872495-4-8 (ebk)

A CiP number for this title can be found at the National Library of Australia.

Top of the World lyrics by Dwayne Wiggins, Eric Baker, Frederick Busby, as sung by Karen Carpenter

Printed in Australia.

DoctorZed Publishing rev. date 12/02/2015

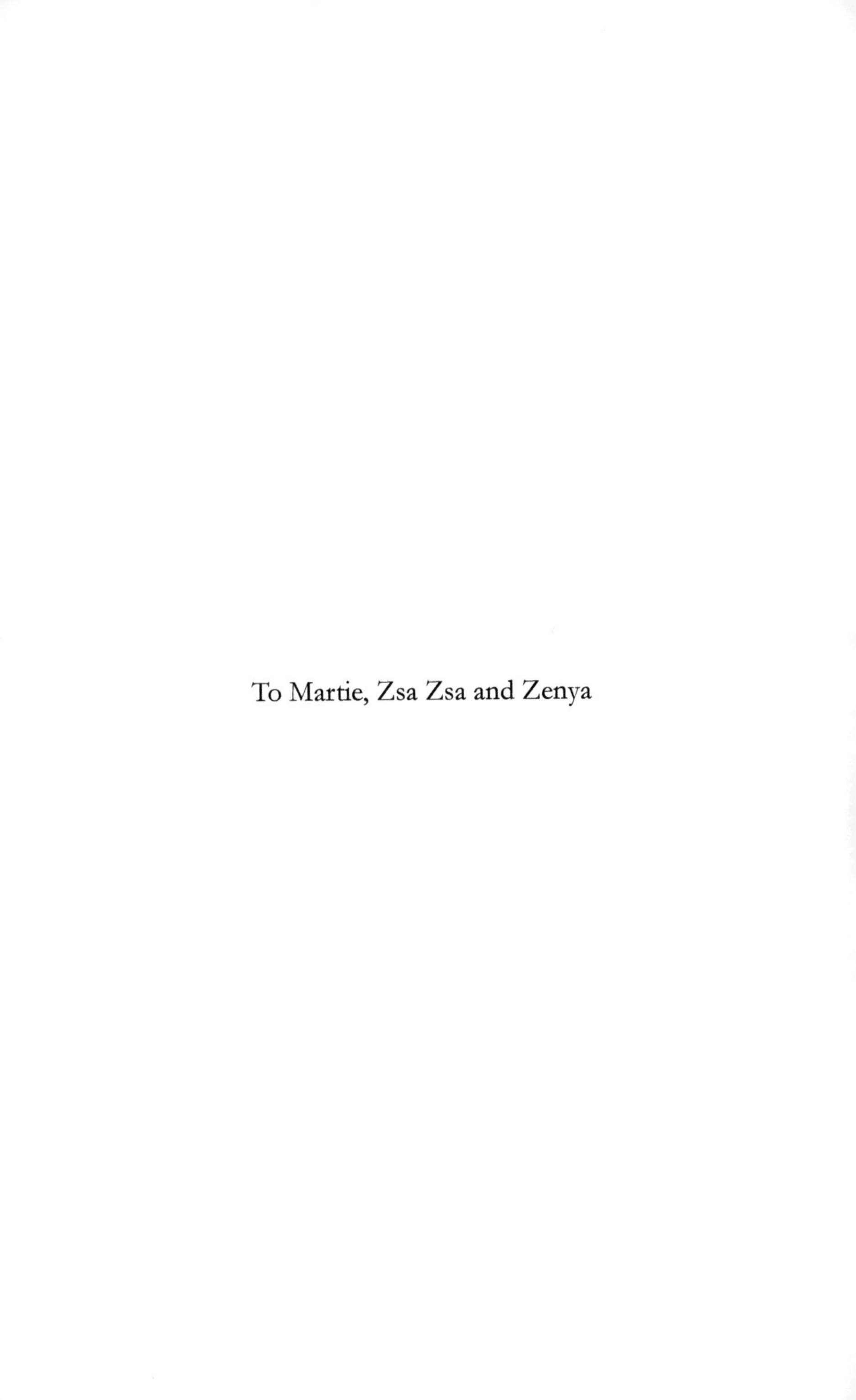

To Martie, Zsa Zsa and Zenya

Acknowledgments

For fifteen years now I have been writing and for fifteen years I've had the loving support of my wife. Without her support this book and others would still be vague images trapped inside my head. Thank you again Martie for helping me give birth to this story.

To my readers who proofed the manuscript, thank you for your time, effort and suggestions. The book is better for your input.

Lastly, to God, thank You for showing me that we make a heaven and hell of our own choosing, especially on this earth, even if I'm a little slow in learning.

"With our thoughts we create the world."
Gautama Buddha

Prologue

The Grand Vision

HIDING his smile at the head of the table, Louis DeVille eyed the suit and ties filing into the boardroom. With a wink and a nod he greeted every one of the Vice Presidents as they sat down. Could say this was what he'd been working toward since the day he began the company, the culmination of his life's work. He basked and took it all in. And why shouldn't he? The company was about to burst onto the big stage. All thanks to him.

"I'd like to call this AGM open," the company secretary said, glancing at his watch, "at 6:04, March 13."

The secretary then read out the minutes of last month's board meeting before asking Louis if there was anything he wanted to say before the vote. To the applause of the VPs, Louis stood and gathered his thoughts. He thanked them and gestured for silence, stretching the jacket lapels over his belly and squeezing a button into the eyelet.

"As you know, when I started out in the late fifties I was just a salesman doing the rounds for one of the drug companies here in New York. One of the 'Big Four' back then."

Next to a pile of dossiers his PA had left on the table was a pitcher of cow juice and from it he poured himself a glass. God, he hated this stuff, but he needed it. Grimacing, he eyed his subordinates over the rim. They were chuckling. Everyone knew Louis DeVille had bought out that company when it hit hard times in the mid-eighties and stripped it of its assets. All that remained was the mahogany table they were now seated around.

He put the glass back down on the table and went on. "I was good at what I did, and what I did was sell the wonder drug of the day: Penicillin." There were more chuckles. "Unlike most of you,

I grew up in Brooklyn. The only education I got was on the street. College was never a consideration. Nevertheless, it turned out to be a goddamn blessing in disguise. Those years were my apprenticeship. I learned what it took to get to the top in the only school that matters, the school of hard knocks."

Several gray and balding heads were nodding. The others, fresher faced and fuller on top, just stared back with polite interest.

"Without wishing to bore you with details," he said, "I hated making money for someone else. Plus, I wasn't getting promoted as fast as I wanted, so I figured the best thing to do was resign and start my own company. Best goddamn thing I ever did." The gray heads chuckled and nodded some more. "The market was tough, let me tell you. I had to plead with the banks to call off their goddamn hounds more than I care to recall. Nevertheless, DeVille Pharmaceuticals was in the black within four years. Within ten we'd broken into the south and Midwest. Within twenty we'd stretched right across the country. We then started looking across the Atlantic, and in the eighties we even changed our name to Global Resolutions Network. Now, almost forty years to the day it was born, the company is approaching another milestone. Listing on the Dow. The goddamn Holy Grail."

Louis brought the glass to his lips again, hesitating before he took another sip. Then he passed around the dossiers from the pile next to him and waited until everyone was ready. He held up his ring-bound copy, a sky-blue cover across which was written in white: THE FUTURE OF GLOBAL RESOLUTIONS NETWORK. Glaring beneath it in red: STRICTLY CONFIDENTIAL.

"Each of you now has a dossier of my vision for GRN," he said. "Everything I've learned about the pharmaceutical industry is in here. The secret of my success. The secret that will rocket GRN to global dominance of the drug market."

The Vice Presidents each picked up a copy and began flicking through it. Louis could see a couple of wry grins. This was going to make every goddamn one of them wealthier than they had ever imagined, and they were entitled to raise a few eyebrows at what they read. They were welcome to the money. Some of them though, the older boys, the ones with a third wife and second coronary understood that it was more than just the number of zeros on the bank statement. The game was about dominance. Proving everyone else wrong. Making a goddamn success of your life despite the odds.

He nodded toward the company secretary, one of the fresher faces with a full head of hair but not too far from hiding the double chin behind the hairy mask of a goatee. "Stop taking minutes for a moment. Go on, put your pen down. Tell me what the gurus at Yale taught you about marketing."

The secretary put his pen to his mouth and leaned back in his chair. "Uh… to identify and target a niche, I guess."

Louis hit the table with the soft part of his fist. "Exactly. Find a gap in the market and exploit it. Give the man in the street what nobody else can, and he'll make you rich. That's basically what it means, isn't it?" The secretary nodded, his eyes darting from side to side, wondering why he was the target of the boss' sudden attention. Louis glanced around the table. "And it's all horseshit. Every one of you who went to Harvard, or Yale, or MIT, you've all majored in horseshit," and he sniffed the air. "I can even smell it."

The secretary wiggled in the seat, looking for a means of escape. The VP next to him hooked down his tie. No one else said a word, staring down at the dossier in front of them, not daring to make eye contact with anybody, let alone the boss.

"But it's not your fault, and I don't blame you for what those idiots taught you." Resting his knuckles on the table, Louis hunched forward. "If you want to earn a lousy million, then targeting a niche might do it for you. But if you want to earn hundreds of millions, even billions," and he trailed off, reeling them in, "then you *create* a niche."

The Vice Presidents looked at one another and shrugged. It was the secretary who broke the awkward silence. "I'm not sure I follow."

Louis had been glaring at some of the grayer heads, hoping they would be the first to catch on and speak up. He flashed his gaze onto the secretary, and said, "How did Bill Gates become the richest man in the world?"

The secretary didn't answer. Louis eyed the rest of them. The question, as he had expected, was met with blank faces.

"Well I'll tell you. He didn't *find* a niche in the software market. His creation *became* the software market." Still nobody spoke, but Louis could tell a few of the older boys were now starting to cotton on. "What about Henry Ford? He didn't find a niche in the motor vehicle market. The invention of the assembly line *created* the market for him."

"So you're saying we have to do the same?" the secretary said.

Louis straightened his back, flattening the length of his tie with his knuckles. "Exactly."

"But how? The pharmaceutical market is flooded."

Louis fisted the table again. "By creating our own *disease*."

The secretary stroked his double chin. At first a blank, his face began to lighten as the concept slowly dawned. Louis smiled, opening his confidential dossier to the first page. The sound of flicking paper filled the room as everyone else did likewise.

"That's the first step in our four-step plan. We need a disease for which only GRN has the product to cure. We have to monopolize an illness, patent it if we have to, and then flood the market with our wonder drug."

Louis lifted his glass and took another sip, a small one, barely wetting his lips this time. When no one offered a comment, he said, "We turn the tables on the current approach to curing illness. Most pharmaceutical companies waste millions in research and development, all competing for the same thing, all hoping to find the magic bullet that will put an end to cancer or AIDS or whatever. We're not going to spend a goddamn cent. We're going to create a disease to fit the drugs we already have."

The silence continued, then the secretary said, "I hope you're not thinking of poisoning the water supply." His candidness elicited a few nervous snickers around the table. "I mean… uh… something like that wouldn't be ethical, would it?"

Louis grinned. "What has ethics got to do with the pharmaceutical industry? We're in the business of making money. Simple as that." He planted his forefinger on top of the dossier. "But to get back to the point, to create a disease all we need do is turn something that's normal into something that's abnormal. Something that has to be treated. You've heard of Münchausen's Syndrome, haven't you?"

The secretary stoked his double chin again. A few VPs wiggled in their seats and pretended to concentrate on the dossier.

"Let me explain. Someone who's a Münchausen is perfectly healthy, but they make the doctors believe they have an illness that needs treating. They're con artists. They have thousands of dollars spent on investigations and medical intervention. And for what? There's nothing wrong with them. So if one individual can divert thousands of dollars from the insurance companies, imagine how much we can make if a whole city like New York, or the whole country for that matter, is convinced they have an illness they don't really have."

The secretary glanced up from his dossier. "You want GRN to create a pretend illness?"

Louis nodded. "A pretend illness with a real drug. We already have a range of anti-depressants. We'll use one whose sales have dipped. Repackage it to save on costs," and he smiled. "Of course we'll have to come up with a savvy name for what it's treating. DeVille's Syndrome, or something like that."

The secretary had the pen in his mouth again. "But… will it work? I mean…"

"Of course it will. The trick is to make the consumers feel worse about themselves than they already do. That our magic pill will take away their problems and make their life more bearable." He paused to take stock. "The pharmaceutical industry has moved into the next phase of its evolution, and we have to move with it, if not take the lead. Pills are no longer just about treating life-threatening conditions. They also improve our *quality* of life."

The secretary had a wry grin. "Pills for a lifestyle?"

The comment was greeted with a murmur of chuckles around the table.

"That's not such a silly idea. People are always looking for something that will make them happier, or increase their sense of security, even feel more popular. Pills already exist to treat anxiety and stress, why not have a pill that can treat our everyday sadness? Or even guilt? You've just cheated on your wife and are feeling bad about it. Take a pill! Wash away those unwanted feelings. Next, take a pill to save the marriage. Even the career that's on the ropes. The consumer needs to believe that a pill will save them in their hour of need. Step in GRN." The flash of an idea momentarily stunned him.

That's brilliant, Louis. Just goddamn brilliant.

"In fact, here's our criteria for the diagnosis of DeVille's Syndrome. A triad of symptoms: sadness, insecurity, loneliness."

The secretary glanced at the dossier. "You're sure the public will fall for it?"

Louis had been waiting for that question and almost jumped on the secretary in his eagerness to answer. "Look at ADHD, Attention Deficit Hyperactive Disorder. According to some statistics over one in three kids have it. We're in an epidemic of hyperactive brats jumping all over the furniture and climbing the walls. Sure, some of them might have an underlying pathology that actually needs treatment, but thirty percent? Goddamn ludicrous. That was a disease created to sell more amphetamines. The medical profession has swallowed a lie and the pharmaceutical companies are making a fortune out of it. Which leads to the next step."

Everyone flipped the dossier to Step Two: BUILDING CONSENSUS WITHIN THE MEDICAL COMMUNITY.

"An integral part of the plan involves winning over the hearts and minds of the medics and any other legalized drug pusher in the community," Louis said. "The basic platform is already established. We don't have to do much more than what we're already doing. I've highlighted the main points on the page," and he pointed to the list. "First, we need a marketing strategy to educate doctors in the triad of DeVille's Syndrome and what to do about it. We'll stress the need for early diagnosis, and of course the correct drug to treat it. Next, we'll foster interactions between our patients with the mysterious 'new disease' and those doctors or scientists we get on board early, the ones who'll become our experts in DeVille's Syndrome. Of course we'll have to bankroll a few conferences across the country to get our message across. Vegas. Aspen. San Fran. Even here in Manhattan."

Louis paused again. He had to stop getting too far ahead of himself. Man, he was flying, but he had to remain calm. He had balls between his thighs, after all, not goddamn ovaries. He asked the table if there were any questions before he went to Step Three: Reaching The Consumers.

When no one spoke up, he said, "The next step involves increasing the public's need for our drug, which we'll call Hypnocal for the time being. As you can see in the dossier, I've outlined a few means of achieving this. We need a tab line. Something to perk the interest like, "By the time you've reached retirement, it's likely you will have experienced the detrimental effects of DeVille's Syndrome at least once." Or even, "Lonely, frightened or blue? Hypnocal's for you!" Anyway, you know what I'm getting at. You've seen it before. Remembering of course we need to use a lot of medical jargon to confuse the average monkey in the street. The more confused they are, the more likely they'll think they've got the disease and need treatment for it. We won't say someone's sad. We'll say they're suffering "severe hypo-affectation." Loneliness will be "intractable agoraphobia." Insecurity will be, what? Help me out here…"

"Psychosomatic Delusional Complex," the secretary said.

This time every VP was laughing. Even Louis smiled.

"You've got the picture," he said. "We'll also use the media to give us free publicity for Hypnocal, just like we've done before. We'll run items in the papers and brief the radio and TV channels. Marketing disguised as news. You know the things. Something like, "A new drug has been found to significantly reduce the harmful effects of DeVille's Syndrome." That usually gets the public going.

We'll hammer home the fact that it's a "breakthrough treatment" and get our experts interviewed on how it's improved their patients' life. Of course, if we can get a celebrity endorsement of the product, someone big who'll come out and say they've had DeVille's Syndrome for years and didn't know it until they improved with Hypnocal, then we're laughing all the way to the bank."

Louis rubbed a clenched fist down his tie, then reached for the jug of goddamn cow juice and filled his empty glass. One of the VPs inquired as to whether or not he was feeling okay. Grimacing a little, he nodded that he was doing fine. It was just a little gastritis. Had had it for years. All he needed was some antacids to calm the flames.

Excusing himself, he went to the intercom on the side-table abutting the wall behind him. He lifted the handset and punched the call button. When his PA finally answered, he told her to fetch a bottle of Kwel-Amities he kept in his office desk. Once done, he went back to the head of the table. "Okay, where were we?" he said, clearing his throat and glancing at the dossier. "Ah yes. Step Three. An important channel for promoting awareness of DeVille's Syndrome is the use of supporter groups. We'll set them up in every major city and town. Forums on the Internet are also the way to go, especially if we want to go global with this thing. We'll encourage free screenings for people who are worried they might have the disease. We'll assist government lobbying for grants to help the poor."

The secretary perked up. "I've just thought of something. What about a National Day for DeVille's Syndrome?" He glanced around the table. "An awareness day. Like they do for AIDS and breast cancer. We can get people to wear a pair of wacky sunglasses to raise money for future research. You know, the ones with the funny nose and moustache that make you look like Groucho Marx."

The VPs chuckled at the thought. At that moment, Louis' PA entered with the bottle of antacids. Ash-blonde with melons like Dolly Parton, and not an inch over five foot, even in sneakers, she made him feel like a giant cat about to pounce on an unsuspecting mouse. While she put the bottle of Kwel-Amities on top of the table, he maneuvered himself so that his elbow rubbed her breasts. Then, as she turned to leave, he let his hand fall to his side and brush her gorgeous ass. Running his forefinger across her skirt, he wondered how long it would be before she would give in to his advances. They always did, in the end.

She lifted her face to stare into his eyes. "Will that be all, Mr. DeVille?"

"For now," he said, absently toying with the ring on his wedding finger.

Once the door had clicked shut, he opened the bottle of Kwel-Amities (one of his competitor's products, ironically, but goddamn it they worked wonders) and took two of the little blue diamonds, chasing them down with a swig of milk. He then flicked the dossier to the last page: RESEARCH AND CLINICAL TRIALS.

"Your last suggestion is more valid than you think," he said to the secretary. "Step Four is concerned with the scientific validation of DeVille's Syndrome and its treatment. Probably the most difficult stage; the scientific community is as cynical as hell. Goddamn bunch of assholes if you ask me, but we need them. If we have to bin research that's less favorable than others, then so be it. It's common practice anyway. If we have to manipulate the statistical data in our favor, then we'll do that too. Again, it's common practice. In today's world, clinical trials are nothing but marketing trials anyway. Every scientist knows that. As long as the data reflects positively in favor of Hypnocal, then we'll do everything we can to push it into the public arena."

Louis took another sip. Every face at the table was turned to him. He then held up the dossier, and said, "Deep down human beings are nothing but an organic process of chemical reactions. Chemicals determine how we feel, how we act, and how we think. Even love is nothing but a chemical reaction. Why not give the goddamn public what they want, control over their own chemistry? Surely we owe them the best possible life they can get. Because you know what, once the reactions stop, there's nothing else."

He felt like ending his talk with a big, hearty "amen." Instead, he put the dossier down and returned to his chair, bringing his speech to a close. The next few minutes would tell whether he'd done enough.

"Well, I think that brings us to the vote," the secretary said, standing and glancing around the table. Louis drew a deep breath, suppressing the urge to fidget in his seat. "I put forward the motion to keep Mr. DeVille as CEO. I need a second."

The VP next to him shot his hand in the air before anyone else got the chance. "I second it."

"Then lets call the vote."

Louis kept holding his breath, maintaining an air of absolute seriousness. How long did he have to put up with this goddamn theatrical nonsense? Not long, it seemed. All thirteen hands shot up in unanimous agreement and it was done. As quick as that; a goddamn rubberstamp. Louis slowly released the air in his lungs and closed his eyes to collect his thoughts, barely heeding the call for votes on the remaining board positions. Should he really have been so worried? Maybe. Maybe not. Despite the feeling that everything was going according to plan, there was always a niggle of doubt in the back of his head. He guessed he had never truly recovered from that time he had almost lost it all in the early eighties, in this very same room, if you could believe it. That was a lesson he wouldn't forget in a million goddamn years. *No sir-ree.* Nothing in life was a guarantee, except death and taxes, if you believed that horseshit. But what the hell, it was all in the past. He was re-elected as CEO and had survived another year. And, oh, what a goddamn year this was going to be.

After the vote for the position of secretary, the meeting was called to a close and the Vice Presidents slowly dispersed, patting him on the shoulder as they passed and telling him what a fine job he was doing; GRN was really going places. Despite the burn beneath his chest, he smiled and thanked them and said he hoped he could count on their support in the coming months.

If not, they'd all be out the door so goddamn fast their feet won't touch the ground.

Finally, the last suit and tie exited the boardroom. Louis opened the bottle on the table and took two more blue diamonds, thinking he had better get his PA to book him in for another checkup. He rubbed his knuckles up and down his chest, wondering what in hell had changed of late. The gastritis just wasn't responding to treatment like it used to.

He let the thought slide. There were more important things to worry about, like how to get his PA into bed before any of the younger VPs beat him to it. He leaned back and clasped his hands behind his head.

Now *that* would be something, wouldn't it?

PART ONE

Chapter 1

Louis' Problems

LOUIS DeVILLE sat behind his desk wondering just what to do. He wasn't outraged. He wasn't baffled. He just had a lot on his mind this morning. A lot on his plate, his wife would have said. Piled right up to the office ceiling, in fact. Piled like a mound of rotting garbage that had been dumped in the IN tray and marked to his attention. It was piled so high he could almost see it spilling against the bookshelves and the filing cabinets. Spilling, still more, out the tenth-story window onto the pedestrians scuttling along Broadway.

Good ol' Lady Di, he mused. She might not be right about many things, but she was right about that; and wouldn't she just love to rub it in? He could see her now at the Beeker Street penthouse. All five-foot two of leanness and exuberance in her leotards and legwarmers, pedaling on her Ezy-Cycle in front of some celebrity aerobics video or the Home Shopping Channel, burning off the calories in some vain attempt to defeat the aging process, stretching muscles and joints he didn't even know existed. He could even hear her nagging at him while she did it.

"It's your own fault. You're a workaholic, Louis," she would be saying. He hated the way she deliberately called him *Lewis.* It was *Lewey*, like Donald Duck's three sons, Hewey, Dewey and Lewey. "You're going to die at your desk one day, believe me." She wouldn't stop there either. "You're never home before eleven. It's not good for a man your age. You should be thinking of retirement, not expanding the business. Leave that for the *younger* men," and she would say *younger* in such a tone that would make him want to throttle that slender neck of hers.

He clenched his fists and thumped the desk. The intercom jumped and the computer monitor flickered momentarily, then switched itself off. Retirement? Hells bells, he was too damn young to retire. He was only sixty-six, and as fit as a goddamn fiddle. Not quite what he was in his mid-twenties when he started the company, but who the hell was when they had been steering the helm for over forty years? Sure, he would pay the price for it one day. There was always a price. Cardiac arrest. Heart attack. Flat line. He had thought about it often enough, whatever name you wanted to call it. Hadn't everyone his age? But he had no concerns except his goddamn gastritis. That was all. Got himself checked up every six months. Still had a good twenty years left in him before he had anything to worry about.

"Do you really think so, Louis?" he heard Dianne DeVille say in his head again. He could even see her taut legs pumping the Ezy-Cycle in a blur of pink and blue in front of the TV, her bouffant hair as motionless as her silicon breasts. "Do you really *think* you've got twenty good years left? I mean, look at your waistline." It was always waistline, never belly, or guts, or stomach, words that were just too crass to ever spill out of her surgically perfected lips. "It's not what it used to be, is it dear?"

He could feel the burn of his gastritis just thinking about her, like he had swallowed one of those stupid party candles that never went out when you blew on it. He rummaged through the top drawer looking for his antacids while Lady Di kept nagging in his head.

"Your poor heart," she said. "I'm surprised it hasn't given up already."

Ha! Really? he snapped back, vaguely aware that he was talking aloud. He had already outlived Peterson, that good-for-noth'n union slob, not to mention several others who she had thought would live to a ripe old age. So much for them, huh? Look who's had the last laugh!

Lady Di had no reply. Her pedaling image began to fade like some overused videotape that could no longer record. Then she was gone and he was alone again, back in his office with his pile of problems stacked to the ceiling.

Walter Peterson, though, stayed fresh in his mind. The old toad who had stolen from the rich and kept every cent for himself, good old Mr. Fat and Ugly with a hairy wart on his right cheek (and probably on the cheek of his ass, too), always sticking his pug-nose in business that wasn't his. Coronary got him a few years ago, no surprises about that. Only surprise was that it didn't happen earlier. Would've saved GRN thousands in "charity donations" if he had croaked it when he should have. That chain-smoking scumbag had taken more money from his pocket than his yoga-stretching wife, and that was saying something. He was better off dead. Never did any good for anyone.

Like that rat from Morgan Divott. Another scumbag he had had the misfortune of sharing business intercourse. He had been the first to go. Now that *was* a surprise. Coronary, too, wasn't it? Or was it the big CA? One of his clients once told him over lunch it was actually that faggot disease, the one all the heroine junkies were dying of too. Whatever it was, the end was sudden, that much he knew. Here one minute, gone the next. Almost too young to die really, still in his forties, but he had never forgiven the little vermin for trying to force him out in the eighties.

Damn near succeeded too. Had almost two-thirds of the board on his side. Bunch of backstabbing mongrels. They had ambushed him in the boardroom with a vote of no confidence and almost succeeded. Taken completely by surprise, too, he was. Hadn't even the foggiest clue his own vice presidents were scheming behind his back. He had trusted them, he guessed. That was his weakness. Too much goddamned trust. Well, it was a hard earned lesson, but he was still here, and where were they? Gone to hell, as far as he cared.

"Ha!" he said. "There you are."

Goddamn bottle of Kwel-Amities hidden right at the back of the drawer. About goddamn time. His gastritis was really fired up and frying the inside of his lower chest. He removed the bottle, unscrewed the cap and peered inside, then grunted and rolled his eyes. Wasn't that always the goddamn way? Just when you really needed two or three, there was only one of the little buggers left. Just typical. Just goddamn typical.

Before he took it, he got up from behind the desk and lugged his hefty frame to the window. Horns blared somewhere downtown, the angry howls of New York's mechanical wildlife. Directly below in the shadows of the highrises and skyscrapers, grazing animals crawled along Broadway. Every goddamn creature in the jungle was down there. A cement truck bull-rhino charged anything that moved. Buffalo buses chewed the cud, not in any hurry at all. Yellow deer taxis moved in herds, nervous and alert, ready to dart away at any sign of danger. Even the monkeys of the jungle were there, scuttling along the sidewalk in office-wear, head down, briefcase in hand, not one of them lifting their eyes to see who was looking down on them.

He imagined a rifle in his hand, picking them off one by one. Not that he had ever shot someone before. God knew he had often wanted to. His wife for instance. Could do it too, and not so much as bat an eyelid. If he could get away with it, that was.

Ah, the perfect murder. Did it exist? Probably not. Everybody got caught at some point, usually when they bragged about it. Which was a bitch, because what was the point if you had to keep it secret? That's what trophies were for, weren't they? But if he could get away with it, ah yes, he had no qualms about picking someone off from his tenth-story window every once in a while, especially when his gastritis was playing up. Like that good-for-noth'n bum at the Metro corner always begging for money. He would be the first to go. Then that jogger who thought he owned the sidewalk. Then the hippies cleaning windscreens at the traffic lights, even when you told them you'd got no loose change to pay them. Ping. Ping. Ping. All three gone to meet their maker courtesy of Sniper Louis, the only CEO with big enough balls to rid the city of its filth.

He laughed a little. Sniper Louis. That was a good one.

While he took a couple more imaginary potshots from the window, the noonday sun peeked from behind a drifting cloud and shone directly into his eyes. He winced with pain. The burning from his stomach had turned up a notch like some goddamned internal boiler running on solar energy. Cursing, he yanked the drapes and tipped the remaining Kwel-Amity straight from the bottle into his mouth, then made his way back to his chair crunching the pill into sharp little shards that stuck between his teeth.

Goddamn it, he grimaced, these buggers tasted awful.

At the desk he chased the bitterness down with a swig of scotch from the bottom drawer, then wiped his mouth with the back of his hand. He slipped his thumb between two shirt buttons to give his sternum a massage. The skin felt hot and sweaty, as if a boiler really had been fired up beneath it. Still grimacing, he took another swig of scotch for good measure, and as he tilted his head he caught himself staring back.

"I know, I know. It's getting worse," he said, thumb-massaging his sternum. He could still taste a lingering bitterness in the back of his mouth, so he took another swig of scotch. "I need to see the doc again."

The portrait behind the desk kept staring its frozen accusation. The painter had captured all his best features (as he had been paid a goddamn fortune to) – his dark hypnotizing eyes; his broad shoulders; his expansive chest – and had managed to minimize his less noble attributes – his double-chin; his overhanging gut (*Waistline, dear, it's a waistline*!); the thinning patches on his scalp. Done a pretty damn fine job, too, he might add. At the time he was posing for it though, he had reckoned the idea of wearing a laurel and toga was kind of prissy, but the painter had assured him that the Caesar look with the backdrop of ancient Rome oozed the essence of success and power he needed in his line of work. Louis had paid him cash straight away. Best goddamn five grand he had ever spent.

He tossed the empty drug bottle into the bin beneath the desk and took a final swig of scotch before putting it back. Just as he sat down, his secretary buzzed on the intercom. The image of her abundant cleavage drifted in front of his eyes like two un-tethered helium balloons. "What is it?" he said.

"David Epstein's on line one for you."

Goddamn it, he had told her he was busy. No interruptions. Wendy would have understood. Now there was a damn fine secretary. Damn fine woman too. Not keeping her at the firm was the only thing he truly regretted. These young women nowadays didn't understand what a boss needed. He should have sacked Sarah ages ago, although he had to admit she was a hell of a lot better than the previous one. Frumpy bitch was nothing but trouble from the day she started. Stirred up all sorts of legal mess the company didn't need, and was still stirring. Damn shame they didn't make secretaries like they used to. In fact, you weren't even allowed to call them secretaries anymore, were you? Personal Assistants, PA's, or some or other bullshit term for someone who didn't type or do anything of the "personal" nature Wendy used to provide.

The red light on Button-1 kept flashing. "What does Epstein want now?"

Sarah's voice fluttered across the intercom: "Didn't say. You know he won't leave a message. He'll only talk to you."

Louis rolled his eyes and said, "Okay. Okay. I'll take it." He picked up the handset and punched the flashing red button. "This had better be good," he said to Epstein. "I don't wanna hear the contract hasn't been signed."

There was a pause on the line from the LA office. Either it was a bad connection or Epstein had taken fright. "That's what I want to talk to you about," Epstein said eventually. Louis had been about to growl at him to speak up. "Collins wants another week to think about it."

"Think about what?" Louis thumbed his sternum. "He's had six goddamn months! We need that signature! We're hedged to our teeth over here. If he doesn't do it today, there won't be any goddamned contract to sign. D'you hear what I'm saying?"

Epstein paused again. "I've been my persuasive best. The guy just won't put pen on paper. I think he's holding out for a higher offer."

"What kind of bullshit is that? We've already doubled our original bid. We're the only ones interested in his goddamned business and we're not offering one more cent than what's already been agreed. Tell him he can take it or leave it."

"Do you really mean that? I thought..."

Louis rolled his eyes and gritted his teeth. "No, I don't really mean that," he said. "Of course we're not going to let him go. We're in too deep." Still massaging his chest as he had, Louis could feel the thumping of his heart against his thumb. Then, remembering his favorite line from *The Godfather*, said: "Make him an offer he can't refuse."

Epstein paused again. "What does that mean?"

"Just do what you're paid to do. Get the signature on the contract."

Louis slammed the handset down and clasped his hands behind his neck. Tilting back in his manager's chair, he released the pent up air with a long exaggerated sigh. Hells bells, he thought, the garbage was really piling up today. It was never ending.

Still, he had faced worst and gotten through in one piece, hadn't he? He was a goddamn survivor. History had proven that.

Chapter 2

Coup-d'etat

HIS memory of the attempted *coup-d'etat* was a little hazy, what, nearly two decades ago now. He couldn't remember exactly who was in attendance or where they were sitting, he couldn't even remember all of their names, but he certainly remembered Johnny Winterbottom and the guy who had almost choked to death on the ice cube. He could actually picture the scene in the boardroom, now that he thought about it. The blinds were drawn, just as he liked it, the bare white walls reflecting the artificial light as though they were glowing with radioactive energy. Suits and ties occupied all thirteen seats around the table (no skirts or "power suits" back then, not on *his* board of control), except for one, the one next to Johnny at the other end of the table, the only vacant bay in the parking lot. He hadn't known it then, but that empty seat had saved him.

"We've… got something else on the agenda," Johnny Winterbottom had said that Friday back in '84.

Louis had already stood, tired and cranky at the end of another long week of eight-till-late. "This isn't protocol. The meeting's over," he said, then hit upon the most likely reason for the delay. "Is it the damn unions again? I thought we'd fixed that last month. Does that greedy bastard Peterson want more money?"

A couple of vice presidents shuffled in their seats and fidgeted with their ties, eyes fixed to the new mahogany desktop. "Not… exactly," Johnny said.

There was something in the way the young lawyer was trying to appease him that Louis immediately disliked, as if he had a poisoned water cooler he wanted the CEO to drink from.

Go on, try it, his look was saying. *It's kind of refreshing. You'll like it.* The look of a lizard trying to coax a fly onto its forked tongue.

One of the VP's on Johnny's immediate left, Louis' right, cleared his throat and took a sip from a glass of water. It was the Irish kid he had employed on Johnny's advice a few years back; a clever mathematician who had already made an impact by halving company tax, but had all the social skills of a frightened guinea pig. He took a long swig and then began to gag on something, turning red in the face as if someone had snuck from behind and started throttling him. Nobody moved to slap him on the back or do anything to help. Nobody did anything except stare. The kid brought his hand to his throat, gagging and gasping for air, and Louis could actually see his temple veins beginning to throb like engorging bloodworms. Then, just when his face was turning deeper crimson, he spat the offending item across the table. An ice cube slid across the mahogany and landed in the empty seat directly opposite, the seat normally occupied by the financial advisor from Morgan Divott. All the VPs watched the ice cube hit the leather upholstery, stunned into frigid silence.

Louis, too, watched the ice cube's route. He wasn't thinking the tax whiz lucky not to choke on a frozen piece of H_2O; rather he was thinking it completely unlike Herbert Grimsby to miss the board meeting. The closet faggot was usually the first to plunk his scrawny ass in his seat. That's what Louis had initially liked about the guy; eagerness, promptness, willingness (not his cutesy-wootsy ass), qualities he wanted – no, demanded – from someone in control of the company funds. Why he wasn't in attendance, he didn't know. Neither did anyone else. Not at that moment, anyway.

All the VPs around the table turned and faced Louis, including the kid who had spat the ice cube across the table. His color had mostly returned, but his mouth was gaping and his eyes were bulging, not quite believing what he'd done in front of the boss.

"*What*, not exactly?" Louis said to the lizard at the end of the table.

Johnny's expression hadn't changed. In fact, now that the atmosphere inside the hothouse had chilled to something like the ice-cube, he didn't like the expressions on most of his subordinates. They looked like members of a jury not sure which way the evidence was pointing, evidence that could send him all the way to the gallows. It was like that movie, *Twelve Angry Men*, his VP's turning on him like the jury who wanted to hang the kid. Something was up. Something rotten. He could smell its stench like Peterson could smell a bribe.

No, he reckoned, *it's not Twelve Angry Men. It's The Dirty Dozen.*

"Are you going to tell me what this is all about?" he said to Johnny, and glared at the rest of them. They all averted his gaze, apart from Johnny, who maintained his stare but still couldn't say what was on his mind. Except he didn't have to; Louis had a pretty good idea what was going down, and company protocol wasn't going to save him. "Go on!" he said, almost growling. "Be a man. Have the balls to say what you want to say."

Johnny glanced at the empty chair, the one in which the accountant's cutesy-wootsy ass should have been parked. The ice cube had begun to melt in a little pool of water.

So that was it, Louis thought, he's stalling for Herbert. Johnny wasn't the leader in all this. That rat from Morgan Divott was, but he wasn't here, was he? Something had happened, something the rest of them hadn't planned on, especially Johnny. That's why they were stumbling all over themselves, why Johnny had taken it upon himself to take control. Thrust the first dagger, so to speak. They had meant to catch him by surprise (and they had, hells bells yes they had), but he'd had a little slice of luck; their leader had gone AWOL, and just for the moment the mutineering sons of bitches didn't know what to do. Goddamn it, the company was his, and his alone, and he wasn't going to let some lizard-kid come in and steal his baby from under his nose.

"There… there's a significant majority of the board…" Johnny began, once again glancing at the empty seat.

Here it comes, Louis smirked. *Et tu Brutus*?

Perhaps he should have seen this coming. When he had employed Johnny straight out of law school his grades hadn't topped the list of candidates, not even in the top ten, but his ambition had stood out like the only vacant seat at the table. Ambition was a two edged sword, though. Louis knew that more than anyone. It could get you where you wanted to go, and fast, but it had its price. In that way, ambition was more like rocket fuel than a sword. Lots of fire, lots of power, but burned out quickly, more than often in a spectacular ball of flames. He had tried to bring Johnny under his wing and control his ambitious nature, help the protégé learn his trade while he climbed the corporate ladder. That was his second mistake, after trusting him. You can't control rocket fuel. It just burns until there's nothing left.

"What significant majority?" Louis said, bluffing. He could see around the table that most had already turned against him. He clenched his fists and rested his knuckles on the table. "You'd better have two thirds. You'll burn in your own fire if you don't."

Johnny's expression steeled. His eyelids hooded and his lips pursed. Coldness emanated from him. The lizard was back. "We've got it," Johnny said.

The kid who had nearly choked to death on the ice cube cleared his throat again, reached for the glass of water, then withdrew his hand. Others around him fidgeted with their ties and scratched imaginary itches on their scalps and noses. Louis had to act now.

"Then call your vote." He undid his top button, hooking down the knot of his tie with his finger. He thought of sitting, then decided against it. If they were going to bring him down, they would have to do it with him looming over them. He needed every advantage he could get, even if it was a psychological one. He knew his size was daunting, but was it enough? He needed to scare the willies out of a few of them, cause them to doubt which way they would go. One vote might be enough to swing it. He only needed one third, or four of the twelve. In fact technically, although Herbert's absence annulled his vote, it worked in the CEO's favor: it counted as a no vote. He only needed three to cling to power.

Louis could tell Johnny knew that too. The rat's absence had made the count closer than he had wanted. Johnny was gambling. He probably had six definites, seven including himself, bought them off with false assurances of pay rises and promotions when the old weasel had been cast out and all the blood had been washed from the boardroom walls. Would probably get rid of the majority within a year if he won, just maintain a handful of trusted friends at his side (and, oh, wouldn't he learn the hard way; there's no such thing as trust in this world) and bring in a fresh group of young lawyers and accountants straight from college, kids that wouldn't dare challenge his power, at least not for seven or eight years. But now he needed two more to be safe, and that was just the problem. He didn't have them.

"I… uh… I need to go to the toilet," the Irish lout said. He pushed his chair back and stood up.

"Gregory, sit down," Johnny said, still as cool as a lizard. "You said you were in."

Gregory's face went as red as it had earlier. "No… uh… to be sure, I never said that, not really. I said I'd think about it." He glanced at Louis, eye-to-eye, and visibly cringed. For someone pushing six foot two, Louis thought, he was kind of weak at the knees. Gregory returned to Johnny and stepped back from the table toward the door, hands flicked up at the wrist, as if in surrender. "I… I don't want to be a part of this anymore." Taking another step back, he glanced over his shoulder at the door, then back at Johnny. "I… uh… I really must be going."

"Gregory, if you don't sit down now your career's as good as over."

Gregory glanced at the door again, and Louis wondered if the lanky galoot knew he would be out of a job by Monday irrespective of who wrestled control in the next few minutes. This was his chance, however, to create another vacant seat, another annulled vote. Once the dominos had started to tumble, who knew how many would fall? Then he summoned his most pleasant *I'm-really-your-best-friend* smile, and said, "Gregory, come and sit at the table." He almost felt sick saying it, like telling Lady Di he loved her, but he needed the tax whiz like never before. "You don't have to vote if you don't want to. No one's putting a gun to your head."

Relief evaporated from Gregory's shoulders like waves of heat above a desert road, and the faintest smile brushed his lips and eyes. "You… you're sure?"

Louis nodded. Gregory stared back at him as if he were Jesus Almighty, the goddamned savior of the entire universe, and took his seat back at the table. Louis suppressed the urge to laugh, then glanced at Johnny. The lizard-kid's nostrils flared almost imperceptibly, the only sign belying his coolness. The dominos had started to tumble; and to add to his woes, Wendy knocked on the door and entered with a note for Louis. She barely glanced at the others, seemingly unaware of what was happening, then left with a wiggle of her curvy hips, a subtle invitation for Louis that they were available whenever he wanted. It was an offer he would certainly take up. Tonight even, right after this sordid little affair was dealt with.

Still standing, he glanced at the memo. "Ha!" he blurted, and chuckled with surprise. The whole situation just got better and better.

He reread the memo, just to be sure. It was a message sent straight from heaven (if you believed in that bullshit), delivered by an angel with a great set of jugs and butts of steel. "It seems, gentlemen," he said, making no attempt to hide his glee, "that your glorious leader will be unable to come to your rescue."

He glanced at the traitors, letting them know he had them by the balls. They were all staring at the note in his hand, even Johnny. Gregory was the only one who wasn't anxious. He was leaning back in his chair with an expression of a passenger smug enough to believe he was the only one safe in a plummeting aircraft because he was the only one wearing his seatbelt. He was smiling. He was actually smiling.

"It says here that Herbert Grimsby has been struck down with a mysterious illness and is currently in a coma in Intensive Care at St. Mary's Hospital. The prognosis isn't good." Louis now let Johnny have the full intensity of his glare. "And the prognosis isn't good for you, either. The game's over. I accept your resignation, effective immediately."

Johnny's hooded eyelids lifted slightly. His nostrils flared, and for a horrid moment Louis thought he saw a forked tongue flick out and lick his lips. "The game's not over, yet," he said, cool as ever. "As you've said, we have to follow protocol. There's still a vote to be taken." He scanned the faces around him. "We don't need Herbert. We can still do this."

The suit and tie two seats up from Johnny's right fidgeted with his cuffs and scratched his balding scalp. "I'm… um… going to abstain," he said.

Johnny stared in disbelief, his cool now rapidly thawing like the ice cube in the seat next to him.

The VP on Gregory's left spoke up next. "Me too. I don't know what we're voting for anymore, now that Herbie's in ICU." He made the sign of the cross on his chest.

Louis now beamed. That was four, five including himself. Johnny had just lost his two-thirds majority. The dominos had fallen quicker than he had expected.

"As I said, I accept your resignation, effective immediately," he said.

Glaring at the two who had just betrayed him, Johnny stood, sniffed contemptuously, and headed for the door. Before he left the boardroom, he turned and fired one last parting shot. "This is not the end. You haven't heard the last of me."

Louis laughed in his face. "The goddamn sky will fall down before you're ever a threat to me again."

Johnny's eyes hooded over. Then he was gone.

Chapter 3

No More Problems

LOUIS chuckled at the memory. History was written by the victor, no truer words had been spoken; and victory was sweet, as sweet as revenge, no matter what anyone else said, almost sweet enough to douse the burning inside his chest. Surprisingly, he hadn't seen nor heard of the lizard-kid since he slinked out of the boardroom and was escorted by security onto Broadway. He had just disappeared. Not that it wasn't hard to meld into the New York shadows, but to completely vanish without a trace was a little surprising. He would have thought he'd have heard something from someone, maybe another CEO who had received his CV, or a client who had been solicited for services, but no, nothing, not even a whisper.

He just wished the mound of problems he was facing would disappear as easily as Johnny Winterbottom. Sighing long again, he heard the muffled ring of the secretary's telephone through the office door. Simultaneously, the red light on Button-1 began flashing again.

Damned idiot thinks we've been disconnected, he grumbled.

He picked up the handset and punched the button before Sarah buzzed to tell him who it was. "Do I have to get on a plane and come over and kick your scrawny butt? Just get the signature on the contract. I don't care how you do it. Just do it."

To his shock, someone other than Epstein cleared his throat before speaking. "Mr. DeVille, this is Sergeant Washington. NYPD."

Louis felt his gastritis burn a path from his lower sternum all the way to his Adam's apple. He leaned forward, resting on the elbow of the hand that held the handset to his ear. The other hand rubbed his chest. He knew what the cop was calling about (and he really should have known it would happen today, shouldn't he?). Just part of the garbage that had been building up since this morning, since two weeks ago in fact. He cleared his throat, and said, "What can I do for you, Sergeant?"

"I think you know, sir," Washington said, and he said *sir* in a way that twisted in his gut like a poker stoking the flames of his gastritis. Louis was sure the cop had been secretly coached by Lady Di to put him off his guard. "We've been waiting for you since half past ten this morning. This is the fourth interview you've failed to attend."

Quashing the urge to slam the phone down, Louis saw the red light of Button-2 begin to flash. An instant later, he heard the muffled ring of the secretary's phone through the door and then Sarah's faint voice talking to the caller.

"I'd like to remind you that sexual harassment is a serious issue," Washington continued. "We need to clear up certain facts before we can proceed with the claim."

"I can explain," he said. "My secretary's new. She's been letting a few things slip lately…"

Washington's voice firmed. "You can explain it to the courts. This is a courtesy call to inform you that because of your frequent refusal to attend police questioning a subpoena has been issued…"

"A subpoena? You're joking." Louis was now rubbing his chest so hard he feared he'd stick his thumb through the fleshy gap in his ribs.

"I'm not joking, sir."

Again *sir* in a manner that snorted down the line: *I've just about had enough of this.* It was Lady Di's coaching, all right. Maybe she was in cahoots with goody-two-shoes Sergeant Washington and that good-for-noth'n cow that had laid the sexual harassment crap against him. "But the bitch is lying."

Washington paused on the end of the line, a pause as long as Epstein's earlier. "I'd also advise you to get a good lawyer before you say anything that may incriminate yourself. Take this as a friendly warning. The subpoena will arrive in the next day or so."

Louis was left holding a dead line. The red light on Button-1 flicked off, but the light on Button-2 was still glaring. He could still hear Sarah speaking through the door and hoped she wouldn't put the caller through. It was bound to be more trash to pile on his plate, and he could do without that at the moment because...

...because, jeez Louise, this pain in his chest was really firing up. Hells bells, he could hardly breathe. The Kwel-Amity had done absolutely nothing. Not a goddamn thing. Worse, he had been rubbing his sternum so hard the skin was stinging raw.

Desperately hoping he had overlooked a bottle of antacids, he flung the top drawer open and rummaged around. There was nothing in there but crap. Blunt pencils. Capless pens. Last year's diary. Used paper. A stapler with no staples. And what was this? A drugstore docket for... for goddamned Kwel-Amities!

He cursed and slammed the drawer. To his horror, the thud of oak on oak coincided with the biggest solar flare of the decade right in the middle of his chest. He flung himself back, arching in his chair, and tried to take a breath. The pain was too intense. So he just sat there, holding still, afraid that even the slightest movement would trigger another monstrous flare.

After a few seconds the pain began to ease enough to take a shallow breath. Then another. Except now he felt the whole of his goddamn neck tingling with pins and needles, including his left arm. Which was kind of strange because he could still move his elbow and wrist and wiggle his fingers, but his shoulder right down to his fingernails had suddenly numbed as if he had been asleep on it or something. A hot, restless sleep too, because his brow was clammy and his mouth was dry like he had had a real horror of a nightmare. What's more, his vision was starting to play up. The room had blurred so much he could barely make out anything in the dim light.

Goddamn it, he thought, he needed a Kwel-Amity. He needed one *right* now.

He scrunched his eyes to see if that would help, then opened them to some kind of sick joke. The room was spinning like a grownup carousel he didn't want to be on. The drapes, the door, the bookshelves, the filing cabinets, every goddamn thing in the room was rotating and moving up and down in an unsynchronized, queasy gyration, slowly at first, then quicker and quicker as the tempo of the music increased…

…Music? Goddamn it, he really *could* hear something. Church bells on a Sunday morning call to service. Yet there was something wrong with them. They sounded, what, out of tune? Almost as if someone was striking a massive gong that had cracked or split, striking it over and over again, faster and faster until the noise was one continuous warble that wormed inside his head and made him want to crush his skull between his hands.

Whatever the hell was going on, he wanted an immediate end to it. He wanted to get off this goddamn ride and throw up. That's what he really wanted to do. The burning in his chest. The numbness in his neck and arm. The gyrating furniture. The goddamn warbling. He needed to puke, and he needed a goddamn Kwel-Amity.

"Mr. DeVille!" Sarah said. "Are you all right? You look pale."

He had only just heard her over the warbling. He glanced over and saw her riding the door as if it were a wooden horse, gyrating up and down and spinning with the rest of the room. Amazingly, her breasts weren't moving. He half expected them to be bouncing all over the place. She also seemed to be holding something in her hand, something yellow and small.

"G'off thagodd'm daw!" he said.

"I can't understand you," she said. "You're slurring."

Louis scrunched his eyes and opened them again. Sarah was still spinning with the room. "Get… off… that… goddamn… *door*!"

Sarah frowned and glanced over her shoulder. He was about to repeat himself when another flare struck him in the middle of the chest. It scorched up his neck to his chin, then down the deadened arm to the hand he was dangling over the armrest. At first he gasped. Then he groaned, a long withering ejaculation that sounded not too dissimilar to the warbling inside his head.

Sarah rushed to the desk. "Mr. DeVille! Are you sure you're all right? Do you want me to call the paramedics?"

Louis sucked in a breath against the pain, held it for as long as he could, then let it out between his gritted teeth, long and slow, hissing steam from his internal boiler. He told her he didn't need the goddamn paramedics. He needed a Kwel-Amity, a whole goddamn bottle of the stuff.

"I can't hear you," Sarah said. She was almost crying. "You're slurring everything you say."

He felt his chest, neck and left arm fizzing in the aftermath of the recent flare. Focusing on her cleavage seemed to help. "Kwel… Amity," he said.

This time Sarah understood. She rushed to his side of the desk and opened the bottom drawer. From somewhere at the back behind the bottle of scotch she removed three drug bottles, then put them on top of the desk. "I thought you knew where I put the spare ones," she said. Louis didn't move, just stared at the bottles in disbelief. "Here, let me open one for you."

He snatched the bottle from her hand and poured the entire contents into his burning gullet. Some of the little white pills spilled onto his desk and lap like popcorn, but most arrived at their intended destination and these he crunched greedily, ignoring the savage bitterness at the back of his mouth and the goggle-eyed surprise of his secretary. He didn't care what he looked like. He had what he wanted. If only he could do something for his eyes. He could barely make out anything beyond the desk, just a swirl of darkness that was once his office.

"Scotch!" he said to Sarah's cleavage.

A pill shot out of his mouth across the table, gobbled by the black abyss. Sarah grabbed the liquor bottle, unscrewed the cap and handed it to him. When he took it he noticed that the yellow thing in her hand was a goddamn Post-It note. He poured the amber liquid into his mouth, crunching and grinding the pills into a sticky paste. Biting into a cake of soap-on-the-goddamn-rope would have tasted better. Worse, sticky foam began to dribble down his chin, but he kept crunching the pills in the hope they would start to do something pretty damn soon. The fire in his chest was starting to build again. The flares were coming in waves and the next one wasn't too far away.

"I'm not sure this is the best time to tell you, Mr. DeVille," Sarah said.

He could hardly hear anything she said now over the god-forsaken warbling. "Huh?" he said through a spray of foam.

"Your wife…"

"Whaddabout mar wife." More dribble splattered onto the desk. At first he thought it was bird shit, then realized his mistake. He lifted his hand to wipe his chin, found that he didn't have the energy, then let it fall to the side. The bottle of scotch dropped to the carpet. "Whadduz the ol cow wun now?"

"The hospital rang while you were on the other line." Sarah was sobbing. She put the Post-It note on the desk in front of him. "That's their details," she said. "You might want to ring them."

He squinted at the memo, a yellow blur with illegible blue squiggles. Sarah hurried to the door that Louis could no longer see, disappearing into the darkness as if she had walked into shadow. He yelled after her, suddenly frightened at being alone. "You call them!" he said. "That's what I pay you for."

"Don't you care about anyone? Not even the woman you've been married to for forty years?" She was yelling from somewhere in the darkness. "She's dying! She's taken an overdose. The doctors don't think she'll pull through."

Suddenly, the warbling intensified into a deafening squeal and the greatest pain he had ever felt smashed through his chest in an explosion of heat and flesh and bones. Sarah was still berating him, but he couldn't make out anything she was saying. He sunk forward, collapsing face down onto what used to be his desk, now a chasm of nothingness. For some reason the last voice he heard wasn't Sarah's. It wasn't even his. It was his wife's.

"I was right, wasn't I Louis?" Lady Di said. "Told you you'd die at your desk."

Then he heard no more.

Chapter 4

Louis' Choice

LOUIS stirred to the sound of scuffling footsteps. He was lying on something comfortable, not what he expected a hospital bed to feel like, lumpy and hard and sheeted with plastic in case your sphincters opened before a nurse slid a bedpan beneath your smelly ass. More like a leather seat with the flip-out footrest, the kind in first-class you can just lay back and sink into with a pillow and blanket all the way to LA or London, or wherever the hell it was you were going.

He then heard scuffles again, though couldn't pinpoint exactly where they were coming from. One second he could have sworn they were to his left. The next, they were to his right. Then in front. Then behind. Then, amazingly, on the ceiling.

When they faded completely, he kept looking around. He saw only whiteness. No door. No window. Just whitewashed walls and a ceiling. A modern building, he reckoned, or recently renovated. Probably St. Mary's Hospital, one of the private rooms in the ITU, which didn't quite make sense either. There was no medical equipment. No beeping cardiac monitors. No whispering artificial ventilators. No bags of blood or fluid over his head. Nothing. Absolutely nothing to suggest where he might be. There wasn't even a call button.

"Nurse! Nurse!" he yelled. "Goddamn it! I need some help here!"

No one answered. *Just good ol' Louis DeVille and this goddamn white room*, he mused. At least that horrid blackness had gone. His vision seemed pretty much back to normal, too. Better than normal, in fact. He could see everything without the need for bifocals. Close, far, in between, everything was as clear as daylight, as if the medics had fixed his eyesight while they were rerouting his clogged up coronaries. Goddamn paid a fortune for medical insurance; they damn well *should* have fixed his eyesight while he was under the knife.

Maybe that explained the bandages. He was covered like a goddamn mummy wrapped head to tail in cotton strips: his arms, legs, torso, just about every goddamn inch of his body. The medics had left holes for his mouth, nose and eyes, but not his ears. He didn't feel uncomfortable, just stupid. What if he had to go to the bathroom in a hurry and there was no one around to help him unwrap? What about that, huh? Which brought him back to the room. He would have to ask the nurses to do something about it. A TV would do for starters. God knew what had been happening while he was infirmed. Another goddamn war in the Middle East could have started and he wouldn't have had the foggiest. Worse, the stock market could have collapsed. How much money had he lost lying unconscious in this goddamn place?

Some things didn't need to change, however. The leather bed, or layback thing, whatever it was, was comfy enough. A pillow and blanket would have been in order, but he was all right for the moment. The temperature was rather pleasant, actually, for a hospital. Damned frigid places, usually. Or worse, damned hot. They were always one way or the other. You either had to wear a coat and gloves like you were stepping into a goddamn refrigerator, or you had to strip everything off like a sauna. This hospital had it just right, though. Nice and cozy. Not too hot. Not too cold.

Still, the light was too damn bright. He would ask the nurse when she came to pull the drapes. But was there a window? He couldn't exactly say. The light seemed to emanate from the walls and ceiling as if they were made of some kind of fluorescent putty, the kind of Glow In The Dark stuff his grandkids used to play with that radiated unnatural lime when the lights were switched off, like it had been bombarded with x-rays or gamma rays or whatever. Not that he thought this room was radioactive. The emanating light almost caressed him, you could say. Bright, but without heat, and it certainly didn't glare his eyes like the low-lying winter sun. The emanation was – dare he say it? – almost cathartic.

It was. He had no more chest pain, and the head-crushing warble was gone. He felt fantastic, actually. Kind of refreshed, in a well-rested kind of way, like he had slept for a whole week or just returned from holidaying in the Bahamas. In fact, he hadn't felt so goddamn good since he was a kid quaffing homemade ice cream on his grandfather's farm just outside Fairmont, Indiana. Ice cream that was exactly what the name implied: iced cream. Not that watered down chemical crap the dairy companies had the gall to sell the kids nowadays. The stuff grandma made was the real thing. Cream churned from cows that he had even helped to milk himself, whipped fluffy and then left to settle overnight in the icebox.

Those were the days, weren't they? Yes sir-ree, he remembered them well. He wouldn't be able to sleep after grandma had set to work. He would lay awake all night thinking of ice cream melting in his mouth, filling his belly until it overflowed from his ears and nose. Then next morning before the rooster crowed he would sneak downstairs to the kitchen and help himself to the tub on the bottom shelf. One spoonful was enough to send him into spasms of ecstasy. Good ol' grandma.

He probably didn't feel quite as good as that now, but he felt pretty damned fine all the same. He wondered what miracle drug the medics had suffused him with, some kind of magic ice-cream infusion that had mended his palpitating heart and put him on top of the world. Not to mention what it had done to his vision.

Scuffled footsteps coming his way brought him back to reality, then kept going. "Nurse!" he shouted. "Don't you leave me here! Don't you leave me!" The scuffles faded, then they were gone. "Goddamn it! I need some help!"

All right, he thought, trying to get off the leather layback, *if nobody's going to help me, I'll just help myself.*

He couldn't get up, however. Something was restraining him. He could move his arms and legs and neck, but something was immobilizing his torso, something like a seatbelt strapped around his guts (*Waistline, dear, it's a waistline*!). He felt around for the offending item, finding nothing save the bandages. Straining against the invisible restraint, he gave up and sunk back into the leather layback wondering what he could do next.

Stuck as a pig in muck, Louis, he mused, staring at the ceiling. That's what his grandma would have said. *Yar gone and put yarself thar. Now yar gone haf't git yarself ait.*

Only he couldn't remember how he had got there. How could he? He had been floating in a goddamn sea of blackness for god knows how long.

Yet that didn't ring quite true. Where he had been was closer to nothing than blackness. Blackness was at least *something*. You might not like it, but you could at least tell it *existed*. Nothing, on the other hand, was nothing. It wasn't even blackness. That's what he remembered. Goddamned nothing. Time and space had just folded in on itself and vanished into nothingness. Then he was here. Wrapped head to tail in bandages and strapped with an invisible seatbelt to a leather layback in a room whose walls and ceiling were made of Glow In The Dark putty. What the hell was he supposed to do next?

Goddamn it, he hated losing control. That's what he hated most about this little prank.

And it was a prank. No two ways about it. Someone – some goddamned medic and his good-for-noth'n nurse – was having a laugh at his expense. Maybe his wife had put them up to it. Maybe they were all laughing at him behind the white walls, having a little chuckle at his expense. Maybe these walls were really two-way mirrors. They could see in, but he couldn't see out.

"This isn't funny anymore!" he shouted, straining against the invisible strap. "Get me outta this goddamn chair!"

No one came, as he had half-expected. He didn't even hear any scuffled footsteps.

"That's goddamn it!"

He arched his back and thrashed his arms and legs, shaking his head from side to side and screaming, "Get me outta this goddamn chair!" After a minute or so (it could have been longer, five or ten minutes maybe, it was hard to tell, maybe even shorter) he gave up and sunk into the leather layback. Though he hated it, absolutely hated it, he would just have to wait until the prankster returned and let him loose.

And wouldn't he give the scumbag a piece of his mind when he did.

Then, just as he felt his eyelids begin to sag, he heard scuffled footsteps approach and stop (from left or right, or up or down, he couldn't tell). This time they didn't fade away. This time he heard whispers. Like the scuffles, they were hard to locate; they were just everywhere. He couldn't catch the whole of the conversation, but there was no doubt who they were talking about. He strained against the invisible strap and yelled, "Who the hell is there?"

The whispering ceased. Then a booming voice almost shook him off his layback, reverberating from all corners of the room. "LOUIS DEVILLE!" He was too stunned to answer. Though loud, the voice wasn't painful like the warbling had been, just something that seemed to *emanate*, the verbal equivalent of the light. "ARE YOU READY?"

Ready for what? he thought.

"It's Lewey. Not Lewis," he said, directing himself to the ceiling. Whoever was talking to him must be talking from somewhere up there. "And you'd better have a goddamn good excuse for tying me up like this. I know my rights. My lawyers will sling your sorry ass to court quicker than you can call your defense union."

He sank back waiting for the retort, but the voice remained silent for some time. For a horrid moment, he thought he'd been left alone again. Then it spoke.

"LOUIS DEVILLE! ARE YOU READY?"

"Stop calling me Lewis! It's Lewey, goddamn it!"

Another momentary pause, then, "ARE YOU READY?"

Struggling to prop himself on his elbows, he said, "Ready for what you goddamn piece of shit?"

"TO SIGN THE CONTRACT!"

Louis kept scanning the room for originator of the voice, failing to see anything past the bright walls and ceiling that were continuing to radiate like some x-rayed slab of Glow In The Dark putty. He wasn't surprised. His first hunch was becoming increasingly likely; he was in one of those two-way mirrored rooms watched by god knows how many medics and professors analyzing his every word and gesture. He had seen the TV shows. He knew what they were doing behind the screen. Still propped on his elbows, he said, "What contract? My health insurance is paid up. I don't owe you a damn thing."

"YOU HAVE A CHOICE."

Two contracts? Now there was a goddamn novelty. "I'm not signing anything until I read them," he said. Then, as an afterthought: "I want my lawyers to go through them, too."

He heard a whisper hushing around the room, above, below, forward, behind, left and right, everywhere in fact. It was difficult to tell whether there was more than one or whether the voice was just whispering to itself. Then: "NO LAWYERS."

"Goddamn it!" he shouted to the ceiling. "Just who the hell do you think you are? I'm entitled to legal representation."

Again, more whispering followed a studied pause. Then: "NO LAWYERS."

Louis took a moment to think. He was in a Mexican standoff. Except he wasn't really, was he? They – whoever *they* were – had him by the short and curlies. They could see him, but he couldn't see them. They came and went as they pleased, while he was restrained like a goddamned psychopath the medics were too afraid to untie for fear of letting loose the devil. He hated it, but he really had no choice apart from accepting their conditions and making some sort of compromise. Still, at least they were offering him a choice. It probably wouldn't do any harm to have a look. Maybe he could stall for time while he tried to work out just what the hell was happening. He didn't have to put pen to paper just yet.

Louis said to the ceiling, "I'll look at the contracts on one condition."

Whispers hushed around the room before it spoke again. "STATE YOUR TERMS."

Louis smiled. *A minor victory, Louis my boy, but there's a long way to go yet.* "Remove these goddamn shackles," he said.

Instantly, the invisible restraint loosened around his waist. He sat up and dangled his legs over the edge. On the floor at the base of the layback were two contracts he hadn't noticed before; one a wad of paper as thick as a telephone directory, the other a single folio scrolled and tied with a purple ribbon. He jumped down, surprised at the ease and litheness at which he landed on the floor, and picked them up. Now that he had the medics listening to him, it was time for the next item on the agenda.

"How long do I keep these bandages on?" he asked, putting the contracts on the leather layback.

The voice didn't answer immediately. "YOU HAVE A CHOICE."

Louis glanced up at the ceiling, slightly bemused. "You're the docs. Aren't you supposed to tell me when they can come off?"

The voice repeated itself.

Louis shrugged. If that was the way it was, then he chose now. He grabbed a loose end of a bandage on his wrist and unwound it. There was another bandage underneath. He unwound that one too. There was another. And another. "What the hell's going on?" he said, growling under his breath. Then to the ceiling: "Get these goddamn bandages off me!"

"MAKE YOUR CHOICE," the voice said. It wasn't a threat, just a simple statement of fact.

Louis glanced down at the leather layback and picked up the scroll with the purple ribbon. He was surprised to read that it wasn't a contract at all. It was a goddamn party invitation: *Louis DeVille is hereby invited to attend the Celebration of Life at the Mansion of Many Rooms.* He reread it, thinking it some kind of childish joke. There was no name, no indication as to who had written it. Nor was it dated; and he had no idea where in hell he was supposed to find the address of the Mansion of Many Rooms. His signature wasn't even required at the bottom. What kind of goddamn contract was this? Something his useless wife would have come up with. It was even hand written in amateurish scrawl. The whole thing was farcical, just like this entire goddamn state of affairs.

When he glanced down at the thick wad of paper, it suddenly clicked what he was meant to do.

Maybe that's it. Maybe this whole thing is a test.

He tossed the scroll over his shoulder and flicked through the other contract. Now this was more like it. Six hundred and sixty-six typed pages of detailed contractual obligations. Though, to his dismay, there were more clauses and sub-clauses than he had seen on any document, more than he reckoned he would find on the latest amendment to the constitution of the United Goddamn States of America. It would take him over a month to get through all the legalese mumbo jumbo.

He skimmed over the first few pages. It seemed the issuing authority, LeMont International Enterprises Ltd, was undertaking a major restructuring program and he was being headhunted to oversee the project, and at his age that was a goddamn laugh. Still, on page thirteen, the contract defined the proposed position as "Interim Management Consultant," IMC, and went on to list the terms of his employment over the next four or five pages. Which was the first thing he needed to negotiate. He couldn't devote himself to another fulltime position whilst remaining head of Global Resolutions Network. Goddamn it. That would mean working around the clock. It just couldn't be done; and though he was flattered at their interest in him, he would just have to tell them that their expectations were a little unrealistic, to say the least. If they really wanted his consulting services, they would just have to accept he couldn't do it at the drop of a hat. It would have to be part-time, once a week at most, or nothing.

He continued reading. On page one hundred and four he saw something about "exclusivity of intellectual property" and made a mental note to query it with his lawyers (and he would, goddamn it, even if LeMont International Enterprises had a problem with getting his lawyers involved). There was more, too. The position of Interim Management Consultant entailed living on site, which was just goddamn ridiculous. He would be buggered before he packed up and left his penthouse on Beeker Street. But it was there, in writing. Clause one hundred and sixty-nine, sub-clause (b) on page two hundred and seventy-three: "It is agreed that the IMC undertakes immediate residency within the premises of LeMont International Enterprises Ltd."

He kept flicking through, shaking his head. From what he could gather, LeMont International Enterprises was some kind of industrial export park where all the employees worked and lived, from cleaners and maintenance workers to administrative and executive staff. It sounded massive, in fact, a corporation leviathan. A corporation *metropolis.*

How hadn't he heard of them before? He hadn't a goddamn clue who LeMont International Enterprises were, and there was nothing in the contract from what he had briefly seen to indicate what they actually produced. They weren't listed on the New York Stock Exchange, that was for sure; something this big he would have known about. They had to be privately owned. When he got out of hospital, he would make sure Sarah got onto it straight away. Find out just who these guys were, and what in hell they had to do with his rehabilitation.

He put the contract back down on the leather layback. All in all it looked like the real deal. It was tempting all right. Tempting enough that he might just take them up on their offer. Maybe he could manipulate the position of IMC for the good for his own business. Maybe this company was the answer to the recent problems he had been facing.

"I'll need some time to go through it," he said to the ceiling. "Devil's in the detail, you know. I'm not just putting my name down on something without going through it with a fine-tooth comb."

Louis heard whispers before the voice answered: "YOU HAVE ALREADY CHOSEN."

"What do you mean? I haven't signed anything yet."

"YOU HAVE REJECTED THE OTHER. YOUR CHOICE HAS BEEN MADE."

Louis glanced over his shoulder at the scroll he had tossed away. He was about to say that the assumption of choice made through indirect action was goddamn ridiculous, and about as legally binding as same sex marriage in the state of Utah, but the voice cut him short.

"LOUIS DEVILLE. ARE YOU READY?"

"What, goddamn it? Ready for what?"

"YOUR JUDGMENT."

Chapter 5

Judgment

WITHOUT any indication of what was going to happen, the room suddenly lit up in a flash of brilliant white light, as though a Super Nova had just exploded over his head. Louis' first reaction was to cringe and bury his head in the crook of his bandaged elbows. "What the hell?" he shouted.

It wasn't an explosion, as it turned out. There was no noise, no cracking boom that burst his eardrums and rendered him deaf. There was no heat surge, though he half expected to feel himself erupt into flames and frizzle to a pile of ash. There wasn't even a shockwave to knock him to his knees or launch him into the wall on the other side of the room. Not so much as a breath of wind, just stillness and silence.

Nonetheless, when he peeked from the crooks of his elbows, he found he had been temporarily blinded. The abyss of darkness had returned, to his dismay, though this time he was fully *corpus mentis*. "Goddamn it you son of a bitch!" he shouted to the ceiling, groping the space in front of him where the leather layback should have been. "I can't see a goddamn thing!"

He kept groping for the layback. At that moment, he heard footsteps scuffling from behind. He spun around, though what really freaked him out was that it sounded more like a scuttling rodent than an approaching nurse or medic. A goddamn *huge* rodent.

"Who's there?" he said. He heard the opening of a door, followed by scuffled footsteps and some sort of scraping noise. "Who's there?" he asked again. The door clicked shut and he heard more scraping scuffles. "Answer me, goddamn it! I know someone's there!"

"Now, now, Mr. DeVille," someone said, and sniggered. "No need to get hot under the collar. I'm here to help."

Louis almost jumped out of his bandages. It wasn't the same voice he had heard previously, the one that boomed from every corner of the room. This was meek and reedy and filled with a false sense of courage, the kind of voice that only dared to make itself heard from the shadows. The voice's manner was kind of familiar too, though not one he had heard for some time, and not one he could immediately put a face to. He figured it wasn't Epstein. That good-for-noth'n Jew-boy wouldn't fly all the way to New York to see how the boss was recovering. Not unless there was something in it for himself. In fact, he was sure it wasn't any of his current vice presidents. They were probably this minute squabbling over who would take over the reins. Well, he had news for them. This CEO wasn't dead and buried just yet.

"Who are you?" he asked. "I can't see. I've been blinded."

"You're not blind," the stranger said, and from the tone of his voice he seemed to have enjoyed scaring him. "The lights are off."

Louis brought his hand to his face and held it an inch away from his eyes. It was true. He could see the bandages wrapped around his digits, though in the near total darkness he thought he could only count three fingers and they looked kind of shorter and stubbier than normal. He let the thought go, blaming it on the lack of visibility, and told the stranger to switch on the lights.

"They're off for a reason," the stranger said.

Louis heard him snigger again under his breath. His high reedy voice was really beginning to give him the creeps. It sounded like the squeak of a mouse, or even a rat; and no matter how goddamn ridiculous it sounded, the idea that he was in conversation with a rodent wouldn't leave his head. He wanted to see who he was talking to. *Had* to see, for his own sanity.

"I don't give a goddamn hoot what the reason is. I want the lights on."

The stranger replied, "They're off for your own protection."

Again, Louis heard the guy (mouse?) snigger. He had heard something else too, a kind of swish, like something (a tail?) trailing across the floor. Something wasn't right here. Something wasn't goddamned right at all. Louis took a step back, feeling his way toward the wall. "I want the light on," he said, taking another step back. "I want it on now!"

This time the stranger snorted in contempt. "I tell you what. Why don't you stop giving the orders and start taking them?"

Louis took another step back. The leather layback wasn't where it should have been. The darkness had him so disorientated he had lost all sense of where he was in relation to it. What's more, the room seemed bigger somehow, as if the walls had stretched apart with the Super Nova explosion. Even the ceiling seemed higher. The dark space was vacuous; and if he didn't think it impossible, he could have sworn he was in a different room from a moment ago.

It even smelled differently. The white room (if he could actually suspend disbelief for a moment and admit that he was no longer in that room), the two-way mirrored room, hadn't really smelled of anything. It certainly hadn't smelled of disinfectant or antiseptic floor wash, the kind of nasal-cleansing reek he expected from a hospital; and neither did this room (the dark room?). It smelled more like he remembered his grandfather's farm, cattle and horses and pigs and poultry, before the old man was forced to sellout to the Office of Roads and Transport and watch the bulldozers level the only property he had owned to make way for a goddamn highway. That's what this room smelled of, animals; and whether they loved it or hated it, that was the smell every kid growing up in the big smoke remembered about their trips to the countryside. The smell that lingered for days in your hair and clothes when you got back to your parents' two-bedroom apartment in Brooklyn, no matter how often you rinsed your head or how hard you pressed your jeans and shirt through the wringer. The smell that made the bullies in the playground rub your face in the mud and call you "Farm Boy" or "Stinky" (*Horseshit, DeVille, you stink of goddamn horseshit!*), then pull your trousers down and fill it with dog turds and tell all the other kids that you crapped in your pants.

Yeah, he remembered that goddamned smell all right. He had never forgotten it; and it was with him again.

Louis backed further away. He could still hear the swish of whatever it was trailing back and forth behind the stranger. A length of rope? For what? To tie him up?

"You can stop backing away, Mr. DeVille," the stranger said, but that was the last thing Louis was going to do. "I'm here to help."

Two steps more, Louis backed into the wall. Though difficult to feel anything through the bandages, he ran his hand over it for a door handle or window ledge. Even still, he could tell that the wall was rough with indented shallows and knobby bumps, as if a pick-axe had gouged the entire face out of rock. That was a goddamn surprise. He thought he was on the upper level of the hospital, where most ITU departments seemed to be located. Except now it seemed he was somewhere underground, in a tunnel or something. Most probably down in the basement with the emergency generators and laundry rooms. Which explained why the room was so goddamn stifling. When had it got so goddamn hot and steamy? It was a goddamn sauna.

He kept running his bandaged hand over the rocky wall. The stranger scuffled closer. "I want my lawyer," Louis said. He had never wished to see that Jew-boy Epstein as much as now. "I know my rights."

The stranger sniggered, scuffling closer still. "You'll get a lawyer in due course." Louis figured the gap between them was no more than two or three arm-lengths now. "As for your rights," and he paused, sniggering, "you have as much as what *The Boss* allows you to have."

Louis pressed himself to the wall. He felt his body break out in sweat beneath the bandages. The stranger was now right in his face, yet he still couldn't see him. Where was that goddamn Jew-boy when he needed him? Where was Sarah? Goddamn it, where was any of his employees? The stranger sniggered and a stench of rotting flesh wafted past his nostrils, a stench so goddamned vile it made him gag and his head start to spin.

"I've waited a long time for this, Mr. DeVille," the stranger said. "Your ass is mine!"

Louis felt the stranger grab him on the shoulder and then a sudden sting in the neck. He squealed, a pathetic noise that sounded alien and far away. Worse, as if he had just been injected with some hypnotic drug, he felt his head beginning to spin. It was happening again. His knees crumpled beneath him, then his ears blocked up and he was suddenly deaf as well as blind. He could still smell, though. That god-awful reek was worse than anything. It was everywhere, totally overwhelming his senses (*Horseshit, DeVille, you stink of goddamn horseshit!*).

Powerless, he slid down the wall and collapsed in an unconscious heap at the feet of the stranger.

Chapter 6

The Mirror of Truth

THE first thing Louis saw when his eyelids creaked open was the portrait. Similar in many ways to the portrait hanging in his office, the one he had paid a goddamn fortune for, it was roughly the same size and had the same gilded frame. Yet it wasn't his portrait. To begin with, there was no Roman Coliseum in the background. Just a plain gray backdrop like on those days when the clouds sheeted the sky from horizon to horizon and drizzled nonstop for hours and hours and hours.

What's more, someone with a warped sense of humor had replaced his imposing Caesar-like figure with a scrawny weasel, still wearing a toga and laurel mind you. A goddamn caricature those two-bit artists at Times Square or Liberty Island sketched for the tourists, the ones that exaggerated your worst features – bucked teeth, bulging eyes, flapping ears – and made you look like a goddamn Loony Toon cartoon. Maybe Epstein had passed the hat around the office and had it made while he was stuck in hospital. Maybe the Jew-boy thought it would cheer the boss up and help him with his rehabilitation. If that was the case, he could afford a bit of a chuckle. He wasn't so uptight he couldn't laugh at himself (hadn't his VPs always called him "the old weasel" behind his back?). As long as Epstein hadn't dipped into company funds to pay for the goddamn thing, it was all right with him.

Thinking of his subordinates caused him to remember where he was and how he had got there. Looking left and right to see if he still had company, he realized somewhat absently that he was on the leather layback again, now propped upright with something digging into his lower spine, a cylindrical-shaped lump, like a rolled newspaper or magazine. Thankfully, he was alone again, just as he had been in the white room. Except now the walls and ceiling and floor were gray, like slate or granite. In fact, it was more like a cave or grotto than a hospital room, and it was still as goddamn hot as hell.

At least the stench had improved. He could still detect the lingering smell of horseshit, but it was nowhere near as bad as it had been when the stranger had sniggered in his face. What's more, and it had almost slipped his attention, the lights were back on. The dark room had turned into the gray room.

He glanced at the roof. A single dusty globe dangled from the end of a tortuous piece of wire. Was it just his mind playing tricks on him, or did the rays from the filament seem gray and sick, somehow *malignant*? Like the tumor that had eaten his grandfather's stomach from the inside out. He didn't know if it were possible for light to become cancerous, it just reminded him of how his grandfather's skin had turned the same miserable gray toward the end. Despite his youthfulness, when Louis had walked onto the hospital ward and seen the limp form on the bed, he had known right there and then that there would be no miracle cure to save his grandfather. Henry Trump didn't even last a week, and the grayness never left his skin. Even the foundation and rouge the undertakers had applied to his face before the funeral couldn't hide it. Once the grayness was in you, it never left. It lingered like horseshit.

Annoyingly, the cylindrical thing continued to press into his back. He wiggled around to try and dislodge it, but it only seemed to roll from one flank to the other. Then he leaned forward and reached behind, and when he did he almost fainted with shock for the second time. The weasel in the portrait had moved.

Frozen, he kept staring at the toga-clad weasel. Likewise, its arm was now behind its back. That was the movement he had caught out of the corner of his eye. Louis didn't dare move. *Couldn't* move. He had heard of people petrified with sheer terror, like rabbits caught by headlights in the middle of the road, but not from simple disbelief. His jaw hadn't even dropped. His eyelids, too, were stuck half-open in the act of blinking, like shutters jammed on rusty hinges. They hadn't so much as fluttered.

Unable to take his gaze off the weasel, his mind whirred with possible explanations as to what in hell was going on. Not for the first time he wondered if he were being set up, if this was just one big joke. Someone was having a goddamn laugh at his expense. Nonetheless, there was really only one explanation, wasn't there? And if that was a mirror in the center of the frame and not a portrait Epstein had arranged for his amusement, and somehow, somewhere between blacking out in his office and waking up in this gray sauna-cave, he had been resurrected as a goddamn weasel, then he would rather find out sooner than later. The proof, he figured, was on top of his head. If the laurel was there, he was a weasel. If it wasn't, he was still good ol' Louis Hugo DeVille, CEO of Global Resolutions Network, suffering husband to Lady Di, and there was nothing to worry about. Goddamn simple as that.

Slowly, he began to reach for the laurel, then stopped, keeping his arm wedged behind his back. Maybe this wasn't really happening. Maybe this was one of them watchamacallit dreams, the ones where you were awake but not awake. Lady Di had had one a year or two ago, about the same time she started yoga classes and mumbling "aum" around the apartment to the point it drove him half-mad. She didn't listen when he had told her to shut her goddamn trap, of course. She kept on doing what she damn well pleased, chanting "aum" here, there and everywhere until he had no choice but to ignore everything she said, which wasn't exactly a new course of action. But he hadn't been able to ignore entirely everything, as he had wanted.

One thing he remembered was the conversation she had had with her good-for-noth'n sister. Something about a dream she had had. "Lucid dreaming," she had described it. He was at the kitchen table reading the Sunday paper trying to ignore her. Lady Di was in front of the TV in the lounge room with the portable handset nestled between her ear and shoulder, shrugging it tight so that it wouldn't fall to the carpet while she exercised on the Ezy-Cycle. She and her sister had been gasbagging since the crack of dawn and he was about to blow his top. Nothing he had tried could block out her constant prattle. Closing the kitchen door. Turning on the radio (even though he couldn't stand the weekend breakfast programs). Not even the TV could drown out her whine. She was just so goddamn *loud.* He was about to get up and go to the bedroom when he heard her mention the dream she had had.

"I tell you, Jennifer," she said, still pedaling on the Ezy-Cycle and watching the Home Shopping Channel, "it was a lucid dream. What? … Oh, don't you know? My yoga teacher has them all the time. It's really strange, you know… Hmm, what? No. Not that kind of strange. More like you know it's a dream but it's as real as when you're awake."

Louis scoffed into his coffee, flicked the newspaper and tried to ignore his wife for the rest of the day. Only people who had nothing better to do with their time would believe that yoga-dreaming claptrap. Except now, believe it or not, he was having the same kind of experience that his wife had had. Maybe he was still unconscious in the office on Broadway and having this god-awful dream about reincarnation as a weasel. Maybe he was laying face down on his desk next to the bottles of Kwel-Amity and the yellow Stick-It note…

Goddamn it, he mumbled, snapping out of his train of thoughts. *I completely forgot. The stupid cow's taken an overdose again.*

He hadn't dreamed that, or if he had everything in his goddamn life had been imagined and no more real than Santa Claus or the tooth fairy.

Daring to return to the weasel in the mirror, he hoped the reality he had once taken for granted and felt so comfortable with wasn't about to take on a horrifying new dimension. His arm was still wedged behind his back feeling for the lump, which, if this wasn't a goddamn lucid dream but a real life nightmare, he had a pretty good idea what it was. If he grabbed it and twisted it, he would feel pain shooting up his spine into his brain as if he had done the same thing to his big toe. Which now he was beginning to doubt he had. Big *claw* was probably more to the point, or whatever a weasel had for digits on its feet.

He decided there was no point in hanging around and waiting for something to happen. He had always considered himself a go-get-it, roll-up-your-sleeves kind of guy; if something needed doing, he would do it. He had no time for pussyfoots and cowards who couldn't make up their mind, who froze to the spot when a decision needed to be made. No time at all. So he went for it.

When he grabbed the thing pressing into his back, he flinched.

It was exactly as he had suspected. He had grabbed his tail.

Chapter 7

The Weasel

LOUIS let go of his tail and put his hand (did weasels have hands?) – his *paw* – on his head. The weasel in the mirror copied everything he did, including removing the laurel and putting it on his lap. He was a goddamn weasel all right. The evidence was plain enough. He was even wearing the toga he could see adorning the reflection, and when he ran his paw over it he was reminded of the silky sheets the maid fitted to the beds at the penthouse. He felt like some idiot at a fancy-dress party that nobody else had turned up for.

Perhaps that was it. Perhaps this was a surprise fancy-dress party in honor of good ol' Louis DeVille's birthday. Perhaps Lady Di, her sister Jennifer, Sarah, Jew-boy Epstein and the whole crazy gang from Global Resolutions Network were going to burst through the door and start singing For He's A Jolly Good Weasel.

"That's the surprise, Mr. DeVille!" Epstein would say. "Your really *are* a despicable little critter."

Lady Di would probably add: "Told you, Louis, didn't I?" and she would call him Lewis, not Lewey, in her smarmy, know-it-all tone of voice. "Always said you'd find out who you *really* were."

Louis snorted and briefly examined the laurel. It wasn't the real thing. Fake plastic bay leaves that looked dull and lifeless in the grim, gray light. He put it back on his head, figuring he couldn't look any more ridiculous than he already did, and glanced beneath the chair at the floor. The six-hundred-page contract was there, next to a pile of tangled bandages. He wondered who had stripped them off and dressed him in this goddamn costume. Nurses? Medics? He doubted it. He no longer reckoned he was in a hospital. He was beginning to suspect he was somewhere else. Somewhere much worse.

For the moment though, he pushed that thought to the back of his mind and jumped off the chair to get a better look at his "new" self. He went to the mirror and stood in front of it, more in resignation to his future as a small carnivorous mammal than in genuine interest with his unplanned metamorphosis. His body seemed long and out of proportion with his arms and legs; and he had fur, goddamn it, the kind of russet all-over-body stuff that his wife would have paid a fortune to drape around her neck or made into a coat. Probably why he felt so hot and sweaty. What's more, he also had a snout with whiskers, which he could twitch with his pointy ears.

All the better to smell you with, little red DeVille! he thought, and sniffed at the reflection a couple of times in jest. To his revulsion, he caught more than he had expected of the stench that lingered in this god-forsaken place. *Just your luck to end up in a place that stinks of goddamn horseshit, Louis.*

He smirked, and was surprised to see the amount of teeth beneath the curl of his upper lip. There were hundreds of the pointy little buggers. Well, maybe not hundreds, but a hell of a lot more than he was used to. He ran his tongue over them, thinking he could do some serious damage with a mouth like this. *All the better to eat you with*! he growled at his reflection, and chuckled.

If only he had his rifle. He looked just like something he would take a shot at in the woods and have stuffed and framed. If he hadn't seen it with his own two eyes (if these beady brown things on either side of this feral cranium were actually *his*), he would never have believed it; and that wasn't the half of it. Besides the laurel and toga, the thing that really pushed this entire goddamn shenanigans to the edge of lunacy was his stance. He didn't even *walk* like a weasel, or like any goddamn animal he knew. He was upright! Standing on his back two legs like some goddamn circus bear, or a human in a…

That was it! He was wearing a goddamn suit. Had to be. It explained everything. Absolutely everything. He yanked the hem of the toga up and splayed the fur of his belly in search of a zip, but to his frustration there was no sign of anything remotely close to one, not even a stitch line or buttonhole. Neither was there anything on his back, as far as he could see in the reflection, just a tail that wagged as easily as he could wiggle his toes.

Claws, Louis, he sneered. *They're not your toes anymore. They're your goddamn claws.*

He sighed and let go of the hem of the toga. It fell over the lower half of his body and upper thighs. Who was he kidding? This was for goddamn real, if *real* meant anything any more, and he had better get his head in order if he wanted to do something about fixing the situation and returning to some kind of normality. He didn't know if getting back to normal was possible, but he wasn't going to give up on the idea just yet. What did his grandfather used to say? "If you don't pull the trigger, you'll never hit the target." He guessed it was the old fella's version of *You've got to be in it to win it.*

While he stared at his reflection wondering what in hell he should do next, he detected someone (or some*thing*) outside the door. More precisely, he had *smelled* it. The stench of horseshit had dramatically increased, alerting him before anything else, which surprised him. His sense of smell was usually the worst of his five senses. Let's face it, he thought, sixty-six years of living with the fumes and garbage and grime of the Big Apple had dulled his sense of smell to something he barely knew he had. Except now, this new elongated snout with whiskers on the end was a highly sensitive organ that could detect aromas many times fainter than he had ever thought possible. The jury was out on whether that was a good thing or not. What was better, having virtually no sense of smell at all or being able to sniff horseshit from a mile away?

He faced the door, pricking his ears. Scuffling footsteps, faint at first, were getting louder, echoing down some sort of corridor or passage. There was more than one, as well. Two pairs, maybe three; and as the scuffles neared, the stench of horseshit got worse. Then they stopped outside the door. He could hear whispers, followed by sniggering.

Louis braced himself. "Who's there?" he asked, though he reckoned he already knew the answer. The whispering got louder. "I know you're out there. I can goddamn smell you."

The whispering continued to ignore him. Louis could definitely hear two distinct voices now (along with his sense of smell, his hearing was a hell of an improvement on what it had been). One of the voices was the high-pitched whine he had had the misfortune of encountering before. The other was unfamiliar: deeper, more masculine. They seemed to be quarreling over who was going in first. Neither of them seemed to want to do it. He pricked his new weasel ears even more. Without them he wouldn't have heard much more than broken syllables and disjointed sentences, TV chatter in a hotel room down the other end of the corridor. Then the unfamiliar voice said, "All right. I'll do it. But you owe me."

Louis considered rushing the guy and pinning him to the floor, then thought better of it. He didn't have his two hundred and fifty pound frame to throw around anymore, just this pathetic lightweight thing of fur and bones without an ounce of fat on it. Plus, the guy about to waltz through the door might be a goddamn monster. Then again, he might also be as scrawny as a mouse. Still, though he hated the thought of being physically weaker than someone else, he wasn't about to take the risk of making a fool of himself. This was a time to be cautious, not reckless.

When the door opened, he was glad he had held back. The guy turned out to be a good head taller than him; and if the goddamn stench didn't stop him in his tracks, then he was sure he would've fallen over laughing anyway. As it was, he had to do all in his power to stop rolling over in fits of laughter now. "What the hell are you?" he asked.

Like Louis, the guy was walking unnaturally upright. He took several steps in and stopped, leaving the door open. He hooded his eyelids, as if he had heard worse a million times before. "What does it look like?" he said, his voice cool and calm. "I'm a lizard. A monitor lizard to be precise. From the genus *Varanus Niloticus*."

"In a suit and tie?" Louis didn't bother mentioning the leather briefcase he was carrying, or that his tail was poking out from the seam of his trousers.

"Taken a good look at yourself lately?"

Louis glanced at laurel and toga in the mirror. He figured the lizard had him on that point. "It's not my fault. I woke up like this."

"It never is our own fault, is it Mr. DeVille?" The lizard flicked out his tongue, licking his lips. "Sometimes we just don't have a choice what happens to us."

Louis was certain the freak was laughing at him behind those dark eyes. Like his first encounter with the sniggering stranger, he wasn't too sure he could warm up to this guy. "How do you know my name?"

The lizard removed what looked like a bottle of Kwel-Amities from his inner suit pocket, but whatever lizards had for hands – Louis decided on claws – it was obscuring the label. "Your reputation precedes you," he said, opening the lid. "The Boss has had his eye on you for quite some time."

Louis glanced at the wad of papers next to the pile of bandages at the base of the layback. "Who the hell is The Boss? The CEO of LeMont International Enterprises?"

He heard a snigger from the doorway, but couldn't see who had made the noise. Outside the room was a passageway or tunnel with rough-cut walls that appeared to have been bored through a mountain. Like the room, it glimmered with dreary gray light. He was beginning to get some sort of picture of where he was. Somewhere underground. Which explained the artificial light and lack of windows, but not exactly *where* he was. Probably not Manhattan. Probably not even in the state of New York. He would get to the bottom of it though. Good ol' Louis DeVille always did. One step at a time.

The lizard popped a pill into his mouth. "Why does The Boss want me to work for him?" Louis said. "And keeping me locked up against my will is no way to start a working relationship. I want a lawyer before I do anything." He pointed to the wad of papers on the ground. "I'm not signing the contract until I have legal representation."

Still holding the briefcase, the lizard snapped the lid back onto the drug bottle and returned it to the inner pocket. Then he stepped forward, holding out his claw to be shaken. Louis was no reptilian expert, but the back of his claw seemed excessively scaly, almost dry and flaky, like a bad case of all-over dandruff.

"That's where I come in," the lizard said, and flashed what Louis thought only as a salesman's smile. Louis wasn't having a bar of it. "Frederick Spank. *Spank'n rich and spank'n good look'n.* But you can call me Flash, or Freddy, or even Flash Freddy. Whatever takes your fancy."

Louis reckoned the lizard had probably delivered that line a million times or more. Probably didn't even realize how goddamn cheap and sleazy it sounded. He shook the scaly claw in any case. "You're my legal representative?"

Flash Freddy kept his flashy grin. "At your service. The Boss has specifically asked me to take care of all your concerns regarding the contract."

"And your expenses, too, I hope," Louis said.

Flash Freddy winked, and said, "Naturally. You don't have to worry about a thing."

The gesture was supposed to have put him at ease, but all it did was send a shudder down Louis' spine all the way to the tip of his furry tail. He drew his paw away and absently wiped it on his toga.

Flash Freddy didn't seem to notice. He opened his briefcase, picked the contract off the ground and put it inside, then snapped the briefcase shut. "You must be pretty special to have The Boss take such an interest in you," he said. "I'm one of LeMont's most expensive attorneys, you know."

Louis heard the lizard's colleague sniggering from the passageway again. He motioned toward the open door with an upward nod. "Why's your friend hiding?"

The lizard glanced over his tail and said, "Smiggins, show yourself to our new friend. He's not going to bite you." Saying nothing, he turned to Louis and shook his head, as if to quell any notion Louis might *really* have had of taking a bite out of his colleague.

Louis heard a hiss and a shuffle of feet. Flash Freddy hooded his eyes and told Smiggins again to show himself. Then again.

Finally, after the fourth time of asking, Smiggins appeared in the empty doorframe.

"Louis DeVille," Flash Freddy said, now beaming. He even pronounced his name correctly. "This is Warren Smiggins. Your personal assistant."

Louis took one look at him and for some reason licked his upper lip. He almost *did* have the urge to rush over and sink his pointy teeth into his neck.

Smiggins was a goddamn rat.

Chapter 8

THE AFTER LIFE

STARING at the rat, Louis felt the grip of revulsion twist in his gut. The stench of horseshit had become overwhelming the instant Smiggins had entered the room. Flash Freddy was still smiling his salesman's smile, but he had another thing coming if he thought the CEO of Global Resolutions Network was going to work with a guy like this. It was a goddamn insult. If this scrawny rat as his PA was a condition of becoming IMC, then there was no way in hell he was going to sign the goddamn contract. Wouldn't even think about it. An eight-figure sum wouldn't be enough to entice him to the negotiating table.

"I think you'll enjoy working with each other," Flash Freddy said, motioning for Smiggins to get closer.

By far the smallest of them, Smiggins was also standing upright, his spine bent like someone three times his age. For some reason, his bony claws were clasping a calculator to his chest. To Louis' relief, he stayed exactly where he was, keeping the safety of the open door at his back.

"The Boss is staking the future of LeMont International Enterprises on your ability to get along with one another," Flash Freddy said, hooding his eyes. "He's invested a lot in getting you here, Mr. DeVille. Had to pull a lot of strings. We wouldn't want to disappoint him now, would we?"

Louis kept eyeing the revolting critter near the doorway. His navy blue suit and pinstriped tie was identical to his colleague's, yet beneath it the rat seemed to be wasting away. The jacket sagged over his shoulders like a baggy raincoat, and the backs of the legs hung like two limp flags at half-mast. His tail furthermore, poking out from the seam of his trousers, jerked like a worm stretched unnaturally long and thin in the throes of death. "You injected me with some kind of sleeping drug," Louis said, rubbing his neck.

The rat sniggered, and like the lizard had done before removed a drug bottle from his inner suit. "For your own protection," he said, swallowing a pill and pocketing the bottle.

Louis cringed with disgust, wondering just how in hell he expected any respect with such a high-pitched feminine squeal. He'd be buggered before he allowed this goddamn faggot to work as his PA.

Flash Freddy flicked his tongue and licked his lips. "Most new clients don't handle the transition very well," he said. "We've found it easier for all concerned to induce a state of somnolence when they first arrive. It… uh, kind of lessens the shock, if you know what I mean. You, by the way, are handling the whole thing extremely well."

Louis glanced at his reflection again, hitching the toga strap that had slipped from his shoulder. The lizard had no idea how much trouble he had accepting this new image of himself.

"Before The Boss established the protocol of sleep induction, we used to do nothing," Flash Freddy went on. "We used to let the *newbies* sort it out themselves, but too many of them went completely nuts." He shook his head and chuckled at the memory of some or other amusing incident with a newbie. "You wouldn't believe what some of them did, I tell you. Head banging. Wailing and gnashing of teeth. Fur pulling and self-mutilation. Some are still staring at themselves in the Mirror of Truth as we speak, thousands of years after arriving. As you can imagine, it became a bit of a problem for The Boss."

Flash Freddy and Smiggins glanced at each other, sharing a private joke. Louis just stared at them. "*Thousands* of years?" he said.

"Hmm? What? Of course," Flash Freddy said. "This is the After Life, Mr. DeVille. Or hadn't you worked that out yet?"

Louis guessed he kind of had. How else could he have turned into a goddamn weasel? It was just… well, he was kind of hoping he hadn't died so soon. There were still so many things he wanted to do.

So many women, so little time.

As it was, he now had a whole heap of questions he wanted answering. "How do you know I'm not just having one of those goddamn lucid dreams? I mean, really, look at the two of you. Who's ever seen a lizard and a rat in a two-piece suit? And what about me? I look goddamn ridiculous in this thing."

With surprising alacrity, in the time it took Smiggins to snigger, Flash Freddy reached out and plucked one of Louis' whiskers.

"Ow!" Louis said. He flinched and took a step back, rubbing the end of his snout. "Why'd you do that?"

Flash Freddy held the whisker up in front of his face, examining it like a kid would eye the head of a grasshopper he had just detached from its body, then let it flutter to the ground. "Do you feel pain in dreams?" he asked. Smiggins sniggered again. "This is real, Mr. DeVille. The After Life is *very* real."

Louis scoffed. "Then where am I? Heaven or hell?"

Smiggins briefly held his eye, then looked away and sniggered. Flash Freddy held out his arm, ushering him to the doorway. "Come now, Mr. DeVille. You're an intelligent being. You don't believe in that nonsense, do you?"

Louis didn't really know the answer to that. He had lived his whole life a goddamn atheist. Thought he had worked out all the answers to life and death and the whole damned universe when he was in his twenties. Life was a jungle, survival of the fittest and all that. You were born, then you died. Whatever happened in between was purely a matter of how much goddamn hard work you put in, sprinkled here and there with a bit of good old-fashioned luck. Anyone with half a brain could see that you came from nothing, and you went back to nothing. Pure and simple.

Except that's not how things had turned out, had it? There really *was* something after death. *Well fancy that and bugger me.* He kept rubbing the dull throb on the end of his snout. *Goddamn hippies and religious freaks had it right all along. Who would've believed it?*

Flash Freddy put his scaly claw on Louis' shoulder. Louis hitched up his toga again and Smiggins stepped back, allowing them plenty of space to pass. "This isn't exactly protocol," Flash Freddy said, "but what the hell, I like you. Why don't we hit the town and celebrate your arrival in style?"

Louis figured anything was better than sitting in this dingy room looking at his reflection in the Mirror of Truth for a thousand years like some newbie gone catatonic stupid. "Why not?" he said, approaching the door. "But one more thing. How long have I been dead? Just for interest sake."

Flash Freddy looked over at Smiggins, who immediately punched some numbers on the calculator he had been cradling to his chest. "One hundred and seventy-three years, two-hundred and ninety-four days, eleven hours, sixteen minutes and…"

"Not that long," Flash Freddy said.

"Not that long?" Louis could feel his eyes bulging out of their new sockets. "I've been dead three times longer than I was alive."

"Eternity's an awful lot longer. You'll get used to it. As I said, some newbies take thousands of years to work out what's going on. You're doing remarkably well. I can see why The Boss thinks so much of you. You've got a smart brain for a weasel."

Before stepping outside, Louis accidentally kicked something on the ground. It was the scrolled contract, the one with the purple ribbon he had tossed over his shoulder when still wrapped in bandages. He picked it up and handed it to the lizard. "Just a goddamn party invitation. Where's the Mansion of Many Rooms, anyway?"

Eying it suspiciously, Flash Freddy shrugged and said that he had no idea. He had never heard of the place. He reached inside his inner pocket and removed a Zippo lighter. On it Louis saw the emblem of a lightening bolt striking a laughing lizard.

"Sure you don't want this?" Flash Freddy asked. When Louis nodded, he lit the lighter. Nothing happened. He tried again. Still nothing happened.

"Nothing lasts long around here. That's the third one this month," he said, and tossed it away. The Zippo slid across the floor and hit the wall, snapping off its lid. He removed another one from his briefcase, which worked first time. Strangely, the flame that sprang from the flint had that same kind of sick grayness as the light in the room. Even the tortured shadow that leapt upon the wall behind him looked dim and gauzy, like some gothic painting faded to the point of nonexistence.

Louis watched the scroll burst into sickly gray flames. Flash Freddy then dropped it to the ground and let it burn until nothing remained but ashes. "You'll let me know if you get any more of these invitations, won't you?" he said, putting his claw back on Louis's shoulder. Stepping into the outside tunnel, he flashed his salesman's grin again. "What say we show you to your hotel before we hit the town? You must be dying to see where you'll spend the rest of eternity."

From a chamber somewhere down the tunnel, Louis heard the faint wails and gnashing of teeth of one of the newbies that hadn't come to terms with who or what they had become. He hesitated, then hitched his toga and continued on.

Better get used to it, sonny, he thought, brushing some flaky skin off his shoulder. *Eternity's a long damn time.*

PART TWO

Chapter 9

Conduit Number 1

LOUIS followed Flash Freddy along the passageway past many closed doorways and branching tunnels. Smiggins scuttled behind at a safe distance, sniggering and punching numbers into his calculator, barely taking the time to glance up from the goddamn thing. Louis put the rat out of his mind and tried to concentrate on where he was going. It was difficult. Every turn, every twist, brought more of the same, and he soon lost his bearings. Like his room, there were no windows, just the stony walls and the dreary grayness that made it hard to see much further than fifty feet ahead. There was no way in hell he would find his way back if he had to. What's more, his sense of smell was of no goddamn use to him either; the stench of horseshit didn't improve no matter what tunnel they took. Flash Freddy and Smiggins seemed completely oblivious to it. He thought of saying something then let it slide, and continued on behind the lizard.

As they went, their footsteps echoed down the passageway, fading away or merging with the muted thuds of a newbie banging his head against the door or wall, or were drowned by his incessant wails. Louis heard no other sounds. He saw no one else, either. It seemed they had the whole goddamn network of tunnels to themselves.

They kept going as they had for over an hour. Not much was said between the three of them, and when they did speak it was brief and hushed. Though Flash Freddy was in the lead, it was Smiggins who had to get them back on course when the lizard took the wrong tunnel or became disoriented at an intersection. They had to backtrack on more than a dozen occasions before the lizard seemed comfortable with where he was.

"Now I know," Flash Freddy whispered at another intersection, nodding to the right. "We're almost there. This way."

Smiggins sniggered and kept punching numbers into the calculator. Not much further on, they entered a massive tunnel. The stench stopped Louis in his tracks, making him gag and bringing tears to his eyes. As before, Flash Freddy and Smiggins were completely unaffected.

"Why does everything stink of goddamn horseshit?" he whispered, wiping his watery eyes with the hem of the toga.

Flash Freddy lifted his snout and sniffed the air. Smiggins stopped punching numbers and did likewise. They then looked at each other and shrugged. "You'll get used to it," Flash Freddy said, removing a drug bottle from his inner pocket. He swallowed another pill and nodded to the tunnel. "Keep following."

As with the other tunnels there was not a soul to be seen, and the absence of anyone else seemed to compound its unearthly size. The tunnel was so long Louis couldn't make out its end in either direction, though when he strained his eyes to the right he swore he could see a faint glimmer of light reflecting off the walls, brighter and whiter than the rest of the grayness around him, like the weak winter sun trying to shine through heavy, gray clouds.

Louis was suddenly reminded of a piece of trivia about the Eskimo language. They apparently had something like fifty goddamn words for the color white, if you could believe it. He supposed that's what happened when there was nothing but snow to look at all your life. This place was kind of similar. Nothing but grayness everywhere you looked, except there was a difference. He could still discern color. Flash Freddy's navy blue suit. His green laurel. The whiteness at the end of the tunnel. The color was still there, painted on a background of grayness. The grayness, though, seeped in and made the color dirty. Like a white drape that had collected dust over the years, or a pair of white socks accidentally washed with the darks. Flash Freddy's suit was still navy, but it was navy-gray. His laurel was still green, but it was green-gray. His toga was still white, but white-gray. All except the bright light at the end of the tunnel, that was. That was still pure.

Flash Freddy, though, began heading in the other direction. In some of the smaller tunnels and passageways, Louis had seen him ducking under a low-lying ceiling or jutting piece of rock to avoid hitting his scaly head. That was never going to be an issue here, not by a long shot. The ceiling was an arching vault so high he reckoned that even if they stood on each other's shoulders like circus acrobats they would never touch it. In fact, not even twenty acrobats standing on each other's shoulders would reach it. The tunnel was wide, too, wider than it was high, and he didn't have to be a goddamn genius to work out that this was the main thoroughfare through this underground maze. All the other tunnels were just tributaries to this, A and B roads connecting onto a major highway.

All roads lead to Rome, he mused, and absently hitched his toga.

"This is Conduit Number 1," Flash Freddy said, swapping his briefcase to the other claw. He had stopped whispering. "It's the original tunnel that was dug to accommodate the influx of new clientele when The Boss established the company. As you saw," and he flicked his head back toward the tunnels they had just passed through, "even this wasn't big enough to meet the volume of newbies that began arriving. We're still digging new tunnels. Even then we're just managing to keep up with demand. LeMont International Enterprises is the most sought after destination in the After Life, you know. You're lucky to be offered such a high-ranking position. Millions of newbies would kill to have your job."

Smiggins punched some numbers into the calculator and sniggered. "It's seems pretty empty for the main tunnel, don't you think?" Louis said. "If this place is so goddamn popular, where the hell is everyone else?"

"You'll see," the lizard said. "First, though, I'd like to show you something."

Not far up ahead, Louis caught movement out of the corner of his eye and stopped to see what was happening. A rat, not too unlike Smiggins, though maybe a little taller and fuller in the gut (*Waistline, dear, it's a waistline!*), and wearing an identical navy-gray suit and pinstriped tie, had just exited the door to a chamber on the other side of the tunnel. Above the door was a wooden sign: CHAMBER OF THE SENSES, that appeared to have been gouged with the tip of an extremely large claw. The other rat sneezed and blew his nose into a handkerchief, then scuttled away, soon melding into the arching grayness of Conduit Number 1. As they approached the doorway, Louis could hear other sounds on the other side, like muffled voices, as though a crowd a thousand-strong were talking all at once. Flash Freddy opened the door and gestured for him and Smiggins to enter.

Hesitant, Louis walked into what he initially thought of as a large cave, looking down on it from up high on an observation landing of some sort. The gray light was the same as elsewhere. So too the goddamn stench of horseshit, which, despite Flash Freddy's assurances, he knew he would never get used to. What *was* different from elsewhere was the incessant mumbling. People or animals, or whatever they were down there, droning on and on and on like his goddamn wife and her good-for-noth'n sister, all of them talking over the top of each other. Not one of them seemed to stop to take a breath, and he knew that if he had to stay here much longer the monotony would drive him half crazy.

Right up these goddamn rocky walls, in fact, Louis my boy.

The other two entered just after him, but he wasn't paying much attention other than what was happening down below, so when Flash Freddy accidentally nudged him with his briefcase he was thrown off balance and pushed forward. Although there was plenty of room for more than a dozen or so on the landing, there was no guardrail, and for a fleeting moment he feared he would be sent sprawling over the edge. He let out a squeal of fright and snatched at the lizard's arm, hanging on for his life.

"Careful now, Mr. DeVille," Flash Freddy said. He had a glint in his eyes. "You don't want to fall down there."

Louis quickly recovered himself. From this proximity, he could see tiny flakes of skin scattered over the lizard's shoulders, like talc. He let go of Flash Freddy's arm and hitched his toga, then inched his way to the edge of the landing and glanced over. There were no steps or ladders as far as he could make out. The chamber was more like a pit that had been dug with the explicit purpose of detaining dangerous criminals or terrorists than a naturally eroded cave. The walls were plastered with scratches up to a level just over the heads of the crowd. The demarcation between the scratch marks and the virgin wall above was as stark as a high watermark on a dockyard pier, but not all the scratches were the result of the prisoners' desperate attempts to claw their way out of the pit. Some were graffiti.

NOW THAT YOU CLAIM THAT YOU CAN SEE, YOUR GUILT REMAINS, he read on the closest wall. It was written well and truly above the demarcation line, the parting message to those below from someone who had managed to escape. There were others, too, hovering above the sea of scratches like seagulls gliding above the surface of the ocean. I SEE WHAT I BELIEVE. Most were too far away to read clearly. He could make out one other, though. I WAS BLIND AND NOW I CAN SEE. Yet it was the mass of bodies crowding the floor that struck him more than anything else.

"How many are down there?" he asked, raising his voice.

Flash Freddy dusted his shoulders and looked over at the rat. Smiggins was keeping a safe distance from the edge of the landing near the door. He punched in some numbers into his calculator, and said, "Forty-five thousand, seven hundred and thirty-four."

"A goddamn football crowd," Louis said, staring at them.

Lizards and rats and weasels were shouting at one another; mice and ferrets and toads were scratching at the walls; even goddamn jackals, as well as a host of other animals he didn't have a clue as to what they were, were colliding into one another like drunks staggering home in the early hours of the morning. For some reason all of them were naked. Not one of them was dressed in a suit and tie, or even a toga for that matter.

"Existentialist philosophers, actually," Flash Freddy said, "and the odd psychiatrist scattered amongst them."

Louis glanced up at the lizard. "Sorry? What did you say? I was in my own world."

"You're looking at over forty thousand existentialist philosophers and several thousand psychiatrists. This is where they choose to live out the remainder of eternity." Flash Freddy pointed below. "This is just the first chamber, what we call a 'High Dependency Unit', or HDU, where we put the most hardened cases, the one's that have been known to cause a bit of trouble in the past. We've had to separate them from the less volatile philosophers and keep them where we can keep a better eye on what they're up to." Flash Freddy now pointed to a doorway at the back of the chamber. "There are over a hundred more satellite chambers behind this one going deeper for miles and miles. Not to mention several hundred more HDU's along Conduit Number 1, each with a hundred or so satellite chambers connected to them as well. You wouldn't believe how many existentialists have walked the planet since Adam and Eve."

Louis did a quick mental calculation. The sizes of the numbers made his head spin, so he gave up. "I don't even know what a goddamn existential-whatsit is," he said.

"Look closely down there," Flash Freddy said. "What do you see?"

Louis shrugged. "Thousands of animals. Ferrets and weasels and toads and things."

"What else? What are they doing?"

"Besides not wearing any clothes?"

Flash Freddy nodded and Louis looked even closer. Many were scratching the walls trying to climb out of the pit. On the far wall, one rat had even managed to clamber above the heads of the crowd, but a jackal reached up and tugged its tail. The rat lost its grip and fell back down, swallowed by the mass of bodies and lost to sight. Elsewhere in the crowd, many were bumping into one another as if they couldn't see where they were going. Though most were mumbling and groaning, some were trying to get another's attention by pointing at their mouth, unable to speak. Others were shouting at the top of their voice and slapping the side of their heads. It was goddamn chaos down there.

"Some are blind," Louis said. "Others are deaf. Others are mute. I'm guessing some can't smell and some can't feel."

"Exactly!" Flash Freddy said, and pointed to a jackal in the middle of the crowd. "Do you see? He has no eyes." He pointed to a toad nearer the back that had had no tongue, then a ferret closer to the front that had no ears. Some animals, Louis now began to notice, were missing both their eyes and their ears. One rat he saw was even missing a snout. "Existentialism is just a fancy word for the worship of the five senses," Flash Freddy went on, "and this is the consequence."

"Ending up in here?" Louis said.

Smiggins sniggered, and out of the corner of his eye Louis caught him popping another pill. Flash Freddy flicked his head toward the crowd. "The Boss just wants to show them the folly of their ways. When they work out that worshipping their senses is the real cause of their imprisonment, not these walls, then they're free to join us as valuable, contributing citizens to LeMont International Enterprises. It's really that easy."

Louis glanced down and saw that another rat without eyes had climbed the wall almost to the graffiti he had read earlier, NOW THAT YOU CLAIM THAT YOU CAN SEE, YOUR GUILT REMAINS, but a weasel reached up and tugged its tail so hard it lost its grip and fell back into the crowd.

"How many actually free themselves?" he asked.

Flash Freddy glanced over at Smiggins. The PA punched some numbers into the calculator, then said, "Twenty-three."

"Every day?" Louis asked.

Smiggins sniggered and shook his head. "*Total*."

Louis kept staring. "You're joking, right?"

Smiggins sniggered and shook his head again.

"You mean to tell me that only twenty-three people in the whole goddamn history of the world have freed themselves from their own imprisonment?"

"From *this* type of self-imprisonment," Flash Freddy said, now ushering Louis to the door. "Humans have devised literally hundreds of ways to tie themselves up. Existentialism is just one way. Let me show you another chamber. You'll see what I mean."

Flash Freddy took Louis to another HDU ten minutes walk down Conduit Number 1. Above the doorway was a wooden sign: CHAMBER OF KNOWLEDGE. Inside, as with the Chamber of the Senses, thousands of ferrets and weasels and god-knew what other creatures were crowded into a pit, mumbling and shouting at one another. Similarly, there were scratches covering the walls to a well-delineated level and graffiti written above – KNOW THY SELF, and THE TRUTH SHALL SET YOU FREE. In here were the worshippers of science and research, Flash Freddy explained. Doctors, university laureates, professors and other lost souls that claimed ownership of knowledge as a possession unto themselves, basically everyone who had ever thought they knew everything there was to know about life. Even fewer than those worshipping the five senses had escaped this kind of self-inflicted imprisonment, Smiggins calculated, just sixteen in the whole history of mankind.

"Remarkable," Louis said, as Flash Freddy ushered him toward the main tunnel again. "They cling to knowledge like a goddamn life raft."

"Except what they cling to is actually drowning them," Flash Freddy said, and laughed.

They headed down Conduit Number 1 to another chamber Flash Freddy was eager for Louis to see. Along the way, they passed several more Chambers of the Senses and Chambers of Knowledge, as well as another Flash Freddy said he would show him at a later date, the CHAMBER OF WILLS. They then stopped at a doorway to a CHAMBER OF POWER. Inside, Flash Freddy told him, he would find the room crammed from wall to wall with politicians, legislators, movie producers and the occasional literary agent. He also told Louis to brace himself. It wasn't going to be pretty.

Then, at the moment the lizard grabbed the doorknob, the chiming of bells down Conduit Number 1 suddenly struck Louis deaf.

It wormed into his skull and clanged around like a four-year old let loose with a set of symbols. He instinctively threw his paws to his head and covered his ears, cursing under his breath. He knew this noise. No two questions about it. Same god-awful sick warbling he had heard in his office the day his heart packed it in and the blackness engulfed him; and by the looks on Flash Freddy and Smiggins' faces, they knew it too. Staring at the brighter end of the tunnel, their eyes had lit up with glee. Smiggins was hugging the calculator to his chest and hopping from foot to foot. Then without a word he darted off down the tunnel toward the god-awful noise.

"C'mon. It's a newbie," Flash Freddy said. "You don't want to miss the fun."

Louis and Flash Freddy chased Smiggins toward the shimmering white light at the end of the tunnel, struggling to keep pace. As they went, they were joined by hundreds of other animals dressed in blue-gray suits and pinstriped ties – lizards, rats, ferrets, jackals, toads – exiting the doorways of what Louis now collectively thought of as the Chambers of Eternity. Coughing and sneezing, many were carrying briefcases and popping pills into their mouths as they ran.

"Hurry up!" Flash Freddy said over his tail. "We want to get a good spot."

Louis hitched his toga and told him he was hurrying as fast as he goddamn could. As they ran, the warbling got louder and louder to the point he thought his head would explode, but because everyone else seemed unaffected by it he pressed on. The light too, got brighter and brighter, until he was almost blinded by the glare.

Then, just when he thought he couldn't go on much further, they came to the end of Conduit Number 1. A crowd had gathered at the base of a golden archway, staring at the bright light streaming through. Smiggins was already there, hugging his calculator and hopping from foot to foot. Flash Freddy grabbed Louis' paw and wormed his way through the pill-popping crowd. As he went, a jackal coughed in his ear. Someone else sniffled and blew his snout. Louis cringed and instinctively covered his mouth with his paw.

When they finally got to the front, he shouted over the warbling, "What the hell is wrong with everybody?"

Flash Freddy hooded his eyes. "What do you mean?"

"Everybody is sick!"

Flash Freddy glanced around. A ferret nearby had doubled over, seemingly struck with sudden abdominal pain. He was moaning and begging the weasel next to him to call the paramedics. The weasel wanted nothing to do with him, eager for only what was about to come through the archway.

"You'll get used to it," Flash Freddy said.

Upon the arch Louis could now make out the ornately etched words: HEREBY LIES THE END OF THE WORLD. TRAVELERS PASS AT THEIR PERIL, and at the top was the cause of the god-awful warbling, a single bell swinging back and forth. Which surprised Louis. It was no bigger than any bell he reckoned he would find at any church in any goddamn city in the country. It didn't seem possible that such a little thing could produce such ear-splitting noise.

Then, just as suddenly as the warbling had started, it stopped. The bell stopped swinging and the crowd hushed with expectancy. "The newbie's coming," Flash Freddy whispered. "Here, take one of these. It'll make the experience more enjoyable."

Flash Freddy shook a drug bottle in front of Louis' face. Its label was unfamiliar: EZPZ, a product of the LeMont Pharmaceutical Company. Louis held out his paw and Flash Freddy tipped a diamond-shaped blue pill onto it, then took one himself. It was the last one, and as the lizard dropped the empty bottle into his briefcase, Louis caught movement through the arches. A murmur of excitement hummed through the crowd. He and Flash Freddy were forced to step to one side as the crowd parted to make room for the new arrival. Smiggins shuffled back to the opposite side, now more excited than ever.

At that moment, the newbie stepped through the arches and the crowd roared with glee. Louis did a double take. Just like himself, the newbie was a goddamn weasel. He wore a white lab coat and a stethoscope around his neck and seemed momentarily oblivious to the crowd, talking to himself.

"I couldn't save her. I don't know what went wrong. It wasn't my fault. I never fail. Never!"

Suddenly, he looked up and noticed the crowd, stopping in his tracks. "No! No!" he said. His eyes were wide with alarm. "This isn't happening. I did everything I could." He then hung back his head and let out a scream that curled Louis' claws. "NOOOOOO! This isn't happening!"

Flash Freddy, Louis saw, had already removed a whip from his briefcase.

Chapter 10

Louis Makes An Impression

LOUIS was nudged forward as the crowd closed in around the weasel with the stethoscope, cutting off every avenue of escape. The newbie cringed, his voice deserting him. The crowd then parted to let through two jackals carrying a large wooden crucifix, then filled in behind before the newbie could make a dash for freedom. The jackals threw the crucifix to the ground.

"Did you really think you were God?" one of them said.

"God? What God? I've always had the power of life and death. I've never failed." The newbie stared at the crucifix. "You… you don't expect me to…"

The jackal motioned toward the crucifix. "Pick it up."

The newbie tilted his pointy chin, as if daring one of them to hit it. "No. I refuse."

To Louis' surprise, Flash Freddy lifted up his whip and jerked it forward. It lashed out with the speed of a flickering tongue and cracked across the newbie's chest, opening up a small red welt. The newbie cried out, as much in surprise as in pain. "Why'd you…" he began to say, but Flash Freddy struck the whip across his chest again, silencing his protest.

The newbie yelped and the crowd around him laughed, including Louis. The weasel deserved everything he damn well got. Just another good-for-noth'n doctor with a god complex.

"Better hurry up," the jackal said, and nodded to the crowd.

Over half were now wielding whips above their heads. Without further ado, the newbie rushed over to the crucifix and hoisted it onto his back, staggering under its weight. The crowd parted but it was some while before he could drag it forward without the crucifix slipping across his back.

Finally, his back buckled and bent, grimacing with every step, the newbie lurched forward. Nobody helped him carry his burden. Instead, as he passed in front of the mass of blue-gray suits, he was jeered and mocked from both sides. A female ferret standing next to Smiggins on the other side to Louis yelled out, "If you're really God, give us a sign!"

The crowd cheered and laughed with glee. Then suddenly, the air was filled with the sound of dozens of cracking whips. Smiggins was hugging the calculator to his chest and hopping from one foot to the other. "Show us a miracle!" he yelled.

Louis began to feel the warm effects of the pill beginning to take effect. It rushed through him in surges of righteous indignation, a feeling he kind of liked, powerful and superior and… well, like he didn't have to answer to anyone, least of all this useless wretch with the stethoscope. Goddamn it, he was once the CEO of Global Resolutions Network, a multi-million dollar company. He had *achieved* something with his life. He was *important.* Nobody – and he meant *nobody* – had any power over him. He snatched the whip from Flash Freddy and screamed at the top of his voice, "Who the hell do you think you are? You're nobody!"

The tip of the whip flashed out and struck the crossbeam of the crucifix just above the newbie's head. Louis cursed and tried again. This time it tore into the newbie's shoulder, ripping the seam of the lab coat and causing him to drop the crucifix. The crowd roared and whipped him relentlessly. As he tried to pick it up, Louis raised the whip and struck him across the back of the head. Out of the corner of his eye, he saw a fat toad in a wheelchair grinning at him from behind an oxygen mask. "Take that!" he screamed. "You good-for-noth'n son of a bitch."

Flash Freddy flicked out his tongue and licked his lips. "That's it, Mr. DeVille. He deserves it. Give him all you've got."

Somehow, in the torrent of cracking whips, the newbie picked up the crucifix and reset it on his shoulder. Lurching forward, step by agonizing step, the crowd herded him down Conduit Number 1. The jeering and whipping continued without letup, ripping his coat to shreds. The stethoscope was flung from his neck like a snake used as target practice, and after ten minutes or so his whole body from head to tail, back and front, had been covered in painful red welts. To his disappointment, Louis could already feel the effects of the pill beginning to wear off. He turned to Flash Freddy and asked for another, but the lizard had run out of EZPZs. He knew of a store near the hotel, however, where they could stock up on more supplies. Until then, they would have to wait.

Louis shrugged and hitched his toga. With all the exertion his arm had become extremely sore and difficult to lift. Fun though it had been, he handed the whip back and told Flash Freddy that he had had enough for one day. The frenzy was almost over anyway. The crowd had stopped at a doorway to another HDU, this one signposted as the CHAMBER OF LIFE. All around him lizards and toads and ferrets were putting their whips into their briefcases and herding the weasel closer to the door, shoulder to shoulder.

Louis and Flash Freddy were lucky enough to have ended up at the front of the crowd with the best view of what was going on. Almost within touching distance, the newbie was doubled under the weight of the cross, staring at the ground in complete shock.

Pathetic really, Louis thought, *goddamn pathetic.*

He felt a surge of indignation, a last dying spasm from the pill, and had to fight the urge to give the loser a smack across the head for good measure. He had said it before, and he would say it again. The good-for-noth'n son-of-a-bitch deserved goddamn everything that what was coming to him.

Just then, Louis heard the jingling of keys and the gruff voice of someone yelling from the back of the crowd. "Out of my way! Out of my way!"

Louis turned and saw a fat toad in a wheelchair being pushed through the parting crowd. Holding an oxygen mask away from his face, he cursed and growled for everyone else to stand back. At first Louis thought the wheelchair was electrically powered. Then, as it rolled past, he saw his mistake. Pushing him from behind was a small mouse with wide staring eyes. She was wearing a long-sleeved, blue-gray dress buttoned high at the neck, the hem of which almost skirted the ground over her sneakers. Louis could even make out the rigid creases that her iron had left behind.

"Out of my way!" the toad yelled. Louis was so close he could hear the hiss of the oxygen mask. "Out of my way."

The mouse pushed him to the door to address the crowd. Like everyone else he wore a blue-gray suit and pinstriped tie, the lapels of his jacket just held across his bulging belly with a solitary button. On his lap was a bunch of skeleton keys. Louis wasn't sure if it was more lingering effects of the pill or not, but he felt an instant surge of superiority to this low-class toad.

Just look at the useless son-of-a-bitch, he sneered. *Goddamn waste of space.*

"That's Rocco Santosa," Flash Freddy whispered, putting the whip in his briefcase. "Grand Pooh-Bah of Workplace Safety and Wages. Been here longer than Smiggins and me. Almost part of the furniture at LeMont."

While Rocco Santosa gestured for the crowd to settle, Louis was drawn again to the petit mouse behind the wheelchair. "Who's the mouse?" he asked.

"Tiffany Tidbits," Flash Freddy whispered. "His PA. Never leaves his side. We call her Santosa's Little Helper."

"Any chance of swapping her for Smiggins?"

At that moment, Santosa opened his gullet and ejected an outrageously long croak. To Louis' disgust, the smell of horseshit intensified, though no one else seemed to notice or worry about it. Instead, when Santosa asked for volunteers, everyone's arm shot up at once. Lizards and weasels and ferrets jumped up and down and climbed over one another, shouting at the toad at the doorway. The weasel with the crown of thorns was still too dazed to do anything save stare at the ground and wait.

Santosa burped and gestured for calm again. "I only want fully paid up members of an officially recognized union."

That didn't do any good. Everybody in the crowd except for Louis had joined a union, and they were now holding up their membership cards to prove it. The shouting and pushing got worse and Tiffany Tidbits' big brown eyes grew even wider than before. Santosa drew a deep breath of oxygen from the mask and said, "A- and B-class citizens keep your arms up."

This decimated the crowd. Only about twenty-five remained eligible for the crucifixion. A ferret next to Louis dropped his arm, monumentally disappointed. "Always the same. Nothing ever changes around here," he muttered, and saw that Louis hadn't moved. "If you're not A- or B-class, mister, there's no point in waiting for a miracle. Better get back to work before The Boss catches you hanging around." When he turned, Louis saw something stuck to his back. A yellow Post-It sized note with I AM AN IDIOT printed across it. Then he was gone, grumbling to another ferret about the injustice as he went.

Santosa burped long and loud again. "Okay, there's still too many. Only those of you who are A-class can stay and help."

Flash Freddy dropped his arm and sighed. So too, Louis saw, did Smiggins. Not hiding their dejection, the rest of the B-class citizens began returning to what they'd been doing before the newbie had arrived, grumbling to one another that nothing ever changed around here. Not including Santosa and his little helper, there remained only a handful of A-class citizens to perform the crucifixion, a ferret, a lizard, two jackals, another toad and a rat. They looked exceedingly pleased and gleeful.

Smiggins ambled up to Louis and Flash Freddy, pocketing his union card. "Same old, same old. You have to be A-class to have all the fun around here. Come on, let's go. We still have to get to the hotel."

Flash Freddy hooded his eyes and licked his lips, then told Louis and Smiggins to wait a moment. He went over to the wheelchair and whispered in Sanotsa's ear.

Smiggins suddenly looked more hopeful. "If anyone can get us in there, Flash Freddy can. He's as smooth as they come. Can charm the pants off a mannequin."

Still whispering in the toad's ear, Flash Freddy glanced over at Louis. Santosa, too, caught his eye. Flash Freddy then reached into his suit pocket, removed a wad of cash, counted off some notes, and slipped them into the toad's webbed hand. In the flick of a lizard's tongue, Santosa had pocketed the money and burped, acting as though nothing had happened at all.

All smiles, Flash Freddy returned to Louis and Smiggins. They were in. "Santosa was impressed with your little cameo with the whip," he said to Louis. "He'd like to arrange a lunch appointment with you. Smiggins will organize it with his PA. Well done. You've made a friend with big connections at LeMont." He lowered his voice to a whisper. "But he's only allowed us inside to watch as observers. We stand back and keep out of everyone's way, got it?" He kept looking at Louis, stressing his point. "Not a word about this to anybody. Santosa's doing us a big favor. If The Boss finds out, it could be us getting nailed to the cross in there. Do I make myself clear?"

Louis hitched his toga and nodded.

Santosa told his PA to unlock the door, then ordered the weasel to enter. Keeping well back so as not to get in the way of anybody, Louis, Flash Freddy and Smiggins followed the crucifixion party inside. Like all the other HDU's, a large pit had been dug beneath the observation ledge. Same gray light too. Same god-awful stench of horseshit; and although there were no scratch marks upon the walls, there were some familiar graffiti floating here and there toward the ceiling: THINE EXISTENCE IS A SIN WHEREWITH NO OTHER SIN CAN BE COMPARED, and WHAT EXISTENCE HAST THOU THAT MAY BE OBLITERATED?

The similarities ended there. Beneath him in neat symmetrical rows, thousands upon thousands of weasels and jackals and ferrets had been nailed to a wooden crucifix. It reminded him of the little white crosses he had seen in pictures of war memorials at Arlington and Normandy. Upon them, every single animal wore a thorn of crowns, above which were small signs: "Here is the King of the Jackals," or "Here is the Queen of the Ferrets." They were moaning over and over again, "Why hast thou forsaken me? Why hast thou forsaken me? Why hast thou forsaken me?"

Still buckled under the burden of his crucifix, the newbie was also staring at the rows of crosses. Eyes bulging, jaw sagging, only now did he realize his fate.

Louis had seen that look before. He had taken his son rabbit hunting one weekend for his tenth birthday, a supposed father-son bonding session. Camp upstate. Shoot some rabbits. Cook them over a campfire spit. Laugh and talk about girls. The kind of thing every kid would love to do with his old man (the kind of thing he used to do with his grandfather on the farm whenever he got the chance). Not Louis Junior, though. A goddamn useless pussy from the moment he was born, a real mommy's boy who couldn't stand the sight of blood and never had the guts to squeeze the trigger on a goddamn rabbit. Though the weekend had been his idea, he should have known better. Still, he had hoped things would work out. One glance at Junior's face after the first kill told him otherwise. Just like this goddamn newbie now. Eyes bulging, mouth sagging, the kid had turned as white as the rabbit between whose floppy ears Louis had just slammed a piece of lead. Goddamn kid then puked all over his boots and trousers. Needless to say, they never went on a weekend away again.

"This way!" Santosa said to the newbie.

His PA reached up to a jutting rock about half the size of a golf ball and smoother than polished marble. She pushed it into the wall as though pressing a doorbell. Almost immediately, the groans and creaks of large machinery kicked into life. Somewhere behind the nearside wall, giant cogs had begun to turn, silencing the moaning from the crosses. All eyes turned up toward the landing. Then, from the wall behind the groaning and the creaking, jutting slabs began to protrude.

So that's how they do it, Louis mused.

It took less than a minute for the groans and creaks to come to a halt. The protruding steps looked like petrified planks of wood, each one wide enough to accommodate three or four weasels abreast and as polished as the button Santosa's PA had pushed into the wall.

The result of god-knows how many thousands of feet staggering down to the pit, Louis surmized.

The newbie didn't move. Though he had recovered his sagging jaw, his eyes were still bulging. One of the volunteering jackals threatened him with a whip, causing ripples of murmuring from the crosses. Just as he expected, the newbie didn't put up any resistance at all. Urged on by the six volunteers, he dragged his wooden cross down the hundred or so protruding steps to the pit, all but resigned to his fate.

Santosa and his PA remained on the landing with Louis, Flash Freddy and Smiggins, burping orders and instructions down to the volunteers. Almost every head in the chamber had now turned to watch the rat and the ferret dig a posthole in a rare free space near the far wall. As they dug, the two jackals held the weasel to the crucifix while the toad and the lizard hammered nails into his paws. His screams echoed around the chamber with each blow, much to the delight of everyone involved. After the rat had placed a crown of thorns on his head and nailed a small wooden sign above it: Here is the King of the Weasels, the six volunteers set the crucifix into the posthole and hoisted it up. The murmuring, Louis noted, had fallen silent.

"If you really are God," Santosa said, looking down at the newbie, "why don't you get yourself down?" He burped long and loud and the six volunteers burst out laughing.

Louis felt a claw on his shoulder and looked over to see Flash Freddy flicking his head toward the door. Louis nodded in reply. He didn't need to see anymore. Hitching his toga, he glanced over his shoulder. Smiggins was right behind, punching numbers into his calculator and sniggering to himself. Behind the wheelchair, Tiffany Tidbits glanced over her shoulder, caught his eye, then looked away, just as the newbie screamed, "God! Where are you when I need you? Why hast thou forsaken me?"

His lamentation triggered the others into moaning all at once, just as when Louis had first walked in. "Why hast thou forsaken me? Why hast thou forsaken me? Why hast thou forsaken me?"

"Do you see the glory of the After Life, Mr. DeVille?" Flash Freddy said, stepping out of the chamber and down Conduit Number 1. "You get everything you wished for before you died. You really can't ask for more than that, can you?"

"They don't really die in there, do they?" Louis asked.

Smiggins sniggered at his heels. Flash Freddy let out a little laugh. "Come now, this is the After Life. They're already dead. They just stay on the cross until they realize their mistake."

"That they're not God?"

Flash Freddy chuckled again and put his claw on Louis' shoulder. "Really, Mr. DeVille. Have you seen anything so far to suggest that God exists? The After Life is all there is. The Boss is probably the closest thing you'll ever see to God, and even then he's humble enough to admit that he isn't. He's just that sort of guy. You'll find he'll give you everything you want, provided you sign the contract and commit yourself to LeMont International Enterprises."

They kept walking down Conduit Number 1 for what felt like the rest of the day. The confusing thing was, Louis couldn't tell whether it was morning or afternoon. There was no sun, only hundreds of doorways and this never-ending dismal grayness. The tunnel made it impossible to tell the time at all. Maybe, when they checked into the hotel, things would be different. Maybe he would see a bit of sunlight. Even moonlight would do.

He goddamned hoped so. This endless grayness was starting to get to him.

Chapter 11

End of the Tunnel

THE closer they got to LeMont International Enterprises, the busier it got inside Conduit Number 1. Rats, ferrets, jackals, weasels and lizards hurried this way and that, in and out of side chambers and tributary tunnels, rushing here and there as if they had a million things to do at once. All of them wore blue-gray suits and carried leather briefcases or sets of keys or calculators. Most were either coughing or sneezing or popping pills, and none of them stopped to say hello or even so much as acknowledge their presence. It was all go, go, go.

Flash Freddy stretched his long neck to see above the busy stream of suit and ties and gauge how much further they had to go. "Not far now. The end of the tunnel's just up ahead."

Louis guessed they had been walking twelve hours since they had crucified the newbie. A dozen hours in the After Life, though, he reminded himself, went a hell of a lot quicker than when he was alive and kicking in the Big Apple. Probably the equivalent of two hours of "live time" (as apposed to what he was now beginning to think of as "dead time"), which really didn't help much anyway; it still *felt* like twelve goddamn hours.

He hitched his toga and sighed. On the wall to his right, a jackal and a ferret were trying to paint over a line of graffiti: WHITE RABBIT FREEDOM FIGHTERS.

"I need to rest. I'm exhausted."

"That's just the after effects of the pill," Flash Freddy said. "Don't worry about it. We'll get you something at the hotel to help."

Two more hours later, to Louis' building frustration, they came to a line of suit and ties five to six abreast that stretched as far as he could see. Most had their heads down and weren't saying very much, as if used to such inconveniences. A weasel immediately in front blew his snout and popped a pill. Next to him, a jackal had something pinned to his back, a yellow Post-It note with: I STILL WET MY BED. Someone else was coughing further ahead.

Flash Freddy told him and Smiggins to wait while he went to see what was causing the hold up. An hour and a half later, he returned. By that time, the line had swelled by several hundred and only moved fifty or sixty yards forward. "Just as I thought," Flash Freddy said. "Random checkpoint's been set up. We'll be here for another ten hours or so, I reckon."

"What the hell are they doing?" Louis said. "A goddamn body search?"

"Checking to make sure everyone's union membership is valid."

Louis was suddenly alarmed. "But I haven't had the chance to join one yet."

Flash Freddy smiled and gave him a wink. "Don't look so worried. We'll sort something out. There are ways to make things happen."

To Louis' unending annoyance, things didn't happen very quickly. The line moved slowly and time dragged on and on. Smiggins busied himself punching numbers into his calculator while Flash Freddy went up and down the line speaking to anyone and everyone. "Just a bit of networking," he told Louis later. "You never know who you'll need in the future."

Not long after, Louis heard Santosa barging through the line. "Out of my way! Out of my way!" Over his shoulder, lizards and weasels and ferrets jumped aside to make room for the Grand Pooh-Bah of Workplace Safety and Wages. His warty face looked flustered and short of oxygen as Tiffany pushed the wheelchair by, neither of them noticing Louis or Smiggins, or even Flash Freddy for that matter. Louis tried to make eye contact, but Tiffany's gaze was firmly fixed ahead as she scurried behind her boss.

"There goes our chance," Smiggins said, watching them disappear into the distance.

Struck with a sudden idea, Flash Freddy darted after them, calling several times before Santosa stopped. The toad turned his head. "What now? I haven't got time for this. I've got an important meeting."

Flash Freddy caught up with the wheelchair and whispered in his ear. Santosa glanced down the line at Louis and Smiggins, thought about what the lizard had said for a moment, then nodded. Flash Freddy then handed over a wad of cash, which vanished instantly into Santosa's pocket. "Hurry up then," he said, burping. "I haven't got all day."

Full of smiles, Flash Freddy trotted back and told Louis and Smiggins to get their running shoes on. The weasel in front muttered to his pal, the jackal who still wet his bed, "Told you. If you don't have friends in high places, you can't do anything. It's who you know, not what you know." The jackal tut-tutted and shook his head in agreement. The weasel wiped his snout with a handkerchief and sighed, "Nothing changes around here."

Louis felt like saying, "Life's a bitch, fellas, and then you die," but Santosa had already moved on. Louis, Flash Freddy and Smiggins had to hurry to catch up as he bulldozed his way down the line. "Out of my way! Out of my way!" It helped that everyone jumped to the side when they heard him coming, parting like water at the bow of a ship, and it wasn't long before they had reached the last of the suits and ties at the end of Conduit Number 1.

To Louis' surprise, there was another arch. Though lacking the bright white light streaming through, it was almost identical to the one at the other end. Its arms glimmered with gold and had an inscription: HERE LIETH THE BEGINNING AND THE END. A plaque on the wall adjacent to it read, "Archway Construction Proudly Sponsored By LeMont International Enterprises. *Your Friend For Eternity.*" Beneath the writing was a large horseshoe omega symbol enclosing a smaller, fish-like alpha symbol.

Everyone's gotta have a logo, he mused.

His gaze then fell to a solitary official behind a desk at the front of the line, a rat with a thick pair of glasses that magnified his eyes to half the size of his skull. He was inspecting a ferret's union card as Santosa wheeled his way past the desk.

"Excuse me sir," the official said, handing back the ferret's card. "Please wait your turn. This is official business."

Santosa burped long and loud. "Wait my turn? Do you know who I am?"

The official held out his paw, his large unblinking eyes staring back at the toad. "Even if you're The Boss himself, I need to see your union card," he said, as the ferret slinked away as unobtrusively as he could. "You're not passing through until I validate it."

"This is ridiculous! I'm the Grand Pooh-Bah of Workplace Safety and Wages. I could have you crucified for this."

The official remained unblinking, his paw still held forward.

Replacing his oxygen mask, Santosa rummaged through his pockets. Louis could hear him grumbling that he had never been so insulted in all the thousands of years he had been at LeMont International Enterprises. After rummaging through his pockets for a second time, he hooked down his mask and said, "I seemed to have misplaced my card. I assure you my membership is current. Do me a favor and let me through. I'll have my PA run it over to you as soon as we find it."

"No card. No entry," the official said.

"Look, I have a very important meeting to attend. You have to let me through."

The official still wasn't budging. Santosa drew another deep breath of oxygen. Then, suddenly realizing what needed to be done, he gestured with a flick of his head for the lizard to join him. Flash Freddy shoved his briefcase into Louis' arms and hurried over. He and Santosa exchanged words before he removed a wad of cash from his pocket and put it in the official's claw. "Just a little donation to the Union Fund," he said.

The rat just stared at it with an expression that of *What the hell is this?*

Louis' heart sank. The official handed back the cash and told Flash Freddy and Santosa that if they wanted to donate money then there was a correct protocol to follow. Forms had to be filled. Receipts needed to be dispatched. They couldn't just hand over cash to anybody. There were cashiers at every branch of the Union Fund to handle this sort of thing.

Louis listened with disgust. Just another smalltime official on a power trip, he thought. He had seen it before on many occasions. At the bank. In the department store. Even at Madison Square Gardens. Anywhere some Mr. Goddamn Nobody could assert a bit of authority and power over someone else, even if it was just to stamp a form or check a ticket. It wasn't about being right or wrong or following the correct protocol; it was about getting even with the world that had somehow offended them. He felt the same surge of outrage as when he had seen the newbie at the other end of the tunnel.

Who in hell did this schmuck think he was? The goddamn Boss?

He opened Flash Freddy's briefcase to get the whip. It was lying on top of a whole array of things, the six-hundred page contract, several legal files (the top one was marked LOUIS HUGO DEVILLE with a slashing red CLASSIFIED INFORMATION stamped across it), a packet of cigarettes, dozens of personalized Zippo lighters, and numerous EZPZ drug bottles. He shook one. Then another. Both rattled like a baby's shaker, stoking his anger to exploding point.

He glanced up at the desk. The rat was now telling Flash Freddy and Santosa that if they didn't have valid union cards, they would have to fill out a 'Lost Card' form and go back to the end of the line. He would assess the claims after he had dealt with everyone else.

Some part of Louis wanted the lizard to suffer for his lies and let him wait at the back of the line. Except, what would that achieve? He would have to wait out every prolonged second with him, and he had just about had enough of this god-forsaken tunnel. This wasn't the time to be spiteful. It was a time to do something about this good-for-noth'n official on a power trip.

He hitched his toga and opened one of the drug bottles. He could feel Smiggins' watchful gaze on the back of his neck, but he didn't give a hoot. He took the pill and removed the whip, raising it above his head and flicking the tip toward the desk. Neither the official, Flash Freddy or Santosa saw it coming. The whip cracked into the desktop just as the rat was about to hand over a 'Lost Card' form to Santosa. The rat squealed in surprise, his wide eyes blinking even wider.

"Let us through or the next one's for you," Louis said.

The rat quickly regained his composure. "What's the meaning of…"

Louis cracked the whip across the official's paw before he could finish. This time the rat squealed with pain and hugged his paw to his chest, much to the delight of the waiting suits. Louis warned him again, actually enjoying the fear in his wide eyes. It must be the pill, he thought. Goddamn thing's working quicker than the last one.

He raised the whip for a third time. "Do I need to use this again?"

Whimpering, and still hugging his throbbing paw, the rat shook his head in short, rapid jerks. Someone from the line yelled out to whip him again anyway.

Louis ignored the request, tempted though he was. "Then me and my friends will just pass through and you can get back to what you were doing," he said.

The official nodded with short, sharp nods.

Santosa was beaming beneath his oxygen mask. Flash Freddy's eyes were sparkling. "Let's go," Louis said. "I've had enough of minor officialdom to last me for the rest of my After Life."

He walked past the desk, but before he handed back Flash Freddy's briefcase he threatened the official with the whip, just for the hell of it. The rat cringed and Smiggins, Flash Freddy and Santosa burst out laughing. Only Tiffany Tidbits said nothing.

Santosa removed his mask, sneering at the quivering official. "Don't think you've heard the last of this." Then to his PA, "Get his name and union number. I want to personally organize his punishment. Something suitable, like the Fires of Oblivion."

The official began whimpering even louder and begged for mercy.

Santosa laughed and told him to shut up. "I'm showing you mercy by not having you punished immediately. You're lucky I have a meeting to attend."

Santosa wheeled himself through the archway while Tiffany took the official's citizenship details. "You did a mighty fine job back there, Louis. You've got the right attitude to make something of yourself at LeMont." He burped long and loud. "I'm personally going to put in a good word for you. The Boss will be very pleased."

Louis gasped and stopped. It wasn't so much as what he had heard as what he had just seen. He had emerged onto a ledge somewhere high on the face of a cliff and was now looking down upon the never-ending sprawl of LeMont International Enterprises.

It was the biggest goddamn thing he had ever seen.

Chapter 12

First Class Service

"HERE we are, Mr. DeVille," Flash Freddy said. "How do you like your new home?"

Louis didn't answer for the moment, just stared. Pinpricks of gray light shimmered from millions of windows and streetlights with the same sick grayness he had hoped to leave behind in the tunnels. It was the sheer size, though, that struck him. LeMont International Enterprises was a mega-city of dreary office blocks, industrial factories, chain stores and apartment buildings that spread beyond his field of vision. He had been to the lookout on the Empire State Building many times and seen the sprawl of New York City stretch for miles upon miles. This was bigger. Much bigger. This was New York City, Mexico City, London, Paris and Tokyo all rolled into one. He hitched his toga and said, "What's the population?"

Smiggins sniggered and punched some numbers into his calculator. "Six and a half billion."

Louis reeled. "That's the entire population of the world."

"Things have moved on since you were alive," Smiggins said, punching in some more numbers. "This is over half the total number of humans that will ever exist."

Louis frowned. "I never thought humanity had a finite existence."

"Ever heard of Global Warming?" Santosa said through his oxygen mask. Tiffany had just stepped through the archway and grabbed the handles behind his wheelchair.

"Of course, but I thought that was all horseshit. What happened to the other half of humanity?"

At that point, Flash Freddy stepped forward and put his dry, scaly arm around Louis' shoulder. "Would you believe everything you see has been excavated from rock?" he said. "You're actually inside the largest underground cave ever constructed."

Louis had figured as much. As far as he could see, the cliff face extended in a shallow concavity and presumably circumscribed the entire mega-city. He couldn't help but think that he had just stepped inside a prison with the ultimate, impenetrable wall. There was also no sky to speak of, compounding this god-awful feeling of internment. He had really hoped to see some daylight. Instead, where the clouds and crisscrossing vapor trails of highflying aircraft should have been, there was just a low vault of gray rock that stretched from horizon to horizon like a permanent sunless winter. From the ledge high upon the cliff face, the ceiling (it was actually so vast it was more like a 'sky-vault' than a roof or ceiling) seemed to sit just above his head, as if all he had to do was stretch up on the tip of his claws to touch it. It merged seamlessly with the upper section of the cliff and confirmed Flash Freddy's statement that they were inside a gigantic, hollowed-out cavern. The sky-vault's proximity was something he wasn't sure he would get used to. He could almost feel the weight of it bearing down on his shoulders, and he had to glance up several times to make sure the goddamn thing wasn't going to fall down around his whiskers.

After one last wary glance upward, Louis turned his attention back to the mega-city and its millions of glimmering gray lights. Everything seemed to have been designed by the same architect. Except for one towering scraper toward the middle that actually touched the sky-vault, none of the buildings were higher than ten or twelve stories; and just as uninspiring, all were symmetrically rectangular or square with sharp, well-defined lines and angles, like buildings made of giant Lego. It was a city of United Nation's buildings. With one major difference, however – this was a city of the dead.

A goddamn necropolis.

"That's LeMont Head Office," Flash Freddy said, pointing toward the tower. "The Boss lives in the penthouse. No one gets invited up there. Certainly no one I know has."

To Louis it looked like a mythical Greek pillar holding up the sky, the only thing from keeping the vault from crashing down onto the rectangles and squares beneath it. A gray neon light blinked on and off from the top. What initially looked like a large, staring eye was actually the LeMont logo, the alpha-fish contained within the omega-horseshoe. He couldn't look at it for too long without feeling an overwhelming sense of dread, as if the sign was watching everything he did and penetrating his innermost thoughts. The others too, he noticed, couldn't look at it for longer than a second or more.

Louis glanced up again, still uncomfortable with the rocky ceiling so close above his head. "What's above the sky-vault?" he asked.

Smiggins sniggered. "Just more rock. What else would there be?"

Flash Freddy hooded his eyes and Smiggins immediately shut up. "Let's not worry ourselves with what we don't know," he said to Louis. "There are much more important things to concern ourselves with."

Santosa hooked down his oxygen mask and burped. "Like my meeting. I'm late enough as it is. If you want a lift in my Limo then you better come now."

Before Louis followed the toad and his PA down to the sprawling metropolis, he took a moment to get his bearings should he ever have a need to return. Chiseled in the rock above the archway entrance was a sign: CONDUIT NUMBER 1. It wasn't the only tunnel he could see. Scattered all over the cliff like black polka dots were hundreds, if not thousands, of dark holes with similar signs above them. Conduit Number 2 was nearby to his right. A little further on, Conduit Number 3; and beyond that, Conduit Number 4. Steps had been fashioned from the ledge of each mouth, zigzagging down the face of the cliff to the buildings below. A constant stream of suit and ties ascended and descended the stairs, like navy-gray ants marching to and from their nests inside the tunnels.

Work never ends, he mused.

He suddenly noticed that the others had already begun the

precarious descent and hurried to catch up. Followed closely by Smiggins and Flash Freddy, Tiffany was pushing Santosa down the slippery narrow steps as though she were on a midday stroll around Central Park, unmindful of the danger. The oxygen cylinders on the back of the wheelchair clinked every time the wheels clunked down each step, like a loud odometer counting down the cliff. Clink. One. Clink. Two. Clink. Three. Nobody was foolish enough to try and pass Santosa on the way up and risk getting knocked off the cliff. Instead, they waited at the only available place to overtake, at an elbow, where the stairs kinked back beneath itself as it zig-zagged down.

Two hundred and fifty clinks later, Louis stepped onto flat ground around two bus-sized boulders embedded in the sidewalk. Santosa was scanning the empty street that ran from the base of the steps toward The Tower. "Where's my Limo?" he said. "It should be here. I'm late enough as it is."

Like a gorge abutted on either side with sheer-faced rock, the street cut directly through symmetrical buildings all the way to LeMont Head Office about twenty or so miles away. Though presumably one of the main thoroughfares, the street was surprisingly empty; with a population of six and a half billion, Louis expected every one of its six lanes to be choked with traffic. Now that he was focusing on it, there were only a handful of pedestrians on the sidewalk too. Maybe it was the middle of the night (he still couldn't get his head around the permanent twilight yet). Maybe it would be a different story when everyone woke up in the morning.

Absolute goddamned mayhem, he reckoned.

He was then drawn to the alpha-omega logo where the pillar-tower merged with the sky-vault. The feeling of dread overwhelmed him again. Only sheer will power enabled him to tear his gaze from its Big Brother stare back to the immediate surroundings. It was difficult not to keep looking back, so he concentrated on the nearest thing, a street sign on the corner building: BOULEVARD 1. Then, grateful for the distraction, he caught movement half a mile or so toward the nearest intersection. A gray stretch Limousine pulled out from around a corner and headed toward them. With his new eyesight the number plate was clearer than newsprint with bifocals: TOAD 10.

"Here it is," Santosa said, and burped. "About time."

The Limo stopped and the chauffeur jumped out to open the door. Another goddamn rat, slightly smaller than Smiggins though no less repulsive. "My apologies, sir," the chauffeur said. "The engine wouldn't start. I had to call a mechanic. Said it was something to do with inbuilt obsolescence. We'll have to think of replacing it."

Santosa harrumphed that he had never heard such rubbish; the engine was less than a thousand years old and still under warrantee. The chauffeur slid a wheelchair ramp from the floor and helped Tiffany push Santosa into the back. "If there wasn't such a shortage of chauffeurs, you'd be looking for a new job by now," the Grand Pooh-Bah said.

Tiffany set to work securing the wheels to inbuilt clamps, then sat down on the back seat, knees pressed together, paws on her lap. Louis, Smiggins and Flash Freddy sat on the seat that backed the driver's cabin. Before the chauffeur shut the door, Santosa told him to drop his friends at the LeMont Hotel. The chauffeur hurried to the driver's seat and the Limo was soon accelerating down the boulevard. Through the tinted glass Louis could hear muffled music from the radio, and if he wasn't mistaken it sounded like Karen Carpenter singing *Top of the World.* Just his goddamn luck. He hated that song, and to cap it off he found himself humming along to the words…

I'm on the… Top of the World, lookin'… down on creation…

"The Boss must think a lot of you," Santosa said. "The LeMont's the finest hotel in the city. Every room has a view of The Tower and the piazza. What's your position?"

"Interim Management Consultant," Louis said, still humming in his head…

And the only explanation I can fiiiind…

"Impressive. Have you signed the contract?"

"Not yet. I just wanted to go over the fine print. Devil's in the detail, you know." He laughed at his own joke, but everyone else remained deadly serious. "It's… uh… practically a done deal," he said. "I'll be signing it soon."

"Good for you." Santosa burped long and loud. The Limo filled with the stench of horseshit and made Louis' eyes water. "Let's celebrate. How about some champagne?"

Tiffany Tidbits popped a bottle of LeMont Imperial Brut from the mini-fridge and filled five champagne flutes, hers less than half. They toasted to Louis' new role in the After Life and an eternity of new friendships. Out through the window he caught a flash of white graffiti on the side of a building: WRFF, from which a drop of paint coursed from the base of the middle F like a long white tear. Louis sipped his champagne. It looked like goddamn dishwater and tasted like bubbly cow juice, but he didn't care. He was on top of the world, you could say.

Limos. Champagne. Five-star hotels. What more could a weasel want?

He sank into the seat and hitched his toga. He was really going to enjoy it here.

Chapter 13

Streets of LeMont

THEY continued to sip champagne as the Limo went down Boulevard 1. Two things struck Louis about LeMont International Enterprises as they drove. Firstly, it was so goddamn clean. Almost too clean. There was no garbage spilling out of trashcans. No TV's or sofas or refrigerators dumped on the sidewalk. No wheel-less cars jacked up on bricks. There was virtually no graffiti, save the occasional WHITE RABBIT FREEDOM FIGHTERS or WRFF hastily sprayed to the walls, and just as hastily cleaned. Not that he preferred garbage to cleanliness (hells bells, when the trash men went on strike in Manhattan the stench was almost unbearable), hell no. Just what he had seen so far was as sterile as a goddamn hospital. It didn't look lived in, kind of like a sofa that had been kept in plastic sheeting for fear of getting soiled. Something his wife would have approved of.

The other thing that struck him was the deceptiveness of depth. The second bottle of Imperial Brut was almost empty and yet, when he turned to glance ahead through the tinted screen, The Tower was still some distance away. He begrudgingly readjusted his initial estimate of twenty miles from Conduit Number 1. It was more like forty or fifty, and even then he wasn't sure. It could be another fifty miles further still. Although LeMont International Enterprises had seemingly been built on a Manhattan-like grid system, which should have made getting his bearings a hell of a lot easier than, say, a tentacle sprawl like London or Paris, every block they passed was identical to the last one. Judging distances was virtually impossible. Each building looked identical to its neighbor. Each intersection was the same as the next. Even the goddamn shops fronting the boulevard were the same between each block, right down to the *sequence*. It was doing his damn head in.

Staring out the window, he decided to play a little game. He reckoned the Limo had driven down enough blocks by now to predict the names of the stores they were about to pass. He waited until the next intersection to test his theory, and sure enough, on the corner just like the last, was a goddamn 24/7 mini-market. "We Never Close," its motto bragged. Next to it, predictably, was a video store, Big Screen Classics. Then something called a Happythecary that had CHEAP WAYS TO FEEL GOOD posted to its window like some kind of fifties drugstore.

As expected, the Limo then went past a fast food outlet with a large, gray neon BB motif flashing on and off: THE BURGER BOSS. *Goodness Is Just A Bite Away.* Hundreds of lizards, ferrets, rats and weasels were lining up along the sidewalk to get in. Some were wiping their snouts with handkerchiefs. Others were coughing. A few even had yellow Post-It notes stuck to their backs. It was the most number of suit and ties he had seen since the end of Conduit Number 1, something he was kind of glad about. He had started to think there was a curfew keeping everyone indoors at the home or office, but the more distance the Limo put between itself and Conduit Number 1, it seemed, the busier the sidewalks were becoming.

"The only cars I've seen are Limos," he said, "and there doesn't seem to be many of them on the road."

Smiggins sniggered and punched some numbers into his calculator. Flash Freddy dusted his shoulders and said, "The Boss only allows A-class citizens to own a vehicle."

"The rest have to walk," Santosa said, hooking down his oxygen mask. "Can you imagine how cluttered the roads would be if everyone had a Limo? Complete anarchy if you ask me. It's better this way."

Six billion Limos jamming the streets was a nightmare too frightening to even consider, Louis thought, glancing back to the sidewalk. The line for The Burger Boss had weaved around the rock the size of a Limo that had seemingly fallen from nowhere and cracked the sidewalk, then continued beyond the door of the neighboring shop, a mobile telecommunications store called LeMont Cellular One. Just as he had guessed. He congratulated himself and sipped his champagne. Five out of five so far. He looked out of the other window to the opposite sidewalk. It was exactly the same, a mirror image of this side.

"Everything is owned by LeMont International Enterprises," Flash Freddy said. "Everyone living here is in its employment. The perfect corporation. Entirely self-sufficient."

Santosa burped and said, "The Boss is an economic genius. He's taken globalization to the next level."

Louis was distracted for a moment by a Limo passing in the opposite direction. Its personalized number plate read: 4 ME. Yet another one close behind read: BIG BOY.

"His previous partner threw him off the board of his original company," Flash Freddy went on. "Nasty piece of business. Take-overs usually are, as you well know. He ended up with nothing. Still, he was sufficiently savvy to form his own company, LeMont International Enterprises, and it's grown and grown into what you see now, a massive conglomerate. He's got more power now than he ever had before."

Louis continued to stare at the passing shops, guessing each one before he saw it. Ties & Scarves. Sox & Jox. Head to Tail Accessories. Shooz-4-U, and LeMont 1-2-3, where he could get a suit for every occasion at a price that was *Cheap, Cheap, Cheap*. The line for The Burger Boss kept going. The Limo passed LeMont Real Estate and the Gadget Emporium, then the Union Bank and Route 666, a coffee shop that for a short time only was doing a large cuppa-chocafrappamochachino for the price of a regular. The line even went beyond the LeMont Travel Center, which had a special three-nights-for-the-price-of-two getaway weekend at a luxury spa resort (conditions applied).

"The spa belongs to the LeMont Country Club," Flash Freddy said, following Louis' gaze. "Best golf course in the city."

"Damn difficult to get a round though," Santosa said, and burped. "Have to be signed in by a member. I've been on the waiting list for over three thousand years. Problem is, nobody dies around here. There's no natural rate of attrition. I have to wait until someone forgets to pay their fees, and that never happens."

Smiggins sniggered and said, "I'm a member."

Santosa's already bulging eyes nearly popped out of his head. Flash Freddy choked and all but spilled his glass. "How can a B-class rat like you be a member of the Country Club?" he said. "It's absurd."

Smiggins sniggered again. "I do their books. Free membership comes with the contract."

Louis turned his attention back to the sidewalk, keeping only half an ear on the conversation inside the Limo. The line up for the Burger Boss eventually stopped in front of a shop selling sportswear and camping equipment. Next to it was a betting agency offering odds on the upcoming derby between the Blues and the Reds. The Blues were hot favorites to win their seven hundredth and eleventh game in a row.

At that moment, a white rabbit hopped out of the LeMont Newsagent next door to the betting agency. Santosa, Smiggins, Tiffany and Flash Freddy didn't so much as bat an eyelid. Even the jackal and ferret that had just joined the end of the line for The Burger Boss walked straight passed it, which was odd because the goddamn thing looked so completely out of place it was impossible to miss. For a start, its naked fur shone almost as brightly as the light through the archway at the end of Conduit Number 1. But that wasn't even the half of it. The rabbit had wings. Goddamn wings!

As the Limo pulled away, Louis stretched his neck to see through the rear window over Santosa's shoulder. The rabbit hopped across the road to the opposite newsagents, receding with every second. "Did… did… did you see that?" he said.

"See what?" Santosa said through his oxygen mask.

"A white rabbit! With wings!" Louis pointed out the rear window. Another Limo passed in the opposite direction heading straight for the rabbit and not slowing down. WHY NOT, its number plate read. "Look! There it is!"

Santosa, Flash Freddy and Smiggins burst out laughing. Santosa burped and slapped his thigh with the palm of his webbed hand. Nobody looked behind to see if Louis was telling the truth or not. "Good one, Louis. Good one," the toad said, hooking down his mask. Tiffany Tidbits was the only one who kept a straight face. She stared into her champagne flute, then took a quick sip. Santosa turned to Flash Freddy. "Your friend's a scream. Where'd you find him? He's in the wrong job. He should be a standup."

"I'm not joking," Louis said. "Look. It's hopped across the road. You can still see it."

Now smaller than a mouse, the winged rabbit had just managed to hop onto the opposite sidewalk before being rundown by the other Limo. Only Tiffany Tidbits shot a glance over her shoulder. Then, seeing nothing untoward, returned to watching the bubbles in her champagne flute. Santosa, Flash Freddy and Smiggins were still chuckling.

"White rabbit!" Santosa said, shaking his head. Smiggins sniggered with him. "With wings! Can you believe it?"

Flash Freddy slapped Louis on the top of his shoulder, and said, "Nobody told me you had such a vivid imagination, Mr. DeVille."

"Goddamn it. I'm not making it up," he said, catching Tiffany Tidbits' eye. She looked straight back down into her champagne glass. "Turn the Limo around if you don't believe me," he said to Santosa. "The rabbit went into the newsagent across the road."

"To buy a flying magazine!" Flash Freddy said, and burst out laughing. Smiggins sniggered and Santosa threw his head back and slapped his thigh.

Louis shook his head in frustration. Again, when he met Tiffany's eye she looked away, unable to hold his gaze for anything longer than a second. In an effort to push what had just happened to the back of his mind, he returned to gazing out the window and guessing which shops would appear next. He felt Flash Freddy pat him on the shoulder again in mock sympathy. He shrugged off the scaly claw and hitched his toga.

"It's not that we don't believe you, Mr. DeVille," Flash Freddy said. "It's… how can I put this? You're exhibiting the classic symptoms of PTDS."

Louis cocked an eyebrow.

"Post Traumatic Death Syndrome," Santosa said, and laughed.

"Don't worry. You'll get used to it," Flash Freddy added. "It's a normal part of readjustment to the After Life. We've all suffered PTDS as some point. Some more than others though."

Smiggins sniggered again. Not for the first time, Louis had to fight the urge to claw his eyes out. "Are you saying I'm just seeing things?" he asked.

"Visual hallucinations are the most common symptom," Flash Freddy said.

"But what about the graffiti?" he asked. "The White Rabbit Freedom Fighters. That's real. I'm not hallucinating that, am I?"

Santosa burped, seemingly irritated, and told Tiffany to pop another bottle of Imperial Brut. "Nothing but troublemakers is what they are," he said. "Outlaws. Crazies."

Flash Freddy hooded his eyes, his smile now gone. "Most cases of PTDS are mild and require no treatment," he said. "Some require nothing more than a few weeks of medication. Few of the more extreme cases, however, are resistant to any treatment. They're the no-hopers. The ones who continue to have hallucinations. The difference between you and them is that you know it's not real."

The Limo pulled up at a red light at another intersection. On the corner was a 24/7 mini-market with WRFF sprayed to its wall. Santosa's little helper began filling everyone's champagne flutes.

"The White Rabbit Freedom Fighters believe they see rabbits with wings. You're not the first," Flash Freddy went on. "They also believe the sky-vault will fall on their heads. That's how crazy they are."

Louis hitched his toga, distinctly uncomfortable with the thought of losing his mind. "You're damn sure the hallucinations will go away on their own? I won't need treatment?"

Flash Freddy smiled his salesman's smile. "That's what usually happens."

"And I've got nothing else to worry about?"

"Nothing at all, although you might hear voices telling you to do things. Just ignore them. They'll go away as well."

Santosa burped and sipped his champagne. "I know of one ferret who heard the voice of God telling him to crucify himself. Completely insane. He begged and begged the authorities until they eventually nailed him up. Still in the Chamber of Life, so I've been told."

Smiggins sniggered. "I've heard of weasels throwing themselves into the Fires of Oblivion, claiming they heard voices in their head telling them to do it."

"Fires of Oblivion?" Louis asked.

"The white light at the end of Conduit Number 1," Santosa said. "Instant obliteration. Which reminds me," and he turned to his PA. "Did you get that official's details?" Tiffany nodded, and Santosa turned back to Louis. "You can see for yourself when we throw him in. I'll make sure you get front row viewing."

Louis recalled the weasel with the god-complex emerging from the Fires of Oblivion, but didn't challenge the toad on the seeming contradiction: *You can check in but you can't check out?* For the most part though, he decided to keep to himself and guess the sequence of shops until they reached the hotel. He was looking forward to putting his feet up and having a rest on a nice soft bed. After everything he had been through today, he could barely keep his eyes open.

Chapter 14

The Money Tree

THE Limo pulled off Boulevard 1 and into the first traffic jam Louis had experienced in the mega-city. Countless Limos were backed up around the Tower Piazza waiting to drop off or pick up from the LeMont Hotel, and they weren't going anywhere in a hurry. He had seen parking lots busier than this.

He glanced at the hotel façade, a little disappointed. It wasn't nearly as grand as he had imagined. From what the others had said, he had been expecting something along the lines of the Paris Ritz or the Vegas Bellagio. Something glamorous. Something luxurious. Something with a little more goddamn character than a drab eight-story shoebox straight from the archives of Sixties Communist Architecture. He certainly hoped the outside was no reflection of the state of the décor inside.

"What's the holdup?" Santosa said through his oxygen mask. "I'm already late for my meeting."

"It's always like this," Flash Freddy said. "It's the most popular hotel in the city."

Smiggins sniggered and muttered under his breath, "It's the *only* hotel in the city."

While they waited to move on, Louis passed the time by scanning the perimeter of the piazza around which the Limos had come to a virtual standstill. Fronting the square directly opposite the hotel was The LeMont Tower, which he tried not to look at for too long. Thankfully the roof of the Limo blocked out most of the upper levels, in particular the staring alpha-omega logo at the top. Somehow, though, he could still feel it trying to pry into his thoughts, as if a pair of invisible claws was scratching at the Limo's roof to rip it off and get inside his skull. The others didn't appear to notice anything untoward. Maybe, he hoped, it was just another hallucination, something to do with Post Traumatic Death Syndrome.

Whatever it was, the sense of attack felt incredibly real and he had to use all his concentrative powers to force his attention to the rest of the piazza. There were a few familiar shops he recognized from the boulevard: The Burger Boss (two of them, if you could believe it, each as busy as the others he had seen on the way here), LeMont Real Estate, Route 666, the Gadget Emporium, and even another Happythecary. There were also a few more eateries and alfresco cafés than elsewhere, he noticed, the tables and chairs spilling onto the piazza in neat rows of six or seven as if put there for an outdoor classroom. Closer still, and dominating opposite corners, were two huge cinema complexes, both showing the same film: PEARLS & SWINE, one he had never heard before.

Santosa hooked down his oxygen mask and nodded his head to the nearest cinema billboard. A larger-than-life ferret wearing a Stenson smiled down on them.

"That guy's got it made," Santosa said. "Riva Sticks, the lead actor. Been with more women than I've had burgers at the Burger Boss."

"I've heard he's been dating the leading actress," Flash Freddy said.

Tiffany Tidbits made to say something, but never got the chance. "Who? Vivian Vixen?" Santosa said.

The Limo crept forward one place. The driver, Louis noticed, had turned off the radio.

"Haven't you seen the latest Hot Gossip?" Flash Freddy said. "They were photographed leaving the LeMont Hotel last week. *Together.*"

"Doesn't mean anything," Smiggins said, and sniggered. "I've heard he's gay. He only dates women to maintain his image of a sex symbol. His agent has set up every relationship he's had. Ever noticed how he starts seeing a new woman when he hasn't been in the news for a while, or when ticket sales are slowing? Bet you a million dollars we hear they're getting secretly married soon. Then, at the last minute, they'll call it off. It's always the same. Nothing changes."

Again Tiffany Tidbits made to say something. "He's still a lucky bugger, either way," Santosa said over her. "Vivian Vixen is one foxy lady. I'd sell my dead mother to wear his hat for a day."

"Why? It's all a sham." Smiggins kept punching numbers into his calculator. "They sign a contract stating the terms of the relationship. They only do it for fame and money."

Flash Freddy flicked his tongue and licked his lips. "What's wrong with that? Everyone wants financial freedom."

Louis chuckled. "No such thing. Financial freedom's a goddamn fallacy. If you don't have a lot of money, you worry you'll never have any. And if you do have a lot, you worry some other bugger's going to steal it. Not much freedom in that if you ask me."

The coldness that emanated from Santosa and Flash Freddy was as powerful as the force he could feel from the top of The LeMont Tower. Smiggins stopped punching numbers into his calculator and looked at him from the corner of his eyes. Louis wiggled in his seat and hitched his toga. "Of course… uh… there is a point where you have so much that you can do anything you like and don't have to worry about a thing. I guess… uh… you could call that financial freedom."

The atmosphere inside the Limo seemed to lighten. "You better believe it," Santosa said. "Money *is* freedom. It gives you the power to have anything you want. Everyone knows that. The more you have, the more freedom you have. It was true before you died, and it's even truer in the After Life." He took a sip of champagne and pointed out the window. "See that Money Tree? It's worshipped for that very reason."

The Limo crept forward another space. In the middle of the piazza was a sizeable gray tree about as high as the LeMont Hotel and utterly bare. Its gnarly limbs reminded Louis of his grandma's crippled fingers in the later years of her life when the arthritis had been at its worst. In fact, the likeness to a contorted hand thrust toward the sky-vault was more than just a little eerie. He couldn't see anything to get excited about. He certainly couldn't understand why the crowd of about a thousand or so had gathered around to worship it. Some of them were bowing. Some were on hands and knees. Some were holding placards like members of a disgruntled union: THE END OF THE WORLD IS NIGH, and MONEY WILL SAVE US. Still more were placing slips of paper in a mound at its base or tying them to the bottom branches, the effect of which was to make it seem as if all but the lowest leaves had fallen to the ground and raked into a pile around its stem. Besides the absurdity of worshipping a tree, there was something else that was odd about the crowd, something he couldn't quite pinpoint at the moment.

"It looks ancient," he said. "In fact it doesn't even look alive. Looks like it's been carved out of rock like everything else in this city."

Smiggins sniggered and Santosa said, "It's an oak tree. The Boss planted it when he established the city. It was the first thing he did, and he made it law forbidding anything else to grow."

Now that it was made obvious, Louis recalled seeing no other oaks or pines in the city, or any other tree for that matter. Not even a shrub, or a rosebush, or even a goddamn weed sprouting from a crack in the sidewalk.

"Legend has it that when the right conditions are met, the Money Tree sprouts cash-leaves and golden acorns," Flash Freddy said.

"Problem is, nobody knows what the right conditions are," Santosa said, and burped. "Load of hogwash if you ask me."

Flash Freddy hooded his eyes and sipped his champagne. "Still hasn't stopped you tying a lotto ticket to its branch every once in a while."

Santosa toyed with his oxygen mask, then burped softly. "You never know your luck." He looked up. "What about you? Never put a Scratch-It or bingo card on the pile?"

Now it was Flash Freddy's turn to feel awkward. "As you so eloquently put it, Rocco," he said, his eyes still hooded, "you never know your luck."

The Limo edged forward again. As far as Louis could make out, they were still nine or ten car-lengths from the hotel. Without any luggage to worry about, it would've been quicker to get out and walk. As it was, despite his constant protests that he was late for his meeting, Santosa seemed to have settled in for the long haul. Another bottle of LeMont Imperial Brut was popped and the conversation turned to the recent hike in insurance premiums, something Louis really didn't want to be thinking about at this point in time.

Instead, he sipped his champagne (*Bubbly cow juice, Louis my boy, but it'll do for now*) and watched the goings on around the Money Tree. Did they really believe it would sprout cash and golden acorns? The idea was too goddamn ludicrous to take seriously. Pigs would fly before that happened. Then again, he admitted to himself, this was the After Life and anything was possible, wasn't it?

Like rabbits with wings.

Chapter 15

CHEAP WAYS TO FEEL GOOD

AFTER more than an hour of staring out the window and listening to the others gossip, Louis was itching for a change of god-damn scenery. The Limo was still someway from the hotel drop-off, stuck behind a dozen other Limos and going nowhere in a hurry. Compounding matters, the champagne was getting a little flat and sour, and the stench from Santosa's burps made his stomach churn. As it turned out, the opportunity he was looking for came like a godsend a quarter of an hour later when the Limo was bumped from behind.

Smiggins nearly dropped his calculator. Santosa spilled champagne on his lap. "What was that?" he said.

Out through the rear window, Louis saw a chauffeur hopping out of another Limo that was obviously the cause of the bump. "I think we've been hit," he said, and scrambled out to inspect the damage with Flash Freddy and Smiggins. He barely noticed The Tower logo chipping away at the back of his skull while he made his way to the rear. The two Limos were gently touching, kissing each other's personalized number plates. He could see no major damage at all. Not even a scratch.

A minute behind, Santosa rolled down the wheelchair ramp with help from Tiffany and his chauffeur, grumbling through his oxygen mask. "Out of my way! Out of my way!" Louis stepped back to allow the wheelchair through. Santosa eyed the smooching vehicles, then the other chauffeur. Hooking down his mask, he said, "Look what you've done to my car! Do you know who I am? I could have you crucified for this!"

The chauffeur's whole body seemed to tremble under the Grand Pooh-Bah's onslaught. Louis felt no pity for the rat. "I'm s… s… sorry sir. I didn't mean to…"

"I don't care what you meant to do, you've done it! I hope you're insured! Where's your employer?" Santosa glanced to the rear of the other Limo. "Is he in the back?"

"N... n... no sir. I'm... I'm... waiting to pick him up at the hotel." The chauffeur wrung his trembling paws. "P... P... Please sir. He... he... doesn't need to know about this. If... If he hears I've had another accident, he'll sack me."

"Do you think I care? Look what you've done to my car. Who's going to pay for the repairs?"

One of the Limos further back hooted angrily. Another chauffeur down the line stepped out of his Limo and shouted at the Grand Pooh-Bah to get a move on.

Santosa barked back, "You're not the only one who's late for a meeting!" Then to the trembling chauffeur, "Well? What are you going to do about it?"

Several worshippers at the back of the crowd glanced over their tails to see what all the fuss was about, saying nothing, then went back to praying. Flash Freddy took Louis' arm and whispered in his ear. "This could go on for a while. How about we pop over to the Happythecary and restock on supplies? We'll be back before they resolve anything."

Louis almost tripped over his toga in his eagerness to get going. He, Flash Freddy and Smiggins left the Grand Pooh-Bah to sort out the problem and circumnavigated the worshipping crowd to the other side of the piazza. On the way they passed an office of LeMont Real Estate. Every house and apartment on the property board had a red SOLD or LEASED slashed across it. "Why do they advertise property that's not even available?" he said.

Flash Freddy shrugged and kept walking. "It's the system. You'll get used to it."

The Happythecary was adjacent to a branch of the Union Bank. CHEAP WAYS TO FEEL GOOD, a sign said at the front as he stepped inside. The ferret behind the cash register looked bored and didn't even seem to notice them. Probably couldn't see a damn thing through his sunglasses, Louis scoffed. To his disappointment, the Happythecary was more like a Dollar Dazzler (*Everything's a dollar! Nothing over a dollar! Come on in and grab a bargain! You won't find better value anywhere! Guaranteed!*) than a pharmaceutical outlet. The aisles were crammed with everything and anything – toiletry goods, party stuff, novelty items, stationary, even suits hanging on a rack at the end of the aisle next to the changing room. The place didn't even have that sterile cosmetic smell all drugstores seemed to have, just your ever-present LeMont stench of horseshit. Nothing more than a glorified warehouse, he reckoned, the kind that sold everything you could think of but nothing you actually needed. Exactly the kind of place he used to avoid like the goddamn plague.

He wanted to tell Flash Freddy that he was no longer interested in getting anything, but the lizard was already ambling down the aisle, grazing the shelves. "Goddamn it," he muttered, and begrudgingly followed. At the toiletry section, Flash Freddy removed a can of underarm deodorant from the shelf, and said, "Degradation Spray. Try it. You'll like it."

Louis removed the cap, shook it, then lifted his toga and gave two quick sprays under each armpit. Suddenly, the smell of rotting salmon wafted up his snout. "What the hell is this?" he said, holding back the urge to retch. "I smell like a goddamn fishmonger."

Flash Freddy had a glint in his eyes. Smiggins sniggered and kept punching numbers into his calculator. Thankfully, the wave of repulsion didn't last very long. Oddly, instead of ebbing away, it grew into an even stronger urge to belittle everything and everyone in the shop. He turned on the easiest target standing next to him. "You! You good-for-noth'n little rat! Why didn't you warn me? You're pathetic. I knew it was a mistake to let you be my PA. You're nothing but a useless piece of…"

Flash Freddy took the can of Degradation Spray from Louis and put it back on the shelf. "I'd say it worked, wouldn't you?"

Louis hitched his toga, liking the warmth of indignation and righteousness flooding his senses. *The goddamn spray made me feel this way?* Still, he scoffed, even if it did he wasn't going to apologize. The sniggering rat deserved everything he got.

The lizard now handed him what looked like a bottle of bath gel. Its label read: SHAMEPOO. "Just wash with it whenever you want to humiliate somebody," Flash Freddy said. "I use it at least once a week. It's amazing how smug and self-important you can feel."

Louis sniffed the cap and recoiled at the reek of brackish water. *Bottled sewage*, he thought, and told Flash Freddy that he would pass for now.

The lizard now reached for a cylindrical container of talc. "Domination Powder?"

Louis shook his head to that too, so Flash Freddy took him down the aisle to the party section. "If you don't like the behavior of your boss or colleagues, just blow on one of these," he said, and put a Whistle Blower to his mouth. The shrill made Louis cringe and think of the warbling bell at the end of Conduit Number 1. Smiggins sniggered, barely affected by the noise. "They're also great for framing anyone who hasn't actually done anything wrong."

Flash Freddy now moved down the aisle and dropped a packet of gray Super Silly-Us Balloons into his briefcase. "I highly recommend these. They're great at office parties and functions where you want to make an impression. The trick is to have the biggest in the room. But you have to be careful. Once they're blown up, they're more fragile than a soap bubble. They'll burst with any mishandling. I've even seen them pop with the wrong word said at the wrong time."

Adjacent to the Super Silly-Us Balloons, what initially looked like a stand of birthday and wedding cards turned out to be something else all together – Discredit Cards. According to the lizard, they were ideal for destroying reputations. The greater the number of signatures collected (and you could even falsify them if you wanted to), the greater the dishonor heaped upon the recipient of the card. "Everybody does it," he said. "They work just as well as a Whistle Blower, even better sometimes." He put a couple in his inner pocket. Smiggins took seven.

Louis hitched his toga. He had no interest in ego balloons or discredit cards or whistle blowing. He still smelled of rotting salmon and just wanted to get his paws on some of those little blue diamonds and get to the hotel for a shower as soon as possible.

Flash Freddy and Smiggins, however, were now heading toward the rack of navy-gray jackets and trousers at the end of the aisle. "You might want to purchase one of these at some point," the lizard said. "Defamation Suits. They're great if you need to get somewhere in a hurry." Flash Freddy took a jacket off the rack and held it in front of Louis, appraising him briefly before hanging it back. "If anyone sees you wearing one, they get out of your way fast. Perfect for anyone in politics or the entertainment industry."

"I'll keep it in mind for when I start work," Louis said.

Halfway up the adjacent aisle, they encountered the stationary section. Apart from the Shame Files (manila folders to store gossip about your colleagues and friends) and Blame Boxes (similar to Shame Files, but here you stored all the negative information about someone you could find – circumstantial evidence, hearsay and rumor mongering, bogus material, forged letters, leaked documents – the list was endless), Louis was drawn to something he had seen before. Snipes, little yellow booklets the size of Post-It notes. Flash Freddy peeled one off and stuck it on Smiggins' back. TAX EVADER! He and Louis laughed.

"Very funny," Smiggins said. When he removed his jacket to get rid of the Snipe, Louis saw how skinny the PA's arms really were.

Goddamn rat's wasting away, he thought. *He's almost anorexic.*

Flash Freddy drew his attention to some more Snipes. The booklets had the same message on each page: I DRIVE LIKE A WOMAN! or FAKE TAN! and others he recognized from Conduit Number 1: I AM AND IDIOT! and I STILL WET MY BED! There were even mixed booklets of cynical Snipes: NICE GUY! and one Louis liked most, TRUST ME. I'M A DOCTOR!

To be effective, Flash Freddy advised, the whole booklet had to be used. "Your target will usually laugh off the first Snipe as a childish prank," he said, "but after the twentieth or thirtieth time they'll get really annoyed and do something completely out of character. It's a real hoot if you stick with it."

Flash Freddy pocketed a booklet of mixed Snipes, then went to the cooler near the checkout for a bottle of strawberry-gray soda. Smiggins took a yellow-gray bottle. "Superiority Soda. Cheapest thing in the store," Flash Freddy said, holding the door open for Louis. "Problem is, the effect doesn't last very long, but it's good while it does. There's Superiority-Lite too, if you're on a diet, or want everyone to think you are."

Louis thought about it for a second, then declined. He didn't have a problem feeling superior, and he certainly wasn't going to pay for it. He was above that sort of thing.

Flash Freddy downed the Superiority Soda in one gulp and went to the counter. On a spiral rack were pairs of sunglasses, similar to what the sales assistant was wearing. *As if you need them in this city, sonny*, he scoffed; but before he could stop him, Flash Freddy had slipped a pair over his eyes. Suddenly, everything looked in miniature. Flash Freddy, Smiggins, the entire store in fact, had shrunk to the size of Lego Land. He felt absolutely massive; a giant with the power to do whatever he damn well wanted.

"Egoroids," Flash Freddy said. He looked far away, like a bug on the floor he could easily squash. Smiggins too. "The lenses have a special filter. They're designed to make you feel bigger than everybody else. Sports stars and TV personalities tend to like them."

Louis considered buying a pair, then slipped it back on the rack. On the shelves behind the sales assistant were the things he wanted, hundreds of drug bottles promising a cure for every known ailment, even Post Traumatic Death Syndrome. Then, to his frustration, his eye caught a sign above the bottles: NO UNION CARD. NO SALE. Just his goddamn luck. He asked for a bottle of EZPZs anyway, but the ferret with the Egoroids rolled his eyes and refused to get off his stool. "I need to see your union card. It's the law." He sounded as bored as he looked. "And don't bother getting your friends to buy you some either. That's illegal too."

Flash Freddy shrugged as if to say the sales assistant was right.

"I'm sorry. There's nothing I can do, even if I wanted to. The law's the law."

Louis closed his eyes and clenched his claws, thinking that the lizard had a certain degree of smugness about him, a look that said *I can buy it and you can't.* It was goddamn humiliating and he hated it.

Flash Freddy showed his ID. "Two bottles of Eezie-Peezies please."

The sales assistant got them and sighed, "Will that be all?"

"Just the Superiority Soda."

Louis eyed the bottles on top of the counter, still smarting at Flash Freddy's unwillingness to help him out. The lizard could have at least tried a bribe, but he hadn't done a goddamn thing. Except, of course, to make him feel small and useless.

"Remember the Ego Balloons," he said, nodding toward Flash Freddy's briefcase.

Although he knew it was coming, he still wasn't prepared for the coldness of the lizard's stare, little arrows of ice that made him freeze when they hit their mark.

"Of course," Flash Freddy said, suddenly smiling at the sales assistant. He removed the packet of Ego Balloons and put them on the counter. "Don't know what I was thinking."

If I'm going to do it, I might as well go all the goddamned way, Louis thought. *It's all or nothing now.* "And the Discredit Cards."

Removing them from his inner pocket, Flash Freddy shot another ice-arrow at Louis. "How silly of me," he said. "I believe that's everything now."

Except for occasional snigger from Smiggins, they left the Happythecary under a cloud of angry silence more menacing than The Tower logo. Louis had no doubts at all that his little act of impetuousness would be returned with interest in the not too distant future. Nevertheless, he wouldn't let that spoil his moment of triumph. He had almost forgotten how good payback felt. As good as any bottle of Shamepoo or Superiority, he reckoned, and to think it hadn't even cost him a cent.

What could be cheaper than that?

Chapter 16

Seventh Heaven

LOUIS, Smiggins and Flash Freddy arrived at the hotel just as Santosa's Limo pulled into the undercover drop-off zone. To Louis' surprise, there was no bellboy to greet and open the door for them. That was left to the chauffeur, who Santosa berated for being too slow and lazy.

Glancing at the rear bumper, Flash Freddy said, "How'd it go?"

Tiffany pushed Santosa past. He patted his jacket pocket and said with a smile, "Just fine. The chauffeur made a donation to the Union Fund."

"I thought you had a meeting," Louis said.

"I do. It can wait for the moment."

Santosa led everyone through the revolving doorway into the lobby. As Louis had suspected, the inside wasn't anything goddamn special. The marble floor needed polishing. Cobwebs dirtied the ceiling and lampshades. Half the chandelier bulbs had blown, and beneath the reek of horseshit the whole place smelled of dusty curtains and rugs. What's more, while they waited in another line at reception, they had to suffer the instrumental version of *Top of the World* playing over and over again in the background; and by the time they were served, Louis again found himself humming the words in his head. *I'm on the... top of the world, lookin'... down on creation...*

"This is ridiculous," Santosa said to the receptionist. "I want to see the manager."

The lizard behind the desk hooded his eyes and licked his lips. It could've been Flash Freddy's identical twin, Louis reckoned, without the briefcase. Similarly, he also had a dermatological condition; but where Flash Freddy had dry, dandruff-like scales flaking off his skin, the receptionist had the worst case of acne Louis could recall seeing. Yellow heads of puss were scattered all over his face and scalp like scabrous pox. "I *am* the manager," he said.

The nametag pinned to the lapel of his navy-gray suit gave his name as Salma Gundi. Probably a goddamn Indian or Pakistani in a previous existence; and now that he thought about it, old pizza face did seem to have an accent. His words collapsed into one another in a kind of concertina effect, each sentence sounding as if it were one long, incomprehensible word. I am the manager became: I-am-the-manager. Melodious to the ear, but at the same time damned annoying.

"In-fact-I-am-the-concierge-the-bellboy-the-chef-the-elevator-operator-room-service-and-receptionist-all-in-one," Salma Gundi said, looking very proud. "I-am-the-hotel's-only-employee. Now-how-can-I-help-you?"

Flash Freddy stepped forward and told him they had a booking for Louis DeVille.

The solitary employee of the LeMont Hotel glanced down at the registry, pressing his lips together in a tight line. "Hmm. I-am-afraid-it-doesn't-look-good. No-No. Not-good-at-all. Not-good-at-all." He wobbled his head in a strange figure-of-8 motion. "The-name-doesn't-seem-to-be-here. Are-you-sure-you-booked?"

Flash Freddy glanced at Smiggins, catching him in the middle of swallowing another blue diamond. With a look of *don't blame me*, the rat sniggered and said, "I made the booking ages ago. I even paid a deposit. With my *own* money."

Salma Gundi glanced back at the registry, shaking his head again in that weird figure-of-8 motion. Louis told him to have a look for Lewey DeVille, not Lewis Deville, but neither name was registered. Salma Gundi lifted the book and showed him the list of reservations. To Louis' dismay, the hotel was solidly booked. There wasn't a goddamn room available for the next two years, and even then he would have to go on a waiting list. "There-is-absolutely-nothing-I-can-do," the manager-cum-bellboy said, shaking his head as he had. "Absolutely-totally-undeniably-nothing."

Louis pulled Flash Freddy to one side and said, "Let's just go to another hotel." He glanced beyond Santosa and Tiffany through the revolving door to The Tower. He could feel the uncomfortable tingle of pins and needles coursing down his spine to the tip of his tail. "It's a little too close to the piazza."

"Precisely why you need to stay here," Flash Freddy said. Smiggins sniggered and punched numbers into his calculator. "Your office is on the twenty-first floor of The Tower. Besides, there *is* no other hotel."

Louis hitched his toga, not too comfortable with the idea of working within the walls of the one place that really gave him the goddamn creeps. Sleeping across the piazza beneath the staring gaze of the alpha-omega logo was unnerving enough. Stepping through The Tower doors was bordering on absolute-total-undeniable insanity. "You sure there's nowhere else I can go?" he asked. "I'll even stay in a goddamn bed and breakfast on the other side of the city. I don't need to be so close to where I'm going to work."

"It's either here or on the streets." Flash Freddy rummaged in his pocket and pulled out a wad of cash thick with single dollar bills. Gray notes too, by the look of them, not greenbacks. Flash Freddy then winked and went to have a word with the manager. A minute later he was back, all smiles and holding a scroll tied with a purple ribbon. "Well whaddya know? He found your original booking. You've got the honeymoon suite. Oh, and this is for you. You've got mail."

Louis took the scroll and began to untie the ribbon, wondering who in hell could have known he was checking in today. When he read it, he grunted and handed it back. He thought it had looked familiar. "Just another goddamn invite to the Mansion of Many Rooms." Tiffany's big brown eyes widened, briefly met his, then looked away. Santosa just burped and Smiggins sniggered. "Did the manager say who'd delivered it?"

Flash Freddy glanced at the scroll beneath hooded eyelids. "Didn't say. It was left at reception marked to your attention. Do you mind?" Removing the Zippo from his pocket, he held it beneath the scroll. Louis shrugged and nodded. The scroll was soon alight with gray flames and dropped into a trash bin at the reception desk. "Okay. Let's get to the honeymoon suite," he said. "Seventh floor."

To Louis' mounting disbelief, the only goddamn elevator in the building was out of order. It meant they had to trudge up seven flights of stairs, all of them lifting Santosa in his wheelchair. At the top, to make matters worse, Flash Freddy led them the wrong way down the corridor. Finally, on Smiggins' advice, they trekked back and found the room. Above a set of double doors was a plaque with fading letters: SEVENTH HEAVEN. Flash Freddy slotted the key into the lock and ushered everyone inside. Tiffany pushed Santosa straight to the mini-bar and removed a bottle of LeMont Imperial Brut. Punching numbers into his calculator, Smiggins went to sit on the modular couch beneath a charcoaled sketch of the Money Tree. Louis, though, hesitated at the entrance while Flash Freddy crossed the room to open the balcony doors.

"This is the life," the lizard said, stepping onto the balcony. "You can see the whole piazza."

Santosa wheeled himself over to take in the view. "You better believe it. I know toads who'd crucify their grandmother to get a room like this. And all of it on The Boss's tab."

Struggling to keep his eyelids from sagging, Louis was more interested in other things at the moment. He went to a door next to the mini-bar where Tiffany was pouring champagne into five flutes, the en-suite bathroom, to his disappointment.

"Where's the bedroom?" he asked, hitching his toga. "I thought this was supposed to be the honeymoon suite."

Everyone suddenly burst into laughter. Even the edges of Tiffany's mouth turned up into a smile. Santosa slapped his thigh and Smiggins sniggered so hard he was snorting like a goddamn pig. Flash Freddy came in from the balcony and shut the doors, smirking. Louis demanded to know what was so goddamn funny.

Flash Freddy put his briefcase on top of the vanity table in the corner. "Why do you need a bed?" he asked. "You're dead. You don't need one anymore."

"Are you telling me nobody sleeps in this goddamn city?"

"Not so much as a catnap. We're awake 24/24."

"You mean 24/7."

Flash Freddy removed the contract from the briefcase and laid it on top of the vanity table. "No. I meant what I said, 24/24."

"What if I feel tired? What if I need to just lie down and close my eyes for a little while?"

Flash Freddy nodded to the flat gray screen on the wall above the mini-bar. "That's what television's for. Or pills. Everyone takes something to keep them awake." He turned to Tiffany, Santosa and Smiggins. They nodded in affirmation. "It's normal. In fact, The Boss encourages the use of anything that'll increase productivity."

Tiffany began handing out the champagne flutes, Louis first. "What does everyone do with the time they don't spend sleeping," he asked.

"Work, of course." Flash Freddy accepted a glass from Tiffany. "LeMont International Enterprises is the ultimate 24-hour corporation. Seven days a week. No holidays. No weekends." He flicked his head toward the wad of papers. "It's all in the contract."

Louis hitched his toga and took a sip of bubbly cow juice. "You mean to tell me I'm expected to be on the game every goddamn minute of the day, for eternity?"

"Could be worse. Look around you," Santosa said, and burped. "It's all about lifestyle. If that's the price you have to pay for a room overlooking the piazza, to pedal a little faster, then isn't it worth it?"

A room without a bed, he might add. It was goddamn ludicrous. "Beds aren't just for sleeping in, especially in a honeymoon suite. If you catch my drift."

"Ha! Louis, you're a scream," Santosa said. Smiggins sniggered and Tiffany's smile dropped from her face. "You really should be a standup."

Flash Freddy read the confusion on Louis' face. "Sex is forbidden between co-workers. And because every citizen is an employee of LeMont International Enterprises, that means no sex at all. It's in the contract."

"Then I just won't sign the goddamn thing. You can't expect me to go without sex for eternity. It's outrageous."

Smiggins sniggered and Flash Freddy went on, "As your advocate, I seriously advise you to reconsider. Besides, what's the big deal? You don't have the equipment for sex anymore. None of us do."

Louis stared at him, momentarily lost for words.

"Have you checked what's beneath your toga yet?" Flash Freddy nodded to Louis' groin. "Go on, have a look if you don't believe me."

With laughing and sniggering in his ears, Louis hurried into the en-suite bathroom and slammed the door. Oddly, there was no toilet, only a washbasin and shower cubicle. He lifted the hem of his toga and grunted in shock; there was nothing dangling between his thighs. He felt around in case it was hidden somewhere in the fur, but no, it was his worst nightmare. He wasn't just a weasel; he was a goddamn eunuch. Shoulders slumped, he returned to the main room and told everyone he was going to kill himself. Throw himself into the Fires of Oblivion, or something. The After Life just wasn't worth living anymore.

"You'll get used to it," Flash Freddy said. "You'll also get used to a lot of other things. Notice something else missing in the bathroom? You can now eat and drink as much as you like without having to use a toilet. What could be better?"

Louis had wondered about that. One of his greatest fears when he had been alive was the thought of dying with a full bladder. For some bizarre reason he had always believed that if there was such a thing as life after death, then he would take with him the feeling of urgency for eternity; hell for him would be getting stuck in a place with no public urinals. Now, it seemed, he had worried himself for nothing. He had had god-knows how many glasses of champagne in the Limo and hadn't felt so much as a goddamn twinge from his bladder. Probably didn't even have a bladder, if what Flash Freddy was saying was true. Probably didn't have a goddamn heart, or lungs, or liver, or any internal organs for that matter. Which only confused the issue even more. Why could he still swallow and smell and taste and feel pain?

Again the feeling this was all a dream washed over him. He reached up and tweaked one of his whiskers. Pain shot up his elongated snout. This was no dream. This was the After Life. He couldn't have sex. He couldn't use the toilet. And he couldn't take a nap.

He was beginning to wish he had read the goddamn contract more thoroughly.

Chapter 17

Mind-Hold

SMIGGINS, Flash Freddy, Santosa and his little helper hung around the honeymoon suite for a little while longer, finishing off the second bottle of LeMont Imperial Brut from the mini-bar before going their separate ways. Smiggins said he had some unfinished business with the Country Club, not that Louis cared where he went or what he did, providing it was as far from him and the hotel as possible. Santosa and Tiffany finally went to the meeting, albeit several hours late, and Flash Freddy went to visit another client on some 'private business' he wouldn't elaborate on. Before he left, he had a quick word of advice for Louis.

"I wouldn't leave signing the contract for too much longer." From his briefcase he removed a pen with his personalized logo and put it on top of the wad of papers. "The Boss likes to tidy up loose ends as quickly as he can. It wouldn't be a good idea to make him wait if you can help it. He's known to have a bit of a short temper, if you know what I mean."

"I'm not sure that I do," Louis said. "He headhunted me, didn't he? I certainly didn't come looking for this job."

Flash Freddy smiled his salesman's smile and closed his briefcase. "How can I put it?" he said, licking his lips. "The Boss is as loyal to you as you are to him. If you don't sign soon, someone else with the credentials for the job might die and take your place. I've seen it happen before. You wouldn't want to end up jobless, would you?"

Louis hitched his toga. He wasn't going to be fast tracked into signing something he wasn't ready to sign. He was too old at this game to fall for that. "And what, exactly, would happen if it did?"

Flash Freddy ambled to the door, his eyes hooded. "Let's just say The Boss controls everything and everybody in LeMont. It isn't wise to disappoint him." He stepped into the corridor. "Remember, Mr. DeVille, eternity is an awfully long time."

Louis watched him leave, straining against the heaviness in his eyes. His brain was like cement: nothing was getting through. He reckoned how he felt gave new meaning to being "dead tired." Admittedly, there had been times when he had felt a hell of a lot worse; and as an ex-CEO who had regularly worked fourteen hours a day, he reckoned he knew a thing or two how to handle fatigue. His second wind would come and he would be as right as goddamn rain. It always did. Granted, he had never been in quite the same situation as he was now, but if he wanted to taste the fruits of success in his new career then feeling like a bucket of horseshit was just one more thing he would have to come to terms with. Then again, there was always the couch. There might not be any goddamn beds in this hotel (it got more ludicrous the more you thought about it), but there was nothing to stop him lying on the cushions and having a bit of shuteye.

Except that was not what he was going to do. There was a degree of edginess underlying his need for sleep, something he could only put down to the aftereffects of the pills he had taken. He knew he wouldn't be able to drift off – there was no point in even trying – so he hunted for the remote to see what was on the television. Between the wall and the sofa he found a book by Miles N. Boon, *Secrets Of A Chambermaid*, the kind of crappy love story – girl meets boy, boy can't commit, girl gets heartbroken – Lady Di used to devour by the dozens. Tossing it to one side, he eventually found the remote in the crack between two sofa cushions, along with a lidless pen that didn't work and a union card belonging to Aldo Fiddler, complete with a passport-sized headshot of a weasel in a suit and tie. The resemblance was uncanny.

He went to the vanity table and shoved the pen and identity card in the drawer for safekeeping. He then pointed the remote control at the flat gray screen above the mini-bar and pushed the power button. The screen flashed on to the Home Shopping Channel, where a rat was urging him to invest in a pair of fur clippers at two-for-the-price-of-one. Unfortunately, the screen was in black and white and he couldn't seem to find the color button to change it. Worse, he couldn't seem to tune into any other channel.

"Goddamn it!" he yelled, banging the remote on the table.

The channel still wouldn't change, so he checked the batteries. That didn't help either. He tried to turn it off, but the rat remained on screen, now telling him to get on the phone and quote his union number before the deal ran out. Louis chucked the remote onto the sofa and pushed STANDBY on the TV screen. The image of the rat and his clippers remained. Even the volume couldn't be muted. "Inbuilt goddamn obsolescence," he muttered, and went to the balcony to clear his head.

The moment he stepped outside, the full force of the alpha-omega logo ambushed him from the top of The Tower. Its magnetic pull was incredible. He tried not to be drawn to it – some kind of instinctive fear told him it wouldn't be the best thing he ever did – yet despite his best efforts not to, his gaze crept up the fifty or so stories and locked into the logo's Big Brother stare.

What struck him was the speed and ease with which it pried into his skull, as though he was being infected with one of those Internet viruses that hacked into your computer and stole all your highly classified documents. He knew what it was doing. It certainly made no attempt to hide or cover its tracks; a smiling cat burglar going through his filing cabinet in broad daylight was the image that came to mind. It didn't care whether it was caught in the act or not. It *wanted* him to know it could do whatever it goddamn liked.

That was the worst thing, the feeling of utter powerlessness. All his secrets were being read. All his private thoughts revealed like an open diary. It was searching through every idea and notion he had ever had. Searching for a weakness. Searching for treachery. It seemed to have him in some kind of mental half-nelson, an unrelenting and disabling mind-hold. The more he struggled, the more it tightened. Nevertheless, he had to do something before the logo turned him into a mindless zombie. He had to stop it siphoning off his thoughts. What he reckoned he needed was some kind of mental anti-virus, a password or something that would break the contact, or at least delay the download and give him some time. He grabbed the handrail to steady himself, and almost at once the password he was looking for spilled out of his lips.

"White… Rabbit," he said, gasping.

He didn't know why or where the thought had come from. He had the surreal feeling that someone else had used his mouth to speak or planted the idea in his mind. Maybe it was another PTDS hallucination. He didn't care. It worked. The link between him and The Tower blinked off the moment he said it.

But then, after a second of mental clarity, it restarted again, searching through his mind, tightening its hold. He fought back, this time with more intent. "White Rabbit!"

The intrusion into his mind dropped out and the searching through his mental filing cabinet came to an abrupt halt. It was like a fresh breeze had blown away the stench of horseshit. He could suddenly think clearly again.

To his horror, as before, it was only momentary. Like an emergency generator kicking in when all the lights had gone off, the connection with The Tower was restored. He gasped, then cursed. Obviously just saying the word wasn't enough. He needed a… a what? He didn't know, and all the while, every second he stood there trying to work out what to do, his thoughts were being stolen from his mind. He felt like screaming and tugging his whiskers out. It was impossible to think straight when someone, or some*thing*, was rummaging though his goddamn head.

At that moment, just when he thought he was going to completely surrender to the will of The Tower, the connection was broken. Something had flown between it and him, allowing him that split second he needed to avert his gaze to something else. He couldn't tell exactly what it had been. It was though he had been staring into the sun and a bird or plane had flown in front of him, just a shadowy blur. But it had been enough.

While he latched onto the first thing he saw, the petrified limbs of the Money Tree, The Tower clawed at his mind, trying to reconnect. He could sense its frenzied intent. It hadn't finished. It hadn't got what it wanted, but there was no way in hell he was going to be drawn back to the logo. He might not have been the smartest cookie in the cookie jar, as his mother used to say, but he had figured that much out: The Tower could only connect when direct eye contact was made. Its power was also greatest at close proximity. When he had first seen the logo at the archway to Conduit Number 1, though still incredibly seductive, it was nowhere near as powerful as right here at the piazza. Back at the archway its power was weaker and he had been able to pry his gaze away (he had also been a lot less goddamn tired), but here in its immediate vicinity he had to fight with every scrap of energy to keep his attention to the Money Tree and the worshipping crowd around it.

Looking down from this height reminded him of the Chambers of Eternity, and once again he had the feeling that there was something odd about the crowd. He followed the stem of the tree, scanning for the bird or whatever that had flown in front of his eyes and broken the mind-hold. As with most of the buildings around the piazza, the topmost branches reached to roughly the same level as the balcony, but there was nothing there, not even so much as a leaf. There was no goddamn way he was going to look any higher, so he glanced back at the crowd, and that's when he saw it. A goddamn rabbit with wings, hopping across the piazza toward the hotel. None of the worshippers seemed to notice it weaving in and around them. He watched it dodge the slow moving Limos across the street to the sidewalk, then hop beneath the balcony and into the hotel entrance, out of sight.

"That's it!" he said, adjusting his laurel. "I want some goddamn answers."

He raced out into the corridor, determined to corner the rabbit before it got away. He rushed down the seven flights and burst into the lobby. Salma Gundi was checking out a jackal and ferret at the reception desk, the instrumental version of *Top of the World* still playing in the background. Backing away almost to the entrance, a long line of navy-gray suits was waiting to be served.

Louis hitched his toga and went to the reception desk. "Did you see it come in?" he asked.

Salma Gundi looked at him beneath hooded eyes. "If-you'd-be-so-kind-as-to-wait-for-one-moment-sir," he said, shaking his head in a figure-of-8. "I-shall-be-with-you-shortly."

The jackal and the ferret glanced at Louis with an impatient look in their eye.

Louis slammed his paw onto the desk. "Damn it! Did you see the white rabbit or not?"

"White-rabbit?" Salma Gundi said. "I-am-afraid-not-sir."

"Are you sure? It's got wings. I saw it enter the lobby."

The jackal and the ferret laughed and shook their heads, then took their receipt from Salma Gundi and headed toward the revolving door. Two rats and a weasel at the front of the line were laughing and snickering.

"As-you-can-see-sir-I-am-very-busy," Salma Gundi now said. "Businessmen-are-already-arriving-for-the-AGM-next-week."

Louis hitched his toga and scanned the lobby once more. The jackal and ferret were almost at the entrance. "You're definitely sure?" he asked.

"I-can-assure-you-sir-that-if-I-saw-anything-remotely-like-a-white-rabbit-with-wings-I-would-let-you-know." Salma Gundi gestured for the rats and weasel to approach the desk. "Now-if-you-don't-mind-I-must-see-to-my-customers."

Louis sighed and turned to go back to his room. Out of the corner of his eye he saw the jackal and ferret step into the revolving door. Right behind them, to his astonishment, hopped the goddamn rabbit. It seemed to have come out of the luggage room.

"There it is!" he said, and pointed.

Salma Gundi looked up from his desk. Everyone else in the lobby turned to the revolving door as well. "I-see-nothing-sir. Absolutely-totally-undeniably-nothing."

Now every pair of eyes had turned toward Louis. The revolving door was empty.

"Goddamn it!" he said, and darted across the lobby. Still wary of his recent experience with The Tower, he ran outside, nearly colliding with a Limo in the drop-off zone, scanning every which way. The rabbit hadn't hopped across the street to the crowded piazza, or fluttered to the branches of the Money Tree. It hadn't hopped to the Happythecary or either of the two Burger Boss restaurants. Nor had it hopped down the street between the dozens of Limos waiting to get to the hotel. It had just disappeared.

He sighed, resigned to giving up on it. Then, as he turned, he saw a large pair of ears sticking in a V above the heads along the sidewalk. It was hopping toward Boulevard 1. "Hey! You! Wait!" he yelled, and scurried after it.

The rabbit continued on regardless. At the boulevard it turned left toward Conduit Number 1. Louis called after it again, and this time it seemed to hear. It looked over its wings, stopped, waited for a second or two, then hopped away.

Surged on, Louis barged through the suit and ties ambling along the sidewalk. He could feel The Tower clawing at the back of his skull, desperate to reconnect with his mind, but he only had eyes for the rabbit. He reached the corner with the boulevard and saw the rabbit hop around a couple of rats arguing outside a newsagent. Continuing to ignore his calls, it then disappeared behind a long line of suits waiting to be served at the Burger Boss.

Hitching his toga, Louis kept his pursuit. The two rats outside the newsagent, he saw as he ran past, were arguing over a lotto ticket. One of them had a Snipe on his back he didn't have time to read. He bypassed the line for the Burger Boss, running along the boulevard then jumping back onto the sidewalk when a Limo sped by (MY BABY was its number plate) and nearly knocked him over. With every step he took, he could feel the power of The Tower diminishing. It was still powerful, but focusing on the rabbit helped to keep it at bay.

He saw it waiting to cross the next intersection in front of a mini-market. No matter how fast he ran he couldn't seem to close the gap. He called out again when the rabbit crossed to the other side. It looked back, then hopped on.

The goddamned thing's teasing me, Louis said to himself. *It wants me to follow.*

He got to the intersection and stopped to wait for a Limo to pass before he crossed. Far in the distance, directly down the boulevard, he could make out the gray cliffs from which he had emerged earlier that day. The rabbit seemed to be leading him back to Conduit Number 1. But for what purpose? There was nothing but endless miles of tunnels and the Chambers of Eternity. It was the last place he wanted to return.

"Hey, Louis!" he heard someone call, then a long croaking burp. "Get in!"

He turned to see the Grand Pooh-Bah's Limo outside a betting agency. Santosa was winding down the window and telling him to hurry up and stop dawdling. Louis was hesitant. The rabbit, he saw, had stopped further down the boulevard and was looking back at him.

"Come on!" Santosa said. "I'm late for my meeting."

Louis figured it would be a cold day in hell before he followed the rabbit to the maze of tunnels inside the cliff. Shuddering at the thought, he hitched his toga and trotted to the Limo. The chauffeur had stepped out and was holding the door open for him, but before he hopped in he looked down the boulevard one last time.

The rabbit was gone.

Chapter 18

Operation White Rabbit

SANTOSA burped long and loud as Louis sat on the opposite seat that backed the chauffeur, as he had done previously, grimacing at the overwhelming stench of horseshit. Tiffany Tidbits reached for the open bottle of bubbly cow juice that was sitting in the ice cooler next to the mini-bar and poured him a glass, briefly meeting his gaze. Though increasingly sick of the taste, he accepted the glass. He heard the chauffeur start the engine, then felt the Limo accelerating down the street and turn a corner.

"Thought it was you," Santosa said over the hiss of oxygen from his mask. "Don't know any other weasel dressed in toga."

"Only goddamn clothes I have," Louis said.

"Tell your PA to get you a suit. Once you sign the contract, you'll have to dress properly you know. Your image is the most important thing." Santosa burped again. "What were you doing on the boulevard?"

Louis hitched his toga and sipped his champagne, grimacing at the sourness. "I was chasing the…" he began, then stopped. "I was… uh… just chasing time. Having a look around. That sort of thing." He shifted in his seat. "How'd the meeting go, by the way?"

"Haven't had it yet. Can't find the building. We've been driving around for ages."

Outside, the Limo passed a Burger Boss and mobile communications store. At first Louis thought they were driving down the boulevard, then realized his mistake. The street had only two lanes and he figured they must be on one that cut across it. At the next 24-hour mini-market, they turned left onto another six-lane boulevard; except he couldn't be sure if it was the same one he had been chasing the rabbit down, or another one all together.

"Chauffeur's completely lost," Santosa said, looking out the window. A Happythecary went by and then another Burger Boss. "I keep telling him to take the same route every time. Same roads. Same turns. Never change. It's the only way to get around this city. But he never listens to me. If there wasn't such a shortage of chauffeurs, I'd sack him."

"Where are we now?" Louis asked.

The Limo passed LeMont Cellular One on both sides of the street. "Boulevard 3, I think. Can't tell for sure."

They turned right at the next 24-hour mini-market, then right once more at the one after. Louis sipped his champagne as they passed another newsagent. Now they seemed to be heading away from The Tower along yet another completely different boulevard. After a few more turns they were heading back toward the piazza, and believe it or not he reckoned he was beginning to get a feel of where he was. Initially, he had assumed the streets of LeMont were like Manhattan, a grid pattern, but now he was getting the idea the layout was more like a giant cartwheel, with every boulevard running from the rim of cliffs like spokes toward the hub at the center, the Tower Piazza. The other image, that of a giant spider web, he pushed to the back of his mind.

"I think we're on Boulevard 9," Santosa said, drawing a breath of oxygen from his mask.

They had just passed an outlet of Route 666. Louis was beginning to think they would be driving around in circles until the goddamn cows came home, when the Limo came to a sudden halt. To his utter bemusement, they had stopped at the piazza on the opposite side to the hotel. "About time," Santosa said. "Come with me. I think you might enjoy this."

Louis asked, "Where are we going?"

"The Tower, of course. Where else would we schedule a meeting?"

Louis set his champagne flute on top of the mini-bar, for the moment taken aback. "Are you sure that's such a good idea? I don't want to jeopardize you in any way. Legally I mean. I'm not technically an employee yet. I haven't signed the contract."

"Just a formality. You'll be signing it soon. Now hurry up and get out."

Sanotsa's little helper pushed the wheelchair toward The Tower with Louis closely following, his gaze fixed to the ground away from the alpha-omega logo. Concentrating on the image of the winged rabbit helped to douse some of the dread whelming in his mind. As they crossed the edge of the piazza, Santosa gave him a brief rundown of the situation he was facing. Louis had to promise to keep everything he saw or heard strictly to himself; they were at a very delicate stage of the negotiations and Santosa didn't want any third parties getting involved.

"I'm in the process of buying my partner out," he whispered, then softly burped. The stench of horseshit, to Louis' revulsion, was no less potent. "Heard of Ties & Scarves?"

Louis said he had seen a few stores along the boulevard but had never been inside.

Santosa drew a breath of oxygen and went on. He held twenty-five percent of the company stocks, his partner twenty-four percent, and, as with all other subsidiaries of LeMont International Enterprises, The Boss held a controlling interest of fifty-one percent. Ties & Scarves, with its monopoly of the accessory market, should have been a profitable company, but things had been going downhill for the last five or six hundred years. Problem was, his partner had let things slide. His mind just wasn't focused anymore. When they first started the company he had been on top of his game, a good partner to have on board, a real whiz with taxation, but then things started happening. He stopped turning up for work. He wouldn't attend board meetings. He practically gave the staff free reign to do whatever they wanted in regards to price fixing and union membership, which was simply unheard of, and Santosa couldn't remember the last time he had seen an end of financial year tax report. The partner had simply shut up shop and stopped communicating with him and everyone else. The Boss, as Louis could imagine, was more than a little concerned with the decline in business.

Approaching The Tower, Santosa drew another breath of oxygen. He suspected something else was going on. There were whispers his partner had been seen in taverns conversing with members of the White Rabbit Freedom Fighters. Santosa had no choice. He had to prevent his good name being dragged through the mud, even if the rumors proved unfounded. The financial consequences were too dire to contemplate.

"This is not the first time I've tried to buy him out," he said.

They had now reached the steps to the main entrance. The power of The Tower was staggering, its attack relentless, clawing and scratching the top of Louis' skull, sapping his energy by the second. He could feel his knees buckling under its force, and did all he could to concentrate on the image of the white rabbit. It was a tough ask, but hallucination or not, Mrs. Big Ears With Wings was proving a damned mighty antidote to the mind-hold.

"Two years ago we negotiated a price for his share in the company," Santosa said. "Then after months of negotiations, the night before we were due to sign the agreement, he rang me up and demanded that I sell *my* share. Can you believe it? He said what was good enough for me was good enough for him!"

Louis helped Tiffany lift Santosa to the top of the steps, fixing his eyes in front of him and whispering, "White Rabbit. White Rabbit. White Rabbit." As a consequence, he almost missed what the toad was saying.

"What I need from you," Santosa said as Louis and Tiffany lowered the wheelchair at the entrance, "is to be an independent arbitrator. Of course you're not, you're on my side, but my partner can't know that. Let him think you're observing proceedings for The Boss. Otherwise he'll stall and make it as difficult as he can. The company won't survive for much longer the way it's going and I've invested too much money to let that happen. I'll tell him I've had enough and that I'm happy to buy him out at a reasonable price. He has to think you're independent, even leaning to his side. Then we'll take him for everything he's got."

"White Rabbit," Louis said.

"What?" Santosa said, and burped.

Louis stared down at the Grand Pooh-Bah, suddenly realizing what had just slipped out. "Uh… Operation White Rabbit. The army and police always name their operations. We'll name ours too. It'll be our codeword for future correspondence."

Santosa was thoughtful for a moment, then smiled and burped. "Good thinking. I like the irony. Operation White Rabbit it is."

Inside, Santosa bribed the rat at the security desk to sign Louis in as a guest, then went to the elevators. All five of them were out of order.

"What's going on?" Santosa said. "I'm late enough as it is."

Tiffany and Louis had no choice but to carry him up the seventeen flights of stairs to Conference Room 1706. Just before they entered, Santosa whispered, "Ready?" To which Louis nodded. Then Santosa stopped and said, "Oh, and don't get too close. Not unless you want to catch fleas."

That's all I goddamn need, Louis mused. "I'll keep my distance."

Santosa's partner, who Louis first mistook for another rat in a navy-gray suit, was waiting impatiently for them at the head of the table. Following Santosa across the room, Louis soon realized his error; the guy was a guinea pig. Tiffany wheeled Santosa to the opposite end of the table, then sat down and prepared to take minutes.

"Frank O'Lynn, this is Louis DeVille," Santosa said. "The Boss' advocate."

"It's Lewey. Not Lewis. Like Hewey, Dewey and Lewey," Louis said, and went to shake Frank O'Lynn's paw. Then, suddenly remembering Santosa's warning, stopped and quickly took a politically neutral seat between the two partners.

"You… you work for The Boss?" Frank O'Lynn said. Louis picked up the Irish twang immediately. It was like he was singing a ditty, sharp and tuneful, like a bird twittering at the break of dawn. He glanced outside the window to the piazza below, then scratched his face and said, "I… I didn't know The Boss wanted to be a part of the negotiations. Why didn't you tell me?"

"I'm telling you now."

Frank O'Lynn eyed Louis with suspicion. "To be sure, this isn't correct protocol."

"Do you have a copy?" Santosa said, to which his partner blushed and shook his head. "Then I'll let you tell The Boss you don't want him meddling."

Frank O'Lynn blushed even deeper and went silent. Though still tinged with the grayness that seemed to seep into everything in LeMont, the redness of his cheeks was the brightest color Louis had seen since waking up in front of the Mirror of Truth. The guinea pig was glowing like a stoplight. Goddamn pathetic. Operation White Rabbit was going to be easier than he thought. Maybe he could have a bit of fun at the same time as helping Santosa with the takeover. Maybe he could make a bit of a profit on the side.

The meeting then began in earnest. Santosa didn't mince his words. "I want a clean split," he said. Frank O'Lynn demurred, thinking they could patch things up, although Louis sensed he was simply holding out for as much as he could. They thrashed things out for over an hour when, out of the blue, he felt the chair beneath him begin to tremble. It wobbled and shook as though he were driving a truck over bumpy ground. Then the table began to vibrate; and he could have sworn the room had started to sway. He wasn't in a truck! He was in an airplane flying through a goddamn tornado. He grabbed the table to steady himself, shouting over the racket, "What the hell's going on?"

Oblivious to his unease, Santosa and Frank O'Lynn continued negotiating while Tiffany kept taking notes. He had to shout again.

Santosa looked at him with an expression of *Why look so worried?* He burped and said, "Excavations. It happens all the time. You'll get used to it."

Louis hitched his toga, unconvinced. He only relaxed when the walls stopped shaking and the room swayed to a standstill, but it was some time before he recovered enough to give his opinion on the matters at hand. "Excuse me for interrupting," he said, "but I think we're going around in circles here. It's obvious to me that there's been a complete breakdown in communication between the two of you. Neither of you has any trust of the other. If this goes on for much longer, there'll be no company left to sell. One of you has to let go, otherwise both of you will be holding onto a share of absolutely-totally-undeniably nothing."

Frank O'Lynn blushed and Santosa burped. "What are you suggesting?"

"One of you has to sell to let the other partner save the company. It's the only way. That way you both come out of it with something and The Boss doesn't lose his investment."

"I'll… I'll sell," Frank O'Lynn said, his gaze fixed to the tabletop.

"What? Like last time?" Santosa said. His partner blushed even brighter. "We've been down this road before. I'm not doing it again. I won't go through months of negotiations and then have you turn around and demand I sell my share of the company."

Frank O'Lynn looked up from the table. "To be sure, that won't happen. This time I'm serious, Rocco." He paused to glance outside the window again, then said, "I want out."

Louis did all in his power to hide his smile. They had the cowardly Irish guinea pig right where they wanted him. Now it was just a matter of turning the screws.

Chapter 19

Louis Signs the Contract

LESS than an hour later, Louis, Santosa and Tiffany left Frank O'Lynn to mull over the offer for his share in the company. Santosa had offered him only half of what they had originally agreed on two years ago. Louis felt no pity for the guy. He had had his chance when the company was in a better financial shape and should have taken it back then. Now he just had to take what was being tabled. And he would, too. Louis could feel it. He didn't know why but Frank O'Lynn wanted out something bad, and he wanted out yesterday.

Louis and Tiffany helped Santosa down the seventeen flights to the ground floor, then outside to the waiting Limo. The chauffeur was busy under the hood tinkering with the engine. Nearby, a boulder the size of Cessna had embedded into the street, as if toppled from the top of The Tower, miraculously missing all vehicles and pedestrians. Nobody except Louis paid it any heed. "I can't see any problems with the buyout. Your partner's mind has gone," Louis said. "He's lost focus. It'll be like taking candy off a baby. The only question is, is the company worth what you're offering?"

The chauffeur closed the hood, then hurried to open the door and slide out the wheelchair ramp. "The structure of the business is sound. I just have to stop the bleeding," Santosa said, as the chauffeur pushed him into the rear cabin. "I might have to go to the bank to come up with the cash, but I'll worry about that when I have to."

Louis hesitated in getting in, eyeing the massive boulder. The invisible force of The Tower logo was scratching at the back of his head, trying to connect with its mind-hold, but he reckoned he could keep it at bay as long as he remembered to focus on the image of the winged rabbit. He stuck his head in through the door and told Santosa he felt like stretching his legs for a bit.

"Your choice," Santosa said. Tiffany had already secured the wheelchair and was now pouring him a glass of champagne. "We should go out and celebrate. I know a great bar around here. The Lounge Lizard. They have a great happy hour."

Louis hitched his toga, scanning across the piazza to the hotel. "I thought everyone was on the job all day every day."

"Entertainment expenses. I'm soliciting business for the company. It's all legal."

Louis always felt perky after a meeting had gone well, so he agreed to meet them back at the honeymoon suite and then head out to the bar. His second wind had come, as he knew it would, and a few celebratory drinks wouldn't go astray. He also reckoned a couple of those little blue diamonds would go down well, too.

Why not? You deserve it Louis my boy. This is the goddamn After Life after all. What the hell do I have to lose?

The Limo pulled away and came to a halt at the end of the jam waiting to get to the hotel. In its wake a used bingo card fluttered onto the street. It wasn't a winner. Nevertheless, on his way across the piazza, he took it to the Money Tree and placed it on the head-high pile at its stem. A ferret next to him made the sign of a five-pointed star on his chest and said a silent prayer, then backed away with reverence.

Louis shrugged and thought, *When in Rome.*

After making the five-pointed sign and praying for more money, he weaved through the rest of the worshippers to the hotel. It dawned only when he stepped through the rotating doors into the lobby what had been bugging him about the crowd: there were no children. In fact, in the entire time he had been here, he hadn't had to give way to an irate mother bulldozing her pram along the sidewalk. He hadn't had to evade any runaway skateboards or scooters. He hadn't collided with a little weasel or jackal that wasn't watching where he was walking; and he hadn't cringed at the sound of a spoiled brat wailing for a toy or ice cream. Not so much as a hungry baby demanding to be fed. An entire city without kids. It was just too perfect to be true.

Salma Gundi called out for him as he stepped around the line of suit and ties waiting at reception. "You-seem-to-be-in-a-jovial-mood-today-sir," he said.

"Damn right," Louis said. Even the background instrumental of *Top of the World* couldn't diminish his joy. "I just realized there are no kids in the After Life. It's heaven."

Salma Gundi shook his head in a figure-of-8. "It-is-whatever-you-choose-it-to-be-sir. But-if-you-would-be-so-kind-I-was-wondering-what-time-you'll-be-checking-out?" He gestured to the line of suits. "As-you-can-see-the-hotel-is-overbooked-for-the-AGM-and-I-need-every-available-room."

Louis' smile faded in a hurry. "What are you talking about?"

Salma Gundi consulted his ledger. "According-to-me-you've-been-here-for-more-than-24-hours. You-must-check-out."

"This is goddamn ridiculous. I need that room. I've got nowhere else to stay."

"The-booking-was-only-for-one-day-sir."

Louis hitched his toga, looking around for a clock. There were none behind the reception desk or above the elevators. Salma Gundi wasn't even wearing a watch. "But I only arrived a few hours ago. I've just booked in."

"Time-goes-a-lot-quicker-in-the-After-Life-sir," Salma Gundi said and pushed the hotel receipt across the desk with the tip of his claw. "I-have-already-given-you-a-late-checkout. There-is-absolutely-totally-undeniably-nothing-else-I-can-do."

Eyeing the receipt with aversion, Louis pushed it back. "I thought The Boss was picking up the tab."

"I-know-nothing-of-that-sir," Salma Gundi said. "You-will-have-to-discuss-it-with-him."

Louis snatched the receipt and told him that he needed some time to make alternative arrangements. Just as he turned to make his way to the stairwell, Salma Gundi called him back to the desk. "I-nearly-forgot-sir. I-have-something-else-for-you." He went to

Louis' pigeonhole and returned with a scroll. "Perhaps-this-is-what-you-have-been-looking-for. From-The-Boss-perhaps?"

Louis took the scroll and untied the purple ribbon, another goddamn invitation to the Mansion of Many Rooms. "Who keeps delivering these scrolls?" he asked.

Salma Gundi hooded his eyes. "I-do-not-know-sir. I-found-it-lying-on-the-desk-like-the-other-one."

"Was it that goddamn rabbit?"

A weasel and a ferret at the front of the line chuckled and shook their heads. Salma Gundi flicked his tongue and licked his unsmiling lips. "I-am-absolutely-totally-undeniably-sure-it-was-not-the-rabbit-sir," he said. "If-you-please-I-will-extend-your-checkout-by-another-two-hours. Then-you-must-pay-and-leave."

Louis climbed the seven floors to the honeymoon suite with the sound of laughter following him up the stairwell. He stormed down the corridor and flung open the door to his room. It banged into the wall and shook the sketch of the Money Tree above the sofa. The Home Shopping Channel, he saw, was still on the screen above the mini bar, the rat now selling timeshare at the LeMont Country Club.

"Goddamn it," he muttered, "that's all I need." What he really needed was to talk to Flash Freddy. He needed him to fix this goddamn mess.

As he entered, he stepped on a folded piece of paper someone had slipped under the door. It turned out to be an unsigned note in neat cursive script: THERE IS NO ESCAPE.

"What in goddamn blazes is this?" he said, slamming the door. "What kind of sick joke is going on around here?"

Still holding the invitation to the Mansion of Many Rooms and the receipt for his stay, he scrunched the note into a ball and hurled it to the other side of the suite. It bounced off the balcony doors and rolled beneath the vanity table. He glared at the ball, then through the doors. The lower stories of The Tower were visible across the piazza, along with half the smiling face of Riva Sticks and the topmost branches of the Money Tree. He stormed across the room and yanked the drapes, keeping his eye on the worshipping crowd below. While he was there, he heard what he thought was Flash Freddy's loping gait approaching down the corridor. He was surprised at how glad he was for the lizard's return.

The footsteps stopped outside his room. Louis put the scroll and receipt on top of the vanity table next to the unsigned contract and was about to shout, "Come in!" when another note was slipped under the door. The footsteps then hurried back toward the stairwell. Perplexed, Louis retrieved the note and unfolded it. The writing was different from the other note, plainer and simpler, as if written by a child: *If you want to know more about the White Rabbit, be at The Lounge Lizard when the music stops. PS. Destroy this note.* It too was unsigned.

Curious, he opened the door and glanced down the corridor. It was empty, so he shut the door and went back to the vanity table. While he considered how to destroy the note, he caught more footsteps approaching the room. Call it a gut feeling or animal instinct, he decided to stash the note inside the drawer next to Aldo Fiddler's union card away from snooping eyes.

Better to be safe than sorry, Louis my boy.

The rat on the Home Shopping Channel was still selling timeshare at the Country Club as the footsteps got louder and stopped outside the room.

Half expecting another note to be slipped underneath, he hurried to the door and flung it open. Flash Freddy was there, his claw raised and about to knock. "Ah, good, you're here," Louis said. "Come in. I've got a problem. I need your help."

Flash Freddy entered and put his briefcase on top of the vanity table, immediately noticing the scroll and hotel receipt. "So I see," he said, picking up the scroll. "You're starting to collect these. Is there something you should be telling me?"

"Not at all. I've got no idea who keeps sending them. Burn it if you like."

Flash Freddy removed his Zippo from his inner pocket and opened the drapes to the outside balcony. "You sure?"

Louis hitched his toga and nodded. "Damn things are starting to freak me out. I feel like someone is spying on me. It's creepy."

"No need to get paranoid. I'm sure there's a rational explanation." Flash Freddy stepped onto the balcony. The lighter didn't work after four attempts, so he tossed it over the railing and removed a spare from his pocket. The flaming scroll was then sent the way of the broken Zippo. "Is there something else you want to tell me?"

Louis glanced at the vanity table, uneasy at the lizard's close attention. He could feel his gaze monitoring everything he did. "I… uh… want to know the meaning of this," he said, picking up the hotel receipt. "I've been asked to check out and pay the bill. You told me The Boss was taking care of the tab. Where am I going to get the money? I don't have a goddamn cent to my name."

Flash Freddy took the receipt, then eyed the wad of papers next to his briefcase. His pen with his personalized logo was still on top where he had left it. "Have you signed the contract yet?" he asked, to which Louis shook his head. Flash Freddy put the receipt down. "I can't be much help to you if you won't fulfill your part of the bargain. The Boss will only take care of you once you're in his employment. You have to sign." Smiling his salesman's smile, he picked up the pen and offered it to Louis. "It's your choice, Mr. DeVille."

"Not much of a goddamn choice, is it?" he said, taking the pen.

"Need I remind you it's unbreakable? Once you've signed, you're committed to LeMont for eternity."

"I know. I know. Where do I sign the damn thing?"

Flash Freddy flipped through the contract to the relevant pages. Louis scrawled his signature where he was asked and initialed LDV in the required paragraphs. The perkiness he had felt upon leaving the meeting with Santosa was well and truly gone. Now he felt deflated and tired, like a general signing the unconditional surrender of his army.

He just hoped to hell he was doing the right thing.

Chapter 20

INBUILT OBSOLESCENCE

LOUIS sighed and handed back the pen.

"Fantastic. You won't regret it, Mr. DeVille," Flash Freddy said, storing the contract in his briefcase. As he did, a folio slipped to the floor. "You're now a proud citizen of LeMont International Enterprises. The Boss will be very pleased. How do you feel?"

"Huh? Me? Oh fine. When do I start?"

"Immediately."

Flash Freddy dusted the fine layer of dry scales off both shoulders and picked up the loose page. Whilst bending, he spied the scrunched ball of paper that Louis had hurled in anger against the balcony doors. He stood up and flattened the note. "There Is No Escape?" he said, eyes hooded. "What's this? A secret message? A code?"

Louis hitched his toga and shrugged. The Home Shopping Channel had moved on to kitchen appliances; all items, the rat reassured, were backed with a thousand year working warrantee. "I thought you might be able to tell me. Somebody slipped it under the door."

"Think someone's playing a prank on you. It's not something I know, a Snipe or a Discredit Card. I'd ignore it if I were you." Flash Freddy laid it on the vanity table next to the hotel receipt. "Is that everything? You haven't received anything else, have you?"

Louis glanced at the drawer. "Uh… no, nothing else, just the receipt. What do I do with it?"

"Send it into the accounts department of The Tower. They'll reimburse you. The whole process takes about fifty years."

"You've got to be joking. I can't wait fifty goddamn minutes. I've got no money."

"Then you've got a serious problem," Flash Freddy said.

Louis was stumped for a moment. Then he hit upon an idea. "Lend me some cash, will you?" he said, holding out his paw. "Don't look so worried. I'm good for it. I'll pay you back as soon as I get my first paycheck."

Flash Freddy threw back his head and laughed. Louis heard scuttling footsteps behind him, then a snigger, and turned to see his PA punching numbers into his calculator at the door. If it were possible, his face looked even thinner than before. "Did you hear that, Smiggins?" Flash Freddy said, still laughing. Smiggins sniggered that he had and sat down on the sofa. "You really should be a standup, Mr. DeVille. You're a scream."

Louis looked at the lizard, then at Smiggins. "What's so funny now?"

Smiggins glanced up from his calculator. "Your position is purely honorary."

Louis just stared at him. "You mean I work for nothing? I'm expected to be on the game 24-hours a day, seven days a week, and not get paid? For eternity?"

"You'll get used to it," Flash Freddy said, wiping a tear from his eye with the back of his scaly claw.

"Damned to hell I will," Louis said. "This is outrageous. It's goddamn slavery."

"I didn't hide anything from you. It's all there in the contract."

"Surely I must get something. What about share options and end of year bonuses?"

The roar of laughter from Flash Freddy and Smiggins drowned out the chatter from the Home Shopping Channel. It was a minute before they calmed down, and Louis almost didn't hear the knock on the door. "Mr-Smiggins-requested-this-for-you-sir," said Salma Gundi, entering with a pressed navy-gray suit in plastic wrapping. "Courtesy-of-The-Boss."

"Thanks, but no thanks," Louis said. "I can't pay for it."

"You don't have to," Flash Freddy said, still chuckling. "The first suit is always free. It's in the contract." He took the suit from Salma Gundi and tipped him. He winked at Louis. "You won't get paid any cash in this job, but you'll find the position comes with a few added perks. The suit is just one of them. Go on, try it on."

While Salma Gundi returned to the reception desk, Louis excused himself and went to the bathroom. As he removed the laurel and unhitched the toga, he caught a faint whiff of rotting salmon from his armpits. "Goddamn Degradation Spray," he muttered, and reached for the faucet at the basin. He turned on the cold. No water came out, so he turned it on full. Still nothing, not even a drip. The same with the hot and cold ones in the shower. Absolutely-totally-undeniably-nothing. "Doesn't anything work in this goddamn hotel?" he said, growling.

Ramming his legs into the trousers, he heard Smiggins snigger through the door. Flash Freddy had obviously said something or made a joke, probably about him. *Now you're getting paranoid, Louis*, he thought, doing up the zip. *Just ignore them.* There was a hole at the back of the trousers he hadn't noticed before, and it felt kind of odd to have his tail poking out through the seam. Nevertheless, the rest of the suit fitted surprisingly well. At least he felt professional again. Santosa was right; his image *was* the most important thing. It felt good to be suited up and back in the game with the big boys. Damn good.

He could now hear the muffled voice of the rat on the Home Shopping Channel telling the audience that if they rang the number on screen and paid for the steak knives, they could get another set at half price. As he knotted his tie in front of the mirror, the photo on the union card he had found flashed before his eyes. The resemblance to Aldo Fiddler really was uncanny, he reckoned, and it gave him an idea how to get out of his cashless predicament.

"How do I look?" he said, exiting the bathroom.

Flash Freddy and Smiggins were putting pills into their mouth, fixated to the screen. "Like you belong," Flash Freddy said, barely glancing at him.

Louis straightened his cuffs and flattened the lapels of the suit down his now slim-lined belly (*Waistline, dear, it's a waistline!*). "Damn right I do! I'm ready for action."

Santosa suddenly burped from the doorway. Tiffany Tidbits was behind his wheelchair. "Me too! Let's hit The Lounge Lizard. The Limo's waiting downstairs." Nobody moved, still glued to the Home Shopping Channel. "Come on. We'll miss the happy hour."

Louis was keen to go, but before he went anywhere he wanted to know who was going to find him alternative accommodation. "I can't live on the goddamn streets," he said.

Flash Freddy snapped out of his daze. "The Boss has no further legal obligation to you," he said, and grabbed his briefcase. "Speak to your PA. That's his job now."

The rat was punching numbers into his calculator and sniggering on the sofa. "Okay. Okay. Leave it to me," he said. "And give me the hotel receipt. I'll fix it for you."

They followed Santosa and his little helper down the corridor and were halfway to the stairwell when Louis stopped, remembering something he had left behind. He told them to meet him at the Limo, then trotted back for the union card and the unsigned note he was supposed to have destroyed. Whilst slipping them into the inner pocket of his jacket, he felt something else. At first he thought it was the crumpled message with THERE IS NO ESCAPE, but that was still sitting on top of the vanity table. It was another goddamn note.

You're Mr. Popularity today, Louis, he thought as he read.

"Do not forget. The Lounge Lizard. When the music stops. Your life is in danger. The White Rabbit will save you. PS. Destroy this note."

Louis reread it, wondering what it could mean. *Save me from what?* He was dead. He had no goddamn life, in the real sense of the word that was. Still, he was curious. He absolutely hated not knowing.

As he made his way toward the stairwell he thought he heard footsteps coming from behind. He spun to see who was there, but the corridor was empty. He shrugged away the thought, but before he went down the stairwell he glanced over his tail again, chuckling at his edginess.

Just because you're paranoid that you're being watched, he thought, remembering the lines of an old joke, *doesn't mean that you're not being watched.*

Downstairs, crossing the lobby, he heard Salma Gundi wishing him all the best and hoping to see him again soon. He ignored him and stepped through the revolving door, thinking that even if it were an eternity before he saw old pizza face again it would be too goddamn soon. Outside in the drop-off zone, Santosa, Tiffany, Flash Freddy and Smiggins were at the Limo watching the chauffeur tinker under the hood. The line of Limos stretched around the piazza, honking at him to get a move on.

"We're going to miss the happy hour," Santosa said. "Come on. Hurry up."

After a few more minutes, the chauffeur tried the ignition. Nothing happened. He tried again. Still nothing happened. "It's no use, sir," he said. "I've tried everything."

Santosa burped long and loud. "What's wrong with it?"

"Inbuilt obsolescence. I'll have to call a mechanic."

Santosa threw his webbed hands toward the sky-vault and said, "Just what I need. This thing gobbles money like a bottomless bucket."

Louis could feel the power of the LeMont logo trying to draw his attention toward the top of The Tower, but felt comfortable enough as long as he remembered to keep thinking of the white rabbit. "I thought you said it's still under warrantee," he said.

The chauffeur shook his head and Smiggins sniggered. Tiffany and Flash Freddy were also smiling. "The warrantee has an inbuilt obsolescence too," Santosa said, and drew a breath of oxygen from his mask. "Not worth the paper it's written on."

Flash Freddy could see Louis was having difficulty with the concept. "Once the engine breaks down, the warrantee's sub-clause kicks in."

Louis scratched his head. "Meaning?"

"The warrantee is only good whilst the engine is working."

Louis kept scratching his head. "You can only claim reimbursement while the engine still works? Why would anyone do that? It doesn't make sense."

"It does to the manufacturers," Flash Freddy said. "It's called business. Everything you buy is covered the same way."

"It isn't called a 'working warrantee' for nothing," Santosa said, and burped. The chauffeur returned to tinkering with the engine. "Looks like we're going to miss the happy hour."

Louis followed Santosa's gaze across the piazza beyond the Money Tree. Next to the LeMont Cellular One, a line was already forming outside a pink-gray door. Two large jackals in suits and Egoroids were using whips to control the eager crowd.

"Couldn't we just walk?" he asked.

"Are you joking? I'm an A-class citizen," Santosa said.

Louis snorted, keeping his thoughts to himself. He had no time for this goddamn nonsense. He had a rendezvous to keep and didn't give two hoots whether or not anyone else was coming. In fact, he kind of hoped the others would stay. They were starting to get on his nerves.

Chapter 21

Un-Happy Hour

THEY waited for over an hour to get into the Lounge Lizard before the jackals on the door let them through. All, that was, except for Louis. He had no membership card.

The others flashed their gold membership cards at the jackals, who eyed them suspiciously before nodding and letting them pass. Music blared out of the club through the open doors. Someone at a piano was banging out *Top of the World*, joined by a chorus of happy club members singing at the top of their voice: *And the only explanation I can fiiiiind...*

"What'll I do?" Louis asked Flash Freddy over the din. "Can't you get me in?"

Flash Freddy turned and shrugged. "Sorry, no can do," he said. Then he was through the entrance after the others, disappearing into the mass of bodies and smoke behind the closing doors.

Louis tried his luck with the jackals. "Come on, let me in guys. I'm new in town. It's happy hour." Plus, he was about to add, he had a rendezvous he desperately wanted to keep. He had to get inside. He had to meet whoever it was that could tell him more about the white rabbit.

"Look, how much will it take to let me in?" he asked the closest jackal.

The jackal didn't answer, preferring to eye him with scorn through his Egoroids. Louis felt really small.

"C'mon. How much do you want?" Louis said, hoping like hell Flash Freddy would lend him the money. "I'm good for it. Just let me in and I'll get the cash for you."

The jackals laughed and threatened him with the whip if he didn't step back. "Go on! Get moving," said the closet jackal.

Louis opened his mouth to protest, but the jackal stepped forward and pushed him backwards. Louis tripped over a crack in the sidewalk and stumbled, landing with a thud on his tail. A jolt of pain ripped up his spine.

"You haven't heard the last of this," he said, standing and dusting himself off. "You better have a good goddamn lawyer."

The jackals laughed again, allowing a weasel and another rat into the club. Music blared out briefly as the doors opened then closed. Louis thought of trying to push his way past the jackals, then thought better of it.

He hung his head to the sky-vault, fighting the urge to tug out all his whiskers. He had no money, no place to stay, not even a goddamn Aspirin to ease his throbbing tail.

Worse, he had missed his rendezvous.

Chapter 22

A Slice of Luck

WHILE he wondered what the hell he was going to do next, Louis felt The Tower logo ambushing his mind and thoughts. He'd expected the onslaught, though he still hadn't quite got used to the speed with which it attacked. Nevertheless, he knew he could hold it off with thoughts of the white rabbit, which now had become an automatic, subconscious reflex. He wished he could block out the stench of horseshit with such ease.

With a rare stroke of fortune, he saw Santosa's stretch Limo parked three cars down. The chauffeur had the hood up and was tinkering with the engine. He got inside to wait for the others, thinking a nap was well and truly overdue. The back seat was more than long enough for his body, and although the ridges poked into his back and hips and his tail got in the way, he managed to find a comfortable position to relax. Almost at once, he could feel the weight of his eyelids pressing down. The last few days had taken a toll he wasn't entirely prepared for. How many days had he been awake? A week? A month? It felt like a goddamn eternity, and he doubted Flash Freddy's words of assurance: there was no way in hell he would ever get used to having no shuteye.

Giving in to the heaviness of his eyelids was easy. Soon he was floating in a black-gray swirl of mist, welcoming the lightness and freedom found only at the utter depths of sleep. The serenity was short lived, to his horror, as the mist thickened into a claustrophobic fog that pressed him from all sides, then condensed and flooded the Limo with gallons of thick sticky fluid. It was like goddamn barbeque sauce, and he began to flounder, flailing his arms and legs. As his head went under, the liquid slosh kept congealing, as if it were now freezing into quicksand. He struggled against its grip, lost, unable to see, his energy sapping with every second. Within seconds it had solidified, like water turning to ice, crushing him in suspended animation. He couldn't breathe. He couldn't move. He couldn't…

"Ahhhhh! Goddamn it!" he yelled, wrenching himself out of the nightmare.

He heard footsteps and opened his eyes. The chauffeur's face peered through the passenger window. "Are you all right, sir? I heard you scream."

Louis shuddered, gathering his senses, then nodded.

"It's better if you don't sleep," the chauffeur said. "They'll only get worse."

Louis sat up, rubbing his throat. "What will?"

"The nightmares. They'll drive you insane. That's why nobody sleeps."

Louis took his paw from his throat to his throbbing temples. Hells bells, he hadn't felt this bad since his last hangover at the GRN Christmas party. "Got anything to help? An Eezie-Peezie or something?" The chauffeur shook his head and apologized. "Thought as much," Louis said. *Nothing changes around here. Ain't that the truth.* "I'll work something out. I'm okay now."

Louis tried to shake off the lingering nightmare as the chauffeur went back to tinkering under the hood. He decided to get out and clear his head while the others were still inside the club. He still had fifty dollars and Aldo Fiddler's union card in his pocket. Maybe he could check out the Happythecary for some EZPZs, anything in fact to get rid of this god-awful headache. Just as he reached for the handle, the two jackals from the Lounge Lizard opened the door and ejected a guinea pig onto the sidewalk. Like Louis before, the guinea pig picked himself off the ground and dusted his suit. Unlike Louis, he never said a word. No threats of retaliation. No words of legal advice. He just picked up the pad of Snipes that had fallen out of his pocket, scratched his face, then ambled across the street toward the piazza.

From his own inner pocket, Louis removed the Snipe that had been left for him at the bar. He reread it, glanced at the guinea pig, and licked his lips. *Who's watching who, now*? His head suddenly felt a whole lot clearer.

Slipping out of the Limo, he followed the guinea pig across the piazza to the other side. Several times he lost sight of the quarry behind the crowd of money worshippers, but once he was around the Money Tree it was a hell of a lot easier to keep track of him. The guy didn't suspect a goddamn thing as he weaved around the boulder that had recently embedded itself in the street outside The Tower. He then made his way down Boulevard 10, essentially the direct continuation of Boulevard 1. More Burger Boss's, more Route 666's, more LeMont Cellular One's, betting agencies and outlet stores; the sequence just went on and on. As he followed, Louis ensured that he maintained a reasonable distance back. At first he tried to keep to shadows, then realized that there weren't any. He glanced up at the low-lying sky-vault.

No goddamn sun!

The guinea pig was now approaching an intersection. He didn't continue along the boulevard as Louis thought he might, instead turning left at the 24-hour mini-market down a two-lane side street. At Boulevard 11 he turned right, then left again, then right down Boulevard 12 past the Burger Boss and video store. Just when Louis thought his zig-zagging route was becoming predictable, the guinea pig suddenly stopped outside a branch of LeMont Newsagents on Boulevard 13 and scanned around. Louis had just turned the corner and had to dart behind the side of the mini-market to hide from view. After a second or two, he sidled against the wall and glanced around the corner. The guinea pig had removed a white spray can from his inner pocket and was shaking it vigorously. Suddenly, something alerted him, and he stashed the can under the flap of his jacket. A Limo had turned onto the street and was heading toward him.

Louis stepped back as the Limo approached (SPUNKY, its number plate read) and turned the corner, obscuring his view of the guinea pig. When he looked back, the guinea pig was gone. In his place, on the wall of the newsagent, were the letters: WRFF.

Two rats in suits leaving the newsagent didn't even notice the new graffiti, too busy quarreling over whose turn it was to scratch the Lucky Lotto card they had just bought. One had a Snipe on his back: I BELIEVE IN GOD!

Fearing that he had lost his quarry, Louis darted across the boulevard, dodging past the squabbling rats and around the corner. There, to his relief, several entrances down the empty side street, he saw the guinea pig approach an innocuous looking door. Louis pressed himself against the wall of the mini-market while the guinea pig knocked some kind of code: *Knock-knock-knock.* Pause. *Knock-knock.* Pause. *Knock.*

The cover to a small viewing hole slid open. The guinea pig then flashed his union card and mumbled something out of earshot, presumably a password. At that moment, the two rats that had exited the newsagent came around the corner, still quarreling over the Lotto card. They didn't even notice Louis pressing himself against the wall.

"It's my turn!" the rat with the Snipe on his back said. "You did it last time."

"That's because I paid for it!" the other rat said.

The first rat made a grab for the card, but the other one wouldn't let go. After a brief tug of war it tore in two, sending both rats sprawling backward in a heap of legs and tails.

"Now you've done it!" the second rat said, staring at his broken half. "It's useless."

"Don't blame me! It was my turn."

Getting up, the second rat growled "Bahhh!" and flung the torn section to the ground. He then stormed back around the corner, his companion close at his heels, still whining and pleading his case.

Louis waited until the coast was clear, then went to the entrance where he had last seen the guinea pig. Along with the absence of a shadow, the green-gray door had no number. He raised his paw, now suddenly caught between two minds. The guinea pig had given himself away with that little cameo outside the newsagent. What did he have to gain by associating himself with an outlaw? Goddamn trouble, that's what, and he had seen first hand what they did to lawbreakers in this city. Crucifixion was just the start. Not that he had a problem with it. If you broke the law, you deserved everything you damn well got. He just didn't like the thought that entering this door could get *him* nailed to a cross or shoved into the burning flames at the end of Conduit Number 1.

Then again, Louis, he thought, his paw still raised, *if you want to find out what the hell is going on, you'll have to take a risk. If you turn around now, you'll never know.*

Louis knew he couldn't spend the rest of eternity justifying the visions of the white rabbit as some kind of delusional symptom of Post Traumatic Death Syndrome if there was any chance at all the white rabbit really existed. Wasn't that a goddamn laugh? He was either mad and was seeing things that weren't there, or he would condemn himself to an eternity of madness not knowing the truth. Mad if he knocked. Mad if he didn't.

"What the hell!" he muttered, and banged the secret sequence. *Knock-knock-knock.* Pause. *Knock-knock.* Pause. *Knock.* He didn't even have time to lower his paw before the viewing hole slid open and two menacing eyes glared out. He could tell straight away they belonged to a jackal, and he wasted no time in showing the union card he had found as proof of identification.

"Password!" the jackal said.

Louis said the first thing that came to mind. "White Rabbit." The viewing hole slid shut, then a bolt turned and the door opened. Louis sighed and stepped inside.

Chapter 23

White Rabbit Freedom Fighters

THE jackal filled up most of the tiny entrance, towering over Louis as he signed the guest registry as Aldo Fiddler. As an afterthought, he counted out twenty single dollar bills and slipped them into the jackal's huge paw, then squeezed between him and the table to get to the staircase. Directly below from a gaping dark hole, the stench of horseshit wafted up the stairs like halitosis from the pit of an ulcerated stomach. He could also hear what he first mistook as gargling noises, a muffled female voice backed by a piano, which turned out to be nothing other than a melancholic version of *Top of the World* (was there any other kind of goddamn version?).

Clinging to the wall for support, Louis followed the stairs to the bottom, emerging into a small chamber beneath the level of the street. There seemed to be no other way in or out. No windows, no other doors, just a dark little grotto illuminated with flickering gray candles. The music was coming from the stage directly adjacent, where the flat-back piano was shoved into the recess beneath the stairs like a worn piece of furniture no one knew what to do with.

"Goddamn blues bar," Louis muttered. "Just what I need right now."

The singer, another goddamn rat, held the microphone to her mouth (*…And the only explanation I can fiiiind…*) and rested her paw on the frail shoulder of the pianist, undoubtedly the most ancient ferret Louis had ever seen. Hunched on the stool, his smile revealed several missing teeth and a crooked snout that had obviously been on the wrong end of a drunken fist. His wrinkled face was dominated by two huge orbs that could probably see no further than the bony claws tapping the keys in front of him.

He remained on the bottom step for the moment, waiting for his eyes to adjust to the lack of light. He could see no booths, just several rudimentary tables with chairs for two or three, most of which were empty. He counted only five patrons in the whole place, all of them alone, plus the lizard wiping glasses behind the bar along the opposite wall. It didn't take long to locate his quarry in the far corner. Scratching a fleabite on his ear and staring into a tumbler of iced water, the guinea pig appeared to be the only one who hadn't seen him enter. Louis went up to the table and dropped the Snipe with I'M WATCHING YOU on top of it, snapping him out of his train of thoughts. The guinea pig glanced at it, then slowly wandered up the contours of Louis' suit, his face beginning to glow bright red.

Caught you, didn't I? Louis grinned. *And there's nowhere to run.*

Meeting his gaze, the guinea pig suddenly began to choke on something he had been sucking on. He spluttered and gagged with bulging eyes, bringing his paws to his throat. Nobody seemed to take any notice. The patrons listened politely to the singer (*I'm on the… Top of the world, lookin'… down on creation…*) and the lizard behind the bar kept wiping glasses. The guinea pig continued to splutter and gag, turning an even deeper shade of crimson. Then suddenly knocking back his chair, he stood in a desperate attempt to dislodge the thing in his throat; but just as Louis was about to slap him on the back, an ice cube exploded from of his mouth and slid across the table. It shot to the other side and slammed into the backrest of the opposite chair, flopping onto the seat.

"Louis!" he said, massaging his throat. "To be sure, how did you… What are you doing here?"

"It's Lewey. Not Lewis. And I could ask you the same question, Frank O'Lynn."

His face still glowing, Frank O'Lynn scanned the room, then gathered his fallen chair and sat back down. If anybody else had overheard their conversation, they weren't letting it show. He now began to whisper. "Please, no names here. We prefer to remain anonymous." He gestured for Louis to sit. "Call me *The Partridge.*"

Louis dragged over a chair and sat, thinking if he wanted answers he would have to go along with the ridiculous charade of pseudonyms and amateur detectives, at least for the time being. He showed him both notes that told him to rendezvous at the Lounge Lizard, and said, "Did you write this?" *The Partridge*, as he wanted to be called, glanced at the simple handwriting, deigning not to answer. Louis pressed him again. Eventually, he got a reply, a simple jerk of the head in affirmation. "Save me from what?" he said. "How can I be in danger?"

The guinea pig scratched his snout. "Are you that naïve?"

If Louis didn't know any better, he sounded almost defiant. "Enlighten me."

Frank O'Lynn took a moment to respond. "To be sure, Louis," he said, "like everyone else in this city, you need to be saved from yourself." Dumbstruck, Louis stared across the table. Frank O'Lynn then leaned forward. "Can I trust you?"

Louis said, "Of course you can." He didn't add: *You don't have any goddamn choice.*

Frank O'Lynn, though, eyed him with suspicion. "Coming from a guy whose motto in life was: Don't trust anyone."

Louis rolled his eyes, wanting nothing more to do with his stupid games. He just wanted answers. "You seem to know a lot about me."

Frank O'Lynn now leaned back, crossing his arms across his pinstriped tie. "I've seen your file. It's not pleasant reading."

"What the hell is this, the goddamn inquisition?"

Frank O'Lynn's eyes shifted from side to side. "Not so loud!" he said, almost hissing. "These walls have ears."

Louis had to suppress the urge to grab him by the collar and shout: *Tell me what in hell is going on or I'll hand you over to the goddamn authorities right this goddamn minute.* Instead, he leaned forward across the table and whispered, "I don't care if the walls have goddamn penises. I haven't done anything wrong. I'm not in any danger from anything, let alone you. Now you better start telling me what's going on – how you know so much about me – or I'm going to go back up those stairs and make my way to the piazza." He pointed to the spray can hidden inside Frank O'Lynn's jacket. "I'm sure someone in The Tower would be very interested in talking to someone who has just graffitied the walls with the logo of an outlawed faction."

Frank O'Lynn began to redden again, getting brighter and brighter until his face seemed more luminous than the table candles. Louis waited while the blues singer came to the end of her song, but when the answer he wanted wasn't forthcoming, he threatened to leave straight away.

"You're being set up," Frank O'Lynn said. He scratched the back of his paw, not looking up.

"By who?"

Frank O'Lynn stopped scratching. Louis didn't like his smile. "Who do you reckon?"

Louis hadn't got to know that many yet, and those he did know, Flash Freddy, Smiggins and Santosa, had been nothing but the model of support. He set his jaw. "I don't believe you. If anyone's setting me up, it's you. Or the goddamn White Rabbit."

Behind him, the blues singer thanked the audience and then restarted the only song that anyone seemed to know. A strand of long hair fell in front of the guinea pig's face, which he flicked away before replying. "To be sure, you're almost right. The White Rabbit isn't setting you up. I am, with a little help from a fat toad. It's an old scam. I'm surprised you've fallen for it so easily."

Louis felt a surge of anger flood through him. "Santosa? How?"

Frank O'Lynn eyed him, assessing whether or not to go ahead and spill everything. "We call it *The Hot Potato.* Whoever's holding it, gets burned." He had the look of someone who didn't care what happened next. He wasn't even bothering to whisper. "We've been scamming newbies for thousands of years. Works every time. We've made a fortune from it."

Louis ground his teeth and clenched his paws. *This guy has a goddamn nerve, doesn't he?*

"We usually take it in turns to pretend which partner is sending the company into bankruptcy," Frank O'Lynn continued. "The other partner pretends he's desperate to buy the other out before it's too late, but that he doesn't have the ready cash to do it. Enter the fall guy. The newbie. He tries for a bank loan but is rejected, being new to the city and without any capital earnings behind him. I presume you're at that stage now."

Louis nodded, a perfunctory jerk of the head. "You could say I was considering my options."

"Thought as much. Anyway, the next step involves arranging a third-party loan from an anonymous source. It's done hastily, as if out of the blue, to meet the deadline of the buyout. All the while, however, the newbie is unaware that the benefactor is no third party at all, but the partner that's lured him into the deal and pretended to have no available cash. The partner being bought out simply sits on the money upon receipt of it, but the newbie is now holding a massive debt he can't pay off. Not at the interest he's being charged, anyway." Frank O'Lynn paused for a moment, then said, "Do you see where this is going?"

Louis snorted, his claws digging painfully into the pads of both paws. Goddamn right he could see where this was going. "The newbie is left holding the hot potato," he said.

"To be sure. A debt he can't pay off, especially with the further slump in sales, which the previous partners had declined, or were unwilling, to arrest. The newbie tries to hold out for as long as he can. Sometimes it's a couple of years, usually no more than several months. But the debt gets too big to handle. He often tries to put the company into liquidation. But because The Boss is the controlling shareholder and has power of veto, the newbie is faced with only one real option: to sellout for whatever he's offered. Miraculously, the first partner suddenly frees up some cash and is able to soften the fall, but not by much. The newbie gets virtually nothing back for his investment. He is only free of the company, but not of the debt, which is of no concern to the partners. They've passed on the hot potato and can now pump the profits of the cheap buyout back into the company and look for another newbie to do it all again."

Frank O'Lynn paused to take a sip of water. "Don't look so glum, Louis. It's not personal. It's business. To be sure, the only way to make money is to take it off someone else. Everyone does it. This time, it just happened to be you."

Louis remained silent for a while, letting his anger cool. His pride had been assaulted, worse than when Mary Callaghan told him to beat it after he had asked her to the prom. Ah, petite Mary Callaghan, the first girl who had set his hormones blazing. The first girl whose mocking laugh had made him want to crawl into the gutter and suffocate in his own humiliation. That had been bad. This was worse. Back at school he was young and naïve, completely forgivable, but at his age he should have known better. Blinded with adolescent lust was one thing. Blinded with greed for a quick buck was another. He had jumped straight in without so much as a clue as to what was happening and broken his own motto, never trust anyone. He was damn lucky to have gotten away unscathed. Still, it left a taste in his mouth more goddamn bitter than if he had crunched a whole bottle of Kwel-Amities.

"The Boss actually goes along with this?" he said.

"Who do you think thought of it first? He wrote the constitution on which LeMont was founded. It's based on three guiding principles: Uniformity, Conformity and Control. What better way to achieve this than to send his employees into the abyss of debt the moment they arrive?"

"You're telling me he's nothing but a glorified slum lord?" Louis said. "That's how he runs his corporation? No wonder things don't work around here."

"You said it, not me."

Louis drew a deep breath. "I just want to know one thing. Why me? I'm innocent. What have I ever done to you, or The Boss for that matter?"

Frank O'Lynn threw his head back and laughed. It was loud enough to put the singer off her guard (*... there's a plee-zant sense of happiness for me...*). Even the lizard behind the bar glanced over.

"You're a scream, to be sure," he said, "and, I might say, a trifle slow. No one is innocent in LeMont. That's why we're here, all of us. Old friends and acquaintances. We *chose* to be here."

"I don't know what you're on about," Louis said. "I was given no choice. I was alive at my desk one minute, the next thing I know I was here in this goddamn weasel suit. I've never met you or Santosa or his little helper before. Not even Flash Freddy or Smiggins for that matter. How could we be old friends?"

"Have you really forgotten everything?" Frank O'Lynn said. "Then again, I guess that's what they're counting on. To be sure, Louis, you're stuck deeper than you know."

Louis ignored the smug expression on the guinea pig's face. "Why are you telling me if you're in on it?"

Frank O'Lynn sighed and scratched his ear again. "I've had enough. I want out. Nothing changes in this city. It's the same thing, day in, day out. There's no hope. Worse, nobody wants to change. Sure, they might complain about it, but deep down all they want to do is maintain the status quo. Everyone's so scared of missing out they won't do anything to improve the situation. I honestly can't see how this city is going to turn around for the better. There's no future here for me. For anyone, for that matter. The Boss has them right under his big fat claw. And you know what? Nobody cares. As long as they have their pills and burgers, they think they've got everything they want."

His confession confirmed the initial assumption Louis had had at the meeting in room 1706. Moreover, thinking of the backstabbing Pooh-Bah and his little helper only stoked his anger further. Hells bells, to think he had nearly bankrupted himself before he had even settled into his job and found a place to live. God help him when he saw that fat toad again; he had better hope there wasn't a free whip in the vicinity when he did.

Frank O'Lynn was now staring distantly at the stage over Louis' shoulder. "No, Louis, I want out. There's only one problem…"

He didn't finish, cut short by shouting at the top of the stairs. Louis spun to see what was going on, just as an upturned table crashed to the floor. The music suddenly stopped midway through the chorus as the pianist's claws arrested on the keys, craning his wrinkly face above. The singer also looked up, still holding the microphone to her lips. The lizard behind the bar tossed his towel to one side and ducked down out of sight. Everyone else in the room was frozen to their seats.

"Peelers! Peelers!" the jackal yelled from the entrance.

The Partridge snapped out of his shock. "Come on! We've got to go. The Secret Police are here."

There were more scuffles and grunts from the top of the stairs. Although fighting a losing battle, the jackal managed to shout another warning down to the patrons.

"What'll we do?" Louis said, scanning the room for an exit he might have overlooked. "There's nowhere to go."

Unbelievably, the weasel sitting two tables over near the stage vanished into thin air. Here one second, gone the next. He even made a small popping sound as he left, like the *Pop*! of a cork from a bottle of Imperial Brut. At first Louis figured he must have dived under the table, but when the old ferret at the piano popped into thin air too, followed immediately by the blues singer, he knew something weird was going on.

At that moment, two rats came storming down the stairs. One of them had a Lucky Lotto card poking from the pocket of his suit. "Nobody leave!" the rat said, taking two steps at a time. His partner was close at his heels. "This is a raid!"

"I don't believe it," Louis said. He watched the remaining patrons vanish into thin air, *Pop*! *Pop*! *Pop*! like muffled firecrackers going off on New Year's Eve. The tumbler another rat had been holding to his lips remained motionless in the air for the briefest of seconds before it fell onto the table and cracked in half.

Frank O'Lynn reached over the table and grabbed his paw. "Close your eyes!" he said. "Quickly!"

Louis instinctively drew away. He watched the first rat leap from the fourth step onto the floor, then point to him and Frank O'Lynn. "There they are! Don't let them get away!"

Frank O'Lynn grabbed his paw again. Louis tried to pull it back, but the guinea pig wasn't letting go. "Close your eyes! Just do it!"

Louis hesitated, stunned with the speed at which the peelers were attacking. Both rats were now sprinting across the floor, maneuvering around and jumping over the tables to get at them. He heard Frank O'Lynn tell him for the last time to close his eyes and complied immediately, just as the first rat leaped over the nearest table, claws outstretched, mouth gaping, fangs bared. He instinctively shrank back and yelped, scrunching his eyes as tightly as he could, fully expecting the force of the rat to hurl him against the back wall.

It didn't happen. Instead, he heard a *Pop*! and felt the briefest rush of breeze ruffle the fur on his head. Then silence, and the horrible sensation he was floating in mist.

Just like his nightmare.

PART THREE

Chapter 24

Fires of Oblivion

"IT'S safe now," Louis heard Frank O'Lynn say. "The peelers can't get you here."

Tentatively, he opened his eyes and withdrew his paw from Frank O'Lynn's grasp, recognizing instantly where he was. Barely a second had zipped by since he had cringed from the peeler's gaping jaw, barely a second to gather his wits that were spilling about like M&M's from the box. How the hell then, in that short space of time, had Frank O'Lynn transported him more than fifty miles to the end of Conduit Number 1? But he had, no goddamn denying it. They were standing near the wall and bright white light was glaring through the golden archway. HEREBY LIES THE END OF THE WORLD. TRAVELERS PASS AT THEIR PERIL. What's more, gathered around in front of them was another whip-yielding crowd of rats, weasels, lizards and ferrets, presumably waiting for another newbie to arrive. Most were popping pills or slipping on a pair of Egoroids, many sneezing and coughing or scratching at fleabites. To his relief, the bell at the top of the arch was motionless and silent, at least for the moment.

"Are you sure the peelers haven't followed us here?" he asked.

Frank O'Lynn nodded and said, "Quite sure."

Louis could still feel the buzzing aftereffects of the near escape. "I… I must have brought them to your club. I'm sorry. They must have seen me enter."

"To be sure, what's done is done," Frank O'Lynn said. "They probably had me under surveillance, as it was. Someone must have tipped them off."

Louis scanned the crowd. "What happened to your colleagues? Where'd they go?"

"They *Popped* randomly all over the city, to wherever came to mind. No place in particular. We'll regroup. To be sure, it's not the first time we've been raided…"

Frank O'Lynn was cut short by something he had just seen over Louis' shoulder.

Louis spun. Trailing the Grand Pooh-Bah like three ducklings behind its mother (Hewey, Dewey and Lewey?) were Tiffany Tidbits, Flash Freddy and Smiggins. "Out of my way!" Santosa said, wheeling himself through the crowd. "Out of my way! This is official business!"

Louis gasped and stepped back, pressing himself against the wall. He wasn't yet ready to deal with the fat toad and his little helper. He also wasn't sure how deep the lizard and sniggering rat had been in the whole *Hot Potato* scam either. As far as he was concerned, better to assume that everyone was guilty. Even Tiffany.

"Don't worry," Frank O'Lynn said. "Nobody can see or hear us. For the time being anyway. *Popping* makes us invisible until we… uh, *Pop* back into relative reality."

Louis watched Santosa push through the crowd to the front. He passed right in front of him and didn't even blink, as did the others. Amazing, considering that he and *The Partridge* could still see each other as easily as they had before they *Popped.*

"How long do we remain like this?" he asked. Oddly enough, this was the first time since he died that he actually felt like a ghost. "Shouldn't we hide before we rematerialize in front of everyone and get arrested?"

Frank O'Lynn scratched behind his ear. "You'll know when the time comes to hide. To be sure, you'll smell the difference."

Louis lifted his pointy snout and sniffed, suddenly elated. The stench of horseshit was gone. In its place a not too displeasing smell of roasted peanuts, reminding him of the jars and jars of homemade peanut butter his grandma used to stack against the kitchen wall before she packed them into crates for market day.

"How did you do it?" he asked. "You know, *Pop* from there to here."

"The trick is knowing you are already where you want to be.

We'll talk about it later. Now's not the time." Frank O'Lynn then stretched up to see over the heads of the crowd. "Aggh, it's no good. I can't see what's going on."

Louis was about to tell him not to bother, that he had seen it all before and wasn't in the mood to watch another public flogging, when Frank O'Lynn grabbed his paw and lifted him into the air. Within seconds they were hovering near the ceiling and looking down on the crowd, like they were perched on the uppermost branches of the Money Tree. His initial start at the unexpected takeoff (he had never really had the stomach for flying) was soon replaced with bemused intrigue. He had been wrong about the reason for the gathering. The crowd wasn't waiting for another newbie to come through the archway; it was waiting to lynch its latest victim. He immediately recognized the bespectacled rat trembling in front of the archway as the obstinate official Santosa had condemned to the Fires of Oblivion.

Frank O'Lynn then warned Louis that he was going to let go of his paw. Louis flinched, fearing he would fall straight on top of the official and give himself away. "To be sure, you'll stick like Spiderman," Frank O'Lynn said, and showed him how to press his back against the roof. To Louis' astonishment, he remained fixed to the rocky vault, even when *The Partridge* took his paw away.

Just your friendly neighborhood Spiderweasel, he chuckled.

"You're probably wondering how your friends got here so soon after the Lounge Lizard," Frank O'Lynn said, and Louis nodded. "You might already know that space and time are intricately woven, like reeds in a mat. So when we jumped across the city we also jumped across time. The bigger the distance we jump or *Pop*, the more time we bypass before we rematerialize. A week has probably gone by since the peelers raided the club."

Well fancy that and bugger me, Louis mused. "Why doesn't everyone do it then? Why do they bother with Limos or walking?"

"To be sure, the same reason they do anything. Comfort. It feels safer to do something you've been doing your whole life than to try something new, wouldn't you agree?"

Louis glanced down, sensing a change in the mood of the crowd. Previously ordered and restrained (wasn't it amazing how a lynch mob could follow correct protocol?), a few of them were now getting restless, flexing their whips, shuffling from foot to foot, muttering to one another their disapproval. A jackal four deep at the back yelled out, "Hurry up! Let's get this over with. We can't stand around all day."

A weasel near Smiggins raised his whip. Flash Freddy and several others did likewise. The official flinched and shrank down, yelping in fear, but Santosa wheeled forward and forbid anyone to act prematurely. The jackal and others muttered in dissent. Louis expected the torrent of whips to come lashing down, but the crowd remained hesitant. Santosa whispered to the cowering official that he didn't have much time. Only Louis and Frank O'Lynn could hear what he had to say. "Do it now and save yourself some pain. I can't control them for much longer."

The official fell to his knees and grabbed Santosa's wheelchair, pleading for mercy, but Santosa plucked his claws from the rim of the wheel and backed off a yard. The rat's thick lenses had magnified his eyes into dark whirlpools of terror, and for the first time Louis actually felt pity for the wretch. He also felt the first inkling of something he hadn't felt for a hell of a long time: guilt. Though it was probably nothing more than what he would have felt for a stray cur he had accidentally run over with his car.

"I can't do it!" the official said, still on his knees. His claws were now clasped like a beggar. "I don't want to be obliterated. I want to stay. I want to work. I promise to take bribes. Honest."

"Have it your way," Santosa said, and burped. He distanced himself further and nodded to the crowd. All at once, whips rained down upon the official. Although he must have known it was coming, he screamed as much in surprise as in pain. He tried to back away on his knees while whips lashed his head and chest and abdomen, ripping shreds from his suit. Another lashing knocked his spectacles off his face, which fell to the ground and broke. He yelped, fumbling around for them on the rocky floor. Another whip lashed his paw, which he withdrew and cradled to his chest, wailing in agony, just as another lash tore a chunk from his right ear. He squealed, shuffling still further backward on his knees.

Louis was fixated. It was something he would have expected in a goddamn gladiator fight. Sensing the end, the crowd closed ranks and edged forward. The bright white rays through the archway now glinted off the official's back like sunlight off the surface of a small pond. He glanced over his tail, clearly feeling the heat, whimpering under the hail of lashes. Still, he wouldn't voluntarily jump through the arch, preferring to curl into a ball and suffer the relentless onslaught. Flash Freddy raised and flicked his whip in a steady mechanical rhythm, each time collecting its mark. Smiggins was hopping from one foot to the other, his tail swishing from side to side almost as fast as the lizard was letting fly with the whip. Only Tiffany remained motionless.

Santosa then burped long and loud and the lashing came to a sporadic halt. One or two eager-beavers got in a last shot while they could before an eerie calm descended on the mob and its victim. The official, still quivering with his head tucked between his knees, didn't move. Santosa told him to get up, but he refused to budge. Santosa told him again. Then, when the official didn't move for the second time, he nodded to two jackals to pick him off the ground.

Only now could Louis see the full extent of the punishment. With a jackal holding him under the arms on both sides, the official looked as if he had just been mauled by a mountain lion. His suit had all but been stripped off, now just torn and tattered, reminding Louis of the old scarecrow in his grandfather's cornfield, the one he used to take potshots at with the air rifle he had been given for his seventh birthday. That scarecrow had had a head that lolled back and forth when the westerly wind picked up and clumps of straw that poked through the old workman's overalls his grandfather had outworn. Likewise, Louis could now see clumps of fur sticking through the holes in the official's tattered suit, and his head seemed to loll from side to side with exhaustion. He seemed even too weak to speak; but when Santosa told the jackals to throw him into the

Fires of Oblivion, he struggled and thrashed about, screaming at the top of his voice, "I don't want to die! I don't want to die!"

"You're already dead," Santosa said, and nodded to the jackals.

"Have mercy! Have mercy!" he screamed, thrashing his head from side to side. The jackals picked him up and flung him into the bright white light, not too unlike Mr. Scarecrow being chucked onto the bonfire of discarded junk and timber the day the officials snatched his grandfather's farm. The Fires of Oblivion swallowed the squealing official whole, cutting short his protests in mid-scream. "Have mer…"

Louis half-expected a cheer to ring through the air in triumph of one more vermin rid from the streets of LeMont. Instead, the obliteration was greeted with demur silence, many in the crowd looking at one another with expressions of *what do we do now*? At that moment, he caught a whiff of something he had hoped he would never smell again. Glancing at the golden archway, he was suddenly struck with horror.

"This is the gates of hell, isn't it?" he said, gulping. "And I'm on the wrong side of them."

Frank O'Lynn, with his back still pressed to the roof, took his attention away from the dispersing crowd and sighed. "To be sure, Louis, I had had my doubts about you." He sighed, but at the same time held out his paw to congratulate him on his newfound knowledge. "You no longer deny the truth of what you see. Welcome. You are now a member of the White Rabbit Freedom Fighters."

"Do I have a goddamn choice in the matter?" Louis asked, though suspected he already knew the answer to that.

"The question is not whether you have a choice," Frank O'Lynn said, "but *what* choice do you make now?"

Louis didn't have to think too goddamn hard about the answer. His whole life had been defined by it. Ever since he was a kid running from the bullies in the playground, escaping to his grandfather's farm from the dreariness of his no-hope parents, resigning from his job to create his own company, there had been one underlying motivation for it all, the one hidden desire that drove him to become what he was. The one goddamn thing he was willing to die for.

"Freedom," he said. "I want out of here."

"Then you're going to have to break a habit of a lifetime and learn to trust again," Frank O'Lynn said.

The smell of horseshit was now more than just a whiff; it was threatening to overwhelm the sanity of roasted peanuts. "Try me."

Frank O'Lynn nodded to the bright white light streaming through the golden archway. "Ever wondered why someone can emerge from the Fires of Oblivion unscathed, but not enter?"

"You're not suggesting that I…"

"Contrary to popular belief, the best kept secret in the world is not that hell does not exist, but that its gates are always open." Frank O'Lynn had that glazed over, distant look in his eyes again. "We walk in and out of them, at our own free will." Then he shook himself out of his daze. "The question you have to ask yourself is this: Do I trust him to be telling the truth? Am I willing to risk obliteration for the chance of Eternal Freedom?"

Louis glanced at the Fires of Oblivion. He could almost feel the heat of the bright white light.

Not yet I don't, he thought. *Not goddamn yet.*

Chapter 25

Awakening

LOUIS and *The Partridge* sought sanctuary in a nearby tunnel to re-materialize before anyone, especially the secret police, caught them adhered to the ceiling of Conduit Number 1. Louis could hear the chink, chink, chink of tunneling going on somewhere at the end of the narrow passageway, interspersed with the occasional wailing and gnashing of teeth from some newbie in his holding cell; but other than that, there was little chance of anyone stumbling upon two renegades emerging out of the ether like developing images in a photographer's darkroom.

Wiggling his snout, he grimaced at the putrefaction worming up his nostrils. Roasted peanuts had been taken off the menu five minutes ago. Gut-turning, throat-wrenching horseshit had been slopped up for mains, and then dessert. Goddamn stench was probably worse now than ever before – probably? *definitely* – given the delight of roasted peanuts and the nostalgia it had evoked; and if Mr. Goddamn Partridge told him he would get used to it, he might just find himself flattened with a right hook aimed fairly and squarely at his pointy jaw, notwithstanding all he had done to save his furry tail from the secret police in the last half hour or so.

"Hope you've got your walking shoes on, Louis," Frank O'Lynn said. "To be sure, the heat's still on and we've got some serious miles to cover before we're safe."

"Why walk? Let's goddamn *Pop*." It wasn't the effort he was averse to; he just wanted an end to the god-awful stench.

Frank O'Lynn started back toward Conduit Number 1, ambulating this time, not floating. "No such luck. We have to wait at least a year before we can do it again." He saw Louis' frown of disappointment. "An ether-channel has been opened between the blues bar and ourselves," he said. "No matter where we are, if we try to

Pop somewhere else before it closes, we'll end up back where we were. The peelers have no doubt set up an ambush. It'd be foolish to *Pop* too soon."

So that was goddamn it then, Louis sighed, for a year anyhow. They had used their get-out-of-jail-free card and now they had to wait to pass Go on the mega-monopoly board of LeMont International Enterprises before they could use another one. At least he had one thing working in his favor: time went a lot quicker in the After Life. He wouldn't have to wait too long; it would be like rolling double sixes to get around the board.

They exited the tunnel after the next bend, emerging into the vaulted grayness of Conduit Number 1 several hundred yards from the archway. Nobody had hung around for a chat and a laugh after the lynching – no friendly beers around this backyard BBQ – the archway now just a deserted beacon of white (*Fires of Oblivion, Louis, that's what it is, and it's the only way in and out of this god-forsaken place*). It drew his attention like the alpha-omega logo at the top of The Tower. Unlike the mind-sapping hold of the logo, however, this he found somewhat comforting, the kind of feeling he could remember as a kid eating roasted marshmallows around the fireplace with his grandfather.

With one major difference, Louis my pal: if you stuck your claw in that fireplace it would more than give it a sting – it would obliterate it like you'd stuck it in a vat of hydrochloric acid.

"Ironic, isn't it?" Frank O'Lynn said, following his gaze.

"Huh?" Louis said, shaking the image of his clawless paw.

"Damned if you do. Damned if you don't." Frank O'Lynn now had a contradictory mix of sadness and mirth across his whiskered face. "Wouldn't you call that the perfect definition of hell?"

In a previous existence Louis might have disagreed. More like spending the rest of eternity with his wife, he would have said; except now he was beginning to think differently. Good ol' Lady Di might have had her faults, and God knew he would have had no difficulty in recalling the hundred or so occasions he wanted to strangle, shoot, horse-whip, poison, or behead her over the past forty years, but compared to the eternity of false promises, inbuilt obsolescence, contractual obligations, mind-numbing logos, spying peelers (was it possible to outrun the law for eternity?), *Hot Potato* scams, no sleep, no sex, no money, 24-hour employment and whatever else the goddamn mega-corporation of LeMont International Enterprises had to offer, then his ex-wife was almost the very picture of heaven.

Good God, Louis, how did you ever get yourself into such a goddamn mess?

Sighing, he trudged with Frank O'Lynn down Conduit Number 1 in the direction he had last seen Santosa, Tiffany, Flash Freddy and Smiggins disperse to after the unfortunate official had been wiped from the face of existence. The gravity of his predicament was only now beginning to be felt. His first reaction was to deny it: if he didn't think about the horrors of his eternal future, it wouldn't be that bad. Denial didn't last long, though, about the length of time it took to amble past the Chamber of Life, where not so long ago he had witnessed his first, and hopefully last, crucifixion. Where now, if he pricked his pointy ears and listened hard, he could hear the muffled moaning of a thousand lost souls through the doorway: "Why hast thou forsaken me? Why hast thou forsaken me? Why hast thou forsaken me?"

He knew he couldn't pretend everything smelled of roses when it really stank of goddamn horseshit. He wasn't an ostrich (*Nope, you're a despicable little weasel, Louis, and don't you forget it*), sticking his head in the ground and convincing himself that if he couldn't see trouble then trouble couldn't see him. Leave that attitude for the hippies and no-hopers of the world. He was a man of action, and proud of it. Sitting on his butt in the land of make believe never solved anything.

"Are you going to tell me where we're headed?" he asked. "I'm not one for surprises."

"To be sure, it's better left unsaid." Frank O'Lynn wasn't in any mood to compromise, Louis could tell. Certainly not the same guinea pig he had met for negotiations in Room 1706. "It's no certainty the peelers have lost our trail. If they catch us, I don't want you spilling the beans on the location of one our safe houses. Our most reliable one, too, I might add."

They had just passed the doorway to a Chamber of the Senses, evoking memories of the last time he had been here. What a difference a goddamn day (week?) made. Then, with Flash Freddy and Smiggins, he had been bursting the seams of his toga like a sixteen-year-old virgin visiting a downtown brothel. Now he wouldn't lose any sleep (*there's a joke lurking in there somewhere, Louis*) if he never saw inside any of the chambers again. The whole scenario made him shudder. It was… well, goddamn hell.

"To be sure, Louis, you look like you've seen a ghost," Frank O'Lynn said.

The attempt at humor wasn't funny, not in the mood he was in. Not a goddamn bit. "Is it the tunnel, or what?" he said, hugging his chest. "I could do with some warmth."

"An after-effect of rematerializing. You'll get used to it." Head down, tail straight, Frank O'Lynn showed no signs of slowing down. "On the other hand, if you're that cold we could always go and warm ourselves back at the Fires of Oblivion."

Another joke that was about as funny as discovering the only so-called friends he had were trying to scam him. Louis shivered and kept hugging his chest, trying to stop his teeth from chattering. To make matters worse, the bell atop the archway had begun to sound its god-awful call. Even at this distance, probably more than a mile or so away, the screeching warbles squirmed inside his skull like maggots burrowing into the once fleshy part of his brain. He shot his paws to his ears, but the warbling only seemed to echo louder down the tunnel and squeeze between his claws. All around, doors were opening and closing as jackals and rats and weasels hurried to greet the newbie emerging through the archway. Next to him, Frank O'Lynn hadn't even broken stride. Louis almost begged him to grab his paw and *Pop* away. Somewhere, anywhere, it was worth the risk of rematerializing back at the club. They could outrun the peelers. Goddamn it, even crucifixion had to be better than this.

Then, just as suddenly as it had started, the bell fell silent. His head was clear and he could hear the excitement building behind him. Sighing with relief, he dropped his paws back to his side, except now he found himself fearing for the newbie and wishing he could do something to help with his transition into the After Life. The shock of the surprised emotion stopped him in his tracks, like he had walked into a glass door he had forgotten was there. It was so foreign, so *un*-Louis.

"What the hell are you thinking?" he said to himself, and shook it off. The newbie would have to defend for himself, like everybody else in this god-forsaken place. What could he do against a ravenous horde? The simple fact was, nothing. That's if he actually wanted to do anything, which he wasn't sure he did. Compassion, like benevolence, was a stranger on his block, something to be treated with wariness and kept on the other side of the street. *The road to hell is paved with good intentions.* Wasn't that how the saying went? It was better to continue down the tunnel and not get involved. He would only get in the way of things.

Yet it didn't feel right. While the suit and ties continued to stream past in the opposite direction, Louis discovered another emotion whelming up from whatever depths he had been suppressing it: helplessness. Something he thought he had goddamn dealt with long time ago. Helplessness belonged to the boy the bullies had pinned to the ground and crammed dog turds in his underpants, then told all the girls in the playground he crapped his pants and stank of horseshit. Helplessness belonged to the lad that had come home from school one day to find his mommy's pretty face covered in fresh bruises and his daddy at the kitchen table shouting at him to get to his room. Helplessness had nothing to do with the man who had started his own business from scratch and built into a multi-national company. Nothing at goddamn all. Except now that feeling was knocking at his door like a long-lost lovechild he thought he had arranged to have aborted years ago. Something he was going to have to deal with whether he liked it or not.

He stopped and glanced over his tail. The bright white light of the Fires of Oblivion was no longer visible, just the steady traffic of navy-gray suits heading away from him. "Shouldn't we do something to help the newbie?" he asked.

"Not so loud," Frank O'Lynn whispered, looking from side to side. "Do I have to remind you that we're running from the law?" A ferret and a rat hurried past, not interested in anything other than getting to the archway before all the fun was over. "To be sure, the newbie's fate has already been determined by the choices he's made. Call it karma. Call it reaping what you sow," and Louis thought: *I call it getting what you deserve. Or at least I used to. Now I'm not so sure.* "Whatever. There's nothing we can do to change the path he's chosen to walk. Just as nobody can change our path."

A roar of thousands echoed down the tunnel, cutting him short.

"I just feel kind of sorry for the guy," Louis said, glancing behind again. Two weasels exiting the nearest chamber sprinted toward the cheering crowd. "I never thought I'd ever admit to something like that, let alone say it out loud, but that's the way I feel."

Frank O'Lynn looked at him the way a father would look at a son who just told him he thought he might be gay, but wasn't sure. The look said: *we better get you some help straight away, before it's too late.*

"To be sure, Louis, if you really want to help the newbie, and everyone else, then you have to come with me. Your job is to spread the word of salvation through the White Rabbit and..."

Another roar from the archway cut over the top of his voice. As if whipped into action, Frank O'Lynn hurried off in the opposite direction. The way ahead was now free of navy-gray suits, with only the occasional stragglers running toward them fearful of missing the action. Louis caught up with him. "And what?" he said. "What else am I supposed to do?"

Frank O'Lynn pretended he was in too much of a hurry to answer, that it wasn't safe to hang around. To be sure, it was better to get to the safe house before somebody recognized them.

Louis broke into a trot, thinking he already knew what he was supposed to do. A shudder of pins and needles rushed down his spine. *He wants me to pave the way for others to follow. He wants me to be a goddamn sacrifice.*

Chapter 26

Louis Seeks Refuge

ALMOST ten hours later they arrived at the archway at the other end of the tunnel. Like before, there was a backlog of navy-gray suits waiting to pass through. Louis reckoned the line to be several hundred yards long; not that he could see the front of it – there were too many goddamn bodies in the way – rather, he took a guess based on the sound of Santosa's voice berating the official whose job it was to check the validity of everybody's union membership. As on the previous occasion, the fat toad was ranting and raving that he would have him crucified if he didn't let him pass, that he was the Grand Pooh-Bah of Workplace Safety and Wages, that he had powerful friends and it wouldn't be wise to stand in his way. Nothing he said, however, had any effect. The official couldn't even be bribed.

"I demand you let me through!" Santosa shouted. "I'm late for the AGM."

Frank O'Lynn stood patiently by as an excited cocktail of sniggering and spitefulness passed down the line. Louis hugged his chest, chilled as much from the effects of rematerializing as what he could hear from others around him. A jackal just ahead sniffled and wiped his snout with the back of his paw, then said, "He deserves what's coming to him."

His pal, a ferret with a walking stick, nodded in agreement: "Officials get right up my nose. They're the bane of my After Life."

Despite Santosa embarking on yet another tirade, the official still wasn't budging, citing protocol as his defense. Santosa's voice lifted over the murmuring, now giving the official one last chance to let him through. A bad feeling came over Louis.

Frank O'Lynn shook his head and said, "They never learn, do they?"

Louis had to agree, though he was thinking more of Santosa and his gang of scammers than the beleaguered official. It was goddamn *déjà vu*.

In next to no time, the shouting stopped and the cracking of whips echoed down the tunnel. Flash Freddy was at work again, Louis figured, and somewhere under the hail of lashes he could just make out the squeals of the terrified official. As he listened, Louis was struck with a sudden sense of dread: these apparently sporadic attacks on officialdom just hadn't happened once or twice, but hundreds, if not *thousands* of times.

Then silence fell, and slowly but surely the line began to move again. Though he was in no way reduced to the tattered scare-crow-like figure of the previous official, Louis saw when he had reached the front of the line, the rat behind the foldout table had the stunned expression of someone who had just been mugged by his own wife. Staring blankly at nothing in particular, pinstriped tie askew, buttons torn from a crumpled jacket, he barely cared for the line of suits trickling past. "Is it me, or is every official in this city a rat?" Louis whispered.

"To be sure, all officialdom and all peelers," Frank O'Lynn whispered back, scratching his cheek. The jackal and ferret Louis had overheard earlier were now approaching the makeshift check-point. "The Boss trusts no one else. Rats seem to have a natural disposition for protocol and corporate security."

"Is The Boss a rat, too?"

Frank O'Lynn glanced around to make sure Louis hadn't been overheard. The ferret and lizard behind were discussing the acquisition of a commercial lease on Boulevard 1. "It's best not to speculate about it," *The Partridge* whispered. "Nobody knows what The Boss looks like. No one has ever seen him. He never leaves his penthouse."

Louis immediately snuffed out the image of the alpha-omega logo that drifted across his mind. "What about my PA, Smiggins? Is he on The Boss's pay list, too?"

"To be sure, it's better to assume all rats are. Smiggins has probably been spying on you from the very start. The Boss likes to know everything about everyone; knowledge is power, you know that as much as anybody."

Louis shifted awkwardly, adjusting the knot of his tie and wondering just how much information Smiggins had passed on. It was safe to assume that everything he had said in his presence had been sent to The Tower to be filtered and analyzed. He then froze at a sudden memory.

"The Boss knows I've seen the White Rabbit," he whispered. "I was in the Limo with Smiggins and the others. I blurted it out. I let everyone know what I saw." He swallowed what felt like a lump of cold rock. "The peelers weren't following you, *Partridge*, they were trailing me from the very start. They knew I'd lead them to your headquarters eventually. It was just a matter of time."

Up ahead, the stunned official waved the jackal and ferret through without so much as a glance at their union cards. Frank O'Lynn's expression was now stern. "Now's not the time," he whispered. "Do you have the union card from the honeymoon suite?"

Louis nodded and reached into his inner pocket. As he removed Aldo Fiddler's ID, the note with THERE IS NO ESCAPE fell to the ground. "How do you know I found the card?" he whispered. "I haven't told anyone."

Frank O'Lynn ignored him, staring at the note. Then snatching it up before anybody else could see it, he put it inside his own pocket for safekeeping. The official was now gesturing for them to approach. "Just show the ID and say nothing." Frank O'Lynn was now whispering so softly Louis could hardly hear a goddamn word. "No doubt the peelers have alerted all checkpoints to be on the lookout for us."

Despite his apprehension, Louis had no choice but to step forward and show his card. To his relief, the official was still in too much of a state of shock to read it; but just when he thought they were through, Louis' gaze fell upon several police sketches on the table. One in particular grabbed his attention, a WANTED picture of a weasel and guinea pig with the names Aldo Fiddler and Frank

O'Lynn printed beneath; and no matter how incriminating his actions might be construed, he couldn't take his eyes off them. What should he do? Should he run? Should he sneak back to the end of the line? The rat only had to glance down and make the connection and they were done for.

Then, before he cracked and made a sprint for the archway, he felt Frank O'Lynn take his paw and drag him out of the tunnel. Only when they stepped onto the ledge did he allow himself to relax. They had been lucky. Now all they had to do was get to the safe house, somewhere down there in that mega-sprawl at the bottom of the cliff. It was best not to think about it though; even here fifty miles away, he could feel The Tower trying to connect with its mind-hold. The damn thing just didn't give up. "Did you see those pictures?" he whispered.

Frank O'Lynn nodded, somewhat calm considering how close they had been to getting nailed to a cross. "To be sure, Santosa and his friends did us a favor."

"A favor? I'm a wanted criminal! Every rat in the city is on the lookout for me."

"For Aldo Fiddler. Not Louis DeVille."

Louis paused to reconsider the situation. Maybe it wasn't as dire as he had imagined. "What about you? I saw your name."

"Frank O'Lynn is just an alias. I've had so many I barely remember what my real name is." He had that dreamy look again. "It's amazing what you get used to in this place." Then he came back from wherever his mind had been and went to the steps. "Come. We're not out of danger yet."

Louis followed Frank O'Lynn down the snaking steps to where a series of Limos were waiting at the bottom. Thankfully, none had its hood up or the number plate TOAD 10. Frank O'Lynn then led him down Boulevard 1, but Louis waited until the mini-market at the second intersection before pressing him about the union card he had found in the honeymoon suite.

"Our guy on the inside planted it," Frank O'Lynn said.

"Salma Gundi? He's a Freedom Fighter, too?"

Scratching behind his ear, Frank O'Lynn scanned the street, making sure none of the pedestrians were within audible range. A Limo sped toward The Tower, its tinted windows fully wound. "You didn't notice him at the blues bar?" he said with a wry grin. "And he goes by the alias, *Miss Elaine*, by the way."

Louis tried to recall the scene inside the bar before the peelers came storming down the stairs. The singer and pianist were on stage. Five or six patrons sat alone at candle lit tables, a jackal, some ferrets, another weasel; none of them monitor lizards. Then he remembered who was wiping glasses behind the bar. The goddamn jack-of-all-trades had disappeared through a trapdoor when the peelers raided, probably into a secret tunnel. "How could you be so sure I'd find it?" he asked.

"What, the union card? It was with the remote, wasn't it?"

Got me there, he mused. Good ol' Lady Di had always said men were as predictable as death and taxes (*TV and tits, that's all you men think about*). The varieties of the male experience were really quite narrow when you thought about it.

Up ahead, a rat and ferret exited onto the sidewalk from a betting agency. Taking no chances, Frank O'Lynn turned off the boulevard and hurried down a narrow side street. A freshly sprayed WRFF adorned the corner wall. "*Miss Elaine* has mastered time control," he said, answering the dilemma that had been on Louis' mind. "That's why he seems to be everywhere at once. I don't know exactly how he does it, although I once overheard him mention that time has a habit of *zipping* by. I guess he *Zips* like we *Pop*. Something like that anyway. To be sure, I've never done it. It's infinitely more dangerous than *Popping*. If you don't know what you're doing, you can get stuck in time, caught for eternity in no man's land between two *whens*."

Frank O'Lynn then shrugged, as if the whole thing was beyond his limited comprehension, offering no further explanation. He then turned into a narrow lane, the kind of alleyway Louis would never have walked down in Manhattan, not even with a dozen armed guards. Several hundred yards at the end, where it intersected with a larger street, Louis caught the flash of a Limo driving past. Not long after, they rounded the corner and headed in the same direction. Two streets past the next boulevard, they turned toward The Tower and stopped in front of a non-descript eight-story apartment building. "Let's just hope *The Master* is in," Frank O'Lynn said.

"Master of what?"

"The Tradition."

Frank O'Lynn scanned the area to make sure they weren't being followed, then buzzed the button on the intercom marked "Basement". A timid voice replied almost at once. Louis' first thought was that a little girl had answered, *The Master's* daughter maybe, but then remembered that there were no children in this mega-city. "It never rains," she said.

Frank O'Lynn pressed his lips to the intercom. "Only rocks and boulders."

"Nothing grows," *The Master* then said.

"Only petrified trees."

She briefly paused, as if nervous. "The sun never shines."

Frank O'Lynn glanced up, then said, "It's blocked by the sky-vault."

The Master's voice now wavered. "Nothing flies."

Still scanning the street, Frank O'Lynn whispered back, "Only rabbits with wings."

Louis then heard a buzz and a click as the front security door was unlocked. With one final glance down the street, Frank O'Lynn ushered him into the communal entrance, then down the stairwell to the basement. As they approached the apartment, Louis could sense the presence of someone watching him through the eyehole. Frank O'Lynn then raised his paw: *Knock. Knock. Knock.* Pause. *Knock. Knock.* Pause. *Knock.*

A bolt slid back, then a key twisted, and then a chain unlatched. When the door finally opened, Louis recoiled with shock.

"Come in," *The Master* said. "I've been expecting you."

Chapter 27

The Prophet

LOUIS was aware that his jaw had flopped while he stared at *The Master*. He hadn't recognized the voice over the intercom because he had never heard her speak until now. Her big brown eyes he had definitely had the pleasure of encountering before. Her long-sleeve, navy-gray dress buttoned high at the neck, along with its rigidly ironed creases and the hemline that kissed her sneakers, he had also seen. He remembered the attraction he had felt the first time he laid eyes on her (*petit, dutiful, just my kind of gal*), and he had to admit he still had a bit of a thing for her, despite his recent misgivings. But this changed everything, didn't it?

"Tiffany?" he said. "What…? I mean… Goddamn it, you're supposed to be…"

She glanced behind him up the stairs. "Not out here," she said. "Come inside before someone sees us."

Louis stepped past her diminutive frame as Frank O'Lynn whispered something in her ear. Seemingly pleased with the information, she bolted and chained the door. Although the stench of horseshit was far better than out on the street, the apartment was not exactly what Louis had been expecting. He had reckoned Tiffany to be the type of woman who lived in a sparse, one-bedroom spinster's apartment (Minimalistic, *dear*, Lady Di said from the depths of wherever dead people were buried in the memory, *the word you're looking for is* minimalistic), where the walls and floor were spotlessly clean, where every kitchen appliance stood side-by-side in regimental order on the sideboard (switched off at the mains when not in use, of course), and where the pantry, though not bare, was thrifty with organically grown, bowel-sensible fodder.

Well, he was half right, he mused, absorbing the décor of the living room. Everything was as clean and spotless as he had suspected, but one thing he hadn't figured on was the incredible amount of collectables on display. There was so much *stuff* it made his head spin. The lack of windows probably made it look worse than what it was, but there was goddamn junk everywhere, cluttering every shelf, tabletop, corner, nook and cranny. A detailed inventory of the room would take years to complete, an insurance agent's worst goddamn nightmare. There were porcelain ducks on the wall to his left, frozen in flight. Boxes piled to the ceiling in the far corner, filled with god-knows-what. Tightly packed animal figurines on the piano, like refugees cramming the deck of a boat. Even circular doilies splayed across the coffee table, one of which was still attached to a couple of crochet needles, half-complete and dumped on the cover of a tatty celebrity magazine. But the corduroy sofa covered with clear plastic sheeting was the goddamn *pièce de résistance.*

While the other two conferred secretly again, he went to pass the time at the inbuilt shelves, where every inch of space was taken with books from a familiar author, Miles N. Boon. Unbelievably, every title was identical. There were hundreds of copies of the same book he had found in the honeymoon suite, *Secrets Of A Chambermaid*, and just as he was about to pull an old, leather bound copy off the middle shelf, *The Master* gestured toward the sofa and asked him to take a seat.

Louis crossed in front of the piano, careful not to upset the figurines on top, and sat down, as irritated with the plastic sheeting under his butt as the lumpy discomfort of his tail. Tiffany politely waited, then sat on the piano stool, her back to the keys, paws clasped on her lap. Frank O'Lynn paced back and forth in front of the coffee table, too excited, or too agitated, or both, to sit. Louis shifted while he waited for one of them to say something, goddamn anything, his butt rubbing against the plastic sheeting and making a squeaky noise that reminded him of something he hadn't heard since he was alive. Something that used to make him laugh until his belly hurt when his grandfather made that same sound at the dinner table (to his grandma's pretend horror). When it was obvious neither of his hosts were going to get the conversation moving, he said, "Won't Santosa miss his little helper?"

Tiffany moved to speak, but Frank O'Lynn butted in. "Who do you think taught *Miss Elaine* how to *Zip*?"

Tiffany smiled patiently, then added, "Mr. Santosa is in row B of the LeMont auditorium right this minute. He thinks I'm sitting right next to him. In fact, I am. We're both listening to your address to shareholders at the AGM. A rousing speech, too, I might add. Everyone is captivated with your remarkable insight and vision for LeMont."

Louis looked at her, then at Frank O'Lynn, then back at Tiffany Tidbits. Though not as melodic or chirpy as the Irish guinea pig, her voice was accented with a likeable European twang, maybe Italian, maybe Spanish. It was only a trace, mind you; he certainly couldn't use it as an excuse for misinterpreting what he had just heard. "Am I to understand that there are two of us? Here and at the conference center?" he asked.

"Not quite. There is only one you and one me, but with *Zipping* we can appear to be in two places at the same time. Would you like me to explain?" *The Master* grabbed one of the doilies with the pattern of a sunflower and began to trace its outline with her claw. "*Zipping* is like a flower. If we start with a central circle, the corolla, then begin to draw its petals, each time starting at the center and returning to our point of origin, then the next, then the next, we can work our way around the corolla until its covered with petals." She continued to trace the crochet sunflower with her claw. "When we *Zip* time, the corolla is our point of reference from which we move out in the same way as we draw a petal. Then, when we've finished what we had to do, we arc back toward the corolla and end up back at the point of departure. The petal – our timeline – isn't compromised, as you might be thinking. Time is always moving forward. It's just that we end up back where we started, free to draw another petal whenever we want, as many times as we want."

Louis eyed the crocheted sunflower. Her claw had stopped tracing its outline. "That's all well and good for a Master. But for your average guy in the street, it's not exactly important in his day-to-day existence, is it?"

Tiffany put the doily back on the coffee table, and said, "Things are not as they seem. Each one of us actually exists in an infinite number of places at any given moment. We just choose which one of the infinite moments we wish to experience."

Louis shifted in his seat again, this time careful not to make the farting sound again. "What would be the point of choosing to be in hell?" he asked. "It's self-defeatist."

Frank O'Lynn stopped pacing back and forth. "LeMont International Enterprises," he said. "It's not hell anymore."

"Whatever. It still makes no goddamn sense why I would choose it over paradise."

Tiffany now answered. "Unfortunately, most of our decisions are made subconsciously or habitually. We're generally not aware of our decision making processes, only the consequences of them. That's why we think things happen to us or against our wishes, why we generally see ourselves as victims of circumstance." Frank O'Lynn was pacing again, scratching furiously at a fleabite on his neck. "Like putting your head inside the lion's mouth and then getting upset when it takes a bite," she added.

Louis had encountered a similar philosophy in one of the self-help books Lady Di had left lying around the penthouse. He had found it on top of the TV next to her reading glasses one night, assuming it was one of the many crossword books she was forever filling in. Then he had spotted the title, *Know Thy Self*, and picked it up, disgruntled at the latest rubbish she was stuffing inside her head. Needless to say, he didn't even get past the first paragraph. "There are no victims," the author had boldly claimed. It was a goddamn joke, pure and simple, the dribble of another backyard guru trying to push his version of the meaning to life onto any fool stupid enough to read his horseshit.

Any goddamn idiot can get published nowadays, he remembered thinking at the time, and glanced at the bookshelf, then back at *The Master.*

"You can't seriously expect me to believe that I'm guilty of things that happen beyond my control," he said.

The Master remained as motionless as one of her many figurines on top of the piano. "You are connected to everyone and everything around you. In as much as you are innocent of what happens, you are also guilty: they are two sides of the same coin. Though the connections may seem invisible, there exists an intricate link between everything."

Louis wondered how long he would have to sit and listen to *The Master* prattle on. Miles N. Boon's *Secrets Of A Chambermaid* had more goddamn appeal than what was being offered to him here. Still, what could he do? As long as this was the only safe haven from the peelers, he would smile and nod and say all the right things and pretend he was interested in what she was saying. Good God, he had had forty years of practice with his wife. This should be a goddamn breeze. Then, when the heat was off, he was out of here. *Make like a tree and leave*, his mom would have said. In fact, he would do more than that. He would be down the boulevard and waving goodbye to the loony Freedom Fighters quicker than a... well, goddamn bat out of hell.

In the meantime, he had no choice than to sit and take it. He watched Frank O'Lynn pace back and forth like a caged hyena while *The Master* remained perched on the piano stool, paws on her lap, eyes big and unblinking. He had to admit she wasn't the meek, timid little mouse he had originally assumed. He'd had her penned as the kind of woman too scared to leave the house without a chaperone, like his mother in the years after his father had died.

What a waste of a life. At sixty-four, Margaret DeVille hadn't had a goddamn clue what to do with the freedom she was given when her husband had unexpectedly collapsed onto the bedroom floor while swinging his size elevens into her head. You would have thought it a cause for celebration, but it wasn't. Although she never said so, Louis knew she blamed herself for his premature demise. Her cage was guilt. Perhaps she shouldn't have let the dinner get cold. Perhaps she should have been more submissive; then he wouldn't have had to exert so much energy in giving her what she deserved. Perhaps her skull shouldn't have been so hard either. But Louis suspected it was more than that – she had been praying for freedom for years, and now that God had answered she suddenly didn't want it anymore. The responsibility was just too overwhelming. Consequently, she turned into a hermit several years before a massive stroke finished off what Hugo DeVille had started all those years before (despite the coroner blaming fifty years of chain smoking, he never explained *why* she smoked a goddamn pack a day). Encamped in the Brooklyn apartment she had lived most of her adult life, she watched TV all day and received no visitors. Even he gave up calling around on the old girl toward the end. In a sense, she had reminded him of one of those budgerigars that could be trained to sit on your finger and talk: after being locked away all her life, she had been too afraid to explore outside when the door was left ajar.

Louis now toyed with his pinstripe tie. He guessed his initial assumptions about Tiffany might have stemmed from the lingering pity he felt about his mother. In some ways they were as similar as sisters. In other ways, they were as far apart as New York and LA.

"My mother always said the same thing," he said, getting back to what *The Master* had just been saying. "Everything's connected. She never spoke of it as karma, and never in front of my father, although that's what I knew she was talking about. She used to call it balancing the books. I called it horseshit."

If *The Master* was upset with his cynicism, she didn't show it. "That's why you are where you are."

Louis kept fidgeting with his tie. "Meaning what, exactly?"

"Meaning, you're here because the choices you made led to the inevitable consequences of you being here."

"All right. Let's say you're correct," he said, and shifted in his seat. "I've made my choices and now I have to live with them. It's not as if I can do anything about it, is there?"

The Master was unmoved. "The gates of hell are always open, Mr. DeVille. Nothing is preventing you from leaving."

Louis wasn't having a bar of it. It was a hell of a lot easier calling the game from the commentary box than making the play on the field, wasn't it? Not to mention a hell of a lot safer. "Besides one tiny little obstacle you seem to be forgetting," he said. "The Fires of Oblivion."

For the first time since she had sat on the piano stool, Louis saw, *The Master* moved. Barely perceptible, mind you, just a faint twitch of the whiskers and a spasm of the shoulders. "Belief determines the quality of your experience," she said. Her expression was as rigidly stern as the creases in her dress. "A veil of illusion shrouds everything you see, and the veil is laid by nothing other than your own eyes. What you believe, you see. What you don't believe, you don't see."

Another moment of silence passed between them. Awkward as any goddamn silence went too, he might add. Even Frank O'Lynn's pacing was silent. "You're talking about a leap of faith," he said. "I only have faith in cold hard facts." Then he added, after a second's thought, "And myself."

The Master faced Frank O'Lynn with her paw outstretched. Louis watched him hand over the note that had slipped out of his own pocket at the archway, the one with THERE IS NO ESCAPE written in neat cursive script. She was smiling with the kind of *I know something you don't* look he used to hate whenever he saw the same thing in Lady Di's eyes.

"I must say, you're the first prophet I've ever heard of that doesn't have faith in something greater than himself."

Louis felt himself disconnecting from his mind, like he was in conversation with someone on a mobile that had just moved out of range. Was this some kind of in-house prank? He had heard of doctors joking about erectile dysfunction and things that went wrong on the operating table. He had heard of pilots joking about near misses and faulty landing gear. White Rabbit Freedom Fighters obviously joked about weasels who became divine mystics and seers.

"A goddamn what?" he said.

Frank O'Lynn was staring at the note over *The Master's* shoulder. He had the look of a Catholic who had just seen a vision of the Holy Mary. "A prophet, Louis," he said. "What else would you call someone who's *communicant* with the White Rabbit?"

Louis glanced at the note, then at Frank O'Lynn, then at Tiffany. When he looked back at the note, a feeling he first experienced as a boy began to tingle through him. The old man's wallet had gone missing from his overalls not long before his twelfth birthday, before his fascination with baseball cards had developed into a fascination with Playboy magazines. Naturally, good ol' Louis was blamed for stealing it and spending the money on useless collector cards. Even his mother sided against him, and he had understood right there and then that his parents had no idea how great his fear of his father really was; yet no matter how much he pleaded his innocence, nothing could change them from believing he was a spineless little thief. Needles to say, he received a thrashing and went to bed with a grumbling stomach. The next morning when he came to breakfast, however, the wallet was sitting on the table next to the salt- and pepper-shakers. It had apparently fallen under the bed when his father had undressed the day before. His father didn't apologize, and neither did his mother; but to Louis, seeing that wallet was proof he wasn't a thief. It wasn't until he was married, however, that he really understood the insidiousness of that feeling, something that was more addictive than the goddamn death sticks his mother committed suicide with. Justification.

The note with THERE IS NO ESCAPE made him feel that way now. It was irrefutable evidence. He wasn't mad. He wasn't suffering from Post Traumatic Death Syndrome. *The Master* and *The Partridge* believed he had seen the White Rabbit, not as some figment of his delusional mind, but as something real and tangible. "I am right!" he felt like screaming. "I am goddamn right!" Better still, better than any blue diamond pill, this feeling had no hangovers.

"I've also received other notes," he said. "Invitations actually. To the Mansion of Many Rooms, wherever that is."

The Master and Frank O'Lynn didn't seem to be listening, just staring at the piece of paper like a couple of paupers who had received a million dollar check from a long lost uncle. Louis sat forward, reading the words upside down, and asked what it meant. Tiffany finally dragged her attention away.

"I was hoping you might shed some light on it."

"Me? I'm not the goddamn Master."

"The message was sent to you. Only you can interpret it."

Louis snatched the note out of her paws and reread it several times. "There Is No Escape," he said, more for his own benefit than the others, as if hearing the words instead of seeing them would resolve the problem. He sat back, slouching into the plastic-covered sofa. "It's no use. I can't think of anything. Except that it totally refutes everything you've both been telling me."

The Master's demeanor didn't change. Not even a Bond Martini, his wife would have said: neither shaken nor stirred. "It is obviously written on different levels. The meaning must be found outside the literal implication of the words."

"A code?"

"More like a key."

Louis sat forward and glanced at the writing again. Was there another way out of LeMont nobody else knew? Was that what the White Rabbit was trying to show him?

"A key to what? A secret door?"

"You could say that."

The Master had that *I know something you don't* look in her eyes again.

"The door to your heart."

Chapter 28

The Ancient Language

LOUIS sat motionless on the sofa, staring at the note and reading it over and over again. There is no escape. There is no escape. There is no escape. It was a key? To his goddamn heart? What kind of Lady Di, self-help horseshit was that?

I tell you what it is, Louis my boy. You've been led into the desert on the promise of finding an oasis and then abandoned halfway there without a goddamn map or water. There's nothing but bleak terrain. No way forward. No way back. No goddamn escape. You're here for eternity and that's that.

He struggled to remember another occasion when his hopes had been dashed more comprehensively than this. The first place he and his wife had tried to buy, a fabulous three-bedroom apartment in the Village. That had been bad. They had signed the contract, got the okay for the bank loan, and were only hours away from collecting the goddamn keys. Except the son-of-a-bitch owner didn't put his signature on the dotted line, did he? Someone else came in with a better offer, literally at the last minute. Their dream had been stolen from under their noses (*Gazumped, dear, I believe the terminology for that is gazumped*). Of course, the owner kindly told them, they could have the apartment if they raised their offer. Tantalizing, except they couldn't. It was just at the time he had resigned from his job and begun the process of establishing the new company; so they had to let the apartment, and their hopes, go the way of the setting sun. Later, they managed to land another apartment, but the marriage never truly recovered from the loss, something he always referred to as their first miscarriage.

Pocketing the message from the White Rabbit, Louis made up his mind to do what he had to do. When stuck between a rock and a hard place, as his grandfather used to advise, there was only one option: go with what you knew. He sighed, knowing it wasn't going to be easy. Eternity was a long goddamn time, but what other choice did he have? "I have an AGM to attend," he said, and stood. His tail made a *rrrrrip* sound as it pried away from the plastic sheeting. "I need directions to the hotel. I don't know where I am."

"I'll do better than that," *The Master* said. "I'll *Zip* you over there. But first, sit back down. There's something you need to hear." Louis sighed and kept standing. What was the point? Nothing they did would make a goddamn bit of difference; the bad news would just keep rolling on for ever and ever. "Before you say anything, just hear me out," she said, and waited for him to sit.

Louis eventually complied, sinking back into the cushions. He might be up the creek without a paddle, but at least he was dry and safe and still in a canoe.

"The White Rabbit Freedom Fighters are more powerful than you may think," *The Master* said, as Frank O'Lynn returned to pacing back and forth between the piano and the door. "It's taken thousands of years, but we've managed to infiltrate the highest echelons of power. The unions. The secret police. Every aspect of LeMont society is crawling with supporters of the White Rabbit, waiting for the right moment to strike. However, we've never been able to get close to The Boss. Nobody has. He's deeply suspicious of everyone. We've been unable to get someone high enough on the inside. Until now."

When she looked at him with those big unblinking eyes, Louis immediately understood the depths to which he found himself. He had been wrong a moment ago; he was up the goddamn creek without a paddle *and* a canoe.

"It's not what you're thinking," *The Master* said, sensing his unease. "We're not hiring an assassin. It's impossible to kill someone who's already dead; and besides, you'd never get near him, even if you could. His demise is not what we're after, only his power. At least long enough to allow as many of the Freedom Fighters to escape, and whoever else wants to join us. We just want to put a hole in his net."

Louis almost jumped out of his seat and blurted, *Are you blind?*

There is no escape! Your own goddamn White Rabbit has said so herself! Instead, he gritted his teeth and watched Frank O'Lynn pace back and forth between the piano and door.

"The Boss only has power over his citizens because they yield it to him. That's why he puts so much stock in signing individual contracts. It serves as a reminder that we've voluntarily signed a working agreement. Only problem is, it's for 24-hours a day for eternity. It's our life, our soul. He has all his citizens nailed to a paper crucifix."

The Master paused to gather her thoughts. Just how did she intend for billions of employees to break an unbreakable contract without ending up in one of the Chambers of Eternity? Louis thought. Mass protests? Strikes? It just wasn't feasible, no matter how many Freedom Fighters there were. The Boss held all the cards.

"The Boss has never in the history of LeMont renegotiated a contract once it's been signed," she said. "Power is all he knows. Without it, he loses his identity, his sense of who he is. Even if The Tower is destroyed and the sky-vault collapsed around our whiskers, he still won't relinquish it. To him, that's tantamount to throwing himself in the Fires of Oblivion."

Behind her, Frank O'Lynn went to inspect the bookshelves, as if had heard it all a million times before. Even though every book was the same, he seemed more interested in browsing through the titles than listening to what she had to say. Finding one that took his fancy, he carefully opened the cover like a librarian researching a delicate manuscript of historical importance, then moved around the coffee table without saying a word and handed it to Louis. Though kept in pristine condition, the yellowed pages felt thin and fragile, like French pastry. Frank O'Lynn drew his attention to several lines on the inside cover. Someone had written a message, maybe the author. "What language is this? It looks Gaelic," he said.

"You're looking at the oldest language in the whole universe, Tongues."

"You expect me to read this?"

"Take a closer look. You might be surprised."

Dubious, to say the least, Louis read the first line: *Grnklpmrph nlw frpztk*. Just as he had suspected, complete and utter nonsense.

"This isn't a language. There's no vowels, no sentence structure, no grammar. Not even a goddamn conjunction. It's nothing but gobbledygook."

As patient as a mother teaching her son the alphabet, *The Master* told him to try again.

Shaking his head, Louis moved down to the second line hoping he would have more luck. It was worse: *Zwlkbdlvrpmh*. He gave up, and offered the book back to *The Master*, but she refused to take it. "What are you laughing at?" he asked Frank O'Lynn.

If Louis had hoped to wipe the smile of the guinea pig's face, he had failed. "Don't get too upset. To be sure, you're making the commonest mistake everyone makes when reading Tongues."

"Which is?"

"You're reading it in your head," *The Master* said. "The language is phonetic. It's meant to be vocalized; that's why it's called Tongues. Interpretation comes from hearing the sounds, not visualizing them."

Louis returned to the first line and read it aloud, stumbling over the unfamiliar sounds, which to his ears sounded like a baby gurgling his first words. "Grnk… lp… mrph nlw frp… ztk." Suddenly, as if by magic (and it really was like goddamn magic), he caught a flash of insight into the meaning of the words. It wasn't a direct interpretation as such, like Italian into English, but more like a visual translation of the words into a picture. Upon hearing the full sentence, an image of a pyramid-like mound of rubble popped into his mind.

"I think I know the first line," he said. "The building is destroyed."

"Not bad for a first timer," *The Master* said, and Louis was relieved to hear no trace of cynicism in her voice. "It actually says: When The Tower does fall. What do you think the next line says?"

Louis was already onto it, reading it aloud. "Zwlk… bdl… vrp… mh." The image he got was of a large man, a *human*, standing before a crowd, but it wasn't clear enough to be sure. "The man addresses the people," he said, then added as an afterthought: "He might be a priest."

"I believe you're a natural, Mr. DeVille. You have the gift of interpretation. With a bit of practice you'll even be speaking it."

The line, Louis learned, actually said: *He will come*, and as he struggled through the remaining sentences, eleven in all, several images came to mind, like he was running his eye over a movie reel one frame at a time. He saw the collapsed building, then the man (priest?) addressing the crowd. Next, the man was in a tunnel, but some of the crowd (Louis still couldn't see the image clearly enough, just shadowy forms) had shunned his invitation and stayed put. Those that had followed seemed to be dancing and singing. For an unknown reason, he was reminded of the early Christians singing joyously in the Coliseum while the centurions released the lions. Then the image seemed to become disjointed and blurry, lost in translation, so he moved on to the last few lines. They evoked images of paradise beyond a wall of flames, which frightened him initially, but then, with the utterance of the final word, an image of a baby cradled in a giant hand came to mind and he was awash with a sense of peace he hadn't felt since the days on his grandfather's farm, when he used to awake to the dawning sun through the bedroom window.

The Master then handed him a piece of paper on which she had written the exact interpretation of the lines. As he had begun to suspect, it was a poem:

When The Tower does fall
He will come
Inviting us to follow.
Take the chance,
Escape the morrow,
Return with him who's lived,
And he'll break with song, 'Lo' thou art a dance."
Belief will take us to a land

Beyond our wildest dreams.
Into the Fire we shall go
To be saved unto His hand.

The Master had even added "Miles N. Boon" at the bottom, like a quote.

When The Tower does fall, he read, *He will come.* It sounded like a goddamn prophecy. Did *The Master* expect him to believe this horseshit? The Tower had been around for millennia and didn't even look like falling down. Of that he was as certain as he was the Money Tree would never sprout cash; and who the hell was the priest referred to in the second line? The goddamn White Rabbit? Some kind of savior, like Moses leading his people out of slavery into the Promised Land?

The Master motioned toward the book. "Did you know that you're holding the very first copy of the very first edition ever printed? It's the most ancient book in LeMont. For that alone it's priceless."

Now that was something he could relate to, worth. Something like this belonged in a bank vault, not in someone's private collection gathering dust on the shelves and losing value. He put it carefully on the coffee table.

"But it's the poem that dwarfs its financial value," she said. "It's proof that the White Rabbit has been with us since the very beginning, before The Tower was even built, when LeMont was still a warren of tunnels and caves in the rock face. We know that because Miles N. Boon was one of the founding citizens, and the only author The Boss allowed into print."

Louis scanned the lines of Tongues on the inside cover again, then glanced at the paper he was holding, the English version *The Master* had written. "But the poem doesn't even mention the White Rabbit."

He heard Frank O'Lynn chuckle, and for a horrid flash thought Smiggins had snuck in through the door. *The Master* told him to look again, so he read the whole thing once more. Still seeing no mention of the White Rabbit, he read it for a third time, now feeling stupid. He even read it backwards, but no, not a goddamn thing. Absolutely-totally-undeniably-nothing.

"You're reading it horizontally," *The Master* said, noting the frustration on his face. "Read down, not across."

Louis followed her advice and was struck with what he read. *Well goddamn and bugger me.* The first letter of each line spelled the word he had been looking for:

When The Tower does fall
He will come
Inviting us to follow.
Take the chance,
Escape the morrow,
Return with him who's lived,
And he'll break with song, "Lo' thou art a dance."
Belief will take us to a land
Beyond our wildest dreams.
Into the Fire we shall go
To be saved unto His hand.

"Miles N. Boon was the first prophet. Not only did he predict the construction of The Tower, but also its demise," *The Master* said. "The White Rabbit inspired him to write that poem, as well as *Secrets Of A Chambermaid*."

Louis remained speechless, and hadn't as yet stopped reading up and down the lines of the verse. "But this is an interpretation. This could just be a freak coincidence."

"That's the glory of Tongues. It's the seed from which all languages sprout, the only language that can be translated directly, word for word, without the subjective interpretation common to all its derivatives. If I were to translate it into German or French, or any other language, even obscure languages that are now obsolete, the word White Rabbit will appear vertically down the verse. Believe me, we've done exactly that. It's there every time."

Louis scratched his snout. It was obvious then; the White Rabbit couldn't be the 'He' referred to in the second line, unless Miles N. Boon was prophesizing the Second Goddamn Coming. But that didn't sit right either. If this poem was genuinely as old as it looked, the White Rabbit had probably come and gone from LeMont as many times as it wished. Good God, he himself had seen it twice already. Which left him with a blank. "I still don't know how I'm supposed to help," he said. "If you ask me, you should be looking for the guy who wrote this. You've got time on your side. You'll find him eventually. There's nowhere else for him to go."

"That's just the point, Mr. DeVille," *The Master* said. "Miles N. Boon vanished shortly after he wrote that poem. He didn't even attend the book launch." Then she shot him a glance that drilled straight through him and left him feeling hollow. "Everyone that's seen the White Rabbit has disappeared. You're the only one that's remained to tell the tale."

Chapter 29

Secrets Of A Chambermaid

LOUIS sat back with a thousand and one things racing through his mind. Despite his best efforts to shrug them off, *The Master's* words remained to taunt him like a Snipe pinned to the back of his jacket he couldn't reach: *Everyone that's seen the White Rabbit has disappeared.* Was that furry ball of fluff some kind of goddamned Pied Piper, hypnotizing the citizens of LeMont toward the cliff and into the Fires of Oblivion? The idea was certainly plausible. Had he not himself been seduced by her allure? Had he not been gripped with total obsession when he chased her down the boulevard?

Louis shifted in the seat and fiddled with his tie. Why couldn't the damned rabbit have left him alone in peace? All he wanted was to get on with his After Life, earn some extra cash on the sidelines, get a nice apartment near the piazza, go to a restaurant or the cinema when he felt like it, and maybe even spend a weekend or two relaxing at the Country Club. That was goddamn it. Nothing else.

Then he was struck with an idea, something that appealed to him immensely. He could just *deny* that he had seen the White Rabbit. Wipe the memory from his mind. Simple as that. Heaven's above, women did that sort of thing all the time, all the women he had slept with that was. "It didn't happen," they usually said when they were getting dressed, sometimes with an involuntary shudder. "We didn't do anything except talk about our work and our partners. Just two adults having a conversation," and that had been just fine with good ol' Louis Hugo DeVille. Except it wasn't. He couldn't deny what he had seen or done, it just wasn't in him. A pragmatist at heart, he knew he could only outrun reality for a finite period before it hunted him down like the lawyer of a pregnant mistress. Like it or not, the White Rabbit was now as much a part of his world as the goddamn whiskers on the end of his snout.

"I was chasing the White Rabbit when you and Santosa picked me up and took me to The Tower," he said.

"I suspected as much," *The Master* said. "You had that look in your eyes I've only seen with two types of emotion, love or desperation. The White Rabbit has that effect on everyone who sees her."

Louis chuckled to himself, still fiddling with his tie. Desperation, he was certainly familiar with that. Love? Well, he wasn't so sure anymore. It was hard to remember ever having those sorts of feelings for his wife. Okay, forty years ago when they had first started dating (*More than forty years now, Louis, my dear. Time goes faster when you're having a ball in the After Life*), love might have been mixed in there somewhere, or what he thought was love, that weird obsession to always have the object of your desires constantly by your side. They had chemistry, she used to say back then, and he would laugh. Dianne Nitro and Louis Glycerine.

"And look where it got you, Louis my boy," he said to himself.

What a goddamn fool he had been. Every chemist knew that a reaction didn't last forever. It petered out when balance was achieved, when all -the excess chemicals were used up and there was nothing left to interact anymore. That was the evolutionary joke. Man and woman, two opposite chemicals, met in an explosion of lust and believed that it would last forever. Granted, some reactions lasted longer than others, maybe a week, maybe a few months, and maybe if a couple were really lucky it would last for a year. But no more. The human condition didn't have enough chemicals to react for any longer. Pretty soon balance was achieved. The love died. Other things dampened the reaction or took its place– children, mortgage, career – and what was once a highly volatile concoction of nitroglycerine was now a drab suspension with as much goddamn passion as a glass of flat Coca Cola. Something you just had to tip down the drain.

He rested his head in his paws. Had he ever felt so goddamn hollow? "Are you sure Miles N. Boon can't be found. He's the key to all this. He has to be somewhere."

The Master, as immoveable as ever, said, "Believe me. The Freedom Fighters have searched every inch of rock and every nook and cranny in LeMont."

Louis dropped his paws and sat back, her words still echoing through his mind. *Everyone that's seen the White Rabbit has disappeared.* The sense of hollowness seemed to be here for the long haul; just one more goddamn thing he would have to get used to in the After Life.

"Even the chambers along Conduit Number 1?" he said.

With Frank O'Lynn standing like a guardian angel over her shoulder, *The Master* nodded in affirmation. "The only place we haven't been able to search is The Boss's penthouse, but I suspect we needn't bother. There's only one explanation that has any merit." She then motioned toward the doily-covered coffee table. The book on top of it was still splayed open to the ancient poem. "The evidence is in there, if you care to read it."

Although he was amused to think that Miles N. Boon had somehow left a trail of written clues to his disappearance, Louis couldn't bare the thought of wading through the pages of some mushy goddamn love story. He was no private investigator, and he certainly had no interest in the rampant affairs of some fictional character.

"Why don't you just give me a synopsis?"

Frank O'Lynn, now scratching a fleabite on his jaw, was aghast. "The story is written on several levels. How can you possibly get any idea of what it's about from a synopsis?"

Publishers make a living out of it, Louis thought, and shrugged.

The Master then interjected, "I'm no literary agent, but let me give it a try."

Louis nodded a begrudging acceptance, noting the displeasure on Frank O'Lynn's face, as though an abomination was about to take place.

The Master drew a breath and said, "The story is set in a small French village. It centers on a poor chambermaid used as collateral to pay off her parents' debts to a corrupt mayor, an indentured servant enslaved to the chambers she keeps tidy and her bedroom in the basement of the manor." She paused for a moment before going on. "The mayor uses the manor to accommodate his powerful associates and make his shady dealings. For years the chambermaid is abused and neglected, until a mysterious stranger comes to stay. Unbeknown to anyone, he is a prince traveling back to his kingdom in the guise of a fur-merchant. He befriends the chambermaid and learns of her debt, which he promises to pay once he has fulfilled his duty to his father. As a reminder that she is in his heart, he leaves behind a white rabbit for her keep until he returns. But he never does. Little does she know, the mayor has ordered his guards to ambush the stranger in the surrounding hills and take his money.

"Months later, she removes the rabbit's collar and discovers a large diamond hidden on its underside, enough to pay for her freedom and keep her happy for the rest of her life. She runs to the mayor to tell him that she's leaving. It's New Year's Eve, and the mayor has prepared a large bonfire in the garden to celebrate. Furious, he tells her that she is a fool to believe she'll ever be free; whatever possessions she owns are rightfully his, including the diamond. To make his point, he tells her that the stranger is dead and then tosses the rabbit onto the bonfire. Despairing that she has now lost everything, the chambermaid throws herself into the flames." She paused, as if wanting to add something more. "The story ends there."

Louis shrugged, and while he fiddled with his tie his thoughts flashed to a sudden despairing vision: book clubs. Groups of women drinking tea and discussing the relative symbolism of *Secrets Of A Chambermaid*, dissecting every single word, compartmentalizing each character over and over again, the scene repeating itself millions of times throughout the mega-city every Tuesday night.

"It's just another tragic love story," he said. "So what?"

"There's something else. I haven't quite finished." *The Master* and Frank O'Lynn shared a look that said *we might as well tell him everything.* Then she said, "From all accounts, The Boss approved of the story from the very beginning. Incurable despair, the reality of everyday hopelessness; exactly the message he wanted to send to his citizens. The problem was, to those who knew Miles N. Boon, the ending didn't fit. Unfortunately, he disappeared just after the first edition was published. No one can say for certain, but the story should have climaxed with the lovers' reunion. The book was not supposed to have been about hopelessness. It was supposed to have been about the saving grace of love and hope. The Boss couldn't allow that – as a symbol of power, the mayor couldn't be seen to have been duped – so he had the last chapter edited out to reflect the futility in resisting authority and privilege."

Is that what he had been brought here to listen to, Louis sighed, a goddamn conspiracy theory? Was nobody immune from believing what they wanted to believe, even *The Master*? It was that line from Simon & Garfunkel, wasn't it? *A man hears what he wants to hear and disregards the rest.* Had truer words ever been sung?

"How can you know for sure?" he said. "It's just hearsay passed down over thousands and thousands of years. You'll never know the truth because the author disappeared, no matter what anyone else says."

Again, *The Master* had that *I know something you don't* glint in her eyes. She motioned toward the book once more. "That's why Miles N. Boon wrote the poem in the first edition, to tell us the truth." She paused to let him weight the facts. "It's also no coincidence that he wrote it in Tongues, to avoid misinterpretation."

All well and good, Louis mused, but what the hell did it have to do with him? "Okay, I've listened to your ancient poem and your conspiracy theories, and they may or may not have any factual basis to them, I don't know, and I don't really care; but quite frankly I've yet to hear the slightest goddamn bit of information that has any relevance to me. Excuse me for sounding a touch paranoid, but why the hell have you dragged me into this?"

Behind her, Frank O'Lynn reddened and pretended to scratch an itch on the tip of his snout. Without the slightest flinch of embarrassment or discomfort herself, *The Master* said, "Not I, Mr. DeVille. The White Rabbit has brought you here. Your coming was prophesized by Miles N. Boon."

Chapter 30

The Prophecy

LOUIS had heard some horseshit in his day – alien abductions, the Holy Grail, weeping statues of the Blessed Mary – but this just about topped the lot. *A prophecy*! *Him*! Surprisingly, he felt no anger, just a stirring rumble in his belly, which escaped as a low reverberating chuckle that wobbled his shoulders and bounced his head until he felt like a doll being shaken by an irate toddler.

The Master waited for him to finish, unaffected by the outburst. Frank O'Lynn, on the contrary, went redder, and the sight of him glowing like a priest who had just been caught leaving the premises of a brothel sent Louis into another fit of laughter. Eventually, he managed to get himself under some sort of control (best goddamn laugh he'd had since arriving in LeMont, he reckoned). "Of course," he said, wiping a tear from his eye with the back of his paw. "I should have known the poem was about me. I'm the goddamn messiah come to save everyone. How could I not see it?"

"We laugh at what we don't understand," *The Master* said. "Ridicule is the easiest way to dismiss something that challenges our perceptions of who and what we are. Just another cheap way to feel good about our self, is it not?"

Louis wiped another tear from his eye. Frank O'Lynn's redness, he saw, had surely peaked. "So it's me against you two, is it?"

"On the contrary, it's you against yourself. We could have turned you over to the secret police if that was our intent. What more do we need to do to prove that we're on your side?"

Louis scanned the poem that had been translated into English. Nowhere did it mention his name. No Louis (not even a Lewis), no DeVille, he was goddamn sure of it. "You could start by proving your ridiculous claim," he said.

Before she could answer, a distant rumbling began to shake the room. It seemed to come from far beneath the floor, muted and threatening, then louder and louder as it grumbled toward the surface. From the kitchen cupboards, Louis could hear the rattle of china plates and saucers. Closer, the figurines on the piano wobbled, at first just one or two, then the whole lot, disco dancers grooving to the beat of the latest Number One hit on the LeMont Top Forty countdown (*Top Of The World*, for a record sixty millionth week in a row!). At the quake's peak, the coffee table was vibrating so violently Louis feared the priceless copy of Miles N. Boon was going to fall apart. One of the porcelain ducks even fell off the wall and snapped a wing, but remarkably *The Master* didn't flinch. Even the guinea pig was unaffected, his redness waning as the rumbling moved onto another part of the city.

"The middle lines," she said, nodding toward the poem. "Six and seven. Your name's there in bold letters."

Louis skipped down the first five lines to read:

> *Return with him who's lived,*
> *And he'll break with song, "Lo' thou art a dance."*

It wasn't obvious, that was for goddamn sure; his name wasn't even in normal text, let alone jumping out at him in glaring bold letters. These had been the lines that were disjointed and blurry when he first read them in Tongues. It had to be some sort of code; and although he had never been one for secret messages and smart-ass wordplays (leave that for the bored housewives of the world), he did make a perfunctory effort to try and crack the verse. "Assuming *him* is referring to me," he said, "then *return with him who's lived* could mean absolutely anybody who has ever been born. There's nothing specific to me."

The Master seemed more moved with his attempt than she had with the quake a few minutes before. "You're on the right track. Are you familiar with cryptic crosswords?"

Familiar, yes, but could he actually solve the goddamn things, no. Lady Di, though, had been a regular addict. She had heard once on TV that there were three things she could do as an elderly citizen to ward off the symptoms of Alzheimer's Disease – learn a new language; learn a new musical instrument; and do lots of crosswords – so on the eve of her sixtieth birthday she made a resolution to follow the TV lady's advice; and that she did, with a vengeance, littering the bedroom and study with god knows how many self-learning cassettes and do-it-yourself manuals. He was forever tripping over them: *Teach Yourself French In Three Months. Learn To Play The Guitar Like A Professional. Cryptic Crosswords For Dummies.* Though she never did manage to conquer the challenges of the Gallic vernacular (her *merci* never got past *mercy*), nor did she ever threaten to topple the genius of Beethoven or Bach with her musical brilliance, he did have to admit that she became more than a competent puzzler. He often saw every square of the Times crossword completed before he even had a chance to glance at the headlines. She also had more than her fair share of success with crossword competitions, twice winning an overseas trip for two, once to London and once to Paris (both times electing to take her sister), which, to his perpetual irritation, she always reminded him of whenever he thought she had done something stupid.

"Can't say I've ever been interested in puzzles," he said. "Don't even like Scrabble."

"Then let me help." *The Master* directed him to the fifth line of the poem. Frank O'Lynn kept silent behind her. "You were almost there when you said 'Go back'. The word 'Return' in a cryptic puzzle not only implies the literal interpretation to follow; it also refers to a word written backwards in the verse. The trick is knowing which one it's referring to. And he gives you a clue."

Return with him who's lived, Louis read. "A clue within a clue?"

"Precisely."

Was he blind, or just goddamn stupid? "I still can't see it."

"He tells you, quite literally, when he writes: *him* who's *lived.* Meaning, not only *him who* has *lived*, but also: *him who* is *lived.* In cryptic puzzles, grammar is used as a tool to hide the true meaning, like a magician's sleight of hand."

"But lived returned spells devil. You're not for one minute suggesting we follow…"

"Of course not. We haven't finished. The *And* of the seventh line is meant as a conjunction, a follow on from the previous word. Ignore the period mark at the end of the sixth line; that's just there to confuse anyone not belonging to the Freedom Fighters who might have stumbled upon the poem. Leave them thinking as you've just done, that it's referring to the devil. You've got to give Miles N. Boon credit for that."

Louis still wasn't convinced. He scanned the seventh line: *And he'll break with song, 'Lo' thou art a dance."*

"The clues are immediate," *The Master* said, and Louis read the line again, this time aloud, though something in his voice told *The Master* he was having more than his fair share of trouble catching on. "Break, here, is referring to the word *he'll*, not the rest of the line."

Up until that moment, his mind had felt like a TV set that couldn't tune into the proper channel, kind of like the fuzzy snow at the end of station transmission. Now, *The Master* had given him a verbal bang to the side of his head and the picture momentarily flickered into focus: all he had to do was "break" the apostrophe from the word *he'll.* "The line really means devil and hell. Is that right?"

The Master nodded. "Remember, with cryptic puzzles there is the immediate literal meaning, and the true, hidden meaning. As with the mysteries of life, there are different layers of truth that are only apparent to whoever has prepared them self to understand the depths of those truths." She paused while Louis tried to retune, but when it appeared he was still somewhat fuzzy, she said, "First you must return the word *he'll* because the conjunction *And* implies that you must, which leaves you with the nonsense word *ll'eh.* Then you can literally 'break' the ends off the word and tell me what you get."

Louis scratched his temple. "L and E."

"Now attach them to the end of line six and spell it out for me."

Louis deliberately took his time. "D… E… V… I… L… L… E."

The instant he said the final letter, he went back to the lines to make sure he hadn't been taken for a ride: *Return with him who's lived and he'll break…* It couldn't be, could it? *Return lived is devil. He'll break is el, which also must be returned, leaving devil and le* – DeVille.

He kept staring at the cryptic sentence for another few seconds, then said, "I'll grant you, it's an extraordinary coincidence. But…"

"But where is the rest of your name?" *The Master* said for him. "Where is Louis?"

"Yes, and not Lewis, either. It has to be spelled L.O.U.I.S before I'll even remotely accept the possibility that the prophecy might be genuine."

Louis didn't fancy the expression on *The Master's* face. Like cryptic crosswords and Scrabble, he had never been interested in chess, or any other board game for that matter, except Monopoly of course (*show me somebody who doesn't enjoy bankrupting their opponents when they land on one of their hotels and I'll show you a goddamn fake*), but now he had a sinking feeling in his gut that he was about to experience his very first checkmate.

"Lo' thou art a dance," *The Master* said, as if it were self-evident.

It still meant nothing; and more annoyingly, Frank O'Lynn was now grinning over her shoulder like he had just backed the Derby winner. God, he loathed smugness.

"The words *with song* tell us to expect a title to follow, which it surely does."

His mind once more fuzzy with TV snow, Louis felt like banging his temples to help him retune (*But there's only one goddamn channel in this hell hole, isn't there, Louis my boy*?) He reread the conclusion to the seventh line, almost hating himself for what he was about to say. "You've got me. I give in."

The Master then said, "Sometimes surrendering is the only way out of an impossible situation." She paused briefly, then went on. "Miles N. Boon tells us that the name of the next prophet is mixed in with the letters of the line, *Lo' thou art.* 'A dance' implies just that. To shuffle them about, to stir them up."

The first thing Louis did was to make a tally. "My name has only five letters. There's nine there."

To his disappointment, the grin that had spread across Frank O'Lynn's pointy face didn't waver. "*Thou* is Old English for what?" *The Master* asked.

Knowing that he had missed out on something obvious, Louis replied, "You."

"Exactly, and in the language of cryptic puzzles it also represents the letter U."

Like SMS messaging, he thought. *Are is R, to is 2, and you is U.* It wasn't rocket science. "I presume *art* is Old English for are?" he said, to which *The Master* and Frank O'Lynn nodded in unison. He went on quickly, now with a faint glimmer of hope that he could finally lay to rest their inane conspiracy theory. "And if *are* is R, then the letters still don't spell my name. L… O… U… R." He nearly added, Q... E… D, but their unwavering grins told him he was a little premature in thinking he could escape the trap. That sinking feeling was back. Checkmate was now just one move away.

"*Art* has a dual meaning," *The Master* said. "It's both plural and singular, which means it also represents the word…"

"Is," Louis said, now shattered. Realization hadn't just dawned, it had landed in a UFO and abducted him to an alien planet in the outer quadrants of the goddamn universe, far away from safe familiarities of his home world. His name was there all right, as she had said, in bold goddamn letters. L… O… U… I… S.

He tried dismissing it to the realms of the ridiculous, but no matter how hard he tried, the letters kept flashing on and off in front of his eyes like a damn Burger Boss sign. This was either a massive elaborate hoax (*Louis DeVille, this is your After Life*!) designed to lure him into the fold of the White Rabbit Freedom Fighters, or he had to accept the prophecy was real and swallow the whole unpalatable truth that there were things he couldn't explain or were beyond his control. But there had to be another explanation. There just had to be.

Admit it, Louis dear, he heard the voice of Lady Di through the hazy snow in his head. *This is checkmate. Take it like a man and admit you've been beaten. As the good mouse said, sometimes surrendering is the only way out of an impossible situation.*

He wasn't ready to tip his king over yet, he told the voice. He still had one last piece to move. Okay, it was a pawn, not a queen, and he didn't fancy his chances, but it was at least something. "I guess my name is spelt in every translation of the original verse?" he said, and as he suspected, *The Master* nodded in confirmation. He closed his eyes and sighed. Checkmate. "Then tell me," he said, "what the hell is a prophet supposed to do?"

When she smiled, he sensed a boulder-like weight lifting off her petit shoulders. Behind her, Frank O'Lynn drew a deep breath. "I never thought you'd ask," she said.

Later, when all was done and dusted, he wished he never had.

Chapter 31

The Grand Plan

PERCHED on the stool with her ramrod-straight back, her head held aloft, and her paws on her lap, *The Master* wasted no time in detailing the plan the White Rabbit Freedom Fighters had devised to escape from LeMont International Enterprises, a plan millions of years in the preparation. Louis shifted on the plastic sheeting, wondering if she realized how goddamn ludicrous it sounded to someone on the outside. To think, he had thought he was suffering from an attack of the crazies.

Post Traumatic Death Syndrome eat ya heart out baby. You got noth'n on this gal.

"Let me get this straight," he said. "You want to tunnel beneath The Tower so that it will collapse and bring down the sky-vault? I understand you correctly, don't I? This isn't a cryptic puzzle or anything I need a PhD to get my head around, is it?"

"It's the only way to achieve our goal," she said. "The Boss won't relinquish his power over us, so we have to wrench it from him ourselves."

Frank O'Lynn had returned to eroding a path on the other side of the coffee table. Pivoting at the door to commence his short return to the piano, he nodded in silent agreement, scratching his chin.

"By creating mayhem and chaos? Killing thousands of innocent victims?" Louis said.

"No one will die. We're all dead anyway."

Louis shifted once more, distinctly uncomfortable. Whatever rationalization she used to keep her pretty self on the straight and narrow, it still didn't negate the manner with which she was trying to achieve her aim.

"It's still terrorism, no matter how good your intentions are.

You're trying to manipulate the masses through fear. I'm not sure I can be a part of that, prophecy or not."

"You've been a part of it all your life. What do you call marketing, if not manipulating the masses through fear? Your morals didn't stop you when your company preyed on society's aversion to infirmity and death to market its pharmaceuticals."

Goddamn it, she was out of order. He had done everything he possibly could to make sure his company had thrived in the cut-throat world of business, and he had been damned *good* at what he did. Sure, he might have bent the rules a little, stepped over the line of corporate responsibility once or twice (what CEO didn't for the good of the shareholders?), but to throw him in the same basket with every goddamn terrorist that had actually killed and maimed innocent victims was more than he could stomach.

"Don't misunderstand me," she continued. "I'm not singling you out. Most corporations are just as culpable, and governments are no different – a society in fear is the easiest society to control – and let's not get started on institutionalized religion, either." Before she went on, another underground quake rattled the chinaware and shook the miniature figurines on top of the piano. "I had hoped with everything that's been said, you would've put aside your prejudice and decided to join us by now," she said, as the shaking and rumbles died away. "We want you, and we need you, to fulfill your role – to fulfill your prophesized destiny – but we can't force you to do something you don't want to do. We can't put a gun to your head; you're already dead. We can't extort you; you have no money. As far as kidnapping your wife and using her as leverage, if she's even in LeMont, I don't think that would work either, do you?"

Louis shrugged, figuring she couldn't be more goddamn right than Ronald Reagan. The Freedom Fighters had nothing over him. He could walk out of here on his own free will and do what he damn well pleased. But the voice of Lady Di, as usual, thought otherwise.

And do just what, Louis dear? I'm sure the secret police would love to hear your version of the Freedom Fighter's plan; and when you've finished, why, they'll let you go as free as a rabbit. They might even help you get settled in a nice apartment just off the piazza…

All right, all right, he got the picture, he said to the voice. It was so clear he had to stop himself looking over his shoulder to see if she was there. She wasn't, he didn't need to look to know that, some part of his subconscious was masquerading as his (ex?) wife. Probably that part where his so-called morals were hidden, popping up to annoy him whenever it suited. No goddamn wonder it sounded like Lady Di.

"In fact, forcing you against your will would defeat the whole purpose," *The Master* added. "We'd play straight into The Boss's hands. We need you to come willingly, no strings attached. It's the only way the plan will work."

Louis wasn't really listening, his thoughts on something *The Master* had just said: *if she's even in LeMont.* Lady Di's whereabouts raised some immediate questions. If, in fact, she was somewhere in the underground mega-city, what kind of spirit-animal would he have to be on the lookout for? A jackal? A lizard? Unlikely. So too a rat or guinea pig. Probably a goddamn mouse, like the one he was staring at across the coffee table. An interesting theory, except for one thing: Lady Di wouldn't be seen dead in a dress that resembled a goddamn straight jacket; she would be in leg warmers and leotards and down at the salon having her hair and nails (claws?) done. Maybe he was onto something there. Maybe searching for her would be as easy as checking out every hair salon in LeMont. It would only be a matter of time before he stumbled upon her, and he had all the time in the world, didn't he?

The Master's voice snapped him back. "When the sky-vault collapses with The Tower, everyone will see that The Boss doesn't have supreme power over everything, most of all themselves. That's where you come in." *The Master* waited for his reply, then, sensing his unease, quoted a now familiar line: "*When The Tower does fall, He will come.*"

"Inviting you to follow," Louis said, beginning to hate Miles N. Boon and his goddamn prophecy. Although he suspected – no, he goddamn *knew* – what the Freedom Fighters wanted him to do, he was still clinging onto the hope that he might somehow be wrong. He eyed the marching guinea pig, hoping for support, but none was forthcoming. Directing himself to *The Master*, he said, "You want me to be the goddamn Pied Piper of LeMont. Lead six billion down Conduit Number 1 and over the precipice into oblivion. Do you know how crazy that sounds?"

Without breaking stride, Frank O'Lynn said, "No more crazy than a city of six billion under the control of one corporation."

Louis clenched his teeth. Just because a shepherd jumped over the cliff, it didn't mean the sheep would follow. "There's just too many variables, too many things that can go wrong. It's just not feasible."

"The plan has already entered the final phase," *The Master* said, and Louis' thoughts flashed to the increasingly frequent underground rumblings. "There's no turning back. We either do it with you, or without you."

Louis was no psychotherapist, but he knew as well as anybody that if someone had it in their head to commit suicide, then no amount of logic was going to make a goddamn bit of difference. He could sit here till the cows came home, a lot of good it would achieve; *The Master* and her Freedom Fighters were going to do what they were going to do. He gave it one last shot, however.

"How can you be so sure The Boss hasn't infiltrated the Freedom Fighters? What if he already knows your plans? What if he's just waiting to ambush you when you make your move, finish off your resistance once and for all?"

The Master said, "The Boss has known about our plan since the very beginning."

Louis bolted upright, making only a pathetic gasping noise in reply. His tie felt like a noose that had been yanked tight around his neck, as though he had just been hoisted onto the gallows and left to dangle.

The Boss goddamn knew?

"The Tower's strength is also its weakness," *The Master* added.

"He thinks The Tower is an infallible fortress, that we are weak, that we are doomed to failure. He allows us to try what we can because it gives him the very excuse he needs to tighten the reins over his citizens, to have even more power. It allows him to enact laws that take away our basic rights. It allows him to pry into our own personal lives, to have anyone he sees as a threat, innocent or not, detained without trial in the chambers along Conduit Number 1. In a way, he uses us to suit his own agenda, but his arrogance will be his downfall."

Any inkling that Louis might have entertained regarding the success of the Freedom Fighter's plans was now well and truly scrapped. They were walking into the lion's den, of that he had no doubt. Nothing bar a miracle was going to stop The Boss chewing them up and spitting them out, and his first instinct was overwhelming and immediate. Run. Save his own pelt. Get the hell out of here, fast. But where could he go? Either direction he faced – going along with the Freedom Fighters, hiding, or turning himself in to the peelers – was a goddamn dead end.

"There's still one thing I don't quite get," he said. "Why do you really need me? You're *The Master*, surely you could do a better job."

"You're forgetting one important factor: you've seen the White Rabbit, I haven't. You're the prophet, chosen to lead us out of the darkness and into the light. You must lead by example. You must be the first to step through the archway."

"But they won't believe me. Everyone already thinks I'm suffering from Post Traumatic Death Syndrome. There's no way they'll follow a madman."

Frank O'Lynn, halfway back from the doorway, opened his jaw to say what was on his mind, but *The Master* spoke before he could even taken the next step. "They will follow if you come back and show them that there's nothing to fear."

"What are you goddamn talking about? Come back from where?"

"Where else do you think?" *The Master* said. "From obliteration."

Her words suddenly took Louis back to his childhood, to the time during and after the war (the big one, the one that nearly shook the world off its goddamn axis). He was reminded in particular of the hard wooden pews and butt-numbing sermons at St. Patrick's Catholic Church, his mother's doing of course. Without fail every week, she would drag him along and force him to sit through mass, including twice at Christmas, three times at Easter, not to mention all the weddings, christenings and funerals that never seemed to end. It was a goddamn production line – in went the newborns, all dressed up in frilly frocks, and out went the old ones, packaged up and shifted out in wooden boxes. Never mind butt numbing, it was goddamn mind numbing.

Not surprisingly, his father never attended, not once in Louis' memory, not even when his only sister finally succumbed to the ravages of polio that had sentenced her to a life in splints and crutches since she was three. "The born-again atheist," he called himself whenever his wife began the ritual of asking whether he would be attending this week (though Louis suspected she was always glad to hear him refuse), "I only worship the trinity of Beer, Wine and the holy Spirits," and if Louis ever so much as chuckled he would receive a clip around the ears, followed by a stern warning that if he kept that attitude up he would be following his father all the way to the gates of hell.

Louis didn't care; he had long suspected his father was onto something Father Gringham and the nuns at St. Patrick's had no idea about, getting what you could out of life while you were still here. At age ten, in a desperate attempt to avoid another morning of utter boredom, Louis summoned the courage to use his father's tried and tested excuse, which he thought infallible. "I'm a born-again atheist," he said to his mother through the bedroom door. "I can't go to church anymore."

Margaret DeVille had burst into the bedroom and had him into his Sunday bests before he even knew what hit him. Which she had, a slap across his face that left a large ruby imprint down the side of his left cheek, along with a puffy eye though which he had to squint for the rest of the day. Injuries that he had to confess to Sister Brady at Sunday school were the result of sleepwalking into the bathroom door the night before.

"The devil loves an idle mind," the nun said, slapping his wrist. "Let that be a lesson for you."

He received many such lessons from Sister Brady over the years, more than he cared to remember. By the time the GI's had trickled home from Europe and the Pacific, Louis had well and truly had the Fear of God beaten into him. Pain and suffering, he came to realize, were part and parcel of being a good Catholic boy. Which was probably why he wasn't a good Catholic boy; he was an extraordinarily *bad* one. He was the last in class to recite the Lord's Prayer by heart. He was constantly overlooked as an altar boy, to his mother's enduring shame. He was never asked to try out for the choir, and he could never for the life of him remember the stories in the Old Testament. The whole genealogy was too goddamn confusing. Everyone was begatting everyone, and he never did work out if Kane killed Abel, or Abel killed Kane? Ask him now, and he reckoned he still wouldn't be able to tell you who was whose brother's keeper. Noah was the guy on the boat with all the animals, at least he knew that, but who the hell was Jacob and Abraham, and why did one of them want to sacrifice his only son instead of a goat? Moses was probably the character he found easiest to remember. Good ol' basket baby was given the dos and don'ts of God on top of the mountain in the desert; but apart from Thou Shall Not Kill, could anyone really list the whole Ten Commandments, and in goddamn order?

Nah, the whole damn thing was just too confusing. Too many things to remember. Too many contradictions. He liked simplicity, and simplicity was anathema to the Catholic Church. It thrived on confusion. The whole institution seemed to be based on the maxim, "God gives with one hand, and takes with the other," and he had often thought of it as an army nurse who deliberately poisoned her soldiers so that she could keep caring for them. He certainly had his battle wounds, embarrassment and disgrace (*You're not wor-*

thy of God's Love, Master DeVille), things he had spent his whole adult life trying to forget; but no scar ever completely healed, did it? Old war veterans, diabetics, chain smokers, anyone in fact who had lost a leg or arm, invariably complained of feelings coming from the limb that no longer existed, pins and needles, twitches, even cramps. Phantom limb pain, the docs called it. Memories were like that. No matter how hard someone tried to lobotomize a piece of history from their mind, there was always a reminder of what had happened, a flash of recollected pain, a grimace of lingering humiliation. Once in, they were always part of you.

One Sunday school memory in particular kept haunting him like a phantom limb. On his way home in the back of a taxi, chairing a boardroom meeting, relaxing in front of the TV, it would ambush him out of the blue just when his defenses were at their lowest. Like now, with *The Master* and *The Partridge* in a basement apartment that was shaking with another underground quake. The memory had hardly changed over the years, a little dog-eared at the edges some would say, but the picture was essentially the same: Sister Brady in front of a class of fifty or so kids that were grouped together like POWs on the carpet. She had a pointer stick she carried everywhere, with which she would slap down on any unsuspecting wrist. The kids cringed every time she came near them. Man, it would sting. "God's little corrector," she called it. The kids baptized it something else, "Brady's bayonet," though later he would come to remember it more as miniature whip.

"Louis DeVille," she said, spinning on her flat heels and making him jump with a start. She always called him Lewis – *Loo-iss-Da-Veal* – not Lewey, her thick Mississippi accent hissing straight from the back of her nose. "What would you have done in the same circumstance?"

Unfortunately, Louis had arrived late to class. His tardiness, not for the first time, made him an easy target. Not only did he have to sit in the only available location, right at the front, it also meant Sister Brady had all the excuses in the world to make a fool of him. He could sense the other kids fidgeting around him, grateful that her attention wasn't trained upon them and yet fearful for what was about to happen to one of their own. Louis, for the time being, was caught in a no-win situation. Whatever he said would probably land him with a stinging wrist. So he decided to say nothing.

"Before you decided to grace us with your presence," she said, speaking above him to the rest of the class, "we were discussing the prophet Moses, and the predicament in which he found himself whilst leading the Jews out of Egypt." She flexed the pointer like she was trying to snap a twig in half, and Louis instinctively sat on his hands. "The Pharaoh's army was hot on his heels. The Red Sea was in front of him. There was nowhere to go. The situation was hopeless." She paced back and forth, still flexing the pointer. "So, Master DeVille, if you were in Moses' sandals, what would you have done?"

Louis knew silence would only save him for so long, so he said the first thing that came to mind. "Run away."

He hadn't meant to be funny, but the rest of the class burst out laughing. He glanced over his shoulder, unable to stop himself smiling with everyone else. When he looked back, Sister Brady was flexing the pointer so hard it was now almost in the shape of an upside down horseshoe.

"Give me your hand," she said.

The laughter immediately stopped. Louis hesitated, torn between outright refusal and submission.

"Give me your hand or it will be your backside, right here, in front of the class."

He heard a few nervous giggles behind him, boys and girls, then held his hand forward. The sting on his knuckles made him flinch and brought a tear to his eye. He absolutely refused to cry, hugging his aching hand to his chest while Sister Brady went back to where she had left off.

"It's a good thing God didn't choose you to lead the Jews out of Egypt, isn't it?" she said.

Louis nodded several short jerks of his head, not meeting her eye.

"The Lord chose a man with faith, a man who wouldn't run away from his responsibilities. Can anybody tell me what Moses really did?"

Louis heard a boy behind him say, "He parted the Red Sea, ma'm."

"Correct. But what did he do before that?"

A girl answered this time. "He prayed to God for help, ma'm."

"Precisely, and God didn't let him down, did He? He saved the Jews and killed the Pharaoh's army. His Will was done."

Absently rubbing his paw, Louis glanced up at *The Master*, half-expecting her to lean across the coffee table and slap him on the paw. The sternness of her posture in particular reminded him of Sister Brady, but that was as far as the similarities went, and as far as he wanted to think about her. He wondered what had triggered the memory, then recalled what *The Master* had been saying immediately beforehand, letting his mind wander to what she was really asking: for him to lead the Freedom Fighters out of LeMont (*And here's the goddamn kicker, Louis my boy,* through *the archway at the end of Conduit Number 1*). Easier said than goddamn done. But if that wasn't frightening enough, he had to prove the Fires of Oblivion were no barrier *by coming back*. Where the hell did she get this insanity?

Delusions of grandeur aside, he couldn't go through with it. No matter how much his ego was impressed with the idea of being a hero, this was an impasse of Moses-like proportions. Probably even bigger, *Lazarus* like, and if it came to the crunch, if he had no other option than to step blindly into the unknown, he knew deep down that he would falter. Sister Brady had been right all along. He simply didn't have what it took.

Goddamn faith.

Chapter 32

The Art of Zipping

"LOUIS! Louis!" Frank O'Lynn said, shaking his shoulders.

With the guinea pig's face barely inches from his own, Louis peeled himself from the mental brick wall into which he had slammed. Frank O'Lynn released his grip and stepped back, eyeing him with concern.

"You okay? You looked gone. I thought we'd lost you."

"I'm still here," he said. "I haven't gone anywhere."

Frank O'Lynn retreated behind the coffee table to where Louis last remembered him, halfway between the piano and the door. "To be sure, you were unresponsive for quite a while. You sure you're okay?"

Louis figured he looked as bad as he was feeling. He was just so goddamn tired. His head felt like a sack of cement on his shoulders. "What do you mean? How long was I out?"

Frank O'Lynn scratched a fleabite on his neck. "Nearly three hours."

Louis stared back at the guinea pig as unblinking as *The Master* herself. A shiver coursed down his back to the tip of his tail, a kind of electric tingle that made his hairs stand on end. It was not too unlike that feeling he always got when he realized his wallet had just been pick-pocketed, that oh-you've-got-to-be-kidding-me kind of feeling.

"You were exhibiting the classic symptoms," *The Master* said. "Staring into space. Impassiveness. Nonsensical muttering. The only thing you didn't do was drool."

"So I am suffering from Post Traumatic Death Syndrome," he said, almost relieved. There was something comforting in knowing that this was all a figment of his delusional mind.

"Heavens no, something a lot more common than that." *The Master* appeared to be laughing at a private joke. "Faithlessness."

Louis glanced at the poem on the inside cover of the book. It was all returning to him, every insane detail. *I'd love to help you, lady,* he wanted to say. *But I can't. Suicide missions aren't my thing. You need the Dirty Dozen, or The Magnificent Seven, guys who've got nothing to lose and figure going out in a blaze of glory is better than fading away.*

"I just can't have faith like that," he said, and clicked his claws. "I just can't believe in something I've never believed in before."

"Nobody is totally faithless. Everyone has faith in something. Money, career, a partner, anything that gives them a sense of meaning."

Louis fiddled with his tie and scoffed. "If you need that sort of thing."

"It's got nothing to do with need. Meaning exists whether you need it or not. It's the ink with which we write. The reason behind existence."

Louis now laughed out loud. "Hippie horseshit! We're here and that's it. There's no reason to exist other than that."

The Master just smiled. "But even no-reason is a reason, don't you see? You can't escape it." Louis made to say that her argument wouldn't hold up in a court of law, but then let it go. "Listen, Mr. DeVille," she said. "If you're going to be with us and help the Freedom Fighters take Miles N. Boon's prophecy to its completion, you will have to tear down the wall of doubt and prejudice you've spent a lifetime building. Remove it brick by brick if you have to. Allow yourself to believe that there's more to life than you can otherwise see. It's not going to be easy."

Damned right it wasn't going to be easy. He had been living in the Kingdom of Old Habits for a long time. His walls were pretty damned tall. "You never got around to telling me what a prophet is supposed to do," he said. "I'm not good at letting things pan out for themselves. I need a plan. Something to follow."

The Master stood, and said, "Then follow me to the hotel. We can discuss what's already been done while I *Zip* you over to the

AGM." She faced Frank O'Lynn. "You know what to do. Tell the others it's begun. We'll rendezvous at the prearranged location. Till then, farewell for now, and good luck."

Without further ado, *The Partridge* left the apartment. He had a skip in his step Louis hadn't previously seen. *The Master* then grabbed Louis' paw and told him to close his eyes. "Ready?" she asked.

Louis hadn't even finished nodding when he heard a *Zzzzzzzip*, like Velcro ripping. Then strangely his head was filled with images of the cinema. Not just any cinema, either. The Odeon, the old converted theatre down near the Hudson he used to frequent almost as often as Sunday school. "I can smell popcorn," he said. "Buttered popcorn."

"Open your eyes," she said.

Some part of him expected to see himself as a thirteen year-old at the box office with his father, waiting to purchase tickets to *Ben Hur*, the very first color film he ever saw. Another part of him would also not have been surprised to see Salma Gundi behind the reception desk in the lobby of the LeMont Hotel. It was neither. Unlike the time he had *Popped* from the blues bar to the archway at the end of Conduit Number 1, he and *The Master* hadn't moved one inch from the basement apartment; but although the contents were still the same – the books on the shelves, the figurines on the piano, the coffee table and sofa – they somehow looked different, as if everything had been removed while his eyes were closed and replaced with stage props.

"Why is the room shimmering? It looks like everything's made of water. Even you."

The Master suddenly raised her paw to slap him across the face. He braced himself for the impact, but it never came. Her paw passed straight through is head; he didn't feel a thing. "You try it now," she said. "Go on. You can't hurt me."

Louis just looked at her. There might have been a few things in his past that he wasn't entirely proud of, things said and done in the heat of the moment, but there was one thing nobody could ever accuse him of being, and that was a wife beater. He had always been a goddamn gentleman.

"That won't be necessary," he said, and reached across to caress her cheek. Unbelievably, his paw passed through her whiskers and fur to the other side, like dipping his paw into a trickling stream. Staring at his paw, he said, "I guess nobody can see us. Like *Popping*."

"Only those who are *Zipping* through this exact period in time, but I wouldn't worry about it. The chances are incredibly small. It's only happened to me once before." She went to the door, which shimmered like a fluorescent light flickering on when she grabbed the handle. "I want you to prepare yourself for what you are about to see."

Louis came over. "Why? What's out there?"

She opened the door and Louis took an involuntary step backward. There was nothing save an abyss of total blackness, as though he were about to step off the edge of the goddamn world. "Shut the door," he said, grimacing. "I'm not going out there. Not for a million goddamn dollars."

"There's no need to worry. Nothing's going to happen. The emptiness you see is not a void, or a vacuum, as you may be thinking. It's the totality of everything that exists in this present moment of now. What you see is time and space frozen, like one giant block of ice."

Still more uncomfortable than he liked to admit, Louis peered through the door, trying to see a familiar landmark – the street at the front of the apartment, maybe a Burger Boss or Happythecary – anything in fact to make him feel more at ease. He would even have settled for a glimpse of The Tower and its logo. "I still can't see a goddamn thing," he said.

"Then you'll just have to have faith, won't you?"

Louis smirked. Bravery was something he was happier witnessing than doing. Unlike all the other kids at school, he had never wanted to be a fireman or policeman; he had just never seen the point in risking his life for someone he didn't know.

"I'll feel better following after you," he said.

Her expression was mocking, but kind. "Ladies before gentlemen? And here I was thinking chivalry had died along time ago."

Despite her words to the contrary, he still expected *The Master* to plummet into the void as if she were stepping over the edge of a cliff. It didn't happen. The moment her sneaker passed over the threshold, a miraculous thing took place – the hallway outside the apartment suddenly blinked into existence. He could even see the stairs leading up to the street; but what really blew his mind, more than the dark nothingness itself, were the numerous frozen images that had appeared out of nowhere, images of *The Master* walking up the stairs with a weasel in a blue-gray suit following close behind. It was like someone had set up cardboard cutouts of him and *The Master*, all at various postures of ascending the stairs. In some, his left leg was raised, ready to step forward, his right leg taking his weight; and in another it was reversed, his right leg raised and his left leg firmly planted. Except there weren't just one or two of these cardboard cutouts, there were hundreds, all of them blurring together. Some were barely indistinguishable from the one preceding or following it, maybe with the left leg slightly more raised, or the right leg slightly lower, as with *The Master*. All of her images were also in some kind of frozen pose of walking up the stairs. It was goddamn stop-motion. Like staring at a series of cartoon stills before they were run through the camera and given animation. The kind Disney and Loony Toons had framed and numbered and then auctioned for ridiculous amounts of money to middle aged men like himself.

"What the hell is going on?" he said.

The Master was now completely outside the door. The hallway and stairs had taken on the same apparition-like shimmer as the apartment, as if she had triggered some kind of light sensor, a kind of supernatural spotlight that followed her everywhere she went. "I understand your concern," she said, "but you just have to put your doubts to one side and trust me."

Louis stepped toward the door to take a closer look, stopping just where it ended and the hallway started. *The Master*, as far as he could tell, was standing on solid ground, not floating in space. Oddly, her stop-motion images seemed to extend directly from her, as if she were walking into a tunnel contoured to the exact proportions of her figure. His closest stop-motion image, he was bemused to see, began on the other side of the doorframe, barely an inch away from his snout, a frozen still of himself stepping forward, left leg out. "How do I know which one is me?" he asked.

"They are all you."

"Yes, but which one is the *real* me? I can't be all of them at once."

"They *are* all really you. What you see is the direct result of the *choices* you are making. Normally, you can't see this because the flow of time veils the future. But now that we have *Zipped* time, you can see the future you are about to bring into existence, all through the process of selecting what you want from the infinite possibilities of what already exists."

"Like choosing clothes from a wardrobe?"

"Precisely. You can't wear what hasn't already been made. An experience is simply a choice of selecting a particular part of the infinite and eternal moment that is already there, an experience that has already been created."

Louis followed the stop-motion images to the top of the stairs, where they faded into the void of darkness like two hikers disappearing into a hillside cave. "My choices don't seem to go very far."

"Every choice leads to another, then another, then another, multiplying to infinitum," *The Master* said, and motioned toward the darkness at the top. "Which is what you see, the infinite multiplicity of every choice you could make from this moment from now. It looks like a formless mass of nothingness because everything you could possibly choose is there, all at once. Essentially, what you see up there is your destiny."

Louis scratched his snout. There was something depressing about having a black hole as his future. "Then why can't I see it?"

"You are too accustomed to seeing only one thing at a time.

That's why everything all at once – *The Plenitude*, as we call it in The Tradition – seems so daunting to the uninitiated. Take a look behind you."

Louis turned around and froze with shock. The bookshelves and piano had disappeared into a similar black void, as had half the sofa and coffee table, reminiscent of the abyss into which his office, and himself, had been swallowed the day of his heart attack. That wasn't the goddamn end of it either. There were more stop-motion images of *The Master* and himself, this time of the past, a still-by-still replay of what they had done in the moments since she grabbed his paw and *Zipped.* He could see stop-motion cutouts of *The Master* coming toward the door and grabbing the handle. He could see himself staring, then grimacing when she revealed what was outside.

I'm looking at my own goddamn ghost, he mused.

Then, while he continued to stare at them, several stop-motion images sparked and disappeared, like light bulbs, brilliant flashes of white as they blew and went dead forever.

"The choices of our past get absorbed back into *The Plenitude* once they've been experienced," *The Master* said. "They haven't been destroyed. In fact, you can revisit them anytime you like, as memories. Which is precisely what we're doing now – *memorizing* – choosing that part of the Infinite Memory we wish to visit and then imprinting it into the reality we call existence. We are all doing it, most of us subconsciously, and we are all doing it in unison with each other."

Louis glanced over his shoulder one last time. Several more images flashed before vanishing into *The Plenitude.* The rest of the sofa and coffee table went the same way. "We'd better get going before we also get swallowed," he said.

The Master cocked her head, as if everything she had said had been a complete and utter waste of time. A slap on the wrist from Sister Brady would have had less effect in making him feel so goddamn small and stupid. "*The Plenitude* is all there is. There is nothing else. You are already in it. You can't escape from it, and you can't be swallowed by it. You can only *experience* it. And what you experience is shaped by your beliefs."

Louis nodded and smiled, trying to give all the non-verbal cues he could to convince her that he understood. *The Master*, however, could see straight through him, in more ways than one. "A Chinese proverb says, 'The journey of a thousand miles begins with the first step.' Are you willing to shed your burden and come with me?"

She held out her paw. Louis was about to take it, but was struck with a sudden flash of insight. "This is all about free will, isn't it?"

The Master smiled. "The power is always within you. No matter what happens. It can only be given away, never taken. Always remember that."

Louis then made his decision. "I can't believe I'm doing this," he said to himself, and stepped across the precipice into *The Plenitude*. Left foot first.

Chapter 33

Sphere of Illumination

WHILE *The Master* led Louis to the closest boulevard through a series of side streets and alleyways, he began to realize that *Zipping* was going to be a lot harder work than *Popping*. Time might have been frozen to a standstill, but it still meant he had to walk every goddamn step of the way to the hotel. Still, he was kind of glad for that. Bad news should be approached cautiously, he reckoned, like an unexploded bomb.

Intriguingly, he couldn't actually see further than forty or so feet in any direction. Wherever he was – ascending the stairs out of the apartment, wandering through an alleyway, crossing the boulevard – his vision came to an abrupt halt at the abyss of nothingness that seemed to have cocooned him and *The Master* in their own, self-contained little world. Cocooned, in fact, inside a bubble of light, as he thought of it ("Sphere of Illumination," she referred to it), beyond which there was nothing to see, in front or at the back, left or right, even above. Just goddamn blackness, like he was walking home through the streets of Manhattan after a meeting that had dragged on much later than he had wanted.

The stop-motion images blinking into existence ahead, and flashing out of existence behind, were also another part of the whole goddamn enigma he couldn't quite get his head around. They weren't solid statues made of stone, as he quickly discovered, or marble, or clay, or even wood; he could move through them like they were wisps of smoke, without the slightest resistance. But the amazing thing was, when he stepped into each image one after the other, they *felt* solid. It was goddamn freaky.

"They represent the highest probability of your immediate future, given the scenario in which you find yourself and the intent with which you wish to move forward," *The Master* added. "They simply reflect the most likely choice you are going to make when you move from one image to another."

Looking at the hazy images blinking into existence at the horizon of *The Plenitude*, it kind of made sense. He could still make out the basic form, maybe with a left leg stepping forward, or a slight turn of the head across the street, but the edges of his body and suit were fuzzy and indistinct, blurred by some ghosted outline you see on a TV with a crappy aerial. Then, as he neared the stop-motion image he was focusing on, more and more details would become apparent – the seams running down the trousers, the individual whiskers at the side of his snout, the creases on the back of his jacket – as if he was twiddling with some kind of inbuilt aerial and the image lost its ghostly halo with the improved reception. Then, when the stop-motion image was immediately in front of him, just as he moved into it, the picture became clear and perfect. One hundred percent reception. *Life, Jim, but not as we know it.*

"From what I can gather," he said, "my body images aren't actually moving. They just blink into existence, frame by frame, and then *I* slide into them. You know what it feels like? Like I'm walking along a conveyor belt. Things are coming toward me, but I'm actually staying in the same spot. It's goddamn weird."

"Because you always considered your body that part of your self which moved," *The Master* said.

"Damned right. If my body isn't moving, what is?"

"Your consciousness."

They continued toward the piazza without saying much more. As they slid through the stop-motion images along sidewalk (he hadn't as yet seen a goddamn street sign to tell him which boulevard they were on), the dark cocoon of *The Plenitude* moved with them, keeping a steady distance all around. Once again he had the feeling that *The Master* was triggering some kind of light sensor, as though the streetlights were switching on one by one as they approached, then turning off behind as they moved out of range. The earlier fear he had when first setting eyes on the darkness was no longer with him. It wasn't as if he was walking through Central

Park after midnight, was it? He was just *Zipping* through the infinite and eternal dimensions of space and time. It was a goddamn breeze, a mere bagatelle.

"My mother always told me to be wary of someone that smiled to them self," *The Master* said, the corners of her mouth turned up as well.

"Now why would she say that?"

"Don't know. She was always suspicious. Then again, she was a gypsy," and Louis suddenly understood the origins of *The Master's* accent. Most likely Czechoslovakian, or Romanian, something Eastern European. "I guess she was a bit of a pessimist when it came to looking at life. Not one to ever wear rose colored glasses. I hardly ever saw her smile."

Louis nodded. "A bit like my mother. But I couldn't blame her; in fact I always felt sorry for her. My father used to beat the goddamn daylights out of her. She had a horrible life. I guess the only thing I never really understood was why she never left him."

"Maybe she feared it would be worse for her children as a single mother," *The Master* said. "Or maybe she didn't know any better. Maybe she was comfortable with what she had."

Louis wasn't buying it. "How could anyone be comfortable living a life of hell?"

The Master opened her mouth to say something, then let it slide and said instead, "Have you heard of the Comfort Paradox?"

"Can't say that I have," he said.

Not too far up ahead, the stop-motion images of himself and *The Master* approached an intersection and stopped before disappearing into the darkness. To his right, a Burger Boss had just blinked into existence. There was no line of eager patrons waiting to get inside. In fact, the whole place was empty, just like every other shop or store they had passed, like they were passing through a ghost town.

It's just like a necropolis, he remembered thinking the first time he had laid eyes on the sprawl of LeMont International Enterprises. *A goddamn city of the dead.*

"There's an interesting fact that explains what I mean," *The Master* said. "When a frog is dropped into boiling water, it jumps out. The heat is too much for it to bear. But when a frog is put into cool water that is brought to the boil, it remains there until it dies. Isn't that fascinating?"

More like goddamn ludicrous. "And you're saying that that's what happened to my mother? She was a frog in hot water?"

"I'm saying that often what we perceive as a level of comfort is actually something that is preventing us from living life to the fullest or to the best of our ability. Something that dulls our awareness and limits our ability to make informed decisions."

"But she was being beaten and battered. Of course she couldn't make informed or rational decisions."

The Master simply reiterated her point. "The Comfort Paradox. The frog stays in the boiling water even though it's dying."

They were now at the intersection. Directly across at the very limits of the Sphere of Illumination, blurring into the darkness, Louis could see the shimmering façade of a 24-hour mini-market. On it graffiti had been sprayed, something that made him baulk: WHEN THE TOWER DOES FALL, HE WILL COME. An unwelcome tingle coursed down his back to the tip of his tail, and he was once again left with the sense that he was being swept along by an uncontrollable force. Then suddenly, while he continued to stare at the graffiti, something strange happened to the stop-motion images. Now there were two weasels in a blue-gray suit. One of them continued with *The Master* across the intersection, disappearing into the darkness beyond the mini-market. The other backtracked (fleeing in panic, if he was goddamn honest) into *The Plenitude* from which they had just emerged.

The Master noticed it too. She abruptly stopped, holding her paw across his chest like a mother protecting her child from an oncoming bus. "What were you just thinking?"

Louis shrugged. "Nothing in particular. Why?"

The Master glanced behind, then ahead across the intersection. He didn't much like the expression that furrowed her brow. "You've reached a crossroad. Literally. You've got some serious choices to make, and quickly."

"What… what are you saying?"

"The future now holds two identical possibilities for you. To turn around and go back to what you were doing before we met, or to break from the past and continue ahead."

Louis stared across the intersection. He had often wondered about the major decisions he had made in his life and the subsequent consequences that followed. Dating and marrying Dianne Trump. Quitting his job and starting the company. It was easy enough to look back and follow the path that had unfolded throughout the course of his life, but what about the path of *unmade* decisions? Or more to the point, the path that led from making the opposite decision, if he had said no instead of yes. What would his life have been like if he had never married Lady Di (or divorced her?), or decided to stick with his dead-end job? Would he still have had children? Would he still be alive?

Now that was a question and a half, wasn't it? Had every decision he made from the time of his birth led to his premature demise, or was it his destiny to have had a fatal heart attack at his desk? Something unavoidable? Something he had no goddamn control over? If not his tenth-story office on Broadway, would it have been someplace else? In the bathtub of some nursing home? Or would he have died peacefully asleep in his bed? He now glanced over his tail at the images of the weasel sprinting away from the intersection and vanishing into the darkness. What he reckoned he was getting at, something that was only now dawning on him, was this: was his destiny written in stone? Did it actually make a goddamn difference what decisions he made throughout his life if he was always going to end up collapsing face first onto his desk as a middle-aged man and then wake up in the After Life as a weasel? Was he goddamn responsible for his own demise?

Responsibility. The word seemed to echo through his entire sense of being, and not in a good way. It felt so heavy, so oppressive. If someone could actually suffocate by just thinking of a word, he reckoned he had found it. "Let's get a move on," he said. "Before I have any more second thoughts."

Amazingly, as soon as he stepped forward, the stop-motion images fleeing in the opposite direction vanished into thin air, leaving only those of himself and *The Master* heading toward the piazza. Furthermore, as though a second streetlight had been triggered, it seemed he could now see further down the boulevard than he had previously been able. The horizon was still only a hundred or so feet away, at a guess, but something had happened for him to now see beyond the mini-market to the store next door, Big Screen Classics. "What's happening?" he asked, stepping onto the opposite sidewalk.

"Your Sphere of Illumination is expanding."

"*My* sphere? I thought it was your sphere?"

"*Our* sphere. We're doing this together."

Well fancy that and bugger me.

With each step he took, the Sphere of Illumination seemed to grow exponentially. Like dawn slowly breaking across the city, the darkness was receding little by little, revealing more and more of the surroundings – the buildings, the boulevard, even the sky-vault was beginning to appear. He could now clearly see beyond the video store and read the sign next to it, CHEAP WAYS TO FEEL GOOD. He felt like an apprentice wizard learning a new trick he didn't know how to control: he was doing something, but exactly what he couldn't say. *The Master* then brought his attention to the other side of the boulevard. Whereas before he hadn't been able to see further than halfway across the street, he could now make out the stores fronting the opposite sidewalk.

"The city's materializing out of nothing," he said.

"*The Plenitude* isn't nothing," *The Master* said, "though it may initially seem that way. It all depends through which eyes you see it, as a nothingness or as a fullness. As an abyss, or as an *Immensity* from which everything in the universe is made real, or realized."

Just her way of saying you either see the dough in the donut or the hole, Louis reckoned. He could now see beyond the next intersection. The speed with which the buildings and street were materializing was extraordinary, and he reckoned within the next twenty paces, about the distance to the next Burger Boss, he might see all the way down the boulevard to The Tower. As it was, over his shoulder, he could already see the pockmarked face of the cliff looming over the images of himself and *The Master*, like a giant wave about to crash onto a couple of unsuspecting beachgoers.

"Let me understand this correctly," he said. "I'm not actually seeing *The Plenitude* retreating from me. That's just an illusion based on my limited knowledge?"

"Precisely. *The Plenitude* is actually revealing Itself within your Sphere of Illumination. You're now seeing more and more of it, not less." They now approached the next Burger Boss, vacant and empty as all the others Louis had seen. "At any one point in time, you can only see a small fraction of everything that exists, the part of the Infinite and Eternal Immensity you are able to experience within the limitations of your mind and body. Your mind establishes the point in space and time where you believe yourself to exist, and your body – your spirit-body in the After Life – establishes the manner with which to get yourself to the next point in space and time. *The Plenitude* waits for you to take the first step, then it provides the direction of your travel. That's why it's important you know where you're going before you do anything else. It's your intent that establishes your path."

"The stronger my intent, the brighter my Sphere of Illumination? Is that right?"

"Take a look ahead. What do you think?"

Louis glanced at the stop-motion images stretching almost beyond the limits of his vision. His earlier prediction was almost spot on. Although he couldn't quite yet make out The Tower at the end of the boulevard, he reckoned it would only be a matter of a few more paces before it materialized out of the dark horizon.

"So it's not just my mind that determines the size of my Sphere of Illumination, but my spirit-body as well?"

"Now you're getting it. *The Plenitude* can only be experienced within a framework. You might not be able to do much about the size of your body, but you can certainly keep it healthy and in good working order. The mind, however, is different. It exists on a different level not bound by the restraints in physical size. That's where choices and free will come in to play. Do you want to experience *The Plenitude* with a small mind, or a big mind?"

"So Dolly Parton was right? Bigger *is* best."

"Bigger just means more. It's up to you to determine whether that's best or not."

Louis had never considered that his mind could grow. Sure, babies grew into toddlers, toddlers grew into children, children grew into adults, and their minds developed accordingly. But once someone reached twenty-one or thereabouts, that was it, wasn't it? Their body had stopped growing. So too their mind. Everyone knew that. In fact, he could almost argue that it got a hell of a lot worse from then on. Once someone reached the beginning of their third decade, once the alcohol and drugs and stress started kicking in, the brain cells began to die at a rapid rate. Before long you couldn't remember the names of your grandchildren or where you put your damned glasses.

And from then on in, it's just a short slide to Alzheimer's and adult diapers, Louis my boy.

They continued on without saying much, passing block after block of mini-markets, video stores, retail outlets and Happythecaries, and he eventually discovered which boulevard they were on, Boulevard 13, his lucky number. The tunnel-riddled cliff face gradually shrank behind them, like a wall sinking into the ground, until he looked over his tail for one last time and saw that it had disappeared altogether, just the buildings and cutout images stretching into the past. Up ahead, The Tower grew from a speck on the horizon to the size of a three-story building, prying the sky-vault away from the ground like a giant jack, inch-by-inch, until before long it was looming high above them. Strangely, the power of its logo was virtually non-existent, as if *Zipping* had completely nullified its mind-hold. The dark horizon, he saw, had also disappeared.

Two blocks from the hotel, he suddenly stopped and said, "I've been thinking. The *Immensity*. I'm part of it, aren't I?"

"You are part of *The Plenitude*, and *The Plenitude* is part of you," *The Master* said, smiling. "There's no escaping it."

Chapter 34

Address to Shareholders

THE lobby of the LeMont Hotel was empty as a supermarket on Good Friday when Louis and *The Master* passed through to the conference center. They entered via one of the rear exits. Looking down the aisle, Louis was surprised to see the auditorium as vacant as the lobby. He had expected to see every seat occupied with suit and ties absorbing the latest figures and forecasts of LeMont International Enterprises. Instead, the microphone on the podium stood alone and Louis was left wondering whether he and *The Master* had missed the AGM all together. The realist inside him was kind of wishing it were true.

"I've saved you a lot of time and boredom by *Zipping* you straight to your speech," *The Master* said, popping Louis' bubble of hope. "The AGM can sometimes drag on for months. I didn't think you'd want to sit around listening to every speaker."

Heading down the aisle and taking position on the empty podium, Louis' stop-motion images parted with those of *The Master*, who sometime in the not too distant future was going to take a seat at the end of row B, presumably next to Santosa's wheelchair. As a backdrop to the podium, a large banner occupied the entire wall: L.I.E Annual General Meeting. Complete with the alpha-omega logo and caption, *Your Friend For Eternity*.

"Where the hell is everyone? You sure they haven't already gone."

"You can't see them yet. We haven't *un-Zipped* and re-entered their timeframe."

A whopping dose of stage fright then suddenly seized him with icy claws. It started right in the middle of his gut, frosty and malignant, then quickly spread to his upper and lower body, as though he was being deep frozen from the inside out. He felt completely rigid, a goddamn ice statue.

"I… I don't know what to say to them."

The instant the words plopped out, his stop-motion images split into two, as they had done along the boulevard on the way here. One set of images continued to deliver the speech behind the microphone, while the other set that had just blinked into existence sprinted for the nearest exit and disappeared from the auditorium.

The Master grabbed his paw. "Look at me!"

Louis only had eyes for the fleeing images. As he stared, they seemed to take on an increasingly firmer, more focused appearance. Those at the microphone began to flicker and fade. As he stared, Lady Di popped up again in the back of his mind, surprising him like someone he thought was still overseas on holiday. *You know what's happening here, don't you Louis? Your internal aerial is tuning into the reality you hope will happen. You have to ask yourself some serious questions, dear. Is this what you really want?*

"Look at me!" *The Master* said again, this time more forcefully.

Even knowing the images exiting the auditorium had him in a mind-hold didn't make one goddamn bit of difference. He just couldn't take his eyes off them, and he knew – he just damn well *knew* – that he wasn't able to go through with the Freedom Fighter's plans.

Suddenly, he caught a waft of horseshit. Then somewhere distant, as though *The Master* was now shouting at him from the podium, he heard her telling him to look at her again. Angry at the loss of buttered popcorn, he sniffed the air again. He was about to turn and complain when he felt a horrendous sting down the side of his face, all the way from his temple to his jaw. Even his ear began to ring.

Louis turned to *The Master*, rubbing his cheek, and said, "Why'd you do that? I thought you couldn't…"

The Master lowered her paw. "We're *un-Zipping*. I had no choice. You'd gone faithless again on me. I thought we'd lost you for good this time."

Louis sniffed the air again and grimaced. He now thought he could hear other voices, whispers coming from the front of the auditorium, though as yet he still couldn't see anyone apart from *The Master*. Even the stop-motion images had vanished. "You should have let me go," he said.

"We need you. *When The Tower does fall, He will come*."

He reckoned if he heard that goddamn prophecy one more time he was going to strangle someone. Someone small and in a long blue dress. "You're sure they'll believe me?"

"This is your forum. This is what they'll remember when the sky-vault collapses."

"What about The Boss?"

"He'll keep his distance. He won't dare show his face, not even in the midst of tragedy. Especially not; he'll be lynched. His citizens will be looking for someone to blame as well as to save them from the mess they'll find themselves in."

From out of nowhere, the walls of the auditorium began to shake. Louis held onto an adjacent seat to steady himself, hoping like hell The Tower wasn't going to collapse right at this moment. He wanted to be a good couple of miles away when it finally happened, somewhere nice and goddamn safe. Like Conduit Number 1.

"You'd better hurry," *The Master* said. The rumbling began to die down and Louis felt confident enough to let go of the seat. "The audience is expecting to see you at the front, not up here. It might look a bit suspicious what you've been up to."

The whispers were getting louder, so they hurried down toward the podium. At row B, *The Master* took the aisle seat and wished him luck. "What do I tell them?" Louis asked. "I haven't prepared anything."

"Just speak from experience. It's what they want to hear."

Louis adjusted his tie and straightened his jacket, thinking of the hundreds of social and professional talks he had given over the course of his life. To his frustration, he couldn't remember the details of a single damn one, not even a title.

You're just going to have to make it up as you go along, Louis my boy. There's nothing else you can do.

"One word of advice, though," *The Master* said. "Speak in the language they understand. There's no point speaking French to the Chinese."

Louis nodded and climbed up the short steps to the podium, getting behind the microphone just in the nick of time. Like someone switching on the lights to a surprise party, the shareholders suddenly blinked into existence. Jackals, rats, ferrets and weasels crammed the auditorium, waiting for him to say something. Santosa was there in his wheelchair, in the aisle at row B next to *The Master* (Tiffany Tidbits, he reminded himself, she's not *The Master* in this crowd), but to his surprise Flash Freddy and Smiggins were nowhere to be seen. The whispering he had heard were the shareholders getting restless. He must have *un-Zipped* at a point in time where he had been saying nothing at the microphone for quite a while. Not the best goddamn introduction he could think of.

"Come on, Louis!" It was the Grand Pooh-Bah, pulling his oxygen mask away from his face. "We haven't got all day."

Louis heard sniggering echo around the auditorium. A jackal in row D shouted for him to get on with it. "Speak the language they understand," he muttered, adjusting his tie and glancing at Tiffany for moral support. She stared back with big unblinking eyes. A weasel in row F yelled out, "Cat got your tongue?" which brought more chuckles and sniggering from the audience. He had to say something. Goddamn anything, before they started walking out on him. Surprisingly, it was Lady Di that got the ball rolling.

Start by telling them what you told me when we first met, Louis dear. You charmed me off my feet. You can do the same to them.

Louis had never considered himself a charmer. He wasn't a Flash Freddy (*Spank'n rich and spank'n good look'n*), capable of sweeping women away with poetic words and a captivating smile. Just a farmer at heart, someone who put in the long hard hours plowing the field until the crops grew, then reaped his reward. It was certainly news to him that Lady Di had been swept off her feet. What he had said at the dinner party where they met was nothing fancy, just…

"Good evening. My name is Louis DeVille."

The whispering and sniggering stopped as abruptly as the shareholders had rematerialized. He thought he even saw the corners of Tiffany's mouth turn up ever so slightly.

"Although, I don't know about you, but since I've arrived in LeMont I've found it difficult to tell whether it's evening, or night, or morning or afternoon. So maybe I'll just stick with good day." Most of the shareholders chuckled, this time in recognition.

That's better, Louis, he sighed. *Just keep it going.*

"As this is my first report to the AGM, most of you don't know who I am. My position at LeMont, as defined in great detail in my contract," and there were a few more chuckles of recognition, "is that of Interim Management Consultant. I've been headhunted to oversee the restructuring of the entire LeMont Corporation." He then pointed to the banner hanging on the back wall: L.I.E Annual General Meeting. *Your Friend For Eternity.* "I guess I'm a bit of a Mr. Fix-It, although my role is a rather simple one: to help maintain the LIE. Goebel, the Nazi propaganda minister, put it succinctly: 'If you tell a lie often enough, people will swallow it.' My job then, is to help The Boss tell the lie as often as possible in as many different ways as possible. And in my experience, the only way to get our message out to the *cosmopolitan* masses is to speak the common language of the masses. Money."

The shareholders applauded politely and Santos nodded in his wheelchair, smiling through his oxygen mask. "Money talks," he said. "You've all heard that saying before. What you might not have heard is that money talks a thousand languages, one everybody can understand. Money cuts through all barriers. Race. Sex. Age. Money is the universal language, the language of the soul."

A good majority were bobbing their heads in agreement and mumbling to one another. *You've hit the right note, Louis my boy. They're warming to you. Keep this up and they'll be eating out of your paw.*

"As LeMont's Mr. Fix-It, there are two questions I have to ask myself," he said. "Firstly, what is good about the system that's already in place? And secondly, what isn't good? In other words, what works and what doesn't?" He straightened the cuffs on his jacket and flattened his tie over his chest and belly. "Let's begin with the first, the things I've observed the LeMont Corporation doing well. In my old job as CEO of a major pharmaceutical company, the negotiation of a contract took precedence over everything else. I did all I could to get the signature on the dotted line. Why, you ask? Well, it's not what's in the contract that's important. It's the transference of power. The Boss knows that. That's why he insists all newbies sign a working contract when they arrive; it forces them to commit to him and the rules with which he governs the corporation, a voluntary handing over of power that becomes legal once they've put pen to paper. And the law, as we all know, is on the side of whoever has the most money."

"You're right there!" a rat in row M yelled.

The shareholders chuckled again and Louis nodded in acknowledgement.

"Have you ever heard of an employee having more money than the employer? No, of course not. That would destabilize the balance of power. The employee would be forced to buyout the employer to redress the situation; and what kind of place would LeMont become if the employees had all the power?" The shareholders along row A shook their head in dismay at the very idea of it. "Not a pretty thought, is it?" Louis continued. "Contracts have to stay. They must continue to be as complicated as possible. Every loophole must be removed. Unbreakable, so that even if an employee did decide to contest it in the courts they would be bogged down for years, or for as long as their money ran out and couldn't afford to continue. Contracts must continue to be to the benefit of the employer. They must continue to be the cornerstone of Industrial Relations, the foundation upon which the LIE is built."

The shareholders erupted in spontaneous applause. Louis flattened his tie against his chest, absorbing the praise, then gestured for them to be silent. "The other things LeMont does well are minor in comparison, but I'll briefly mention them anyway," he said, as the applause died down. "It goes without saying that a monopoly is the ideal for which any corporation should strive to achieve. Globalization achieves this aim. With globalization comes control, and with control comes power, and with power comes money. The circle is complete. Not only must a corporation take control of a market, it must grow so overwhelmingly huge that it *becomes* the market. There must be no room for anyone else, for with competition comes a loss of power, and a loss of power equates to a slow and protracted death. A part of our philosophy in maintaining the LIE should therefore be: smother before we are smothered." He paused briefly, eyeing the auditorium. "Globalization is the blanket with which we will smother our competitors."

"Hear, hear!" yelled a ferret in Row M, followed by mumbles of approval from the other shareholders.

"The promise of instant wealth," Louis said, cutting in. "Now there's something else LeMont does extremely well. Lotteries. Betting agencies. The idea that all our problems can be solved with money is brilliant, just brilliant. The only improvement I can suggest would be the construction of a casino and improving access to gaming machines. They should be everywhere. Mini-markets, shopping centers, restaurants, bars and clubs. The more the better. Churches, mosques, temples too; get them on board." Louis paused. He was starting to get a little ahead of himself. "Oh, and I should also add that worshipping the Money Tree is a spark of genius. Religion. I couldn't have come up with anything better to help maintain the LIE. Everyone needs to believe in something bigger than them self. It gives them hope. Why not money? Is there anything bigger?"

A jackal in row P held up a lotto ticket and waved it about. "I believe!"

"Hallelujah brother!" Louis said.

The biggest laughter of the speech so far rocked the auditorium, and Louis chuckled. *Santosa is goddamn right. You're in the wrong job, Louis my boy. You should be a standup.*

"Seriously though, two last points on what LeMont is doing right before I move on to where we need to improve." Louis flattened his tie across his chest and toyed with the buttons on his jacket. "Protocols. The Boss has it right, yet again. They should be just as complicated and confusing as contracts. Think of them as another layer of control. They force the employee to follow a set of instructions laid down by the employer, preventing them from using common sense and taking initiative. An employee must be trained to think how the employer wants them to think. Or even better, *not* to think, to become a robot, for everyone here knows that an employee with initiative is the most dangerous kind of employee of all."

The shareholders chuckled and Louis glanced at the seat next to the Grand Pooh-Bah. Tiffany's expression was deadpan, giving nothing away. He just hoped he was doing the right thing.

Goddamn it, I don't know what else to say. You told me to speak from experience and talk in the language they understand. That's exactly what I'm doing.

Just as he was about to continue, another minor quake shook the auditorium. The podium trembled beneath his feet and the microphone teetered back and forth. Louis grabbed it, as much to steady himself as to prevent it toppling over. *Please, not now. Not yet. I'm not ready.* The audience stared back, not bothered at all, and after a moment the rumbling moved on and the floorboards calmed beneath his feet.

"I've probably saved the best to last," he said, regaining his composure. "Inbuilt Obsolescence. A concept I wasn't totally familiar with until I arrived at LeMont. Now I see the beauty in it. If everything breaks down, the consumer keeps buying, the monopoly is reinforced and the LIE is maintained. Goddamn poetry in motion. I just wish I had thought of it when I was alive."

He cast his eye over the shareholders. That was the easy bit done. Now he had to give the hard sell. Make them believe he was the real deal otherwise *The Master's* plan was going to collapse around his whiskers like The Tower. As it was, she wasn't looking happy with the way things were preceding.

Not damn happy at all.

Chapter 35

When The Tower Does Fall

LOUIS continued to scan across the heads of the shareholders, going over his mind several things he wanted to say before he got the hell out of here. That they were hooked on every word he spoke wasn't in question. Whether they went the whole way, hook, line and sinker, well, that was another question all together. It had been one thing to get the board of a rival company to sit down at the negotiation table and to listen to his sales pitch when he was CEO of Global Resolutions Network, then something completely different to get them to sign on the dotted line. The difference couldn't be quantified or manufactured and sold in a goddamn Happythecary. It was like Flash Freddy's charm, or the X-factor all the movie producers looked for in a future star. You either had it, or you didn't.

"As I've said, in my short time at LeMont I have observed many things that are being done well to maintain the LIE." He motioned once again to the banner hanging behind him. "There are a few things, however, that I feel have room for improvement. Think of what I'm about to say as advice from a financial manager. Not as a criticism, but as a few tricks of the trade from someone who knows the game. Someone who's been there, made the mistakes, and learned from them."

A few shareholders in row A shifted awkwardly in their seats, especially three rats sitting closest to the aisle.

"From what I've seen, everything happens a little too slow in LeMont. To use a colleague's turn of phrase, everyone is too comfortable. The problem is age. We have an ancient population and it's only getting older. Too much dead wood. I notice there are no children in LeMont. Why is that? Is it a policy decision? Or is something that's just happened? I'm not suggesting we get children into the workforce – they're not efficient, no matter what anyone says – but I am suggesting an infusion of youth. There's an unwritten law I have termed, for want of a better name, Lady Di's Law. It says: *Age is inversely proportional to the economic benefit of society.*"

He didn't say how he came to that conclusion. The first draft of the law he came up with when Ronald Reagan was still the president and not the airport. It went: *Women* are inversely proportional to the economic benefit of society. Based purely on his own experience of watching his wife spend every goddamn cent he had. But he didn't have time for that now.

"Youth is the way forward for any corporation," he said. "Why? Because they inject pace, and pace is the key to success. Give me pace in my legs than a wise old head any day."

Santosa was nodding, Tiffany, however, continued to stare back with big doubtful eyes.

"LeMont needs an injection of speed if it wants to continue being Number One. It needs faster food, faster travel, faster services, faster everything. Fast. Fast. Fast. Especially things that get employees into debt, like banking and insurance. Loan approvals in ten minutes. House and contents insurance in less than five." He pointed to a ferret in row L. "You, sir. What day is it today?"

The ferret scratched his head. "Um... I think it's..."

"Too slow!" Louis pointed to a rat in row A. "You, sir. Can you tell me what day it is?"

The rat stared back at him with blank eyes, but Louis didn't wait for an answer. He moved onto a weasel way up the back in Row W, someone who probably thought she would never be asked. The weasel also took her time, too much time for Louis. He moved on to a mouse closer at hand, one who was sitting next to a toad in a wheelchair. She didn't answer, as he thought she wouldn't, but Santosa pulled his oxygen mask down beneath his double chin, and said, "It's Satanday. What's your point?"

"I thought it was Fryday," said the rat in front of him.

Someone else in row F thought it was Moanday.

"This is exactly my point," Louis said. "Everything must be done at a pace that's so quick nobody knows what day of the week it is. The faster our lifestyle – and I'll get more onto that in just a minute – the more confused everyone will be, and the easier it is to maintain the LIE. No one will have the time to sit down and think about what's really going on. They'll continue to live as they are told to live, no questions asked."

The three rats in row A ahead of the Grand Pooh-Bah glanced at one another and nodded. Louis breathed a sigh of relief.

"An emerging trend I noticed in the years before I died, something I think will catch on in LeMont, is the idea of *lifestyle*. By lifestyle I mean anything and everything from the clothes we wear, to renovating the kitchen and bathroom, to the career we have, to where we dine and drink our cocktails. It's the whole kit and caboodle, all rolled into one. And it's perfect for maintaining the LIE." He took the microphone off the stand and held it to his mouth. "Here's how it works. We'll have a two-stage marketing attack. Hit them in waves. Firstly, we blitz the city with advertising – billboards, radio, TV, cinema. Basically, our aim is to sell the actual concept of a lifestyle as a *product*. Specifically: how to get *more* out of life by upgrading to a better one than what we already have. If Mr. and Mrs. Jones next door have more than us, then we need to do something about it. The employees of LeMont have to feel that their current lifestyle is inadequate, that there's always something bigger and better."

Louis moved closer to the edge of the podium, dragging the microphone cord behind him. He was beginning to feel like an evangelist preaching to the congregation. *Forget standup, I should be on TV. Have my own goddamn station. Entertainment Religion. Now there's an idea: "Louis DeVille's Hour of Praise." The money will roll in.*

"The next phase of attack," he said, closing the lid on his runaway thoughts, "is to then sell the idea that our products will give our employees the lifestyle they are now seeking. We'll package it all together and call them, say, Lifestyle Choices."

He nodded to himself. *That was good. That was damn good. Maybe I should forget religion as well. Maybe I should get into advertising.*

Keeping the microphone to his mouth, he went on: "What

we're really doing is hooking the employees into an eternity of non-achievement, of constantly believing that they can't be happy or safe or appreciated without our Lifestyle products. Happiness isn't something that comes freely from within; it's something that has to be acquired. You see, we can't actually maintain the LIE without the voluntary involvement of the employees. It's *them* that perpetuate it. We just get the ball rolling and give it a nudge now and then when it looks like slowing down. We literally have to be on the ball ourselves. Always watching. Always coming up with new ideas on how to keep believing the LIE."

He moved along the edge of the podium, almost dancing the Fox Trot with the microphone. Man, he was flying. Now he knew how rock stars felt. He could almost feel a song coming on... *And she's buy-yigh-yigh-ying a stairway to heaven*...Where were the screaming women? Where were the lady's underpants thrown on stage?

You old romantic, Louis, he chuckled. *Now you're just getting carried away*.

"And just how do we keep the ball rolling? I hear you ask. It's not as difficult as you may think. Once the system is set up, it's virtually self-perpetuating. Once we've convinced the employees that their lifestyle is a product to buy, maintaining the LIE then simply involves reminding them that the key to having everything is money. In the old days it was called brainwashing. Nowadays it's called targeted marketing. Did you know that the average child sees twenty thousand junk food adds a year? Twenty thousand! That's the level to which we have to strive."

He paused only briefly, letting the facts sink into the minds of his audience. "Our marketing pitch will be both direct and indirect. Direct is easy. We already have the Home Shopping Channel doing exactly that, and the only thing I'm going to elaborate on is that it should be more entertaining. In fact, everything should be an entertainment – newspapers, religion, banking, home improvement, education. Entertainment should become an integral part of our lifestyle. It should be the oil in the engine. Why? Because if we keep the employees laughing, they'll keep working for us." He paused again. "It all comes back to control, in all its multitude of forms."

He had now reached the end of the podium. He spun adroitly and headed back toward the center where he had started, stepping neatly over the lagging cord like he had done this sort of thing a million times. He could feel every set of eyes following him.

"TV is a vital medium of control. We should have more channels. Fill the airwaves with entertainment. Perpetuate the LIE with game shows – Wheel of Fortune, The Price is Right, Who Wants To Be A Millionaire?" His pace quickened in step with his flow of ideas. "But in my experience, it's the indirect, subtle approach that works better. We transmit our message in such a way that it seeps into the psyche of the employees and actually becomes a *part* of who they are. Once it's ingrained in the mind, the message begins to direct how they think, and how they think is how they act. Which is our end goal, is it not? Mass manipulation for profit?"

Out of the corner of his eye, he caught Tiffany making sure that Santosa's oxygen mask was correctly sited over his face. "Marketing, as I have already said, is about mind control, and the mind is controlled easier and longer when a scalpel is used instead of a sledge hammer. Maintaining the LIE, ladies and gentlemen, is the removal of free will in such a way that nobody knows that it's gone."

He had already reached the other side of the podium. The auditorium was so quiet he could hear someone sniffing in the back row.

"How then, do we fool our employees into believing they still have free will when in fact we have already taken it away from them?" He was almost finished now, building up to his climax. He spun, head down, returning to the center of the podium, then faced the audience and said, "We make the employees believe they still have the power of choice. But here's the clincher. We provide them with choices from our own range of lifestyle products. Freedom of choice therefore becomes an *illusion*, because we control the very menu from which they make that choice. They don't know it, but everything they choose is to LeMont's benefit. The system always wins. LeMont will continue to profit for eternity. The LIE has been maintained for ever and ever. Amen."

The ovation was spontaneous and thunderous. Shareholders in every row stood and cheered and called out his name. Some punched the air, whooping and hollering. Even the whole of row A was standing and applauding. Louis bowed in appreciation, taking it all in.

"You're the weasel!" he heard someone yell.

A loud cheer went up. A section of the crowd in the back row started stamping their feet. "LOUIS! LOUIS! LOUIS!"

Louis straightened, glancing along the aisle to row B. The Grand Pooh-Bah was applauding in his wheelchair, his oxygen mask dangling beneath his chin; but the cheering crowd, to Louis' dismay, had swamped Santosa's little helper in a sea of ecstasy. It was useless to even try to keep looking for her.

He put the microphone back on its stand and waved to the crowd. The foot stamping spread down the rows to row D, causing the podium to tremble like the quake that had passed through earlier.

It's a goddamn stampede, he mused.

"LOUIS! LOUIS! LOUIS!"

The stamping got louder and louder, quicker and quicker. Whooping and hollering. Yelling and screaming. He couldn't hear himself think. All he needed were the red, white and blue streamers, the confetti, the balloons, and he could run for the goddamn presidency.

"LOUIS! LOUIS! LOUIS!"

The podium was now trembling so much it was difficult to keep his balance, like standing on a trampoline with fifteen goddamn kids bouncing all around. He made a grab for the teetering microphone, but it fell over just before he wrapped his claws around it. Dust dislodged from the ceiling and floated down on all the shareholders, coating his jacket.

There's your confetti, Louis.

"LOUIS! LOUIS! LOUIS!"

He still couldn't see Tiffany, and it was starting to concern him. He had done what had been asked of him and now he didn't know where to take it next. Goddamn it, he needed her. He needed direction.

Then at that moment, something large fell from the ceiling. It smashed into the middle of the auditorium with such a force he was thrown off his feet, hurling him backward. The banner was dislodged from the wall, crumpling to the podium like a mainsail that had been ripped loose by a sudden gust of wind. The stamping and chanting fell into silence. One second they had been screaming his name, the next as if *The Master* had *Zipped* them out of existence.

Louis propped himself up, wondering what the hell had just happened, then dragged himself to his feet. Had the stomping and chanting loosened a chandelier from its bolts? Is that what had fallen? He dismissed the idea immediately. He had only seen chandeliers in the lobby. Besides, this thing was massive, at least half the size of the goddamn room. He shook his head, trying to clear his thoughts. It was difficult to see even to row A. Dust was everywhere. He could hear a few splutters and coughs coming from somewhere behind the swirling cloud. Someone else had started to moan, a confused sound, like someone knew they were hurt but didn't know how the hell it had happened. He staggered to the edge of the podium and cleared his throat.

"Is everyone all right?" he shouted.

Nobody answered. Just more spluttering coughs and moans.

He repeated himself, and again he wasn't answered. "Tiffany! Santosa! Can you hear me?"

When neither answered, a surge of dread swelled up inside and began to overwhelm him. He looked up to see where the thing had come from, and for a brief second was struck with confusion. Then he understood the cause. He was no longer looking at the ceiling. He was looking at the goddamn sky-vault.

"What the hell?" he said.

Almost the entire ceiling had vanished, like he was now standing in the middle of an open-air amphitheater. From the dust cloud more shareholders began to moan and splutter and cough. What was he supposed to do now? This wasn't in *The Master's* plan. He figured the first thing he had to do was leave the building. It wasn't safe to hang around.

Got to look after Number One, Louis. You know the drill.

He cautiously made his way off the podium to the aisle, feeling his way along the seats of row A, wondering where the hell the shareholders had gone. There should have been bodies at least. At row B, Santosa's wheelchair was also missing, so too his little helper. He didn't even get to row C. A massive crater had swallowed half the goddamn auditorium, and the only thing that had prevented him from stepping over the edge and plummeting to its depths was the twisted frame of the aisle seat. To his despair, the crater was between him and the only way out. He took a step back, trying to peer into it, but the dust made visibility almost impossible. "You have to test its depth," he said to himself. "You have to find a way through it."

Summoning his courage, he shuffled forward, careful not to slip over the jagged rim. He still couldn't see, so he crouched on his knees. "Hello! Anyone down there?" he called. Strangely, his voice seemed to echo, but nobody replied, only the moans and coughing from the auditorium. Looking around for something to drop, he found only the twisted wreckage of the aisle seat.

It'll have to do, he thought, and pushed it over the precipice, listening to it fall.

It didn't drop very far, less than two seconds for it to thud into the bottom. He shuffled on his knees to the edge as far as he dared to go. At that moment, a draft of warm air blew away the swirling dust inside the crater. Then the air fell still and the dust began to close in again, but it was more than sufficient to give Louis a sight of what had fallen through the ceiling. He froze, locked in a mind-hold.

The alpha-omega logo was staring straight back up at him.

Chapter 36

He Will Come

THOUGH he knew the logo had no power other than what he gave it, Louis still couldn't find a release from the mind-hold. It was as if some lingering fear was still exerting itself over him, a ghost of the past he couldn't exorcize, telling him that he had no choice than to give in to it.

There is no escape. There is no escape. There is no escape.

Something then moved at the bottom of the crater between him and the logo, breaking the mind-hold. The dust was still settling and he couldn't quite see through the goddamn stuff. Nevertheless he got off his knees, not quite believing it could happen for a second time, hoping all the same that it had.

"Who's down there?" he asked. "Show yourself!"

Nobody answered, though several seconds later, at a rare silence between the moans and coughing, he heard the sound of rubble dislodging inside the crater. Then he saw a flash of movement through the dust, something that looked like a long tail. He had been right. Someone was definitely down there.

Behind him, several shareholders started moaning again. He tried to ignore them, focusing on what was happening in the dark hole in front of him. He heard a scrape, and then more rubble dislodging to the bottom. His eyes blinked open with alarm. Something was climbing the walls of the crater. Maybe it wasn't the White Rabbit. Maybe it was the goddamn peelers. But what did they want? Surely they weren't still after him. Not after *that* speech. He deserved a goddamn promotion, not an interrogation.

"Who… who's there?" he said.

Out of the settling dust a face appeared. Louis took a step back. "Louis? I don't believe it. Is that you? To be sure, you're a sight for sore eyes."

Louis stared at the guinea pig peering up out of the crater. "Frank O'Lynn? What the hell are you doing down there? Are you hurt?"

"To be sure, I'll live," Frank O'Lynn said, but it was a joke Louis didn't find amusing. Scratching a fleabite on his cheek, Frank O'Lynn glanced around at the auditorium, then up at the gaping wound that used to be the roof. His eyes were big and round and Louis could see in them a flood of incomprehensibility, a sudden realization that he had been an integral part of the cause of this destruction. All around, the moaning and coughing was swelling by the second. Visibly graying at what he was hearing, Frank O'Lynn found his voice. "We must leave, Louis. To be sure…" He cleared his throat, though it didn't seem to do much good. It sounded like an old LP record found in his grandfather's attic, scratchy and covered in dust. "To be sure, it's not safe."

Louis reached across to help him out of the crater.

"No. This way." Frank O'Lynn kept scratching his cheek as he had, then disappeared beneath the rim. Louis looked over as another warm draft cleared the dust inside the crater. Frank O'Lynn was already standing on top of the alpha-omega logo, but there was absolutely no way in hell he was going down there. The guinea pig then pointed somewhere to the side that Louis couldn't quite see. "There's a tunnel. To be sure, it's the only way."

Louis glanced over his tail. It was still difficult to make out anything inside the auditorium through the dust. "What about *The Master*? She's gone. I can't find her or Santosa. They might be hurt."

"She's probably *Zipped* somewhere before The Tower collapsed. To be sure, she'll be all right." He was now scratching his other cheek. "Come on! Hurry! The peelers will be here any minute."

Another moan nearby made Louis jump, jolting a memory: *When The Tower does fall, He will come.* "Shouldn't I stay and help? Isn't this the prophecy?"

"Forget the prophecy," Frank O'Lynn said, clambering off the logo onto surrounding rubble. To Louis' surprise, a Snipe was stuck to his back, one he couldn't yet read. "To be sure, the whole thing's a massive failure. Why do you think *The Master* didn't hang around?" He now pointed to the open roof. "The sky-vault is still there. Can't you see? The plan didn't work. If you don't come with me now, I'm leaving you. Give my regards to the peelers."

Louis peered further over the rim. He could see the cone of rubble Frank O'Lynn had used to clamber up to the top of the crater and then down again, figuring he didn't have much choice.

Here we go, Louis, he chuckled to himself. *When The Tower does fall, He will run away.*

He slid his bottom half over the edge, feeling for purchase with his feet. His first foothold dislodged a small rock, which bounced to the bottom and cracked in half. His next was okay, firmer and more stable, and within less than a minute found himself standing on top of the alpha-omega logo.

"This way," Frank O'Lynn said from the tunnel.

Louis' eyes took a second to adjust. The problem wasn't so much the lack of light, but the dust. From what he could gather, the logo had crashed through the roof of the auditorium and then through the floor weakened by the underground tunnel. "I presume this is the tunnel the Freedom Fighters used to undermine The Tower," he said.

"One of them." Now scratching a fleabite on his snout, Frank O'Lynn headed further into the tunnel. At his feet, the head of a pick lay next to its broken shaft. "There's one beneath every boulevard."

Louis headed off after him, almost at a trot. He was now close enough to read the Snipe: I BELIEVE IN MIRACLES. As they followed the tunnel away from the piazza, the moans from the auditorium grew fainter and the dust less irritating. He saw more evidence of the Freedom Fighter's tunneling scattered here and there – picks and shovels, the occasional wheelbarrow tipped on its side, even crude benches hacked at regular intervals out of the wall. The tunnel could easily accommodate three jackals side-by-side, with plenty of room above, and seemed to head in a perfectly straight line, like the boulevard above it. He was not surprised to see the walls radiating that same shadowless, Glow-In-The-Dark grayness he remembered from his original holding cell.

"Are you sure this is the best way? What if the peelers find it?" he said. "We'll be trapped. We can't *Pop* yet; the ether-channel is still open. And none of us knows how to *Zip*."

Frank O'Lynn didn't break stride. If anything, he went faster. "What do you suggest? It's madness outside. The streets are crammed. You can't move. Anyway, that's the first place the peelers will be looking for us." He shook his head, now scratching his flea-bitten ear. "To be sure, it's better this way. By the time the peelers discover the tunnel, we'll be long gone."

Louis hurried behind, finding it difficult to keep up and hoping to hell *The Partridge* was right. They continued at a frantic pace for hours. The tunnel didn't deviate from its line. There were no tributary tunnels branching to either side, no air vents to the surface, just an interminably long pipeline that Louis figured must have taken thousands and thousands of years to chisel out with pick and shovel.

And for what? The whole affair is a goddamn mess.

"Where are we going anyway?" he asked.

"Plan B. We have to regroup and go into hiding. Bide our time. Wait until the heat is off. It could be thousands of years." Louis didn't like the graveness of his expression, and with every step he liked it less and less. Although they could use eternity to wait it out, time was not on their side. It was like having a million dollars in the bank but not being able to use it. Rich but poor. *The Partridge* suddenly halted in his tracks and peered over his tail, his ears pricked.

"Did you hear something?"

Louis faced down the tunnel. A warm draft breezed past, bringing with it an unbearable stench of horseshit. *I'm in a goddamn sewer*, he thought, almost gagging.

"To be sure, it's probably nothing," Frank O'Lynn said, and hurried off. An hour or so later, he stopped again and pricked his ears. This time, Louis could have sworn he had heard something too. A voice, or voices, echoing down the tunnel. "To be sure, they've found it quicker than I thought." Frank O'Lynn was now whispering. "Come. They're still a way behind. We can still make it before they catch up."

Louis goddamn hoped so, but after three more hours of hurried trotting the voices got noticeably louder. No more than harsh whispers, but Louis didn't need to be an Olympic sprinter to know they were losing ground. Frank O'Lynn was getting increasingly nervous and the end was nowhere in sight. "How much further?" Louis asked.

"Not far. Trust me." He was now running.

Four hours later, however, they were still fleeing down the goddamn sewer. Louis could now distinguish at least half a dozen voices behind, although they hadn't gained as much as he had initially feared. The echo was distorting his judgment, making them sound closer than they actually were. At that moment, before he could ask how much further, they stopped at a sheer wall. Footholds had been gouged into it, cupped with the wear and tear of thousands of years of use. He followed them up to the tiny mouth, three-quarters or so of a mile above.

"What's wrong?" Frank O'Lynn asked, one foot already purchased in a foothold.

"I don't think I can make it. I'm exhausted. I feel like I've done back to back marathons."

"To be sure, you probably have. We're now beneath Conduit Number 1."

Louis kept staring upward at the tiny mouth. "But… but that's impossible."

Frank O'Lynn was already several yards up the wall and looking down on him. "This is the After Life. Nothing's impossible. To be sure, you're only limited by your attachments to your past existence."

Louis sighed and took a deep breath. *Just one last effort, Louis my boy. You can do it.*

He slid his claw into a foothold above his head and somehow found the energy to pull himself up. Then another. Then another.

They were smooth but not overtly slippery, enough to get a good grip and allay his fears of falling. He didn't look down, too afraid he might see a gang of peelers grinning back up at him, and he didn't look up. Instead, he kept focus on one foothold at a time, and he was soon climbing the wall as easily as he would a rope ladder.

At the top, Frank O'Lynn helped him out. They were now inside a large cavern, Louis discovered, an abandoned Chamber of the Senses the Freedom Fighters had requisitioned in the guise of LeMont Tunnels and Bridges.

"It's amazing what you can hide from the authorities behind the mask of a fake company," Frank O'Lynn said. "It's even listed on the LeMont Stock Exchange. And guess who's the majority shareholder?" He then trotted to the steps protruding from the sidewall. "Not far now. To be sure, we're almost done."

They ascended the steps to the viewing ledge and out into domed expanse of Conduit Number 1. It was eerily quiet. Louis had expected it to be mayhem, suit and ties running everywhere like headless chickens, but there was not a soul to be seen. Frank O'Lynn closed the door to the abandoned chamber and told Louis to follow. Suddenly, from the chamber directly opposite, a dozen rats burst into the tunnel, yelling and pointing. "There they are!" one of them yelled, the first one out of the door and leading the charge.

"Peelers!" Frank O'Lynn hissed, and froze to the spot.

Louis scanned left and right for a route to escape, but it was too late. The peelers had crossed with frightening speed and surrounded them in a horseshoe. Frank O'Lynn backed himself to the wall. Louis did likewise.

"Got you at last," the peeler said. "There's no escape now."

Louis felt Frank O'Lynn grab his paw. "Close your eyes," he whispered.

Louis wanted to argue that there was no goddamn point, but did as he was told. Immediately, he heard a *Pop*! Then the heavenly smell of roasted peanuts. Then almost as immediately it was gone and his snout was inundated with horseshit. For some reason rematerialization was instantaneous. He opened his eyes to the blues bar, exactly where they had left it at the table near the back wall. The room had been turned upside down, almost unrecognizable. Backless chairs were sprawled across the floor. Topless tables upturned. Glasses smashed and broken. Even the piano looked as though someone had taken a sledgehammer to it, splintered and toothless. There was certainly no plee-zant sense of happiness anymore.

"There they are!" he heard someone shout.

As he had feared, several peelers were waiting in ambush near the staircase. Two of them now rushed over the broken tables and chairs, baring their teeth, and with less than a few yards to go leaped at them with snatching claws. Louis flinched, scrunching his eyes, shielding his free paw in front of his face. His scream got stuck halfway up his throat, silenced by another sudden *Pop*! Again he caught a waft of roasted peanuts, and then just as swiftly, to his disgust, more goddamn horseshit.

"Welcome back," he heard.

Louis lowered his paw and opened his eyes. He was back in Conduit Number 1, his back to the wall with peelers closing in. "Why aren't we invisible?" he said to Frank O'Lynn. "Why did we rematerialize so soon?"

"Because the original ether-channel is still exerting its effect over us. To be sure, until it closes it treats every *Pop* we make as a continuation of the first. But I had to try." *The Partridge* then spoke to the peeler in command. "You had orders to wait until we were at the rendezvous."

"They've been changed."

"By who?"

"By the very top."

Louis looked at the guinea pig, then at the peeler, then back at the guinea pig. "You… you're a double agent?"

Frank O'Lynn scoffed, scratching a fleabite on the back of his paw. "Don't be ridiculous."

Louis felt the first prick of indignation, an itch that started in his chest and worked its way through the rest of his body, including his voice. "No wonder everybody thinks guinea pigs look like rats," he growled.

Frank O'Lynn sighed and his shoulders seemed to sag with an invisible weight. "To be sure, I had no choice. They made me an offer I couldn't refuse."

"You betrayed the Freedom Fighters. Your own friends."

Two rats grabbed Louis by the shoulder. "You're coming with us," the peeler in command said. Then he pointed to Frank O'Lynn. "I'll be back for you in a minute. You're going to take us to the others."

Louis tried to shrug the peelers off. "You know what?" he said to Frank O'Lynn. "You're a goddamn coward. You know the right thing to do and yet you don't do it."

Frank O'Lynn shrugged, still scratching the back of his paw. "Takes one to know one."

Louis tried to wiggle loose, but the peelers tightened their grip. "You're damn right," he said. "That's why I know the worst thing for a coward is to be found out; and you've been uncovered in all your ugly nakedness you good-for-noth'n son-of-a-bitch." He felt himself being picked up and dragged away, but he kept up his struggle. "You've sold yourself out. For what, false friends and promises? It'll only bring you misery. But you like that, don't you Frank? You're a goddamn frog in boiling water. Misery's the only thing you know."

When Frank O'Lynn and the remaining peelers fell out of sight, Louis stopped struggling and gave himself to his fate. There was no fight left in him anymore. What was the point? His captors dragged him through one of the tributary tunnels to a holding cell identical to the gray-room in which he had woken up after his heart attack. He let the peelers strap him to the leather layback in front of the Mirror of Truth without a word, wishing he had never woken up in this godforsaken hellhole.

They didn't take long, but before he locked the door, the peeler in command said, "Don't look so glum. The Boss has taken an extra-special interest in you. He's going to personally oversee your punishment."

Then he was gone, his laughter fading down the tunnel, and Louis was left to stare at his pathetic reflection. He then did something he hadn't done for an eternity.

He began to cry.

Chapter 37

No Escape

LOUIS didn't know how long he had been staring at his crying reflection. He hadn't dared fallen asleep, although that was exactly what he needed. He didn't dare risk another nightmare; that would have tipped him over the edge, and he wasn't prepared to fall into the abyss of insanity just yet. He was teetering, though, and it wouldn't take much to push him over. He wondered what was stopping him from jumping anyway. Become like all the other newbies strapped in front of their Mirror of Truth, wailing and gnashing his teeth for eternity.

Hope, he figured. That was probably it. He hadn't yet given up on being saved.

Was that the difference between sanity and insanity? The sane still cling to hope while the insane let it go? Or maybe it's the other way around...

Louis then heard the sound of a muffled discussion outside. Someone was talking to the peelers posted at his door, which he couldn't see in the mirror so he twisted his neck as far as he could. The knob turned and Smiggins entered, punching numbers into his calculator. Close behind him came Flash Freddy with his suitcase.

"Thank God you guys are here," Louis said. "Get me out of these goddamn shackles will you?"

Smiggins and Flash Freddy went straight to the end of the layback, standing between it and the Mirror of Truth. They had expressions like a couple of undertakers burying someone they were glad to be rid of.

"Sorry, no can do," Smiggins said.

"What? You're my goddamn PA." Louis strained against the restraints. "You'll do what you're goddamn told."

"Things have changed, Mr. DeVille. You're in no position to tell anybody what to do."

Louis turned to Flash Freddy. "Help me out here. I can explain."

Flash Freddy remained as he was, solemn and grave. His eyes were hooded. "Smiggins is in charge. As your legal council, I advise you to seriously consider what he has to say to you."

Louis stopped fighting the straps and let himself sink into the layback. "And that would be?"

Smiggins punched some more numbers and sniggered. "An offer you can't refuse."

Louis rolled his eyes. "By whose authority?" Flash Freddy and Smiggins shared a look that said, *Should we tell him now or later?* Nothing was said for several seconds. "Come on. I'm all ears."

Flash Freddy said, "Smiggins is his own authority. He's in charge of LeMont International Enterprises."

Louis stared at the rat with the calculator, suddenly blank. The void, he knew, would soon be filled with fear. "You... You're The Boss?"

Smiggins sniggered, and said, "I'm not The Boss, just the caretaker. I do the books."

"Then... what...?"

"The Boss has been missing for thousands of years. It's a secret only Flash Freddy and myself know. Now you do too."

"But... I don't understand..."

Smiggins sniggered and swished his tail from side to side. "All we have left is the system The Boss established. We've kept it running until we could find a suitable candidate to fill the vacancy. Nobody seemed to have the right credentials. Until you came along." He added with a snigger, "By all accounts, your address at the AGM brought the house down."

Louis moved from the rat, to the lizard, then back to the rat again. Their expressions hadn't changed. They were deadly serious. "Let me get this straight. You're offering me a promotion? The next CEO of LeMont, The Boss?"

Smiggins punched some numbers into his calculator. "Actually, it's a demotion," he said. "All major corporations work that way. You know that as well as anybody."

Louis recalled an argument with Lady Di one evening over dinner. He didn't remember what he had done wrong, but she was furious. *You know, Louis, in every other profession the cream rises to the top. Not in business. There* scum *rises. And you, Louis are…*

Smiggins' sniggering severed the memory. "Although the system runs pretty well without someone at the helm, it's pretty much run its course. We need someone with a vision to take LeMont into the future. You're just the weasel we've been looking for."

It beggared belief, but Louis wasn't going to be suckered in that easily. "What's the catch?"

This time the corners of the rat's mouth tweaked into something of a smile. The undertaker was back. "You'll be under house arrest for eternity," he said, and Louis felt his eyes bulge as he swallowed the words, then choked on them. "We'll build you another Tower, but you'll never be able to leave the penthouse. Flash Freddy and I will be the only contact you have with the outside world." Smiggins paused, letting him think it over. "It's as good a deal as you're likely to get. Considering your affiliation with the Freedom Fighters."

Louis took his time to chew it over. *Like a cow, Louis my boy. Digest it nice and slowly.*

Nonetheless, it was still difficult to swallow, like eating a bowl of horseshit. He had to take it though. There was no other choice, was there? Sure, he would live in absolute luxury for eternity, but at what cost? Was it better to give in and jump over the edge into the abyss of insanity now, or toss over a rope and abseil into it? Make a steady immersion into madness?

"I can't betray my friends," he said.

Smiggins glanced up from his calculator. Flash Freddy's eyes hooded into ever thinning slits. "What friends? The ones that betrayed you?"

Smiggins motioned for the lawyer to leave it be and told him to unfasten the restraints. "I want to show you something before you make up your mind," he said, and Louis hid his smile. He had managed to buy himself some time.

In less than a minute, he was off the layback and making his way through the tributary tunnel to Conduit Number 1, glad to be free again, even if it were under the escort of half a dozen peelers. He had no intention of making a dash for it, or *Popping*, or *Zipping*, or trying to goddamn fly. There was no point. He would see what they had to show him and then make his decision. He had virtually made up his mind in any case.

Smiggins and Flash Freddy said nothing until they arrived at one of the chambers. The same Chamber of Life, Louis recognized, in which he had helped to crucify the newbie when he first arrived. Through the door he could hear muted moaning and groaning: "Why hast thou forsaken me? Why hast thou forsaken me?" Not too far to his right, the pure whiteness of the Fires of Oblivion reflected off the gray conduit walls. He removed his gaze from it, not wanting to think about the prophecy any more than he had to.

That's in the past now, Louis my boy. All in the past.

Smiggins told the peelers to wait outside, then took Flash Freddy and Louis onto the observation ledge. When Louis looked down onto the first row of crucifixes, his jaw dropped. The Grand Pooh-Bah was nailed to a cross next to *The Master*, his wheelchair tipped onto its side beneath him. Next to her was Salma Gundi. They didn't see Louis at first because they were watching five peelers hoist a cross on which they had just nailed a guinea pig. He was thrashing his head from side to side and squealing at the top of his voice. The Irish accent was unmistakable: They had the wrong guy: He wasn't supposed to be here: It was all a mistake.

"Don't put him next to me," Santosa said. "He's got fleas!"

Smiggins sniggered, punching some numbers into his calculator. "As you see, Mr. DeVille, no good deed goes unpunished."

Frank O'Lynn heard the rat's voice filter down into the chamber. He looked up, spotted Louis, and screamed, "It's his fault! He betrayed us all!"

Santosa, Tiffany and Salma Gundi turned their faces up. "Why'd you do it, Louis?" Santosa said. Louis closed his hanging jaw, not knowing what to say. "What happened to Operation White Rabbit?

We were partners. I was going to give you fifty percent of Ties & Scarves. The legal documents were already drawn."

Louis turned to the cross next to Santosa. Tiffany met his gaze with big accusing eyes, saying nothing.

"See that vacant cross next to the guinea pig?" Smiggins said, and when he put his claw on his shoulder Louis was suddenly struck with a wave of revulsion so strong he almost retched. "It's got your name on it. Unless…" and he let it hang in the air for a moment.

Louis dropped his chin onto his chest and closed his eyes, trying to block out the incessant moaning and quash the nausea inside him. "I don't know what to do anymore."

"Come now. You have a career for eternity, what everyone wants. I can organize membership at the Country Club if you like, and you won't even have to go on the waiting list. You won't be able to use it, of course, but at least you'll *have* it," he said. Louis wavered, and Smiggins sensed the confusion inside him. "Do you really want to throw it all away? For what? A prophecy? A twisted sense of loyalty? You were fooled, Louis." He pointed at the fat toad on the cross beneath. "Miles N. Boon and his Freedom Fighters took you for a ride. You owe them nothing."

Louis suddenly looked up. "Santosa is Miles N. Boon? I thought…" His shoulders sagged. What did it matter? Everything he had been told was a lie.

"You were made to think whatever they wanted you to think. It's not your fault. You trusted them. They were all in it together."

"Doesn't anybody tell the goddamn truth around here?"

Smiggins sniggered and patted his shoulder. "Does anybody really know what the truth is? It's all relative anyway."

Louis turned to Flash Freddy and said, "And I suppose you're the goddamn White Rabbit?" The lizard and rat both laughed. Louis shook his head and drew a deep breath, glancing one last time at the chamber of crucifixes. "Okay. I'll do it. I'll be The Boss."

"You've made the right decision," Smiggins said, and ushered him and Flash Freddy toward the exit. "You won't regret it."

Louis stepped through the door and into the conduit. "On one condition though. You have to let them go. You can't let them suffer like that, no matter what they did."

Smiggins swished his tail and locked the door behind him. "Everybody suffers, Louis. There's no escaping it. Better to get on with what you need to do and stop worrying about it."

Louis stopped in his tracks. When he was a kid, so his mother told him, he used to sleepwalk almost every single night. Most times he would wander through to the lounge room where she was ironing or watching TV, or both, and just stand there staring up at her with sleep-drugged eyes. *The lights were on, but nobody was home*, she used to say. It never bothered her. She would simply take him by the hand and lead him back to his bedroom. Most of the time he would climb back into bed by himself. The next morning, of course, he would have absolutely no recollection of what had happened. Not even a dream.

One night, however, he apparently scared the living daylights out of her. She almost called the doctor to rush over and do something for her little boy. Louis had wandered into the lounge room wielding a large kitchen knife and demanding to know where *he* was. *He*, of course, was his father, and he wanted to kill him. Thankfully, it was poker night with his work buddies, as almost every night was. He never heard about this incident, and Louis was only told once, when she poured a vase of cold water over his head to wake him up.

"Why'd you do that?" he had said, shivering. As far as he knew, he had been sleeping. He thought he was still in bed.

"You were going crazy, Louis," she told him. "You were sleepwalking again. I couldn't get the knife off you."

Louis looked at the knife, not remembering how or when or where he had got it. He was gripping the handle so hard his knuckles were white. Then he dropped it and ran back to his bedroom, slamming the door. It wasn't the fact that he wanted to kill his old man (the good-for-nothing son-of-a-bitch deserved whatever came to him), what sent him into the grand old house in Loony

Ville was that he could walk and talk and do things and not even know he was doing it.

It was something that had bothered him for the rest of his life, but now he stared at the rats and Flash Freddy with sudden understanding – he had woken up in the gray room in front of the Mirror of Truth, and yet he hadn't woken up at all. He was still sleepwalking. Still going through the motions without realizing it.

"Everybody suffers," Smiggins had said. The words were a vase of cold water tipped over his sleep-drugged head. "There's no escaping it."

Smiggins and Flash Freddy, he saw, were staring at him. The peelers just looked at one another. They had no idea whether to laugh or tackle him to the ground.

"What's so funny?" Smiggins asked.

Louis wiped a tear from his cheek with the back of his paw. He felt so goddamn joyous, like he had just drunk a bottle of happy juice or something. "There is a way out of all this. There really *is*," he said. Suddenly, his mouth seemed to open of its own accord, effortlessly, as if he no longer had any control over what he was saying. "*Grnklpmrph nlw frpztk. Zwlkbdlvrpmh.*"

Smiggins eyes flew open and dropped his calculator. It broke into three pieces next to his feet. Flash Freddy caught his briefcase just before it slipped out of his grasp.

"What did you just say?" Smiggins asked.

"You heard me," Louis said, though he had absolutely no goddamn idea why he had quoted the first line of the prophecy. The peelers waiting by the wall seemed to tremble, and in a sudden flash of clarity he knew his opportunity had come.

Make hay while the sun shines, Louis. It was his grandfather's voice this time, and without waiting another second, while his captors were still reeling, he darted for the archway at the end of the tunnel.

Smiggins was the first to react. "Stop him!" he yelled.

Lucky for Louis, the archway was only a hundred or so yards away. He had sprung them by surprise and opened up enough of a lead to know he couldn't be caught. He was going to do it. He was really going to do it. He was going to keep running and running and running until… BAM! Instant obliteration. It was the only way out.

Smiggins shouted again, directly to Louis. "Stop! Let's talk! You don't know what you're doing."

Louis didn't look back. The archway was now less than forty yards and nothing was going to get in his way. Light was streaming through. He could feel its warmth caressing his cheeks, liking the way it made him glow from the inside out.

I'm going to do it. I'm really going to do it.

Smiggins shouted again. "Louis, stop! You're being unreasonable!"

Twenty yards now, and he could read the inscription on the golden arms. HEREBY LIES THE END OF THE WORLD. TRAVELERS PASS AT THEIR PERIL. He could almost take a flying leap and dive straight through it, but Smiggins had one last roll of the dice.

"Louis, stop! You've signed a contract!"

Louis stopped in his tracks. He was less than five yards from the wall of shimmering light; if he tripped he'd fall face first into it. Damn it! He couldn't believe he had forgotten about the contract.

"Don't do it, Louis," Smiggins said, closing in behind. "Think about what you're doing. We need you."

Louis turned his back to the Fires of Oblivion. Smiggins, Flash Freddy and the peelers had caught up but not one of them dared to come any closer.

A good old-fashioned Mexican standoff, Louis my boy. As long as you keep close to the archway, they won't dare make a grab for you.

Smiggins could sense the hesitation on his face. Not taking his gaze off Louis, he flicked his paw toward Flash Freddy. It was a few seconds before the lizard cottoned on to what he wanted. Hugging the briefcase to his chest, he removed the contract and handed it over.

"That's right, Louis," Smiggins said, holding the thick wad of paper forward. "The contract you signed at the hotel. You're an employee of LeMont International Enterprises. For eternity. It can't be broken."

Smiggins dared to take a step forward. Louis instinctively stepped back, keeping the distance nice and safe at three yards.

Smiggins froze. "Stop!" he squealed, then recovered himself. "Come now, let's be reasonable about this. Obliteration isn't any good for anybody. Nobody wins."

Suddenly, making him jerk with a start, Louis felt something brushing the back of his legs. Something fluffy and soft, like a cat rubbing itself against him. He assumed at first it was one of the peelers creeping around him while his attention was on Smiggins and Flash Freddy.

"What the…" he began to say, then stopped. He was staring into the beautiful dark eyes of the White Rabbit. Although the bell atop the arch remained silent, she must have emerged from the light behind him.

Be not afraid, she said.

Her mouth hadn't moved. He'd heard her voice telepathically inside his head, one he knew all too well.

"Dianne?" he said. "You… you're an angel?"

Be not afraid, she said again. *Follow me. It's the only way.*

Louis glanced at Smiggins and Flash Freddy. They and the peelers hadn't moved. "Do you see her? She's goddamn real. I'm not making her up. I'm not crazy."

"What are you talking about?" Smiggins said, and sniggered.

It's no use, Louis dear. They see what they want to see. Come, follow me. We must go now.

Louis glanced out of the corner of his eye at the White Rabbit (his ex-wife, a goddamn angel?), then again at Smiggins. Though the rat was staring back with savage intensity, his eyes shifted subtly toward Lady Di, a faint twitch, no more than a blink, then refocused onto Louis. Louis could feel the hatred in that stare, but he could also feel something else. Fear.

"You see her, don't you?" he said. Flash Freddy was deadpan. "You're a goddamn liar."

Louis then felt the White Rabbit brush against his side. "See what?" Smiggins said with a grin Louis didn't like. "There's nothing there."

Louis followed his stare and saw the empty space by his side where the rabbit had been. *Or where you thought she had been, Louis my boy.* He glanced over his sagging shoulders at the white light streaming through the archway. Had he just made her up? Had he made goddamn everything up? Was this all just a figment of his pathetic, weak mind?

Smiggins sniggered and held up the contract. "Come now, Louis. Let's stop all this nonsense and get back to reality. You've signed a contract with LeMont. It's your legal obligation to work for the corporation."

Suddenly, Louis felt the shackles of legality loosen its strangle hold. In a flash of instant enlightenment, everything made complete and utter goddamn sense. He felt light and free, like it used to when he sat on the back of his grandfather's tractor while he plowed the cornfield, the sun shining down on his hair, the breeze licking the freckles on his face, the feeling that something greater was nurturing and sustaining his very being, something joyous and strong and completely accepting.

"You said it yourself," he said. "Like everything else in this godforsaken city, the contract has an inbuilt obsolescence. It's a 'working contract': it's only valid for as long as I work." He smiled and stepped back, welcoming the heat that flooded through him.

"NO!" Smiggins yelled. "You can't!"

"I can, and I will," Louis said.

Two peelers made a desperate snatch for him, but they were too late. Their claws ripped the lapels of his jacket just as he fell into the abyss of light.

Obliteration was instantaneous.

Epilogue

Lo' Thou Art A Dance

LOUIS jolted awake at the sudden loudness. Goddamn warbling again. Drilling its way into his skull, shredding in his ears like an angle grinder.

WOOOO-WEEEE. WOOOO-WEEEE. WOOOO-WEEEE.

His eyelids flung open. He was flat on his back, lying on something covered in plastic sheeting. Two rats were ripping open his jacket, tearing the buttons on his shirt, yanking his tie out of the way. Trying to stick something on his chest, electrical leads or something. They'd been torturing him! That's why his chest was on goddamn fire.

WOOOO-WEEEE. WOOOO-WEEEE. WOOOO-WEEEE.

He flung out a numb left arm. It was heavy and awkward, but he managed to hit one of the dirty rats in the head. "Keep your goddamn claws off me!" he shouted, but his voice was muffled. Something was over his face, gagging him. A mask, like Santosa's, hissing and gurgling and making it impossible to speak. He tried to rip it off.

"Keep it on!" one of the rats said, grabbing his arm. "It's for your own good."

"I've heard that before," Louis shouted, fighting back control.

"He's confused," the other rat said. He was holding a syringe and needle. He depressed the plunger and a mist of fine droplets sprayed from the tip of the needle. "I'll give him this to calm him down."

WOOOO-WEEEE. WOOOO-WEEEE. WOOOO-WEEEE.

Louis struggled even harder, thrashing his head from side to side, wrenching back his arm. He suddenly stopped. On the end of the arm was a fist. It was unmistakable. A goddamn hand!

"That's better Mr. DeVille," the rat with the syringe said.

Louis opened and closed his fingers, counting them. One, two, three, four... five of them! Goddamn it, he had fingers. He brought his other hand up to his face and stared at it. Un-goddamn-believable! He opened and closed that one too, now racked with hysterical laughter. He then saw a clear plastic tube worming its way into the crook of his left elbow. It was attached to a bag of fluids above his head on a drip stand.

"What the hell?" he said to himself. "Where am I?"

WOOOO-WEEEE. WOOOO-WEEEE. WOOOO-WEEEE.

"I think you'll need something stronger," the first rat said to his colleague.

"Nothing stronger than this," his mate replied. "It's morphine."

Louis tore his gaze from his hands. They weren't rats. They were goddamn humans! Paramedics. In green overalls. Green! Not sickly gray-green, but beautiful goddamn green, like the grass, like the leaves on a tree, like the colour of freedom – the Statue of Liberty. He wanted to kiss them. He wanted to shout for joy. He was in an ambulance on his way to hospital. He was back! Goddamn it, back in the Big Apple, good ol' New York, New York, back where he belonged. It was too glorious to be true.

"Give me all the morphine you've got!" he screamed with uncontrolled laughter. "Give me everything! Absolutely-totally-undeniably everything!"

The bag above his head swayed with the motion of the ambulance while the rat with the syringe (*He's a paramedic, dear, he's saving your life*) punctured the needle through the rubber stopper, administering the drug. "I've never seen anything like it," he said.

WOOOO-WEEEE. WOOOO-WEEEE. WOOOO-WEEEE.

"I have," the other paramedic said. "Post Traumatic Hallucination Syndrome."

Louis squealed with laughter and told them to keep pumping the morphine into him. After less than half a minute, he could feel it doing its work on his body. *My overweight, aging, glorious human body*! But there was one last thing he had to do. Lifting the oxygen mask an inch from his mouth, he took a big sniff. The horseshit was gone. Just the smell of disinfectant and traffic fumes. Sighing, he let his head sink into the pillow and gestured for one of the paramedics to lean forward.

"Do you think it's possible to turn off the goddamn siren?" he asked.

The paramedic nodded, and said, "We're almost at the hospital. Shouldn't be a problem."

He then disappeared, and after a few quick words with the driver the sirens fell blissfully silent. In the background, Louis caught a familiar tune on the radio, and chuckled. The Carpenters were singing with a plee-zant sense of happiness, *I'm on the… Top of the world, Lookin'… Down on creation… And the only explanation I can fiiiind…*

The paramedic returned, squatting next to Louis' gurney, and said, "You've had a heart attack, Mr. DeVille. We're taking you to St. Mary's. You're going to be just fine."

Louis nodded through the morphine haze. He was so goddamn tired he could hardly open his mouth to speak.

"I know… I know," he said. "We all are."

The Pilgrim Chronicles

Samantha Honeycomb
by Scott Zarcinas

ISBN Parent: 192120702-7
ISBN International: 0 9775969 3 1
eISBN: 097759630-3
Publisher: DoctorZed Publishing

Available in print and ebook.

"Enchanting and full of joy." ~ Inner Self magazine.

Wrongly punished for breaking the ancient laws, Samantha Honeycomb is expelled by the queen into the wild and untamed Crazy Lands. Her only hope of redemption is an impossible quest—to find the fabled hive of Beebylon and bring back its secret of Infinite Richness. But there are others who would see her fail.

Evoking the wisdom of the ancient sages, Scott Zarcinas reveals through the trials and tribulations of Samantha Honeycomb that the surface appearance of unpleasant and torturous experiences are, in fact, essential ingredients in the melting pot of our future joy, security and acceptance—our destiny.

www.samanthahoneycomb.doctorzed.com

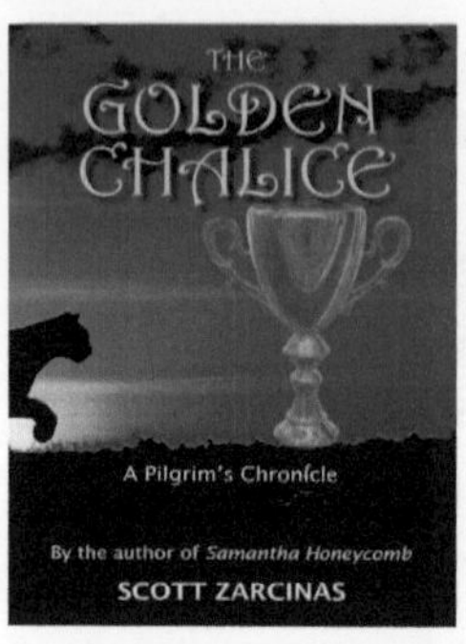

The Golden Chalice
by Scott Zarcinas

ISBN: 978-0-9875975-9-5
eISBN: 978-0-9775969-2-8
Publisher: DoctorZed Publishing

Available in print and ebook.

Fleeing the dreaded plague that has struck his village, the orphaned Giacomo heads to the mountains and its mysterious Golden City in search of the Elixir of Life, the only thing that can save the village and the woman he loves.

His quest brings him face to face with the Six Thieves, cunning enemies who will stop at nothing to see him fail, and even with the Angel of Death herself.

In the tradition of The Pilgrim Chronicles set by *Samantha Honeycomb*, *The Golden Chalice* is a compelling adventure story of self-discovery.

www.thegoldenchalice.doctorzed.com

www.ingramcontent.com/pod-product-compliance
Ingram Content Group UK Ltd.
Pitfield, Milton Keynes, MK11 3LW, UK
UKHW040022200726
13854UKWH00001B/310

9 780992 447359